FIRST KISS

In one long stride, he'd reached her and closed his arms about her. She put both arms around his waist and leaned into his chest, eyes closed, a smile on her face. His embrace was everything she had needed. Safety, security, friendship . . . and maybe something more.

For a long second they stood, silently melded together.

"Are you all right, Sarah?" He leaned back just a fraction and tipped her chin up with one hand. "Did they hurt you?"

"I'm scratched and I'm dirty and I'm a bit frazzled and ropeburned, but no, I guess I'm really not hurt." *Oh. He smelled so good.* She tried to lean into that comforting masculine chest once again, but he wasn't having that. He held her chin and lowered his lips. She stared at the sculptured lips. He was going to kiss her. She hoped he was going to kiss her. Gently, then more strongly, he let his mouth cover hers. *He is kissing me, she thought dreamily.* The incandescent heat from his lips radiated from her head down to her toes.

"Hey, Miss Schoolmarm, that was mighty nice, but let's try it again. This time you just open your mouth a tiny bit."

Oh. Was that how it was done? She stretched to put one hand at the back of his neck, and when his lips touched hers, she was ready. . . .

TODAY'S HOTTEST READS
ARE TOMORROW'S SUPERSTARS

VICTORY'S WOMAN (4484, $4.50)
by Gretchen Genet
Andrew—the carefree soldier who sought glory on the battlefield, and returned a shattered man . . . Niall—the legandary frontiersman and a former Shawnee captive, tormented by his past . . . Roger—the troubled youth, who would rise up to claim a shocking legacy . . . and Clarice—the passionate beauty bound by one man, and hopelessly in love with another. Set against the backdrop of the American revolution, three men fight for their heritage—and one woman is destined to change all their lives forever!

FORBIDDEN (4488, $4.99)
by Jo Beverley
While fleeing from her brothers, who are attempting to sell her into a loveless marriage, Serena Riverton accepts a carriage ride from a stranger—who is the handsomest man she has ever seen. Lord Middlethorpe, himself, is actually contemplating marriage to a dull daughter of the aristocracy, when he encounters the breathtaking Serena. She arouses him as no woman ever has. And after a night of thrilling intimacy—a forbidden liaison—Serena must choose between a lady's place and a woman's passion!

WINDS OF DESTINY (4489, $4.99)
by Victoria Thompson
Becky Tate is a half-breed outcast—branded by her Comanche heritage. Then she meets a rugged stranger who awakens her heart to the magic and mystery of passion. Hiding a desperate past, Texas Ranger Clint Masterson has ridden into cattle country to bring peace to a divided land. But a greater battle rages inside him when he dares to desire the beautiful Becky!

WILDEST HEART (4456, $4.99)
by Virginia Brown
Maggie Malone had come to cattle country to forge her future as a healer. Now she was faced by Devon Conrad, an outlaw wounded body and soul by his shadowy past . . . whose eyes blazed with fury even as his burning caress sent her spiraling with desire. They came together in a Texas town about to explode in sin and scandal. Danger was their destiny—and there was nothing they wouldn't dare for love!

Available wherever paperbacks are sold, or order direct from the Publisher. Send cover price plus 50¢ per copy for mailing and handling to Penguin USA, P.O. Box 999, c/o Dept. 17109, Bergenfield, NJ 07621. Residents of New York and Tennessee must include sales tax. DO NOT SEND CASH.

PARADISE FOUND

PEGGY FIELDING

ZEBRA BOOKS
KENSINGTON PUBLISHING CORP.

ZEBRA BOOKS are published by

Kensington Publishing Corp.
850 Third Avenue
New York, NY 10022

Copyright © 1994 by Peggy Fielding

All rights reserved. No part of this book may be reproduced in any form or by any means without the prior written consent of the Publisher, excepting brief quotes used in reviews.

If you purchased this book without a cover, you should be aware that this book is stolen property. It was reported as "unsold and destroyed" to the Publisher and neither the Author nor the Publisher has received any payment for this "stripped book."

Zebra and the Z logo Reg. U.S. Pat. & TM Off. The Lovegram logo is a trademark of Kensington Publishing Corp.

First Printing: December, 1994

Printed in the United States of America

*For my good friend
Cleo Reeves
who taught with me
in the Republic of the Philippines*

One

Sarah Collins was melting.

She just knew it, could feel it. Her carefully starched and ironed white shirtwaist was a mass of damp wrinkles, the tall collar slumping, no matter how high she kept her chin. She wouldn't even let herself *think* about what her body was like under the blue serge skirt and the embroidered linen petticoat her mother had insisted she wear for the wedding. Her boned corset was as wet as it had ever been when her mother had occasionally put it into the weekly washtub back home on the farm.

Her blond hair, including the wire nest under her pompadour, was so damp that it dripped lines of sweat onto her already moist face.

But her new hat was dry.

She reached up to reassure herself once more. The stiff straw wide-brimmed sailor had received only a few tiny drops of seawater as she and all the other American teachers had disembarked from the ship, the United States Transport *Thomas*. She had a quick moment of panic. Was she doing the right thing? Her mother had trimmed the fashionable new sailor-brimmed straw hat with yards of sky-blue velvet ribbon. With the jaunty forward tilt in front, the long streamers of ribbon hanging down in back looked very smart. Her mother had helped her check for exactly the right slant in the mirror in her bedroom back home.

She sighed with just a touch of homesickness, then immediately pushed it away. She must be doing the right thing. Her parents had seemed reassured. "No decent unmarried young woman would go so far away from her parents," her mother had said. "After you're married, then you're your husband's responsibility."

Anyway, they both trusted Robert. "He's a good Iowa farmboy," her father was fond of telling everyone as she was hurrying to get things ready for her wedding on the other side of the world. Never mind that she had always found Robert a bit of a know-it-all stuffed shirt. Her parents thought he would take good care of her, even in an unknown place like the Philippine Islands. Her mother had even given Sarah the two real gold hatpins her grandmother had left to her mother.

"Blue's a good color for brides. That's why I picked that color for your hat's trim . . . and the gold hatpins are my wedding present to you." They embraced, and both her parents had cried a little once again at their acknowledgment that their Sarah would be having her wedding ceremony far, far away, in a strange country . . . and without them. For a second, Sarah longed for her mother and father and Iowa.

Sarah brushed aside the memories of home which had darted into her mind. "I have to think of the here and now," she'd told her teacher, Miss Arnold. Miss Arnold had considered answering the President's call to volunteer to go to the Philippine Islands to teach also, but she'd thought better of it and decided she was too old to be traipsing around the world. Sarah knew Miss Arnold was at least forty, so probably she was right. Anyway, and just the same, it would have been mighty comforting to have had one well-known face at her wedding. Sarah sighed and touched the new hat once more.

I'll certainly be a wet and crumpled bride, Sarah thought, *but I'll keep my promises.* She relived for an instant her father's growls about how "no decent young woman would go alone to work in a heathen country. If that boy Robert wants you to come over there," he proclaimed, "you and he'll have to agree to marry on the day you arrive."

She'd agreed to that condition. "If Robert has arranged everything, I'll marry him the instant I get there," she'd promised them. That was also what she'd told her new friends on the *Thomas* during that interminable trip in the government ship.

She clenched her fists in her lap. Marriage wouldn't be so bad. She had to keep telling herself that. All women wanted to be married, didn't they? At least, as a married woman she would have some control over her own life. Perhaps even a little excitement. And it was all working out. Here she was, ready for a new country, a new husband, a first job, and all these adventures were awaiting her right here in Manila.

She tilted her chin just a fraction higher so the ribbons would hang straight. Anything would be better than staying in her parents' house in Iowa until she was a dried-up old spinster like Miss Arnold. Her teacher all through grade school, Miss Arnold had been not much older than Sarah was right now when she'd first come to River Crossing to teach . . . and now look at her. Old and skinny and at the mercy of the whole community. Nothing to look forward to but more teaching and more boarding in someone else's house. Never a home of her own. Sarah sighed. Anything would be better than a life like that.

Miss Arnold had said something very strange just before Sarah left. What was it? Something about Robert? "Robert is a man, Sarah. Older than you. You don't really know him all that well." When Sarah had protested that she'd had several classes with Robert and that he'd always been a perfect gentleman, the teacher had sniffed and said, "Men are often different after dark than they are in the daytime hours." Sarah had assured her that she was aware of her duties as a wife and that had been that.

The fragrance of a tropical flower wafting on a warm breeze jerked her attention back to the Manila Harbor. The small brown man who sat paddling the boat toward the customhouse wore a string of tiny white flowers around his neck. Somehow a delicious-smelling floral necklace seemed exactly right for him and for this tropical city. The boatman seemed to be studying her wilted shirtwaist, her soaking skirt, her brave new hat. Suddenly, he smiled and spoke. *"Mabuhay, Maestra."* He glanced back at the other young women behind her and called out the strange word to them, also.

"Mabuhay, mabuhay, mabuhay."

"Mabuhay!" Sarah felt very bold speaking the word in answer to the stranger, but the widening of his smile made her feel good. Maybe the word just meant hello. *Maestra* certainly meant *teacher* in Spanish.

Of course, she'd stood right on the front porch of the family farmhouse and promised her mother that she would not speak to strangers, but what could she do? He seemed such a sweet little person. Anyway, he was three inches shorter than she was, and with his fragrant floral neck decoration and his two front teeth missing, he looked like a skinny child who'd been playing in the garden.

She forced herself to turn her thought away from herself and Iowa and away from all the promises her parents had extracted from her. She was here! In the Philippine Islands! She'd slipped from the noose of family and home and now she could allow herself to pay attention to the sights around her.

Ugly bargelike boats lined the banks of the River Pasig. Each boat carried its own set of children, goats, roosters, and plaited bamboo masts. She realized with a start that she was looking at people's homes, that the people lived on the boats, that everything they owned was probably right there on the boat with them.

To the right she could see Fort Santiago, and behind the fort were the ancient city walls. Ahead she could see the gilded top of a huge building. The customhouse? It must be. The men who had come out to meet the *Thomas* before they'd docked had told them they would be going to a building with a golden dome where their luggage would be checked.

Everything was happening too quickly now. Sarah felt torn, excited to see her new home, afraid to see her new husband-to-be.

It's just Robert, she told herself. *You know he's an upright, pleasant, friendly person. He goes to church, even sang in the choir. What could go wrong with being married to him?*

She pushed all thoughts of Robert and marriage from her mind and clambered out of the small boat with the other American teachers. Once on the wooden dock she looked back and down at the man who'd been working the paddle.

"*Mabuhay,*" she called, and smiled.

He laughed and said something to his fellow paddler, then he shouted an answering "*Mabuhay.*" His shout was almost lost in the clatter and noises of the pier. The air was distinctly thick with the smell of rotting fish and unwashed human bodies and some other odors Sarah couldn't identify.

I wanted something different, and this is surely different than Iowa, she thought. She wished for a second she could show everything to Miss Arnold. The teacher had urged her to come to this country. She'd said, "I'm too old to change now, Sarah, but you can see the world for me."

Sarah ducked a swinging rope net filled with trunks and suitcases. As she straightened, a man in an American Army uniform grasped her arm.

"Miss Sarah Collins?"

Sarah shook her wrist from his grasp and met his frowning gaze with a frown of her own.

"Yes. Who are you?" Sarah, used to looking most men in the eye only a few inches above her five feet two inches, was shocked to realize that the dark-eyed soldier stood at least a foot taller than she.

"I'm Captain Markham Nash." The captain's frown deepened. "I am supposed to be in Manila on business, but I find myself acting as a bridesmaid instead." He gestured toward the passageway to the door that led to the street. "I've already arranged for your luggage to be put into a *carramato.*" He studied her hat, then her face, then the length of her body. "I suppose, like most women, you've brought a ton of useless stuff with you?"

Sarah drew herself up to her full height.

"I demand to know where Mr. Robert Zumwalt is."

She stared up into the piercing brown eyes which were set in a tanned and chiseled masculine face.

"Robert, uh, *Mr. Zumwalt,* if you prefer, is waiting for you at his leisure, back at the parsonage, or whatever they call it over here." He gripped her arm again and urged her none too gently through the crowd and toward the door. "He's got the wedding-day jitters, I guess. Anyway, he didn't feel so good, so guess who was elected to fetch you?" He jerked her arm a bit. "And now I can't get the bride to shuffle on over to the church." He dropped her arm and stalked ahead of her. "Come on, lady, let's get moving. I've got work to do before we head out for the bush."

The army man had almost disappeared from sight before Sarah could make her new patent-leather slippers move to follow him. Fear choked her under her wet collar. She had to go with this man. He was probably the only person around who spoke her language. An arrogant bully, of course, but perhaps being in the Army fostered such behavior. She remembered that Robert had a quick temper. He would soon put this brash soldier in his place. Why, why, why hadn't Robert come for her himself rather than sending this oaf after her.

On the street a small man who might have been a cousin to the man in the boat except that he wore no flowers, tossed her valises and boxes and bags into a cart, jumped in atop her grandmother's wedding trunk, then whipped up the tiny pony who pulled valiantly at the huge load.

"Those are my things, sir! Where do you think you're going with them?" She ran a few steps after the cart before the captain called after her.

"Miss Collins! I engaged that *carramato*. He's taking your things to the church. Here is another vehicle for your riding pleasure." He gestured to a second, seemingly identical cart pulled by an identical pony and guided by an identical little man. "Just calm down."

"Oh. Well. I'm not going anywhere until you've answered my questions."

Captain Nash rolled his eyes and sighed.

"I have a passel of things to do, but go ahead. Speak." He took off his wide-brimmed tan felt hat and fanned himself with it as he leaned against the cart. "Ask your questions, little lady."

Sarah's mind whirled. There was so much she needed to know. Where to start! She was shocked to hear herself ask, "What does *mabuhay,* mean?"

Markham Nash's teeth glowed white against the tan of his face.

"Well, well. The meaning of *mabuhay* is so all-fired important that you can hold the U.S. Army from its duties while you get a translation?" He chuckled, and she could see his wide shoulders in the dark-blue woolen shirt relax against the wooden cart. "I guess you'd say it means something like 'greetings' or 'welcome.' " He moved his hat brim lazily against the heated air. "Satisfied? Can we head for the church now, lady?"

The top third of the man's forehead was pale under his thick black curly hair and above his suntanned face. *He usually wears his hat,* Sarah thought, and she, too, smiled. He seemed much more human, not so military, with the pale strip of his forehead revealed. She shocked herself by wondering if the skin on his body was pale like his forehead.

"There are one or two more things I need to ask, such as why did you come to meet me and how did you know me. And again I ask where Robert is and . . ."

"Hold on." He clapped his hat back onto his head and put both hands up in the air as if to stop the tumble of words. "Your bridegroom is at the church, keeping cool. He asked me to come and fetch a slim, blue-eyed, blond young Iowan to him, and that's all I know. You were the only blonde I could see, at least the only slim one." He bowed. "Your carriage awaits, ma'am." He held out his hand to help her up to the cart seat. His fingers were warm and strong, his palm dry.

Sarah settled herself into the narrow seat, and at the captain's shout, the Filipino man put his small horse into motion. Sarah could see the cart carrying her belongings trundling along about twenty yards ahead.

The cobblestoned streets were lively with carts much like the one in which she was riding, as well as with people on foot and a few on bicycles.

The swaying of the cart didn't seem so strange to her. The many days on water had finally given her what the men on the *Thomas* had called "sea legs." Several days of seasickness had made her pay dearly for the last few weeks of feeling right at home on the bobbing deck of the boat. *"Ship,"* she corrected herself. She leaned into the peculiar waddling movement of the cart with the ease of a practiced sailor. From her perch on high she could see and hear peddlers hawking their wares with strange chants. Sea birds swooped down on the piles of refuse that dotted the beach area. Palm trees lined the wide avenue on each side.

She looked back to see Captain Nash swing himself up into the saddle of a huge roan horse. Soon he was riding the handsome steed back and forth between the two lumbering carts, trying unsuccessfully to speed up his small caravan.

Sarah hid her smile when she heard what she assumed were army issue curses muttered against the heads of each of the cart drivers, their mothers, and their ponies.

For a second he let his horse prance a side step near Sarah's primitive wooden throne.

"What were your parents thinking of to let you come halfway around the world to marry some stranger?"

"My parents like and respect Robert Zumwalt, sir. When he wrote and asked me to marry him . . . for the second time, I might add, Captain, I said yes. They did everything correctly, I assure you. They made Robert promise to marry me the instant I arrived in Manila. Which he agreed to do. Which is why we are on our way to a church." She touched her new hat to be sure of the tilt. "Does that answer all *your* questions, Captain Nash?"

The frowning brown gaze seemed to bore into her inner being.

"I think they were crazy to let you come, but I think you are even crazier to do this without finding out a lot more about this man Zumwalt." He tipped his own hat, and again took up his back-and-forth coaxing-for-speed between the two drivers.

What more do I need to know about Robert? she asked herself. *He is kind, well spoken, well educated, proper. Too proper, if anything. And I'm nearly twenty-one years old. Time to be married. Everybody thinks so. I'll admit I'd never have said yes if we were both still in Iowa, but the invitation to a new world . . . I just couldn't resist.* Was that wrong? Miss Arnold, her parents, her school chums . . . everyone had urged her to accept. "And they were right," she murmured. Robert's proposal of marriage was probably the best one she would ever receive anyway.

She eyed the carnival of the Manila streets and listened to the blistering invective issuing from the woolen-uniformed soldier. The right wheel of the *carramoto* dropped into a chughole and Sarah clutched her wooden perch more tightly. See? Her life was already more exciting and she'd only just arrived.

She looked at the sweating army man. He sat tall in the saddle, a part of the horse, his knees guiding the big animal with no conscious effort. His frowning face glowed harshly masculine in the tropical sunlight. A picture of a sedentary, white-faced Robert rose behind her eyes and as quickly vanished, pushed from her mind by the vitality and energy of the man on the horse.

"I shouldn't be looking at him," she murmured. She could feel a flush rise to her cheeks. "I shouldn't even be *thinking* of another man on the very morning of my wedding."

Captain Markham Nash felt like digging his heels deep into his horse's flanks and fleeing the city and everybody in it, especially the beautiful, blond-haired, blue-eyed, rosy-cheeked, Iowa farm girl. The big horse laid his ears back and loudly exhaled his displeasure at the slight touch of the captain's spur.

"Sorry, Jonas." Markham Nash leaned forward to mutter into the roan's ear. "But you're getting fat from hanging around a stall and eating all day. We need to get back to camp. You'd better buck up, boy. This town living is ruining both of us."

Again he looked back at the young woman forcing herself to sit with a rigidly straight backbone in the clumsily rocking cart. This was not a happy wife-to-be.

She looked plain frightened to him. Just an innocent little country girl venturing into the lions' den. He gritted his teeth.

"Looks like she's bound and determined to marry herself up with that cad of a clumsy, bumbling clodhopper, Zumwalt." He cursed as he imagined what Sarah Collins's body would look like under all those sweaty clothes. A picture of that gorgeous alabaster body stripped for the hungry eyes of the male schoolteacher rose to taunt him. He swallowed the dust in his throat.

"I can't believe I'm doing this. I sure didn't join the Army just to deliver up country maidens to a fate worse than death," he muttered to himself. He trotted the roan back toward the wide-eyed bride. He opened his mouth, then closed it and turned his horse away. "I know that her *Mr. Robert Zumwalt* is seven kinds of bastard . . . and I can't just tell her. First of all, it's none of my business." He patted the roan horse on the neck. "I'd sure like to make it my business, Jonas, but I can't. There's really nothing I can do, nothing at all." He straightened in his saddle. "I only have to do my duty and quit worrying about her. Delivering her is all we're required to do, Jonas, and that's what we'll do, then we'll head for the woods and never see her again except as Mrs. Zumwalt, the teacher's wife."

Jonas nodded his head as if agreeing with his master, and the captain's hand tightened on the animal's reins. It was an old story. Innocent female delivered up into the hands of a smooth-talking bad guy. But this time *he* was the one doing the delivering. Maybe he could talk her out of the whole thing. Maybe.

Two

All the twists and turns the carts had made had finally moved them into a quieter, shadier residential area. Sarah happily realized that it was several degrees cooler on the narrower street. Many of the large, airy-looking wooden houses on either side of the roadway were almost hidden behind tall stucco or cut-stone walls. Others were tucked into nests of verdant shrubbery.

Few pedestrians were in this area, and fewer still were the peddlers who called out their wares, although their carts did have to skirt around an informal market which one enterprising woman had laid out into the street itself. A cloth covered several square feet of cobblestone and the seller squatted against a concrete wall that fronted one of the houses. Sarah craned to see the kinds of fruits and vegetables the woman was selling. She recognized carrots and onions and squash and bananas. Pineapple, Sarah had seen in pictures, but many of the other items were completely unrecognizable to the former farm girl.

Far ahead, a group of children played a street game. Sarah glanced at them, then pulled her gaze back to

PARADISE FOUND

her escort. He looked at her at the same moment and pointed to indicate they were going to turn right. He shouted something, which Sarah couldn't catch over the creaking and groaning of her cart, then he put his horse into a gallop and disappeared around the corner. Sarah held her breath for a moment. When he didn't return, she felt panic rising inside herself again.

What would she do? She didn't even know where they were going. She knew only one word of the language. *Mabuhay.* He couldn't just *leave* her here like this. She would never be able to find her way back to the custom house by herself. She had a shuddering moment of terror that she'd have to go back to Iowa and tell everyone she had not been able to find Robert, that he had not met her ship as he had promised to do.

She bit back her fear and gritted her teeth. She would *never* turn back, she would only go forward, wherever *forward* might be. The carts continued their steady rumbling and creaking procession toward the corner where the captain had just disappeared, then they, too, lumbered into the sharp right turn and onto a slightly narrower and definitely shadier street. She could look up into the tree limbs that met in the middle of the road. The greens pierced with the jagged points of strong sunlight made her feel as if she were looking up into a slightly tattered green umbrella.

But there was no captain. No big American horse. Sarah rose shakily and stood staring out, holding on to the seat as if she might spy her lost guide if only she were taller. A shocked over-the-shoulder look from her driver caused her to reseat herself. *Where was Captain Nash?*

The cart in front pulled to the left and it, too, turned out of sight. Sarah closed her eyes and forced herself to stay calm. Maybe soon they would arrive at the church. Soon she would be with Markham . . . *no, with Robert.* Her eyes flashed open with shock. Her mother might have asked, what ailed her?

The picture of the tall soldier on the roan horse was engraved clearly on her inner sight. She tried to bring up a likeness of her fiancé, but for a long moment she couldn't even remember what Robert looked like.

Markham Nash swung down off his horse and tossed the reins across the twisted floral design on an iron gate. He stomped across the cobblestoned courtyard, pushed open the small door built into the huge wooden one, and stepped into the vestibule of the church. As soon as his eyes had adjusted to the near darkness of the building, he strode forward through another door and crossed the back of the sanctuary toward a smaller open door, his spurs jangling against the terrazo floor. His boot heels rang as he stamped up the three stone steps which led to the room he sought.

He took off his hat before speaking to the sweating, shirtsleeved man seated in a wooden armchair in front of a carved and polished desk where a priest sat on the opposite side.

"She'll be here within the next two minutes. You'd

better get yourself ready, Bobby boy. She's expecting to get married the minute she sets foot in the church."

The smaller man nodded and slipped into the jacket that hung from the back of his chair. The priest also rose. They both moved to another doorway.

"I'll just lead her right down to the altar, shall I, *padre?*" Markham knew the priest didn't speak English, but he couldn't resist the hint of sarcasm. "I'll bring her right on down like a little lamb to the slaughter, right?"

Robert Zumwalt looked back and passed a brightly figured silk handkerchief across his forehead.

"I'll thank you to keep your lip buttoned, Captain. This is none of your business."

"None of my business. Yes, indeed. That's just what I told the major, but he insisted on giving me these stupid orders and *making* it my business, Robert, old boy, so I guess you're just going to have to put up with me . . . all the way back to camp. I'll be the judge as to what this young woman needs to know." He stepped back to return to the courtyard. "This is the most unjustified use of army time that I've ever seen."

He wanted to say more. He wanted to knock the teacher flat on his back. He wanted to tell the priest to tend to his prayer book. He wanted to kick something. He wanted to take the girl from Iowa into his arms. Shocked at his own thoughts, Markham drew back his booted foot and vented his fury against the solid mahogany rectory door.

The other American looked back to give him a thin

smile of triumph before he continued his slow walk toward the sanctuary. He didn't say a word.

The little brown man smiled back at her and pointed. *"Iglesia."* His voice barely carried over the squeak of the large wooden wheels.

Iglesia. Wasn't that Spanish for church? Sarah strained to see, but only blank cement walls met her gaze. A bit ahead, she *could* see wide iron gates opened from the street. The baggage cart turned in between the two gates. As her cart drew nearer, Sarah was thrilled at the sight of the big roan standing hitched to the inside of the decorative iron twists of flowers. Her eyes lifted to the building. A church. Three crosses on top of three high spires. One set of huge wooden doors opened inwardly as she watched.

When the cart stopped in the churchyard, Sarah allowed the Filipino driver to help her down. As she tried to smooth out her wrinkled woolen skirt, her eyes searched for the captain.

A young man in a priest's robes, who looked paler and much different than the Filipinos she'd seen so far, gestured from the doorway, and Sarah forced herself to move toward him. A priest. This was a *Catholic* church. The man, the priest, was probably Spanish then.

What would she tell her parents? Of course, they'd surely realized that she'd be married in a Catholic church in the Philippines. It was, after all, the national religion. Sarah nodded to the man of God, then followed him into the darkened vestibule. He motioned her forward toward another large inner door, then turned and walked ahead of her toward the altar.

The huge space was silent, the scent of incense hovered in the air. Their little wooden church at home wouldn't take up even a third of this cavernous room. A bird startled her as it flew above her head and then darted out one of the high open windows near the distant roofline of the church. Sarah shuddered. Wasn't a bird inside a room a sign of bad luck? Hadn't Grandma once said that it was an omen of death?

Behind her she heard the clink of spurs against the stone floor. Her heart lurched. Captain Nash. He tucked her hand through his arm and smiled down at her.

"Ready to do this?"

She nodded. There appeared to be no pews in this grandiose structure, but she could see Robert sitting on a kitchen chair just to one side of the altar. He seemed even thinner than she'd remembered. He wiped sweat from his face and neck with a yellow-red-and-white striped silk handkerchief. She remembered that someone had told her only gamblers and roundabouts used colored handkerchiefs. And silk? All the men she knew used cotton bandanas in the field and white linen for church and all other places.

She felt as if she were looking at him through the wrong end of a telescope. He seemed so tiny, so far away.

Her knees buckled slightly, and the captain slowed and drew her arm even closer.

"Are you sure you want to go through with this,

Sarah Collins?" he whispered. "You don't have to, you know."

"I promised," she murmured, her gaze forward, staring at the man who would very soon be her husband. All of her years of knowing Robert Zumwalt as a classmate in River Crossing School, three grades above hers, all that time seemed wiped from her mind. This was a stranger sitting on that kitchen chair. Her body felt chilled, icy . . . in every part except her warm right hand, which Captain Markham Nash held in both of his.

She looked up at the army man and whispered again, as if to reassure herself, "I promised my mother and father."

"They're not here. They don't know what you're feeling right now. They'll understand."

"No. I promised."

"Then I guess I'll have to be the one to give the bride away."

They continued their slow journey toward the three waiting men. To Sarah, their advance to the altar seemed to go on forever, yet not nearly long enough.

Robert Zumwalt rose from his chair, and as Captain Markham Nash stepped aside, Robert moved into his place to greet her with a light kiss on the cheek. "Sarah," he said and nodded. But he didn't say anything else. He took the hand the captain had been holding into his own hand.

Robert's hand was soft, moist, sticky hot against her own. She wanted to pull away, but she didn't. Robert said nothing more, just turned and looked at the priest, so she kept silent also. She tried to smile and she, too, turned to look at the priests who had begun the wedding ceremony in a language Sarah couldn't understand. After a time, the younger priest indicated the kneelers just below where the priest stood, and she and Robert knelt for the wedding blessing. She could feel the captain's disapproving presence all through the ceremony.

Sarah's tremulous smile from under her new straw hat caused a ripping pain in Markham's chest. *By God, she's doing it!* he realized. *And they haven't even let her take the time to wash her face. The girl's got grit . . . or she's really loco.* His hands were trembling as much as they did when he first got the fever down in Cuba. He put his hands into his pockets to keep them still. *She didn't love Robert,* he was sure of that. But she'd made him a promise. Even more important, she promised her parents.

Well, I guess I know something about this girl, he mused. *You can by God depend upon Sarah Collins's word. Sarah Collins Zumwalt's word, now, I guess.*

Robert gave Sarah another chaste kiss upon the cheek at the end of the ceremony. He fumbled a slim silver band onto her finger with a whispered explanation. "I don't believe the wedding ring is a part of the marriage ceremony over here."

The priests picked up their symbols of office and

turned away, the captain with them. Robert kept Sarah's hand tucked into the crook of his arm as they followed the three men.

"I suppose you've wondered why I didn't meet you at the boat?" Robert swiped at his forehead, then his neck. "I do believe I have a touch of the summer complaint, so I thought it best that I stay quietly in the parish house whilst Captain Nash fetched you."

"Why are you being so strange with me, Robert?" Sarah asked in confusion. "So formal?"

"We'll talk, my dear. Later." He sniffed into the gaudy handkerchief. "I'll answer all your questions when I'm a bit more myself."

Sarah nodded and watched the priests, then the blue-clad soldier step up and disappear into another room. She quelled her momentary panic by reciting silently to herself, *I'm all right. I'm a married woman now. I'm with my husband.*

"I will need to go to bed again as soon as we've finished signing all the papers." Robert sighed and patted her hand. "I suppose you won't mind?"

Sarah shook her head that she wouldn't mind. Did that mean he expected them to go to bed right away? In the daytime? Her mother had explained how marriage was after the lights were out when you were in the bed at night. But it was barely after eight o'clock in the morning. Mama hadn't said anything about the daytime. Sarah fought the nausea that rose in her throat.

Three steps up and they were in a room where the three waiting men stood in a semicircle at the end of the large desk. Robert dropped her hand and flopped into the lone wooden chair facing the desk.

"I hope you don't mind, Sarah dear. I seem to be completely worn out from our strenuous jungle trip. It was a goodly distance from our village to Manila."

Sarah nodded. She was glad that he didn't seem to expect an answer. She knew she couldn't have spoken if her life depended upon it.

After a word from the priest, Robert signed the documents, then Sarah followed suit as they were passed to her. They were all written in Spanish, weighted down with fancy borders and printed flourishes and gold seals. The younger priest and the soldier signed as witnesses. The older priest rolled the papers into a tube and tied the bundle with a red ribbon. He looked at Robert, then nodded, smiled, and handed the papers to Sarah.

"Señora Zumwalt."

Sarah nodded. *"Gracias, padre."* Her new name echoed strangely in her ears.

"If you will excuse me now, my dear." Robert stood. "I will go to my room and rest for a short time."

Does that mean I'm supposed to go, too? Sarah walked behind him toward the door. She almost bumped into him when he suddenly stopped and turned with a frown. "Oh. Yes. I should tell you. I've arranged for a separate room for you, Sarah. Perhaps you'd like to have a moment or two to rest also? I'll be calling for you shortly. Captain Nash is determined that we head back into the bush in the morning, so we will need to make our preparations."

Sarah was shocked to see that Robert's glance toward Markham Nash was filled with venom. But she decided she'd been mistaken when the gleam of hatred disappeared almost as soon as it appeared.

"That was the deal you made with my major, Zumwalt." The captain's voice was low but hard-edged. "You could have me as your guide on your wedding trip if you could work it into the Army's schedule. You agreed to his stipulations." His deeply tanned face looked dangerous to Sarah. "I have all the Army's supplies, and I've taken care of their other business. The Army wants me out of Manila. You can come with me or not."

"Fine, fine." Robert wiped his face again. "We'll be ready."

"Why do we need a guide, Robert? We could go by ourselves, couldn't we?" Sarah made her voice as imperious as possible. "I don't think we really need the captain's help, do we?" There. That would put Markham Nash in his place.

"Oh, my dear," Robert turned his face away from her. "I'll explain it all to you later. Right now I must take to my bed for just a short time." Her new husband left abruptly through a door behind the desk.

The young priest motioned Sarah to follow him. She looked at Markham Nash, but he only shrugged as if she were no longer his problem. She followed the priest from the rectory office and down a long, shadowy hallway. At the end of the hall, he opened a door and gestured her in.

She found herself in a narrow, whitewashed, high-ceilinged room containing a cot, a straight wooden chair, and a small wooden table. High up on the most distant wall a dark-brown crucifix hung above the bed. Two walls of glassless, unscreened window openings kept the room from feeling too closed in.

A white china chamber pot under the bed and a matching pitcher and washbowl on the table completed the room's furnishings.

Sarah walked to the nearest window. She found herself looking down at the back churchyard. A smaller building, probably an outhouse, she thought, lay at the very back of the large square piece of property, which was bordered with the usual high, blank, cement walls. To the left she could see a cobblestoned space which she was certain was used as a laundry area since she spied a huge black iron pot on legs, a place for fires under the pot, cut firewood stacked head high against the outhouse, and several tubs and a washboard leaning against the building. A tall red clay jar stood near the black pot. Water, she thought. Farther to the left she could see a carriage house and what she surmised to be a stable. She had to lean far out the window to see the stable well, but she could hear the stomping sounds that horses make when they're restless. A loud snorting and one triumphant whinny confirmed her surmise. Horses for sure.

To her right, a large tree shaded a well-swept wide-open hard earth yard as well as her corner of the rectory.

Not wonderfully exotic, she thought, but not too bad, either. Kind of homey. She turned back to the room and carefully removed her new hat, pressed the two gold hatpins into the blue velvet ribbon trim and placed it on the chair. She longed to remove her wrinkled blouse, her soaking skirt, and her underclothes, especially her pinching corset. She debated a moment, then decided against it. Robert had said he would be calling for her soon so they could prepare themselves for their trip back to his assignment in Zambales Province. She wanted to be ready when he came for her.

She chanced unbuttoning the high collar on her shirtwaist and removing her patent-leather shoes. She wished for a cloth of some kind to clean the no longer new-looking slippers. She had wanted French kid leather, but her mother had persuaded her that "patent-leather is so modern and it cleans up so easily, Sarah."

For a moment she gave the problem some thought, then lifted the hem of the hideously warm serge skirt. Inside the hemline. That would work. The skirt certainly could not look much worse than it already did. She busied herself dusting each black patent-leather shoe with the inside hem of her skirt. She placed the slippers on the floor below her hat. She had to smile. Her fashionable hat and her gold hatpins and her clean shoes looked so pretty, so worldly. They looked just like what a bride should wear.

Sarah dropped a small curtsey to the still-life arrangement of her things before she sat on the edge of the cot to wait.

She didn't have to wait long.

A young Filipina woman knocked and entered before she could get up. The woman carried a tray holding a bowl of fruit, a pot of tea, a thick mug, and a large handbell.

"You eat. You drink. Ring bell. I come."

"Oh, wonderful. You speak English. Where is Mr. Zumwalt? The captain? Are they ready for me?"

The woman smiled. "You eat. You drink. Ring bell. I come. Captain say ring." She handed the bell to Sarah. "You ring."

Charming, Sarah thought as she placed the well-polished silver bell into a window niche, and quite a lovely girl. She suddenly realized that all the Filipino people she had met so far had been small but very pleasant to look at and extremely kind in their limited conversations. She smiled at the woman and lifted the tinkling bell to shake it with her answer.

"Thank you." The silvery jingle she caused made the young woman giggle. "I will ring." She nodded at the servant, realizing she would be able to get little information from the young woman.

The little maid left and Sarah poured herself some tea. That was what had been wrong. She was unbearably thirsty and hadn't realized it. She drank one cup of the pale tea quickly, then perched herself on the side of the bed to drink the second cup slowly so she could savor it.

She tried to sample several of the peeled fruits but somehow couldn't make herself eat much. She settled for the tea, then stood to ring the bell.

When she comes back I will ask her to show me to Robert's room, she decided. *We can talk while he rests. He and I need to get reacquainted.*

She looked up, surprised at the swiftness of the maid's answer to the bell. But it wasn't the maid. Markham Nash was framed in her doorway. She stood quickly and glanced at her shoes, but he was too fast, she, too slow. He had already looked at the spotless pair of slippers and then at her stocking feet. He smiled at the neatly laid-out display of wedding finery on the chair before the frown returned to his face.

He looked at the young woman's blond halo that stood in disarray around her pompadour and the once tightly bound high chignon. Her guileless blue eyes seemed to beg for his attention. Her small feet in black cotton stockings peeking from under the horridly stiff blue serge skirt made her look even more artless. He closed his eyes to block out her expectant smile, then stepped to the nearest window to look out. He looked, but he was blind to the courtyard below. He opened his mouth to speak, then closed it and turned once again to look at the disheveled new bride who stared at him so expectantly.

How the hell am I going to tell this girl that her new husband may have the cholera?

Three

"Cholera!"

At that word Sarah sank back against the footboard of the cot. Her hand moved against the air as if she were batting away a bothersome insect. "I don't believe you."

Markham felt a rush of pity for her. He stood silently looking down at Sarah a moment before he decided to downplay the ugly news he'd been asked to deliver.

"Uh, Sarah, it's true the doctor didn't say *cholera* straight out, but he *did* say he thought Robert was in pretty bad shape."

"Well, then," Sarah lifted her chin and gave him a sunny but unfocused smile. "If he didn't say the *word* then that means he really didn't know. *Robert does not have the cholera.*" She straightened and rebuttoned her high collar. "We were officially married and afterward he was standing there and talking with us. That was just two hours ago." She swooped her hat up and pinned it to her uncombed blond hair. "You were there. You saw him."

Markham nodded and surveyed her closely. She seemed to be acting and talking strangely, as if she were not really there, as if she were not really seeing him as she talked.

She strode through the door ahead of him, then turned and beckoned.

"You will show me to my husband's room, please, Captain."

He nodded and motioned her to precede him down the hall. He wanted desperately to smile at the black stockinged feet marching off the distance with soft determination. The two sky-blue velvet ribbon streamers on the hat seemed to be marching also.

"To the end of the hall," he directed, "turn left," then, "up the stairs," and "on the right." Soon they stood outside a closed door.

She looked an inquiry at him. He nodded.

She straightened her shoulders, smoothed her skirt, touched her hat, then knocked with forceful authority. The captain looked down at her feet. Her toes were curled against the black cotton stockings, counteracting the demanding sound of her signal. Her knock was the action of an imperious woman. Her feet were still those of a scared little girl.

Markham felt another surge of pity for the young woman. Life was handing her more adventure than she'd bargained for. All those days in a train, then weeks on an Army Transport and now this. Most newcomers he'd seen, even new soldiers, acted either tired or crazy the first few days in the country. Sarah was holding up pretty well. She'd probably sleep for a week once she let herself fall into a bed. Or maybe she'd be one of those crying, crazy-acting women he'd seen more than once at the postings in Manila. God, he'd hate to see her fall apart like that.

No. This Iowa farm girl would hold up better than most. He was sure of that. She'd probably sleep around the clock for several days. That's what the strong ones usually did.

The same young maid who'd brought her the food opened the sickroom door. Before she allowed Sarah to come in, she looked back at the army surgeon for permission. He nodded and she allowed Sarah to enter the large bedroom.

Sarah's hand flew involuntarily to cover her nose. The stench was overwhelming. Robert Zumwalt lay stiffly stretched upon a twisted, sweaty sheet. His eyes were closed and he mumbled in delirium, his weak arm movements sporadic and seemingly at random. He called out something. Names? Sarah couldn't recognize the two words. Mad? Late? Was he saying he was mad because she was late?

"You're his wife?"

Sarah nodded.

"Don't worry. You don't have to be quiet. You won't disturb him. He can't hear you, ma'am."

"Can't I do something to help?"

The doctor shook his head. His gray hair fell across his forehead and he shoved it back with spread fingers.

His eyes told Sarah everything she needed to know, but she asked anyway.

"Is it cholera?"

"Yes, ma'am. It is." He waited for her next question, sympathy for the new young wife written across his face.

"Will he die?" Her question whispered across the room. She clapped her hand across her mouth. As soon as she'd said the words, she'd wanted to call them back.

The doctor nodded without speaking. His face had already told her the truth.

Sarah turned and walked back into the hall and into the arms of the waiting captain. He pulled her face against his chest and she let her tears flow.

"I hardly got to say hello to him."

"I know." He patted her on the back as if she were a sorrowing child. "This is a pretty big shock for you, Sarah. You go ahead and cry."

He searched his back pocket for a handkerchief. He handed the still-folded khaki-colored cotton square to her.

"Isn't there anything I can do?" She gulped the words against her sobs.

"You heard the doctor, Sarah. There's nothing *anyone* can do now. Everyone who gets cholera has a fast ticket to the hereafter. It's the same for Robert Zumwalt. What we have to do now is think about what you can do for yourself."

She stiffened and pulled away from him.

PARADISE FOUND 39

"What do you mean?"

"Well, this is an example of what I was talking about when I said I didn't like cities. Bad as it is, the jungle is always preferable to the open gutters of a crowded town." He pulled her back against him, a prickle of guilt caused him to frown as he felt pleasure in the roundness of her shoulders under his hands. "We have to think about what is best for you now. And the open sea will be the healthiest place in the world. For sure, there's no cholera back in Iowa."

She jerked away from him, scrubbing her swollen eyes with the wadded handkerchief.

"Iowa?"

"Yes, Sarah. I know this sounds callous, but we have to think about you. I've seen cholera." He gently pulled the gold hatpins from their anchoring spot and lifted the straw hat from her head to hold it in one hand while he smoothed her back and shoulders with the other. "The *Thomas* will be in port here for several more days they told me, and it's pretty sure we'll have Robert in the ground long before they leave." He patted her again. His hand wanted to clasp her closely to his chest. He forced himself to make his touch light. You can go home. Be with your family." Her shoulder blades felt so fragile against his hand.

"But I don't want to go home. There's nothing there now for me except being Mama and Papa's daughter. Maybe teaching and later on, boarding with a family in a place that's just like home." She sniffed loudly, like an unhappy child. "Just an old maid schoolteacher."

"Well, girl, that's not quite true. You'll be an old

widow woman schoolteacher now. And you'll be alive. How about that?"

"Oh, you don't understand."

Behind them, the door to Robert's room opened and the gray-haired doctor stood looking at them.

"Mrs. Zumwalt . . ." The doctor hesitated, then lowered his voice. "I don't think your husband will last the night. Why don't you go on down to your room and try to get some rest? I'll take care of him as best I can."

"But I want to stay and help. Maybe Robert will need me."

"That's not a good idea." Markham handed her the hat and the two gold pins. "I promise I'll come and get you if there's any change." He awkwardly patted the hand that held the hat. "I'll just stay nearby here so the doc can call me to move the patient or do whatever he needs me to do."

Sarah nodded.

"Can you find your way back to your room?"

She nodded again and drifted toward the stairs with both men watching until she disappeared from their sight.

"Bad luck for the girl, that wedding this morning, Captain."

Markham nodded. "You don't know how bad, Doc."

Back in her tiny room, Sarah placed the hat on the chair just as before, then removed her shirtwaist, and skirt and her stockings. She considered taking off the punishing corset but decided against it. She wasn't even aware that she'd forgotten to wear her shoes. Her mind an exhausted blank, she fell onto the small cot. *I'll just rest my eyes for a while, then I'll go back upstairs and make them let me stay there. A woman should be with her . . . husband.*

A stab of guilt pricked her conscience that she could feel a need to rest but she couldn't cry. All her tears were gone. When she'd talked to the captain, had she been crying for Robert or crying because she might have to go back to the boredom of her life in Iowa?

"Never," she said aloud. "I'm not going back." Her hands clenched into fists. She had come all this way on a crowded ship, suffered days of seasickness, eaten swill, slept on a hard bunk in a room with a bunch of snoring female strangers. No. Returning on that ship or any other ship was out of the question.

"Robert needs me here." She repeated her promise to herself and in seconds she was asleep.

Later, when she awakened, she didn't recognize where she was nor why she was there. The early-evening twilight had left her room in almost complete darkness. She looked around, thinking herself to be back in the attic bedroom she'd slept in all her life before she'd left for the Philippines. But no. Her Iowa room was large, with cabbage roses on the walls. This room was tiny, painted white.

In an instant the whole day flooded back into her memory. She was in a room in the church rectory in Manila. The gloaming light outside subtly darkened almost to nightfall as she watched. The tropical moon made its way into the corner of one of the window openings. The quickness of the change from day into night and the appearance of the huge molten silver moon seemed unreal to her. She rose and drifted toward the windows.

The churchyard lay bathed in moonlight as Markham strolled toward the outhouse. He opened the door of the small building and immediately wrenched it closed again.

"God damn."

The stench overpowered him, drove him back toward the high wall. Even there, the smell of urine hung strongly in the air. He considered crossing to the stable. At least the smell there was the good earthy smell of healthy horses.

He decided he wasn't the only one who preferred to piss in the open air. In fact, in one of the stairwells *inside* the rectory, he'd had the distinct olfactory impression that someone, or perhaps several someones, had relieved themselves inside the building, under the stair.

The dark-blue cup of sky above him held bouquets of stars along with the artificial-looking moon he'd thought so unusual when he'd first arrived in the country. He threw back his head to try to catch some cleaner smelling air into his lungs. Sometimes he felt himself longing for the changing seasons of home.

A leisurely unbuttoning of his gun-metal blue army trousers gave him time to think, time to dream, time to plan.

He pictured himself lying next to Sarah, looking down at her. He felt his groin tighten and his member stiffen in his hand. He cursed under his breath. Pesky little woman. Now he couldn't even urinate. Damn. He was letting his body take control of his mind and that wasn't like him.

Back to Iowa. That was the only answer. She'd just have to reboard the *Thomas*. He'd see to that. He'd put this girl, this young woman, this Sarah, right out of his head. It was several minutes before he was able to do what he'd come to the courtyard to do.

Above him in the dark, narrow room, Sarah watched the captain flinch away from the outhouse to move to stand facing the tall concrete wall. For a second he stared across at the stable, then turned to face the wall again.

She wanted to get away from the window. She wanted to stop staring at the man, to give him his deserved privacy, but she couldn't make herself step back.

He fumbled with the front of his woolen trousers, then threw his head back as if he were howling at the moon. Long moments later she heard water splashing against the wall, after which she heard him groan.

His wide shoulders slumped for a moment, then squared again as if he'd come to a decision. His long legs striding back to the rectory displayed determination in every step.

Sarah rested her arms on the sill and filled her gaze with his military bearing. She closed her eyes. She had to force herself to tear her thoughts away from the soldier.

What am I doing? She spoke to herself inside her own head. *I'm just newly married and here I am, mooning over this man I hardly know. A man who most surely hasn't given me a thought . . . except perhaps to consider me as some sort of nuisance which was thrust upon him.* She watched him race toward the rectory, then leap up the wooden stairs two at a time and disappear into the side door.

She lifted her chin as she reiterated her promise to herself. She would help Robert get well. She would go with him to Zambales Province. She would be an honor to his name. She would do her duty. She would help teach the Filipino children and be a credit to her husband, to President McKinley, and to her country. What she would *not* do was waste any more time or thought on this person. She *would* put this intrusive man, this captain, this Markham Nash, straight out of her mind.

Four

. . . she nodded at Robert from across the classroom inside the one-room school. What was he doing at River Crossing school? He'd already gone on to the Normal Institute. But there he was. In his best suit. Holding a figured silk handkerchief that looked as if it belonged to a gambler. His note read: "I want to speak to you after class." She glanced at Miss Arnold to see if she had noticed, but the teacher was involved with reading class for the primary children.

Robert's note piqued her interest, but she also felt a tiny thread of resistance. *He's going to ask me something I don't want to answer,* she told herself.

Her schoolhouse double desk turned into a *carramato,* trandling along a Manila street, a tiny Filipino man driving. She worried that she wasn't going to be able to meet Robert, that she wouldn't be able to answer his question, that he would be angry because she was late. Beside the cart, a dark male face glowered at her. The soldier. His whiplash words of anger whirled in the air above her head.

"Silly girl. You're marrying a stranger!"

A priest's Latin and Spanish words wove themselves into the tableau. The wedding ritual sounded as if it were echoing from a distant point.

"Señora Zumwalt, Señora Zumwalt, Señora Zumwalt."

Another voice picked up the words. "You'll be Señora Zumwalt today. We're putting you on a ship tomorrow."

Her mother and father smiled from the porch of their Iowa farmhouse. Her mother waved. "We trust you, Sarah. We want you to marry him. We know you'll do what's right."

No. That wasn't where she was. She wasn't at the farmhouse. She was lost. She was in the corridor at the Normal School. No one else there. No classmates. No teachers. No light. Lost. She looked again at her listed daily schedule. She knew she was supposed to be in a class, but she couldn't find the right room. She was lost. Late for an important class. Late for everything. Late . . . and lost . . .

Sarah whimpered in her sleep. "Lost!" The sound of her own voice crying out woke her to the narrow room and to the dark blue light of a tropical evening.

"Oh, no. I've allowed myself to fall asleep again," she wailed aloud. The dream receded and she leaped from the cot to the table to splash tepid water against her face. She felt a scrabbling impatience with her own slowness. "Hurry. Robert needs you." Her frustration mounted when she found she had to search for her clothing.

She finally scrambled into the almost dry shirtwaist

and skirt. This time she slipped into her new shoes before she tidied her hair. Why was she sleeping so much? she wondered. Maybe because of the seemingly never-ending trip on the *Thomas* and the long nights awake in her wooden bunk during the crossing? Her sense of time seemed to have been turned upside down.

She jerked open the bedroom door and once again stepped out into the hall and into Markham Nash's arms.

"Hey, Sarah. Slow down."

"I can't stop. I have to get to Robert's room. I'm sure he needs me. Let me go."

Markham pulled her close for a moment before stepping back. In the pale moonlight from the open windows, her blond hair was a silver halo around her face. She smelled clean. And womanly. Her body seemed to fit perfectly against his own. Guilt ricocheted within his chest as if he had been caught stealing something. He put one hand on her shoulder.

"Sarah, honey, I came to tell you . . . the doctor sent me to tell you . . . Robert . . . Robert is . . ." His facial expression conveyed his meaning.

"Dead" she finished for him, and she slumped against his broad chest. "He's dead. I let him die without helping to make him well. That's what my dream meant." Anger flashed through her mind. She drew back from his touch. "You. You and that doctor. You sent me away when he needed me." She pounded her fist against his chest. "I didn't even get to say much more than, hello." A sob rattled in her throat. "He might have needed me, but you wouldn't let me . . ."

"Believe me, Sarah. He didn't need you. There wasn't anything you could have done." He caught her fist in his own hand and raised his voice. "He was never conscious after you saw him in his bedroom." He closed his eyes. "Sarah, it's like I said. Cholera is always a death sentence. Anyway, I was right there the whole time."

"And *I* wasn't!" The words were bitter, but Sarah realized that her shortcomings as a wife were certainly not his fault nor the fault of the doctor. The guilt lay entirely within herself.

"I'm sorry, Captain. I shouldn't have said that. It was not your fault."

The barefooted young Filipina woman slipped silently up the hall behind them, her hands laden with a tray bearing a tureen of soup, bowls, spoons, and a long oval-shaped loaf of bread. A lighted candle in a holder rode between the tureen and the bread. The woman's smoothly tan skin glistened a warm golden color in the glow of the candlelight. She smiled, but her liquid brown eyes held unspoken pity for Sarah.

"You eat, señora. You eat, señor."

Sarah stepped closer to the hall window. Then Markham turned his back. She reached toward the soldier as if she meant to touch him, but she let her hand drop before it made contact.

"Will you eat with me?" She didn't look up at him as she spoke in a near whisper. She wasn't aware of the wistful note in her voice. "I don't think I can eat alone."

"Well, I believe the padres expected me to keep you

company at supper, ma'am. They said as much. Here, Luz." He took the tray from the maid. "Let me have that." He used his chin to point. "Put the pitcher and the bowl on the floor. Pull the table close to the bed." He said several words in a strange language and the little woman scurried to obey.

Sarah stood watching helplessly from the hallway. *He just called me "ma'am." Earlier he called me "honey" when I was acting like a child. Did he call me ma'am because I'm married.* She raised her chin defiantly. *No. It's because I'm a widow,* she decided.

In seconds the meal was arranged, the candle centered, the tray set out to wait beside the door.

"You ring." The maid pointed to the handbell resting in a window niche, then sang out her usual order before she scuttled back down the dark hallway. "You eat. You ring."

"What was it you called her?"

"Luz. That means light, I think."

"That's pretty." The fact that he obviously knew the sweet-faced Filipina quite well pricked at Sarah's consciousness. She had to remind herself that it was certainly no business of hers *whom* he knew. Soldiers were notorious for their womanizing, weren't they? Anyway, *she* couldn't concern herself with the details of a soldier's social life. She had to look to the future, had to do the job she'd been sent to do. Captain Markham Nash was only her guide, appointed by the U.S. Army. Nothing personal, not at all.

When they were settled, she on the bed and the captain on the chair, Sarah was surprised and somewhat shocked at her strong appetite. *My husband just died and I'm hungry!* She pushed her guilt aside. She'd make it up to Robert by accomplishing what he'd just started. She'd work very hard in his school.

The soup, the crusty bread, the molten moon peeking above the palm trees, the tiny table, the candle, the man across from her—everything conspired to make her feel happy. She tried to quell the joy that seemed to spring from nowhere, but she couldn't dampen it entirely.

"I love this bread." She tore another piece from the loaf. "Spanish *pan,* I think. We had such awful biscuitlike stuff to eat on the ship. Not even good biscuitlike stuff, something hard as rocks." She paused. "We always had delicious biscuits or cornbread back home . . . Mama is the best cook in the county and Papa loves her biscuits. But we almost never had any lightbread. I love lightbread. It's so . . . so sophisticated." She waved the crust toward the glowing window opening. "I think this is a beautiful country and they have exquisite bread."

"It *is* a beautiful country." He smiled across the table and pulled off a chunk of the bread for himself. "And they do have pretty sophisticated bread." He smiled at her. "I'll have to tell my Filipino aide that you said so."

"You're teasing me. But I'm serious. This is a beautiful country, I think."

"The Philippine Islands are a whole lot prettier outside Manila. Too bad you won't get a chance to see the countryside."

PARADISE FOUND 51

Sarah frowned.

"Oh, but I will see it, Captain."

"The Filipino countryside? Or what do you mean?"

"I'm keeping my part of the bargain I made, Captain. I'll keep my promise and I'll most certainly get to see the Filipino countryside. After the fune—the funeral." She choked a bit on the word, then recovered. "After that, I shall, of course, go with you to Zambales Province to take over Robert's work, Robert's school." She took another sip of the clear soup, then waved the empty spoon airily in his direction. "I'll just move into his house and carry on with the school and with any other project he had started."

Markham's eyes flashed a warning.

"You're going nowhere but back on the Transport *Thomas,* and then back to Iowa, miss."

"Not Miss. *Mrs.* Captain Nash. That's *Mrs.* Señora Zumwalt. Remember?" She held out her left hand bearing the plain silver band which Robert had slipped onto her finger earlier. "I came here at the behest of President McKinley and I don't believe *your* official authority extends to telling a government employee, a married American woman schoolteacher, what she can or cannot do." She smiled up sweetly at his frown. "I believe that also holds true for American widows, sir. Am I right?"

"We'll see about that." His voice was grim.

"We shall *certainly* see about that." Her voice rang with determination.

Five

Both continued to eat. Long moments passed. Neither spoke a word but their eyes continued the argument. Sarah felt her resolution to stay, to work in the Philippines, growing stronger as she stared defiantly into the soldier's equally defiant brown gaze.

By the time they'd finished their soup, the younger Spanish priest who'd first greeted her at the church had tapped lightly at the open bedroom door and then stepped into the room. He asked Captain Markham something and the captain nodded.

"He wants to talk to you and he wants me to translate for him," Nash explained.

"You speak Spanish, Captain?" She felt her eyes widen in surprise as she surveyed the soldier's deeply tanned features with a more avid interest. An educated soldier!

Nash grinned and flushed a bit.

"You gotta know what your enemy's thinking, I always thought, ma'am." He placed his spoon on the plate before him. "If you know his language you can better tell what he's likely to think."

He stood and motioned for the priest to take his vacated chair at the table. The sleek, well-groomed young Spaniard looked tiny, almost feminine, next to the tall, broad-shouldered American whose hair stood up in a chaotic whirl of carelessly tangled black curls.

"So when they sent us to Cuba to fight," Nash continued, "I got right to work on it and picked up some of their lingo."

"Captain Nash, I'm impressed. Truly. I'd already made up my mind that I was going to try to learn the Filipino language while I'm here." She put down her own spoon and nodded at the young priest who waited patiently for their attention. "Maybe you can help me learn Spanish, too?"

Markham Nash's face darkened.

"We'll talk about that later." His lips carved a grimly straight line across his face. "As to learning 'the Filipino language,' as you call it, you're going to have a hell of a time at that, if you'll pardon my French."

The priest waited quietly, seemingly content to sit there until they were ready to listen to him. The soldier pointed to the young padre, drawing Sarah back to the matter at hand.

"We can talk about your language problems later. I expect you'll want to hear what the parson here wants to talk to you about."

Sarah nodded, then smiled at the priest.

"Yes, Father?"

He spoke for some moments before turning expectantly to Markham for the translation. "He says they want to bury your husband's body early in the morning, to avoid the heat of the day." He shifted uneasily. "Uh . . . he doesn't want to be indelicate, but he wants you to understand that they can't wait around for burial here in the tropics. Are you agreeable to the arrangement? And he wants to know if you're Catholic."

Sarah shook her head to the last question.

"My family is Methodist and I went to church because they expected me to go. I think Robert was Methodist, too. He didn't go to church much after his parents died. Does that matter?"

"Yeah. They have some kind of rule in the Catholic Church, he says. Seems like they can't bury a non-Catholic in the church burying ground but they can arrange to have him taken to the American cemetery. Do you want a ceremony out by the grave?"

Sarah closed her eyes for a second. She felt as if she'd been forcibly pulled from a pleasurable moment back to an all too unpleasant grim reality. She nodded.

The priest spoke and Markham translated for him.

"You do understand, Sarah, that they aren't allowed to say a mass for him?"

"I know that, but couldn't they just say a prayer? I guess we don't want a big ceremony. Unless *you* want to say something, Captain Nash? After all, you were his only friend in Manila."

Markham Nash leaned down to look into Sarah's eyes.

"Understand this, Sarah." His hard brown gaze glittered into her own. "Mr. Robert Zumwalt was no friend of mine." He straightened. "Excuse me if I sound harsh to you, but I barely knew the man."

PARADISE FOUND

He turned and spoke in Spanish to confirm the arrangements. As he did so, Sarah could feel the winds of anger rising in her once again. She broke into their conversation without an apology.

"You didn't like Robert, did you? You didn't even try to like him. I could tell. And now he's dead and you're acting like he's . . . like he's . . . like he was . . ." Sudden tears streamed from her eyes. Angry tears? Sad tears? She couldn't tell. She sat as tall as she could and forced herself to speak with dignity. "I want everything to be perfectly correct for my husband's burial. You just tell him that."

She stared at the cross which lay against the white-robed chest of the priest on the other side of the table. The large cross seemed to glimmer and move as she watched, but she knew it was only because of the trembling candlelight and because she was staring at the symbol through a veil of tears.

"What about a coffin? What about money ? . . . But no, I think I have enough to pay for everything." She picked up her pocketbook and searched for the small leather money purse her father had given her before she left. "I have twenty dollars, right here." She held out the small leather purse.

"You came around the world with only twenty dollars in your possession?" He seemed angry.

She nodded. "I knew I wouldn't need any money after I married and started work."

The captain spoke quickly in Spanish, then translated. "They had a box here and your husband's body is already resting in it. The Army will take care of all the expenses here at the church. I'll see to that." He lowered his gaze to continue. "I don't know what it costs for a burial plot, but Robert had a little money with him, as well as some other things you might want. They've put his money and his jewelry and all his other personal belongings with your luggage."

"With my luggage?" She felt puzzled, then remembered. "Oh, I'd almost forgotten about that. I do have some luggage, don't I? Where is it, by the way?"

"Well, there was a small sitting room connecting with Robert's bedroom and they've put everything in there. I'd told them to do that right after the wedding, when we first got here." He glanced around. "I didn't know what else to do. This is a pretty small room."

The young priest patted her hand and spoke in a softly sympathetic tone. Again Sarah felt tears rush to her eyes. She wished he hadn't tried to be kind. Even as a child, any sign of sympathy from her mother or her father or from Miss Arnold had always been enough to tip her over the edge and into tears. And now, everything was just so wrong, so sudden, so sad.

She, too, looked around the room. Apparently Robert had already arranged for this separate room for her before they were married. Had he not meant for them to stay together? She wiped her hand across her eyes. There was too much to figure out right now.

Both men shifted uncomfortably at the sight of her tears. Sarah, angry at her own loss of composure, confused by her situation, stood and walked to a window so she could turn her back to the two men. The nighttime air carried the scent of the small flowers she'd smelled at the dock. That, and a faint trace of the ammonia odor of urine. As she watched, the moon hid its face behind a passing gauzy cloud for just a second or two, just long enough for her to calm herself.

"We'll take him to the American cemetery and I'll read from my Bible for the burial." She pulled a small leather-bound volume from her purse. "I guess that's the last thing I can do for my husband." Her tears had slowed, but she didn't yet dare to turn around. "I'll do that with pride."

Markham spoke in Spanish, then the priest answered him at length. Markham mumbled. "Oh, hell" before he translated. Sarah turned back just in time to see him grimace at what the priest was saying.

"He's telling us the doctor doesn't want me to leave for Zambales for three or four days. He's afraid I might fall ill on the trail or you on the ship." He shrugged. "Well, Doc outranks me, so I guess I'm stuck in this place until he lets us leave. I'll just have to deal with my commanding officer when I get back to camp."

"Anyway, Captain Nash . . ." She took a step toward him. "We couldn't just have a funeral and leave here that very instant, could we? Somehow that wouldn't be right, would it?" Again she wiped her face with the back of her hand.

He shrugged. "I could. My packtrain is all but loaded. It'd be plenty all right with me to leave right now. I'll talk to the doc tomorrow about how soon I can deliver you back to the Transport."

"Don't you dare!"

Markham raised his hand, palm out, toward Sarah,

as a gesture for quiet, so he could listen to the priest. After a long exchange of conversation, the younger man glanced quickly at Sarah and stood to leave. He nodded to her as he spoke.

"Buenas noches, Señora Zumwalt."

"He's saying 'good night,' Sarah."

"I know what he said." Sarah let her irritation creep into her voice. "I'm not a complete idiot." She nodded to the priest.

"Buenas noches, padre."

When the young priest had gone, Markham Nash took a step closer to Sarah as if to comfort her. She turned her back to him again.

"He asked you to be ready at about five o'clock in the morning. That's when they're going to be moving the body." He took another step closer to her.

"The body? Again you're calling him 'the body'? Can't you even say his name?" Bitterness and rage seemed to swirl in equal parts through her soul. "He wasn't an important soldier like you, but he *was* a man, a human being. His name was Robert Ellington Zumwalt."

She laid her pocketbook and the Bible on the window ledge and turned away from the opening to see the wide, masculine, blue-clad chest right there waiting for her. Waiting to give her a place to cry her eyes out.

"I don't know what's causing me to fall apart this way," she sniffled against the solid woolen comfort he offered. "I'm usually not a crier or a whiner."

"What you *are* is a tired young woman who has had too much happen to her in the space of only one day." He smelled of sweat and horse. He smelled American. He smelled like home. His voice above her head was gentle. "You've had things happen to you that have forced you to grow up whether you wanted to or not . . . and almost in the twinkling of an eye." He pulled her a bit closer.

He gave her a few awkward pats on the back as he continued to talk. "Few women could move to a new country, get married, and make plans to bury their new husbands all on the same day, without crying . . . or maybe even going crazy." He was silent for a moment. "The whole thing is about to make *me* cry, Sarah. Just thinking about it. And I reckon *I* was already a little crazy."

She had to smile through her tears. She knew she would never see this rawhide-tough soldier cry. The mere thought of such a thing was amusing. She sighed and leaned against him. The gentle circle of this man's strong arms around her shoulders made her feel as if this were the only place in the world she wanted to be at just this moment.

When he dropped his arms and left the room with a low "Good night, Sarah," she felt bereft for a moment. She stood staring into the space where he'd been. She grasped the roll of legal papers the priest had given her so many hours earlier and stood silently pondering the red-ribboned tube.

She nodded as if she'd come to a decision, and placed the marriage papers on the table. She blew out the candle, removed her sweat-dampened clothing, left her new hat on the floor, placed the shoes at her bedside, put her totally wet whaleboned corset on the windowsill to dry, and folded everything else across the chair. And then, wearing only her white cotton shift, she dropped onto the hard cot with a sigh.

She fell into sleep as a stone falls into water, hardly moving throughout the remaining hours of the tropical night. If she dreamed, she never remembered it.

Markham stalked the halls of the rectory to the side door, then stepped out into the darkness. At the stable, his mind replayed the scene he'd just been a party to.

"She's in a foreign country where you're the only person she knows," he mumbled to himself as he inspected the hooves of each of the patient horses and the string of packmules. "You, Markham. You're the only person in this strange world who speaks that little woman's language."

His Filipino dogrobber, Bong, struggled up from his straw pallet to stand at attention. "At ease, Bong. Go on back to sleep. I just needed to get outside for a while." The young Filipino soldier nodded and fell back into the straw nest he'd arranged for himself and in seconds he was again snoring loudly.

Markham sighed. He wished his own life could be as uncomplicated as he imagined Corporal Bong Manawe's to be. A few jars of the local drink and it was back to quarters to sleep peacefully with the horses. No woman needed either his protection or his extended attention. That's what a soldier's life should be.

The women Markham Nash had known along the way in his army career were mostly able to take care of themselves. Most didn't want anything from him but a little money or a lot of passion-filled nights, or vice versa or both. And now this blond complication. She didn't want either money or passion, but she was the first one who'd needed comfort. From him. And he was the one who was officially appointed to give her that as well as protection. Damn.

His thoughts carried the idea a step further. *That's the reason why she's always cozying up to you, leaning on your chest and crying against your tunic. It has nothing to do with you. Just get any other ideas right out of your mind.*

"That's right," he whispered into the ear of his roan horse. "Old Markham here is just like you, Jonas, a government-supplied convenience so far as little Miss Proper-young-lady-from-Iowa is concerned and we all better remember that." He lifted an army issue curry comb from the wall, and with hard, downward swipes he began grooming the surprised animal.

Six

The clear light of the early tropical morning still offered a few shreds of low-lying mists. Second by second the sky above Manila began to lighten to a pearly, sunwashed blue. Sarah took a deep breath of the city's air which carried woodsmoke, the fragrance of exotic flowers and something she couldn't identify, a buttery, yeasty smell, almost like fresh bread baking but somehow richer. She'd have to ask Markham.

She heard roosters crowing from every part of the city and realized she'd heard their loud chorus before. Just yesterday. She'd heard, but she hadn't really noticed that homelike sound as she was trundling through the streets toward her marriage ceremony.

I was afraid. Panicked really, she thought. *Everything seemed to be happening to another person . . . a Sarah I didn't even know.* A quick picture of her strange wedding ceremony rose behind her eyes. "We never had a chance, Robert." She whispered so only she could hear the words, then bent toward the opened rectangle of ground that held his casket. "And I wasn't the only one who was at fault. Were you afraid, too? You acted as if I were someone you'd just met."

Scrubby-looking clumps of damp seagrass felt harsh against the thin soles of Sarah's new shoes as she stepped forward and dropped a handful of earth into the grave where his body now lay. The sound of the chunks of earth thudding on the top of the wooden box echoed in Sarah's ears. The sound made her feel hollow, then angry, then sad. Although it was still barely dawn she was already aware of the heat that had begun to ooze from the tightly hooked confines of her corset.

Her reading and the priest's prayer had filled only a few moments. The captain, the young priest, the doctor, and the maid, Luz had listened with bowed heads. Oh, yes . . . Captain Nash's helper . . . what was it Markham had called him? His dogrobber. The man was called Bong. Why had he acted so strangely during the whole thing? He'd frowned and been silent, but there had been something in the man's eyes, something accusatory.

Sarah was certain the frown wasn't directed at her. Maybe he was angry with his boss? she speculated. Captain Markham Nash wasn't always easy. She certainly knew *that*.

Anyway, that wasn't her business. Here were the *carramoto* drivers and the grave diggers, each waiting . . . waiting for her. It was all over. Completely over. It had never even begun. She stood dry-eyed at the rim of the grave a moment longer, then raised her gaze to meet the steady brown eyes of the man whom she hoped would help guide her to her new destiny.

"I guess we're finished now, Captain." When she stepped away from the grave, all the others turned to leave. The two Filipino men carrying shovels, the ones who had stood just outside their small circle during the makeshift funeral, moved forward, ducked their heads toward her in what she took to be gestures of respect, then immediately bent to their task of filling the earth in above Robert's mahogany box resting place.

Swinging from the neck of one of the men was a necklace of the small, sweet-smelling flowers. The circlet was exactly like the ones she'd seen on the Filipino men the day before.

"What's the name of the flower so many of the men wear here?" she asked the captain.

"Ilang ilang," he informed her. "They're sold everywhere on the street. Would you like a string of them?" He smiled down at her.

She nodded.

"But not for me. I want to put one on Robert's grave." She nodded again. "Yes, that would be right. He wrote me about how much he loved the Philippines and how well he liked the Filipino people. I think that the *ilang ilang* would be a proper flower to mark his passing, don't you?"

Markham Nash's face hardened and he frowned, but he turned without a word and strode briskly to the nearby road. Sarah watched him talk with a woman who was offering green coconuts for sale and a second later the woman reached to take the delicate green-

and-white wreath from her own neck to hand it to the soldier in exchange for a coin. He strode back just as quickly and handed the flowers to Sarah, still not speaking.

After she thanked him, she asked him to tell the others to go on. "I can tell they're all eager to get on back to their own affairs," she explained, then turned her gaze away from him. "You go on, also, Captain. Just tell the *carramoto* driver where I want to go and he can take me back to the rectory later. I want to stay here just a few minutes longer."

"I can't leave you here alone in a graveyard."

"Please. I need to do something in private, something that's just between Robert and me. I'll be all right. The Filipinos I've met all seem to be kind and gentle people, so I'm not afraid. Do please go on with the others."

"Are you sure?"

"Yes." She turned away and moved to stand near the spot where the grave diggers were finishing up their task. She didn't look back, but she could hear the tall soldier explaining her request in both Spanish and English and then the sounds of all of the mourners leaving.

Mourners? Not really. Even *she* wasn't a proper mourner. She hadn't loved Robert, had she? She hadn't really wanted to marry him, had she? She'd been using his offer of marriage as a path to a more adventurous life, hadn't she? She must now find a way to make up for all those things. And she would. She'd make it up to Robert even though he was dead. She had a lifetime ahead of her in which to make up for her shortcomings as a wife. She'd do it with her work.

Captain Nash stopped his big roan at a massive planting of deep pink flowering hibiscus bushes. He could see Sarah, but she probably wouldn't notice him.

"We can't leave the Widow Zumwalt all alone, Jonas, now can we?" He patted the horse's neck to quiet him.

He watched her turn and walk again to the filled hole. The two workers stepped back respectfully. She bowed her head. Praying, he thought. Then he realized she was talking to the grave itself. Frustration filled him. "Why the hell is she so set on talking to that dead sidewinder?"

She still wore the crumpled blouse and the ugly serge skirt she'd worn for the wedding. Her wedding hat still rode valiantly atop the glowing blond hair, but the little patent-leather shoes had been badly dampened by the early-morning dew.

She placed the flower circlet onto the dirt mound, then read something aloud from the Bible before replacing the volume in her pocketbook. Markham grunted. Good idea. If anyone needed an angel's intercession, it was old Robert. Now, maybe the bastard could sleep peacefully and the beautiful Sarah could go on back home and live a good life in Iowa. The idea of taking her to the ship to send her away made an almost physical pain clutch at his chest.

"I must find a way to get her on that ship," he nevertheless whispered to Jonas. "It's the only decent thing to do. There's no other way."

As she approached the waiting cart, the roan horse stepped into view. Sarah felt an inner shock at how glad she was to see the animal, and the man on him. Of course, it wouldn't be proper to let either the horse or the man know that.

"You've been spying on me, Captain Nash. You and your big old horse. I told you to go on, that I would be all right."

"I didn't stay to spy on you. I stayed to protect you. That's my job."

"But I don't need protection. The Filipinos I've met have treated me well."

"Well, Mrs. Zumwalt," his tone was dry. "You haven't met all of them. Ever hear the word, *ladrone?* They coined that one right here. Your first Filipino word. *Ladrone* means robber in Tagalog."

Sarah continued to walk toward the cart, the roan sidestepping daintily beside her.

"There are quite a few Spaniards still around, and even though they may not say anything to you, to them, you're the enemy . . . or at least the enemy's woman."

"The enemy's woman!" Sarah made a rude clicking sound with her mouth. "I'm *nobody's* woman, be it friend or foe. I'm my own woman." As she stepped up into the cart with the driver's help, she felt more at ease because she was now eye-to-eye with the soldier. "Anyway, how can you say such a thing? The two priests at the very church that's giving us both a place to stay are Spaniards. They've been both generous and helpful."

"Well, preachers . . . what do you expect?" He swung down from the horse to stand closer to the cart. "They're getting plenty of silver from the Army for what they do, believe me. But not all the Spanish leftovers here are priests, Sarah. Anyway, never mind the Spaniards and the Filipinos. There are thousands of American men roaming around this country who would just love a little blond morsel like you."

"Blond morsel! I'm a blond *morsel?*"

"To them you would be. A beautiful, bright haired, Caucasian woman. Every soldier's dream. I protect you, Sarah, until I know you're safely on your way home."

"We'll see about that." Sarah waved the driver to put the cart in motion. She trembled against her rising inner heat. *Captain Markham Nash thinks I'm a "blond morsel." That I'm "every man's dream?" That I'm "beautiful!"* Warm as the day already was, she couldn't help giving a shiver of excitement.

"Yes, ma'am." He raised his voice to be heard over the creaking of the cart. "We *will* see about that. I'm gonna get you onto that ship in spite of yourself."

Sarah kept her face forward, her back straight, her chin thrust forward with determination. *We shall, indeed, see about that, Captain Nash,* she thought.

From the churchyard Sarah strode resolutely into the priest's office to find the army doctor's whereabouts.

PARADISE FOUND 69

The younger priest called to Luz to speak English for him.

"Father say Doctor upstair," the young woman explained. "He sleep now."

"When he awakens please tell him I wish to talk to him."

"You eat now."

"I speak with doctor now."

"Father Gomes say you eat now."

Sarah realized she would get nowhere without a translator who really knew the language. She turned at the sound of Captain Nash's spurs against the stone floor of the church. *He's probably coming in here, too,* she thought, *I suppose I can trust him to translate for me.*

"Captain, would you explain to Luz and the Father that I would like to have a word with the doctor?" She compressed her lips before she asked the next question. "Are you translating exactly, Captain Nash?"

"I am." With exquisite courtesy he nodded and spoke to the others. His eyes gleamed with laughter.

"Anything else I can do for you, Mrs. Zumwalt?"

"No, nothing. I just need to speak to your *superior officer.*"

The priest spoke and Markham again gave a half bow. "The priest says that the doctor is resting now but if you would have the kindness to take a bit of refreshment at your own comfort in the room assigned you, he will send the doctor to speak to you, madame, forthwith, upon the officer's awakening hour." He bowed again. "I have translated as exactly as I could, Mrs. Zumwalt."

Sarah had to suppress the laugh that rose at his pompously literal translation.

"Thank you, sir. You may tell Luz that I will be glad to have something to eat." She paused on her way out the door and turned back. "Please tell the priest that I want to send my marriage certificate to my parents. I would like a sheet of paper and some ink so I can write a letter to them. Is that possible?"

Markham Nash spoke with the padre and bowed again. "That will be possible, madame. Luz will bring the equipment you have requested within this very moment. She will also return for your missive and will see that all legalities are mailed to your father and mother in their far-off country."

"Again, thank you, sir." She let a smile slip onto her lips before she turned to make her way to her own room.

She didn't turn around when she heard Markham say, "Upon his awakening, I will, if you've no objections, of course, accompany the doctor, my superior officer, to your quarters, madame."

She had to release one small giggle in the hall. Sarah Collins from Iowa was being called "madame"?

Hours later, Sarah, again in her stocking feet, stood arguing with the doctor while Markham Nash stood in the open doorway as an interested bystander.

"But Doctor, I'm an employee of the U.S. government . . . just like you and Captain Nash. President

PARADISE FOUND 71

McKinley sent me here to help the Filipinos and here I shall stay!"

"You're not required to stay, ma'am." The doctor ran his fingers through his hair.

"Doctor, I *want* to stay in the Philippines. I *want* to do the job I was hired to do!"

"This is no place for a young girl."

"If you'll recall, sir, I'm not a *young girl*. I'm a married woman . . . a widow. I'll soon be twenty-one years old and I'm just not going back to Iowa and that's final."

The doctor looked at Markham Nash and shrugged.

"She's got us there, Captain." Again he ran his fingers through his unruly silver hair. "I think you better plan on taking Mrs. Zumwalt back to Zambales Province with you."

Markham tried not to betray the sudden joy that worked to overpower the fear he had for her safety. He quashed the rising pleasure. *Better watch yourself,* he told himself. *You're getting too involved with the little widow. I'll just do my job,* he promised himself, since it seemed the matter was totally out of his hands. So be it.

"How soon can we leave, Doc?"

"Two, three days. That'll give you time to load her stuff and time for me to give you both a physical examination. If you pass, you can head on out for the boondocks."

"Head where?" Sarah asked.

"Boondocks. That's a Tagalog word meaning 'beyond the trees' or 'out in the mountains' or something like that. All our soldier boys over here have just picked it up. It means you're leaving civilization behind, little lady."

"That's quite all right with me."

"It may not be so all right as you think it will, Mrs. Zumwalt, but it'll be an experience you won't forget." The doctor ran his hands through his hair and smiled at Markham. "Right, Captain?"

Markham kept his face solemn. "Right you are, Doc." He turned his gaze to look down into Sarah's face. "If you're going to insist on going with me, we're going to have to unload some of the pack mules and repack them. You can carry a lot of your stuff in the *carramoto*. Then, when we send the cart and driver back to Manila, we'll do some more repacking down the trail after you switch to a horse. There'll be some tough riding later on."

"Switch to a horse?" Sarah's voice quavered.

"No problem for you in riding a horse, is there? You being a farm girl and all."

"Oh, no. No problem at all." Sarah clamped down on the fear that swept her. Riding Papa's plow horse around the barnyard when she was eight years old while Papa looked on was a great deal different than controlling a strange horse on a jungle trail. "But why must we dispense with the *carramoto?* I'm sure it would come in handy for our work at the school."

Both Markham Nash and the doctor laughed.

"No roads where we're going, Miss . . . uh . . . that is, *Mrs.* Schoolmarm." The captain turned in the doorway to leave with the doctor. "No roads at all. Not even any trails. Lots of trees and vines and monkeys and rocks, and mountains and rivers and snakes and spiders and mosquitoes, but not even one little tiny road."

He and the doctor found his last speech uproariously funny. Their mirth floated back down the hall to the tiny room where she stood, stocking feet welded to the floor. Had he said *snakes?*

By the following morning she had persuaded herself that the threat of "snakes" had simply been the two officers' way of trying to rid themselves of her, but she was still determined to stay, to take up her dead husband's work. That was what Robert would have wanted, surely.

The next morning, before the sun had risen too high she was already searching out Captain Nash to ask him to take her to the National Office of the Board of Education. She had to make her own decision official so she could receive her monthly teaching stipend and her school funds or supplies without difficulty.

"I need you to take me to the Board of Education, Captain Nash. My orders were to report there immediately upon arrival, but as you know, with what has been happening I've not been able to follow those orders."

"You have been pretty busy around the rectory, I've noticed."

"What hour would be convenient for you to make the trip to the Office of Education, Captain?"

His sarcasm was not lost on Sarah. "Pretty busy"

indeed. Yes, she'd gotten married and yes, she'd had to arrange for her new husband's funeral, but he was making it sound as though she'd just been idly doing whatever came to her mind.

"No hour would be convenient for that, Mrs. Zumwalt. If you have even a lick of sense you'll let me take you and your luggage straight to the dock, then put you back onto that ship. They're leaving today or tomorrow, I understand. You should be on it, girl."

"I've made my decision. I'm not going back to Iowa and that is that, Captain." She felt like stamping her foot even though the patent-leather slippers wouldn't make much noise. This man was being so difficult and she couldn't fathom the reason for his stubborn behavior. "Now let us discuss the best time for the trip to the office where I am required to make my presence known. Do you know where it is?"

"I guess I could find it if you're dead set on this." He stared at the floor before he raised his gaze to hers. "And I guess you are. Dead set, I mean?"

"Yes, I am. I want to do the right thing." She wished he could understand the emotion that was driving her. She would be ashamed to do anything other than her very best. She'd agreed to this job. The President had recruited her. "The right thing for myself and for the children who are in the school at San Miguel."

Sarah tried to tell herself that squiring her around Manila was a part of the U.S. Army captain's duty. After all, he had been ordered to attend to Robert and to her as well during their trek through the jungle, back to Robert's school in Zambales. Reporting Robert's death and getting herself registered with the Board of Education was certainly part of what she had to do before she could pick up the schoolroom reins from Robert, so what was the captain's problem?

When they alighted from the *carramoto* in front of the building which housed the Board of Education, she looked up at the grim face of Captain Nash and all her righteous claim to his time slid away from her. He didn't want to be here, he didn't want *her* to be here, or even in the Philippines, for that matter. It was a bit scary to be *forcing* this silent, solemn army officer to do her bidding.

"I'm sorry, Captain Nash, that I had to take you away from more important duties."

He nodded, as if to say he agreed. He *was* being taken away from more important duties. Sarah pushed back her indignation at his behavior. She was totally dependent upon him and he knew it. She glanced wistfully out at the busy street. She would love to have a chance to see just a bit more of Manila, but she knew she couldn't impose upon this man for a moment of time that wasn't strictly duty.

"I should not be more than a half hour or so if you'd care to wait, Captain. If you can't wait, I'll see if someone here can help me find my way back to the rectory."

"I'll wait." His voice was so low that it was almost inaudible over the sound of the street traffic.

"I'll hurry." She pointed to a row of chairs in a hallway outside the office. "That seems a reasonably cool and airy place for you to wait, Captain Nash. If it seems I'm going to be very long I'll come and tell you."

There now, Mother would be very pleased at how she had handled the bad-tempered captain. Sweet, thoughtful, and well mannered, yet firm in her directions.

He nodded and, with a sigh of resignation, headed toward the row of straightbacked chairs in the hallway and plopped himself down in the first chair.

"Don't be fooling around gabbing with a bunch of female schoolteachers. If you're determined to go back to Zambales with me, we need to get everything repacked and ready to go." He looked toward the piece of sky that was visible through the entry. "Sunny today, but probably rainy tomorrow, or at least soon."

Sarah settled her hat more carefully on her head and tapped at the office door. The captain was such an impatient man. But there was no help for that. She'd just have to continue to speak sweetly to him. Her mother's admonition still rang in her mind.

"Remember your manners, be kind to the people whom you deal with and remember that a smile will do more for you than will a frown or a sharp word."

Sarah prepared her smile when she heard a male voice say, "Enter."

She found herself facing a young American man behind a paper-stacked desk which faced the door. He looked at Sarah with interest and rose from his chair.

"How may I help you, ma'am?"

"I need to speak to someone about my husband's death and about his school as well."

"I am Allen Haynes, secretary for the School Board.

Perhaps I can help you." He reseated himself and pulled a sheet of paper toward himself, then looked up at her as if to let her know he was ready to take notes as she talked.

Sarah explained her arrival, her marriage, Robert's death and, lastly, her desire to continue Robert's work in the school in Zambales. The secretary wrote rapidly as she spoke.

When she mentioned the school in Zambales, he frowned and held up one hand.

"Just a moment Mrs. . . . Uh . . ." He glanced down at the paper he'd been using for notes. "Mrs. *Zumwalt*. Would you excuse me for a moment? I'd like to see if I can find Mr. Zumwalt's file." He tapped his pencil on the side of the desk. "It seems to me we've had a letter or two from the commandant of the army camp near Zumwalt's assignment." He nodded and scurried through a door in back of his desk.

Sarah looked at a lone chair in the corner. She could just move it to the front of Mr. Haynes's desk and she could sit comfortably while they talked. But he hadn't yet asked her to have a seat, so maybe she'd better remain standing. Was this the Board's way of prompting supplicants to make their stories short and to the point?

She couldn't resist cracking the door to get a peek at the captain sitting in the hallway. He was slouched in the chair, which was tilted back against the wall on two legs. His campaign hat was pulled forward to cover his eyes. His long legs were crossed and stretched out in front of him. He looked as though he were asleep. Good, maybe he wouldn't be so stridently impatient if he napped a little.

Mr. Haynes bustled back into the reception office carrying a file folder.

"We have no record of a school started in the barrio of San Miguel, Zambales, Mrs. Zumwalt. However, we *have* had a report or two of your husband's presence there." He looked at her over the edge of his glasses. "Am I to understand that you are willingly taking your husband's place in starting a school there?"

"Oh, I'm sure he has already started a school. He has been here for several months. I'm a qualified teacher... I was Sarah Collins, from Iowa. I arrived several days ago on the USS Transport *Thomas*. I am not only willing to work, I am eager to do so. Do you have a record of my employment contract, Mr. Haynes?"

"Oh, indeed we do." Mr. Haynes graced her with his first smile. "We need more teachers like you." Mr. Haynes sketched a bow. "The board offers condolences on your husband's death and they are willing to have you take up the job originally assigned to Mr. Zumwalt, if that is your pleasure."

"Could you tell all this to the army officer who will be escorting me through the jungle? He doesn't much want me to go with him, but I'm sure he'll do his duty if you'll point it out to him, Mr. Haynes. Will you tell him that I am appointed by President McKinley and that I am authorized by the Board of Education to teach at the San Miguel school, sir?"

"Certainly, Mrs. Zumwalt."

Sarah whirled and took two steps to open the door to the hallway.

"Captain Nash!" she called.

His chair crashed to the floor and he looked both ways along the hallway before he looked at her.

"You through?"

"Almost." She smiled at the slightly disoriented officer. "Mr. Haynes wants to speak with you and then I think we can be on our way."

Sarah couldn't keep her eyes from the military man's long strides. The uniform really became him. He was so tall and strong looking. No doubt he'd be the perfect guide through strange country. All she had to do was convince him that she belonged in San Miguel, and she felt Mr. Haynes could accomplish that much more easily than she. She stepped aside to let him enter the secretary's office.

"Captain Markham Nash, this is Mr. Haynes, secretary to the Board of Education. He would like to speak with you for just a moment." The two men shook hands. She noticed that the captain had to bend somewhat to put himself on Mr. Haynes's level.

Mr. Haynes looked down at the file in his hand and was silent for a moment before he spoke.

"Mrs. Zumwalt, if you'd sign here," he pointed to a space on a printed form, "I'd like to speak to Captain Nash for a second."

Sarah signed and stepped back.

"Thank you, Mrs. Zumwalt." The secretary didn't look at Sarah as he made his request. "I wonder if I could speak to the captain in private, ma'am. There are chairs in the hallway." He made another small bow, still without looking at her, almost as if he were ashamed to look her in the face.

"Of course." Sarah closed the office door on the captain's questioning look. She wondered what in the world the secretary of the Board of Education could have to say to Markham Nash that had to be so private.

She sat in the chair the soldier had just vacated and waited a bit uneasily for the men to conclude their secret powwow. Was Mr. Haynes pulling some kind of double cross? He'd told her she could go to San Miguel. Was he telling Captain Nash that she could *not* go?

When the door opened and the stormy-faced captain stepped into the hallway, Sarah thought she had her answer. He'd told the soldier in no uncertain terms that he must guide her to her new job. Hurrah!

She followed the military man out to the street where their cart waited.

"What did he say to you?"

"Just army business. Nothing you'd be interested in hearing."

"Am I still going with you to the village?"

"You're still going." Markham helped her swing up into the high-wheeled cart, then pulled himself up afterward. "Oh, yes, you're still going, little lady. More's the pity." He didn't speak another word to her during their return trip to the church rectory and he wore his frown all the way.

Sarah hugged herself with excitement. It was official now. He *had* to take her to Zambales. She was a teacher, a widow, and she was going to live in an ex-

PARADISE FOUND 81

citing new place and have her own village school. She'd write her parents and Miss Arnold this very evening and tell them everything that had happened.

Seven

Captain Nash lifted an elegant pair of gray-striped gentleman's morning trousers high into the air and stared at them before speaking his mind to Sarah.

"You sure as hell aren't going to need any fancy-pants hammer-tailed men's formal clothing in Zambales. Why don't you just give all Robert's wearables to Luz?" He let the trousers drop back onto the mound of stuff Sarah was sorting through. "I can guarantee you that she's got a raft of uncles, cousins, and brothers who could really use them."

"Oh, that's a good idea. But you did say I'd be riding?"

"Yeah. I have a nice gentle mare for you."

"Then I'll take some of Robert's clothing to wear on the trail. I'm certainly not going to wear my new lavender suit that Mama made me." Tears again rose to her eyes, but she controlled herself. "Mama meant for me to wear *it* to get married in." She held up the striped lavender woolen skirt and jacket. "See, the tiny blue stripe matches the blue ribbons on my hat." She turned the jacket so he could admire the pleated pep-

PARADISE FOUND 83

lum that would jut out over her skirt and her new modified petticoat bustle when she wore it. "She made me a pretty linen bustle petti—" She stopped her words and felt herself flushing.

She'd almost said *petticoat* to this man. What would he have thought of her then? She folded the suit and put it back into her carpetbag, her voice subdued. "I didn't even have time to change into it before the ceremony."

"Your mama must know someone in the Army."

"What do you mean?"

"That pretty suit of yours was made of wool. Mighty hot for this climate. But the Army doesn't care about our comfort." He ran his fingers around the inside of his stand-up tunic collar as if to let some cooler air inside his uniform. "They're just like your mama. She was thinking about your appearance and nothing else. They don't know how hot it is over here, and I have a sneaking hunch they don't care. Every time we soldier boys get into our dress uniforms we have to sweat our guts out in a woolen straitjacket. You've seen me walking around in this gold-buttoned horse blanket for three days now, haven't you?"

"I think it looks nice."

"That's what the recruiters say. Nothing like a uniform for catching a girl's eye." Markham smiled. "I'll be getting a whole lot more comfortable after we move on down the trail."

"That's what I intend to do. If I have to ride astride I'm going to wear trousers." She smiled at his shocked expression. "Trousers, Captain. Trousers will be much more modest on a horse than a dress would be. Don't you agree?"

She held out a pair of heavily starched white linen trousers.

"Robert must have had these made up over here. He would never have worn such a thing back home."

"You're probably right." Markham bent his gaze to the pack he was redoing, as if he didn't want her to read his expression. "Bong ought to be back any minute with the rest of our things, so if you think you've got everything you want packed, we can leave in the morning."

"Where will we put my things when I transfer from the *carramoto?*"

"Oh, the four of us will be eating along the way and so will the animals. We'll clear out some space as we go along. Your carpetbags can go right from the cart to hang behind your saddle."

"Four of us?"

"You, me, Bong, and the cart driver. That's four." He strapped a leather pack tightly closed. "It's going to be pretty nice to have some trail food cooked with the 'woman's touch' for a change."

"I'm going to be cooking?"

"Well, I knew you'd want to be pulling your share of the load along the way, so I thought you could do most of the cooking with Bong as your assistant." He strapped the other side of the pack firmly closed and placed the bulging leather object on top of the growing pile of finished packs. "How does that sound to you?"

Sarah nodded, but she quaked inwardly. He was

right. She did want to do her share. Maybe cooking on a campfire wasn't so different from cooking on the woodstove at home. Anyway, she'd keep busy. Wasn't that what she wanted?

"I hope Bong won't mind working with me. He seems to disapprove of me."

"Disapprove?"

"He looks at me so sternly."

"Never mind, Bong. He has things on his mind. He'll loosen up on the trail. He's just the right person to have around."

"Oh. Well, then. I'll get everything ready." She swept up an armload of Robert's clothing, keeping back the morning trousers, two collarless white shirts, and the white linen trousers for herself. She was sure Robert had meant the striped morning trousers for their wedding, along with the tail coat she'd found. She couldn't take the heavy tailcoat, but she would take the trousers.

His pen knife, his money clip with three ten-dollar bills and several one's, a handful of silver dollars, his shirt studs, his gold watch and chain, and the ten leather-bound books were the only other things she'd carry with her. Luz's family would suddenly find themselves well dressed in the American style, starched collars and all!

Indeed, later, in the kitchen, Luz colored with pleasure at the gift of the men's clothing. "My father like. Thank you very many, miss."

Back out in the yard Sarah saw that the corporal had returned. She stretched and was again aware of her corset digging into her sweating flesh. Sometimes being a woman was a curse. She looked at the two soldiers. Even though they were wearing wool they didn't look as if they had any body parts that were *hurting* inside their clothes. They were sweating, but they looked perfectly comfortable with their uniforms and with each other.

Corporal Manawe had returned with cages of live chickens, baskets of fresh vegetables, bags of rice, and packets of dried beans. Unaware of female scrutiny, the two men worked in a companionable silence, each doing what was required for a safe and secure trip. As Markham worked at the repacking, Bong began the cleaning and sharpening of what seemed an arsenal of weapons.

"Must we take all these guns and knives, Captain Nash?"

"The Army wouldn't much like it, ma'am, if we just up and left their equipment in a churchyard in Manila." He looked at Sarah inquiringly. "Are you afraid of guns?"

"The Army requires you to carry pistols, rifles, *and* huge knives?"

" 'Allows us to carry' is more like it. But yes, almost all these weapons belong to the Army." He picked up the largest knife. "Except this one. This belongs to Corporal Manawe. It's what the Army calls a 'machete,' and for me it's just a tool. You have something like it in Iowa, I think. Y'all call it a corn knife." He traced the sharpened edge of the knife and nodded at the corporal.

"Of course, I can cut a little jungle with a thing like this, but for Bong here, this machete is a good deal more than just a tool. Eh, Bong?"

The young Filipino soldier nodded and grinned and caught the heavy machete when the captain tossed it back to him.

"Now for me." He picked up a rifle. "For me, this is the baby that's gonna get us through the jungle and keep us all alive." He ran his hand along the wooden stock of the army rifle in a slow, sensuous movement. Sarah felt a tiny prick of envy toward the weapon. "I've been using a rifle since . . ." He looked at her appraisingly, "I expect since before you were born."

"I'm twenty years old, Captain. Do you mean you used a rifle as a tiny child?"

"Sure did. No general mercantile stores in the Territory, Sarah. We went to the woods for our meat. But I have nearly fifteen years on you, girl. Just turned thirty-four." He picked up two revolvers.

Sarah gasped and stepped back when he suddenly whirled each of the guns around a finger, then stood holding them cocked and aimed and at the ready. The barrels pointed steadily toward the smelly privy. Sarah felt glad that the deadly things weren't turned in her direction.

"My birthday presents to myself. These beauties don't belong to the Army. They're mine. Felt like I deserved them. I just let the Army feed me while I saved up my pay for them. Didn't take long to add up, since I don't have a wife and kiddies to support."

Sarah's heart shifted in her chest. Oh. He wasn't

married. She took one step closer to the arsenal. He held the two new guns up for her inspection.

"Yep. They belong to me. They're Brownings. The latest in handguns." He hefted the two revolvers with an easy intimacy. "Old Bong's mouth waters every time he sees these beauties. Right, Corporal?"

Again the corporal grinned and nodded. Sarah could see that the smaller man adored the big officer. She could also see that Markham liked him, too, and he certainly respected Corporal Manawe's abilities.

"Are your things ready to pack, Mrs. Zumwalt?"

"Oh, Markham. You've been calling me Sarah. Why not continue with that?"

"Well, you've been so all-fired adamant about being a wife and a widow, I thought maybe you wanted us to use your title also." He squinted down the barrel of one of the revolvers, one eye closed. "You get your marriage papers sent home all right and proper?"

"Oh, yes, with a letter telling them everything. Mama and Papa will be sad about Robert's death, of course . . . but they'll be pleased that I am doing the right thing. Now, all I want to do is get out into the country and start working." She studied his sun-browned face for an instant. "I knew you'd do everything you could to get rid of me, so I had to use my marriage or my widowhood or whatever weapon I had."

"To get your way."

"Yes. I suppose it was to 'get my way,' if you want to put it in those terms."

"Well, you won, girl. I just hope you aren't sorry for it."

"I won't be." She lightly traced the smooth wooden stock of the rifle with her hand much as Markham had done earlier. "Tell me, Captain, where were you born? Or what place do you call home? I know you're not from Iowa. Do my ears detect a slight southern flavor in your voice."

"Well, a little, I reckon. I'm from the Territory."

"Indian Territory?"

"Yeah. Oklahoma and Indian Territory. They're soon gonna become one state, they say. But, hell, I don't pay much attention to the politics back home. Can't do anything about it anyway."

"Indian Territory. Your parents are still there?"

"Yeah. My daddy's a white eye from Kentucky. Mama's a full blood. Cherokee."

"You're an Indian?" Shock coursed through her. "But you look, you look . . ."

"I look like my daddy, but I think like my mama . . . and that's good. I always thought she was the smarter of the two. She's the one who made me go on to school." He stood silent for a moment. "She's the one who persuaded me to give up riding around the Territory with a pretty wild crowd of carousing old boys.

"She told me I might as well get my wild oats worked out on army time . . . where riding and shooting and raising hell were all legal, even required." He hefted one of the pistols as if he were weighing it. "She knew I'd never be content to be chained to a store nor to stay hidden behind a desk, either. Daddy agreed with her. He said the redskin in me would love all the wandering around that the Army does and the white eye in me would make me want to work myself up in the ranks. They both knew their boy pretty well."

"I didn't know whites were allowed to live in Indian Territory." She clapped her hands over her mouth. The words had come out before she thought.

Markham lowered his gaze and grinned.

"Daddy never was one to stick too close to the law. He's like most of the other white men in the Territory married to Indian women. Mostly hiding out. Maybe he wanted to run away from something in Kentucky. Probably had a family there. Maybe he couldn't get along with them. He never said." He raised his gaze to smile down at her. "Most likely he just wanted to be with Mama. He still gives her a pat on the fanny whenever he passes near her. Those two old folks are still mighty in love, I think."

"My parents, too, I believe." Sarah felt a wisp of homesickness rise. "I don't think they've been apart for as much as one day since they married." Of course, Mama and Papa had never *touched* in public, but she'd seen them looking at each other the same way they'd looked at her. With great love.

It seemed years rather than months since she'd seen home, since she'd seen her mama and papa. They might not be the most exciting people in the world but they had been good to her. She truly loved them. And she loved Iowa, even if she was bored there. And there was the big comfortable family farmhouse. And Miss Arnold. And her friends from school.

She sighed and swallowed the lump that had caught in her throat. Could she just go on back to Iowa and learn to live with her guilt about Robert? Were adventure and duty to the President and helping the Filipinos all that important?

Maybe she should just take Captain Markham Nash up on his offer and let him deliver her straight to the U.S. Army Transport *Thomas* for the return trip home? Should she? No one would blame her for such a choice. Never mind that she had signed those papers in Mr. Haynes's file. She could still go home if she wanted to. Markham would be glad to tell the Board of Education that she had changed her mind. He'd be *happy* to do that. What should she do? She had to make her decision right now . . . and she had to live with it forever.

Eight

Early on her fifth morning in the Philippines, Sarah paused to take one last long look around the tiny whitewashed room which had been her home for the last four days and nights. She was surprised that she felt almost as sad to leave the rectory as she had been to leave her family's house in Iowa.

"Goodbye, little room," she whispered. "And thank you." She smoothed both hands down the full skirt of her blue-and-yellow cotton print dress, touched her wedding hat to be sure it was on straight, picked up her smallest carpetbag, then walked briskly down the hall toward the turn that would take her to the rectory side door and outside. She resolutely descended the stone steps, crossed the side yard and slowed to walk toward the stable area.

She stood looking silently at the melée caused by the restless, stamping horses and mules. Markham shouted something she couldn't understand and Bong shouted an answer in return. She couldn't help noticing how neatly military both he and Bong looked. Their woolen tunics were clean, brushed, and buttoned to the last button, their trousers and leggings pressed and immaculate. Each wore a wide-brimmed felt military-style hat with a strap under the chin. Bong's campaign hat reached to the shoulder of his captain, who towered over everyone and everything in the yard. He was huge, no question of that. Fit and slim where it counted, but huge nonetheless. As always, his size and his military bearing intimidated Sarah just a bit.

She lifted her chin, drew her own blue velvet hat ribbons tight under her own chin and forced herself to remember that she was now a teacher, a widow, and the equal of any person in President McKinley's army even though she wasn't as big as some of them.

The tiny maid-of-all-work, Luz, stood giggling with a young Filipino man Sarah hadn't seen before. The two laughing people stood within the narrow strip of shade cast by the stable roof. Sarah felt a quick stab of envy at the pretty little rectory maid's freedom to flirt without guilt. She instantly shook the feeling from her mind. Who would she want to flirt with, anyway? She looked up at the captain's hat once again.

After another second of silent observation she whirled to take in the noisy scene, a smile pasted on her face. This was what she wanted . . . wasn't it?

"I thought the Army uniform included a blue-billed cap. Are you and Bong wearing something special for the Philippines or are they just because of the sun here?"

"I have a cap, yes, but the Army is discontinuing them. They're also getting away from the blue. This campaign hat is what most of the troopers and officers wear over here." He reached to touch the tilted brim of her straw hat. "Believe me, you'll be glad of the shade your hat affords."

Sarah couldn't see the cart she'd be riding in, but she knew it was parked on the other side of the rectory. Only hours before, just before going to sleep, she'd packed the last of her belongings into it. The man with Luz must be the *carramoto* driver Markham had said he was going to hire.

"I'm ready, Captain," she told him.

"Good. Let's head out."

He shouted, and Bong and the young driver began the movement of the animals toward the gate. Markham nodded to Sarah, mounted, and swung his horse in to lead the parade of overloaded horses and mules. Bong brought up the rear of the packtrain.

The cart driver gestured to Sarah. "Señora," he said. Sarah let herself be helped up to her seat, her small bag beside her, then the driver leaped to his own perch and they fell in behind Bong. Sarah turned to look at the extra horses tethered to the back of their conveyance. Her eye caught the smile of the maid who'd been so helpful to her.

Before she'd waved her last to Luz, Markham and the big horse, Jonah, were in the far distance down the cobblestoned street. Soon the cobblestones gave way to hard-packed earth and the large houses hidden behind walls and compound gates became smaller wood-and-bamboo structures without the high coral stone walls. After an hour, the packtrain was out of

PARADISE FOUND

Manila and in the country, with only an occasional thatched bamboo hut standing sentinel beside the road.

Sarah always waved to the tiny, almost naked, brown children who clustered in play at the base of each of the cabins which were usually set up on stilts. On a few of the larger thatched roofs of the huts, the family dog stood full-time sentinel duty.

"I've never seen dogs tethered to the roof of a house before," she mused aloud. No one answered. No one heard her. The thud of the wooden wheels, the shouts of the men, the plodding hooves, the squeak of leather, and the clank of harness chains created a moving cacophony which easily covered any sound she might make.

As they moved into the edges of the jungle proper, the sun was, after awhile, blocked by the foliage overhead. Only a few bright spots of sunlight were able to penetrate the madly riotous greenery. By the time two hours had passed, her crisp cotton dress had wilted to a wet rag, her corset punched a whole new set of bruises into her ribs, and her legs screamed to stretch if only for one moment. Worse than the heat was the dust which clogged her nostrils and lodged in the pleats on her dress.

"Hold on, Sarah," she spoke aloud. "You can stand it." She tried to distract herself by staring at the beauty of the passing countryside. The sugarcane fields had been left behind by late morning and the wide dirt road gradually became a rutted trail through a thickly wooded, hilly tropical forest.

At the very moment that her legs had begun to feel

as if they were filled with a thousand gnawing insects trying to get out, Markham raised his hand to stop the caravan. She saw that his tunic was now unbuttoned and showing his white underwear-clad chest. As he buttoned his coat again, he pointed to a huge tree which shaded a dusty, cleared area at the edge of the forested hillside. A crystalline stream gurgled only a few feet down the hill from the open spot.

"We'll stop here for a few minutes," he called out. Sarah felt a rush of gratitude at his words. She let the driver help her to the ground, and for a moment she had to hold onto the cart and stamp her feet to force her blood to circulate freely again.

"What's your name?" she asked the driver. When he only stared, she pointed to her own chest and said, "I'm Sarah," then pointed toward his chest. "You are . . . ?"

"Ah," he smiled. "Rudolfo, señora."

She smiled and repeated his name. Markham shouted the name also. The driver turned at Markham's call. Sarah looked at the captain as well. Was she supposed to cook? Sarah trudged toward Markham. He already had Bong and Rudolfo carrying pails of water for the animals.

"What shall I do?"

Markham looked at Sarah. His eyes seemed to hold a speculative gleam.

"What do you want to do?"

"Anything. Walk, bend, stretch, run . . . anything but sit."

His smile grew.

"You can stand and eat while the rest of us sit down for our dinner. How about that?"

Sarah looked about for a likely place for a campfire. Now. Right here. This was going to be her proving ground. Could she do it or not? She compressed her lips and nodded. She could and she would!

"Where would you like me to build the fire?"

"Well, if you're going to be the cook you're always going to have to be your own best judge of where to put the fire." He pulled a sack from the corner of her cart. "But right now we're not going to have to cook anything. Luz fixed us a pretty hefty bunch of vittles." He handed the heavy cloth bag to her. "You just parcel out something for each of us and we'll fall to." He walked to pull several leaves from a nearby banana tree. "Here are your plates."

The huge leaves felt cool and moist in her hands. Eat from a leaf? She looked at the wide green fronds very carefully. They looked clean. Maybe they'd work.

Markham pointed to the base of the tree.

"We three old boys'll just sit and put our backs against that tree trunk right there. You can put your own leaf on the cart seat and pace between bites if that's your pleasure. Course, we won't stay around here but a short time."

"A short time?"

"Yeah. We're just barely getting started. Gotta make some more miles before dark."

Sarah nodded her understanding and placed all the banana leaves on the cart.

"I'll just step down to the water and be right back."

"Okay, but keep your eyes open. Don't go more than a few steps from where at least one of us can see you. Lots of things could happen to a girl in a jungle."

Sarah nodded and pushed her way into the bush. She slipped into the deep shade between two huge mahogany trees. The shadowy darkness seemed to offer as good a hiding place as any. She squatted. When she rose, she stepped toward the running water and took a deep breath. As she stretched, she felt the hated bones dig into her again. On impulse she undid the row of pearl buttons that ran down the front of her dress and let the dress drop to the cluttered forest floor. She then dropped the sweaty linen petticoat. She bent her head in order to be able to see to unhook the punishing corset.

"You're staying behind," she said to the boned instrument of torture. For a second she could imagine her mother's horrified face, but she continued the unhooking. Her fingers steadily worked down the front of the garment. She remembered how shocked her mother and Miss Arnold had been when they'd first heard of Amelia Bloomer and of her idea of women wearing pants.

Some of the more sophisticated women in American cities had started wearing the silken, ankle-length blousy trousers under their dresses. Nowadays, a few adventurous souls had started wearing their "bloomers" with the elastic pulled clear up above their knees, leaving their lower limbs with nothing covering them except their stockings and their outer skirts. "Hidden sinfulness," some whispered.

PARADISE FOUND

"Easy women," Mama and Miss Arnold had called all the female bloomer wearers. Sarah grunted and yanked at a recalcitrant hook. She'd trade her corset anytime for a pair of bloomers They sounded like practical garments to her.

"Bloomers!" Her mother had snorted the word. "Amelia Bloomer was doing nothing but the devil's work. A good woman wears shifts and petticoats under her skirts, not trousers."

Sarah peeled the wet corset from herself, and with both hands held the garment up to the light as if she were reading from a book. "Latest modern comfort from New York," she quoted the ad in the Montgomery Ward catalog. "Comfort indeed!" And she hurled the boned body controller as far into the brush as she could. She then pulled her white linen shift off each shoulder and stepped out of it.

Naked now, except for her shoes, her gartered black cotton stockings, and her wedding hat with the blue velvet ribbons tied carefully under her chin, she looked both ways then backed cautiously down toward the rushing stream. She turned and quickly scooped up water from the moving liquid to pat her face and splash on her body, then just as quickly she stepped back to pull on the shift and the petticoat and rebutton the dress. In seconds she stood, almost cool, and in unimaginable comfort. Her dress felt a bit tight at the waist but nothing, *nothing,* compared to that wretched "modern comfort from New York."

At a scolding sound she peered up into the branches of the trees. For a moment she was frightened. A group of five reddish-brown monkeys sat staring down at her. She stared back at them. Braced to run, she soon realized they weren't going to hurt her, were only curious. They seemed to be making faces at her, so she made one back at them.

"Ah ha!" She jumped to the right, then to the left, and flung her arms up into the air. The monkeys scattered.

A female carrying a baby swung down a jade vine to once again become an audience to Sarah's antics. Sarah shook her finger at the mother animal.

"Understand this. I am never going to wear one of those things again. Ever!" The monkey raced back up into the high branches, carrying her baby and chattering all the way. Sarah watched for a moment, then smiled.

She kicked each leg as high as she could, then felt her hat to make sure it was still straight before she walked sedately into the clearing to serve a picnic to her "family" of waiting men.

Markham watched Sarah's dreamy smile as she served fried chicken, quarters of fresh onion, chunks of bread, and small mounds of sticky rice onto each leaf plate. She also handed each man a small red banana from the bunch he'd taken from the tree where he'd found the plates.

Walking to deliver the food, she seemed to pay only scant attention to what she was doing. She appeared to be almost totally enveloped in some pleasurable reverie.

Wonder what's making Miss Iowa grin like a Chessie Cat? Markham smiled, too. She might have her secrets, but he had a pretty good secret himself. His smile stretched to a wide grin. He felt so expansive he even allowed Bong and Rudolfo to take a few minutes of siesta time before they again began their trek toward Zambales.

While the men slept he taught the schoolteacher how to cut a ripe mango by scoring and turning each half of the oval-shaped fruit inside out so she could eat the peachlike flesh without dripping and smearing the juice all over herself. He decided with a hidden smile that her tiny mm-m-mm-ms and other sounds of enjoyment for the sweet, juicy treat were more than enough payment for the lesson he'd given her.

For Sarah, the afternoon proved to be even worse than the morning had been, even though she wasn't being punched and prodded by corset stays. Twice the cart dropped one of its wheels into a deep rut and the tiny pony was unable to move farther without the help of the men and the other horses. Tiny orchids and other exotic flowers beckoned to Sarah and she hopped from the cart as often as she dared, but Markham barked at her whenever she tried to walk. He didn't seem the slightest bit excited by the bands of monkeys which traveled along the forest umbrella as the packtrain jangled along on the trail below.

"You'll just slow us down. You sure can't keep up with horses on foot and we aren't planning to wait around while you take your little strolls." He'd gestured toward the jungle growth as if he were sweeping it away. "There'll be plenty of monkeys and flowers where we're going. We gotta keep moving, schoolmarm."

She knew he was right, but her legs couldn't seem to understand. They wanted to walk!

The late afternoon passed in a blur of heat, dust, and the lengthening shadows cast by the trees and vines of the forest. Sarah heard the cries of the monkeys on every side. Were they from the same band of animals who had watched her disrobe earlier? They looked the same.

The deeply musky smell of the jungle was spiced with the sweetness of hidden flowers and piqued by the sharp note of torn greenery that broken vines lent to the heady brew.

When Markham stopped the packtrain the sudden silence hurt her ears. For a few seconds the whole train—mules, men, cart, and horses—stood frozen in a silent tableau. Above them a bird's shriek broke the spell and then the horses and mules stamped, their harnesses jingling and clanking. Markham slid from his horse and walked toward Sarah who sat, still mesmerized, in her cart. The sound of his spurs was muffled against the cluttered ground.

"Wake up, girl. Sun's almost gone. We'll spend the night here." He held up both hands toward her and waited.

She looked down into the dark eyes that stared at her. For a second she felt lost in the brown gaze. She leaned toward the compelling stare and put her hands onto the wide shoulders of the waiting soldier. He lifted her gently to the ground and stood with his hands at her waist until she stumbled back against the wheel of the cart.

"We're not even off the trail. What if someone wants to pass? We're in the road."

"Well, it's not as if we were on a highway in Iowa where the wagons, buggies, horses, and bicycles are just bustling back and forth night and day." He pointed into the dark tunnel of forest where the trail led. "Anyone comes up that road, we'll make room for them to get by, somehow."

She knew that her questions made her sound childlike and ignorant, but she didn't know any other way to find out what she needed to know. She remembered Miss Arnold telling the classes that it was "never a disgrace to ask questions. That's how you learn!"

"Will I be cooking tonight?" The feel of his hands around her waist made her feel slightly breathless, but she stood as still as she could. His touch made her feel so secure.

He shook his head. "We'll finish up what Luz sent first. No use letting all that cooked stuff go to waste." He lowered his hands from her waist. "You can go into the woods, but keep us in sight." He turned to look at Bong and Rudolfo leading the horses and mules into the jungle. "They're going to the river, but you better not wander off that far away unless one of us is with you."

Sarah felt herself flushing. She turned without speaking toward the jungle growth, her gaze still fixed on his brown-eyed stare. Still without speaking, she slipped sideways. She looked down at the humus-covered ground to break the sight line that had connected them for long electric moments. She parted the heavily palmetto undergrowth and turned to look back at Markham Nash. He was still looking at her.

"Watch yourself. Eyes up, down, and sideways, Lady Iowa. Remember those snakes!"

Sarah stood rigid, greenery touching her arms, her face, her skirts. Snakes? She couldn't make herself move either forward or backward.

"Can you still see me?" She could hear his voice quite clearly. She swiveled her gaze back toward the tiny open area. Markham Nash stood staring at the spot where she'd disappeared. Yes, she could still see him and hear him. Could he still see and hear *her?*

"Answer me." His voice was sharp.

"I can see you. I'll be out in a moment." She kept all her senses alert and tried to be as quiet as she could. In moments, she was able to reemerge from the heavy growth. She nodded to Markham and accepted the cloth bag which he again swung down from the cart.

"No banana trees around here. I'll get something else for us to use to eat on," he said, heading for the jungle growth. When he emerged a few minutes later, he handed her pieces of curved brown chunks torn from a nearby tree. "Use this bark. We'll camp by the cart tonight. No fire."

"We'll sleep here?" Sarah wondered why she hadn't even given a thought to where they would all sleep.

"Did you think we'd be putting up at a hotel? We'll

PARADISE FOUND

put you under the cart. The three of us will sleep around you. You'll be fine."

He reached into the cart and pulled out the bedroll he'd had Luz make up for her. "You'll have a roof over your head. Pretty luxurious for a night in the Philippine jungle." He grinned at her.

Later, from her place under the cart, Sarah could just make out a strip of velvety, navy-blue sky studded with stars that flashed white or green or pink fire. *I'll bet Markham can see the whole sky,* she thought, and twisted closer to the wheel to try to see whatever it was he was looking at with his eyes wide open.

His head was resting on his saddle. He'd changed to a khaki-colored cotton shirt and his body was stretched full-length, his legs and arms still. To see more clearly, she lifted the edge of the white mosquito netting he had hung from a ring on the bottom of the cart.

"What are you looking at, Captain Nash?"

"I'm not looking at anything. I'm thinking." When he turned his gaze toward her, his eyes were only a few inches away from her own. "Actually, right now, I may be seeing a young lady who will soon be covered with mosquito bites unless she keeps that netting tight around her bed."

"I didn't have a mosquito net at the rectory."

"The Army's trying to clean up all the skeeter breeding places in Manila. They're doing a pretty good job, too. Anyway, you were so tired you might not have noticed if a whole fleet of flying teeth had invaded your room."

"You and Bong and Rudolfo don't have nets."

"We don't smell quite so sweet to the pesky devils. When they see all that pink-and-white skin . . . Yum yum. They'll call in their families and friends from miles around to chew on you, girl."

She continued to keep the net up just enough to see him.

"Never mind about the mosquitoes. Can you tell me what you're really thinking?"

"Just that this sky is beautiful but that the sky back in the Territory is even more beautiful in its own way."

"Why, Captain! Are you homesick?"

"Nah. Not really. It's just that you got me to thinking about the place with your questions. Course, the Army's my home now and I'm pretty happy wherever I am." He inched a fraction closer to the wheel that stood as a spoked wall between them. "How about you? Are you homesick yet?"

"Maybe a little. But I'm not sorry I chose to stay if that's what you're asking."

They kept their voices low so they wouldn't disturb Bong, who was sleeping next to the cart on the other side. Rudolfo sat on his blanket for what Markham had called "first watch." Sarah decided that it was just Army custom to always have someone awake and watching. There was really nothing to watch out for.

"Maybe you will be sorry later on, little lady. Things are different in the Philippine Islands."

"I don't think so." She gave him a curious glance. "Were you sorry you left Oklahoma Territory to join the Army?"

"I guess I really left home when I went back East

PARADISE FOUND

to school. Massachusetts. Mama made me promise I'd join the Army there and I did. She's a pretty wise old girl."

"Why did she want you to join up in the East?"

He smiled, the light from the stars allowing her to see the white glint of his teeth against his tanned skin. He turned to lie on his stomach and put both his hands under his chin. "All they knew about me up there was that I had a diploma from a good school, that my name was Nash, that my father came from Kentucky . . . that my skin was white."

"Oh." Sarah felt herself flush. Of course. He probably couldn't have joined the Army if they'd known he was an Indian. Certainly he could never have become an officer. "I'm sorry."

"No need to be. I've had the best of both worlds. I spent my childhood as an Indian . . . best life in the world. Hunting, fishing, free to be outside all the time and free to be a part of nature." Again she saw the white gleam of his smile. "I've spent my life as an adult leading and teaching other men . . . still mostly outdoors, but always in the Army's controlled environment." He turned to lie on his back again, his eyes turned toward the stars. "Life's been mighty good to me."

"Do you miss the freedom of Indian life?"

"Oh, I had it while it was still there for us. I hunted or fished every day . . . stayed out in the woods all night with my friends, swapping stories of the old days across the campfire." She could see his smile. "That way of life is all gone now. Indian boys have to live like white eyes now or be left behind, buried in the scrapheaps of the modern world." He was silent for a moment. "We have to change or put up with sickness, drunkenness, and slavery of one kind or another, whether on a reservation or in a big city." He grunted. "The Territory is about the only place I've seen where Indians still have the chance for some dignity."

He tossed a pebble into the nearby clump of oleander bushes. Wings fluttered, then the jungle stilled except for the chirps and clicks of some sort of insects. Maybe one of the three-inch bamboo beetles Rudolfo had pointed out to her earlier? Somehow she hadn't felt afraid of those bugs. They'd looked like some sort of primitive jewelry rather than like scary insects. Markham's low voice brought her back to their conversation.

"My children, if I ever have any, will probably never be able to experience what I did. Even if I go back to the Territory. The Indian's time is over . . . at least the Indian way of life as I experienced it and the Indian customs and language as my ancestors knew them." He sighed. The sound spoke resigned acceptance to Sarah's ears. "Like Mama says. 'Gotta take on the white world's trappings to get ahead these days.' "

Sarah lay silent for a moment.

"You're not at all what I would have thought an Indian to be. I mean . . ." She paused in confusion. What did she mean?

He gave a quick laugh, then quieted himself when Rudolfo stirred and looked toward them from the other side of the cart.

"You mean I'm no naked savage? Because I'm all buttoned up in a high-collared tunic?" He rose to lean on one elbow so he could face her once more to tuck the mosquito netting in around her pallet. "Maybe that's because you don't yet know the real me, Sarah. Oh, yeah, I'm an educated redskin. Probably had more schooling than you, teacher, but sometimes, *sometimes,* that savage inner man . . ." His strong, square hand tapped his chest, "sometimes he gets pretty close to the civilized surface."

He laughed again, more a chuckle this time. He turned to his side, his back toward her now, his voice a whisper. "Better close those curious blue eyes and get some sleep, lady. The easy part of our trip is just about over."

Nine

At their last stop on their fifth day, the trail had narrowed to a twisted, barely there, path. Vines, bushes, and brambles of every kind desperately conspired to erase all signs that either two-legged or four-legged animals had ever passed this way. The little *carramoto* pony was willing, but the high-wheeled cart couldn't be forced farther forward into the jungle growth.

"Time for you to become a horsewoman, Sarah. We'll do some repacking here and Rudolfo can head on back to the city tomorrow morning."

Bong cleared a small space for their camp with his machete, then Markham and Bong and Rudolfo took all the bags and bundles from the cart while she prepared the ring of stones for the evening fire.

She suddenly caught a glimpse of her hands and stopped work, spread her hands in the air in front of her as if showing them to a stranger. They looked ugly to her . . . browned by the sun, short, broken fingernails, calloused palms. Working hands. Mama always said white hands and tended fingernails spoke volumes about a woman's station in life.

PARADISE FOUND

Sarah gave a mental shrug. What did that kind of thing matter to her now? She was going to dedicate her life to teaching young Filipinos to read and write, wasn't she? Her hands were just tools for her use. Beauty wasn't a requirement. So far, her hands had been pretty good tools.

Strange, she thought. *I'm doing this as if I've done it every day of my life. Unpacking, cooking, cleaning, repacking . . . every movement now seems natural, easy.* Cleaning with sand was just another way of cleaning. The oilskin packets which she used to carry the leftovers for the coming day's dinner now seemed perfectly acceptable as food vessels.

And she'd become a fish lover. She'd never cared for fish when she was back in Iowa. Her change of heart was because of Bong. The corporal seined up fish, tiny fish, nearly every night after they'd camped. The fish were so small they required no cleaning, no gutting. He'd taught her to simply impale the live bodies on pointed sticks, then to stand the sticks in the sand just outside the fire ring so the fish could brown over the heat from the hot coals. The first time she'd eaten them, Markham had had to insist that she try one. After that, the delicately crisp, little two-inch morsels had become Sarah's favorite part of the meal . . . heads, tails, eyes, bones and all.

As for rice, Sarah ate it, too, but sometimes she had longed for potatoes for supper.

"We have to have rice with every meal if we can," Markham had explained. "It's part of the contract with the native soldiers. They'll eat almost anything we can offer them, but they *must* have rice. It's like bread and potatoes are for us, I guess." Now she was proud to say she could cook rice to the sticky consistency that Bong and Rudolfo loved.

Sticky rice was only right, she thought, since they were eating it with their hands. Picking up the fluffy single grains cooked the way her mama cooked rice wouldn't have been an easy task on the trail. Yes, rolling little mouthsized balls for each bite, as Bong had taught her to do, required something gluey . . . which was what her cooked rice now was.

Actually, Mama would be proud of me, she assured herself.

The coffee boiled up and out the spout of the blue graniteware pot. Sarah grabbed it, using her skirt as a potholder. Scalding black liquid suddenly spewed out and across her hand. She screamed and stood up with tears in her eyes.

That's what you get for thinking you're so smart, she whispered as she blew against the long, reddening burn on the back of her right hand.

"You all right, Sarah?" Markham, gun in hand, skidded to a breathless stop in the grass in front of her. "What is it? Snake?"

She shook her head no and silently held out her hand in explanation. He smiled but pulled her toward the water bucket.

"Stick your hand in there. Cool water's the best thing for a burn."

"I just brought that bucket up from the spring. It's for drinking and cooking."

"Do it. I'll go get more water if we need it." He pulled her hand down and plunged it into the half-filled container. "Anyway, your sweet little hand won't ruin the water." He grinned and dipped a tin cup into the water, lifted the contents and drank from it. "Ah-h-h-h. See? Makes it taste sweeter." He squatted across from her with a bemused expression on his face. "Feel better?"

The water *did* calm the pain. She lifted her hand out and the pain returned, so she hurried to put it back into the soothing coolness.

"We always used butter back home. Mama said it was the very best burn remedy."

"Sorry to dispute your mama's word, but cool water's better." He shifted closer to her. "Anyway, we don't have any butter. In the field most soldiers have access to water so we've always used it for campfire burns."

"I think I'm learning something new or doing something I've never done before almost every hour of the trip."

"You are doing a lot of things you've never done before, aren't you, Sarah?" She couldn't read the expression in his eyes.

"If you mean I've never burned my hand before, you're wrong. Any woman who cooks has burned herself plenty of times."

"Especially when she's first learning, you mean?"

"I was learning to cook by the time I was six years old."

"Not on a campfire."

"You can tell?" She felt her face warm. Her earlier

paean of praise for herself had now become nothing but a prickly inner embarrassment.

"I've gathered from what you've said that you are the cossetted only daughter of well-to-do farmers who wanted you to be a teacher so you wouldn't have to get your hands dirty." He grinned at her and his white teeth flashed contrast against his tanned face. "Am I right?"

Sarah had to be honest. He'd pretty well learned the truth about her. She nodded shamefacedly, but then she lifted her chin. She was going to make a difference in this new world, no matter what she had to learn in order to do so.

"Your upbringing is nothing to be ashamed of, but just remember, practically everything you do from now on for the next few months is going to be something you're doing for the first time. Don't be afraid to ask for help if you need it." His white smile gleamed again in the light from the fire. "We're going to ford a river tomorrow. I'll need help from you and Bong for that and I can tell you, I'm not afraid to ask for it."

He'd reached out to hold her good hand in his as he talked, smoothing the back of it with his other hand. Her hand felt so good cradled in his that she practically forgot the burned hand resting in the water. She closed her eyes. She wanted the smoothing to go on and on. She wanted to put her head against his chest. She wanted. . . . Her eyes blinked open. No. She wanted to be independent. She wanted . . . she jerked her good hand away from his solid grasp and her burned hand out of the water. She stood up and faced him.

What was wrong with her, anyway? She was no child. She was a married woman, a widow. She didn't need to be catered to or entertained or sympathized with. She could carry her share of the load.

"Thank you, Captain Nash. I'm fine now."

"Oh, so we're back to Captain Nash, are we? What's the problem now, madam?"

"There's no problem. I just know that I'm keeping you from the repacking and I have to get back to finishing the supper. The burn was really nothing. I just reacted too strongly to it." She moved toward the fire, and, using her skirts again, lifted the covered iron pot which held their cooked rice for supper and for the first two meals of the next day. She placed the pot toward the other edge of the fire. "The rice is ready, just needs to simmer for a few more minutes."

There was no comment from behind her, but she heard the soldier pick up the tin bucket and head toward the spring.

After they'd eaten, Markham said only a few words to her. "Sleep well tonight," he advised. "Until we get home this is your last night under a roof, Madam Schoolmarm."

Bong and Rudolfo talked in their own language and Markham joined in their conversation occasionally. He seemed to be joking with them, because the two Filipino men burst into laughter at whatever he said. She thought he and Bong seemed so much more at ease in the open-necked cotton shirts they'd worn for the past few days. *She'd* certainly been cooler and more comfortable without that rotten corset. She wished she could be included in their conversation. She strengthened her resolve to learn to speak the native language.

Bong rose and brought a pottery jar from the cart back to the fire. He and Rudolfo drank from it. Markham drank, too, though it seemed he wasn't swallowing as deeply as were the other two men. Once in awhile Sarah felt as though they were talking about her, but she never caught them actually looking at her or using her name.

Sarah renewed her vow to learn to speak the native language and to do it at once. Tomorrow morning would not be too soon. Once Bong looked at her and lifted the jar as if he were wishing her good health and he said something. Before she could answer, Markham shook his head and spoke words that made them all shake with laughter. None of the three looked at her again and none of them offered her another drink from the jar.

When they finally retired for the night it took her a miserably long time to go to sleep within her net cocoon beneath the tilted cart. She could hear a mosquito whining around her ears, so she knew she'd probably receive a number of itchy bites throughout this night. And she was still hungry. A picture of a bowl of her mother's mashed potatoes heaped up with a valley of melted butter in the center of the white mound rose behind her eyes to taunt her.

Her burned hand throbbed and her head ached and the ground felt especially hard and pebbled beneath her. She hoped Markham would say something to her before he went to sleep, but on the other side of the wheel, the captain kept his back turned toward her until she finally dropped off.

Sadness filled the early morning for her. Sarah hated to see Rudolfo driving the cart and moving into the jungle going back through the sea of island bamboo, just the way they'd come. It was like losing an old friend even if he hadn't spoken a lot of English. They'd carried on whole conversations with her speaking English and a few words of Spanish and him speaking his native language and a few words of Spanish peppered with bits of Englaih. Their hands and their eyes and their smiles had done most of the talking for them. He looked so alone in the cart!

"Goodbye Rudolfo." She waved and called to him one last time. She turned to walk toward Bong, who held the horse he had saddled for her. She felt a bit strange in the starched white trousers and the collarless white shirt. She was conscious that Markham Nash's eyes were focused directly upon her. The starched linen felt a bit scratchy on the tender places between her legs. Not unpleasant, but *different.* She'd let her wedding hat hang down her back from the blue ribbons that tied beneath her chin.

She would never have believed that any garment would be more comfortable on her body than was her long cotton dress with no corset underneath . . . but the rolled-up trousers moved so easily with her every movement. Of course, she could see that the perfectly starched and ironed surface of each leg was already yielding to linen's impulse to wrinkle. No telling what she'd look like by day's end. But it didn't matter. Maybe she *looked* strange, but she *felt* deliciously comfortable. She didn't have to watch out for things that might catch on her skirt. The wind couldn't hook under her petticoat and pull it high into the air. And the pants and shirt were way cleaner than that filthy dress she'd worn all the way from Manila. That in itself was enough to recommend the two garments to her. Of course, she couldn't use a trouser leg as a potholder, but she'd manage.

So far, pants were certainly proving to be cooler than skirts and petticoats. All in all, most satisfactory. Miss Amelia Bloomer was onto something and Sarah had the suspicion that American women were eventually going to learn to wear bloomers and love them.

It couldn't possibly matter what Markham Nash thought about her new attire. She was happy and clean and he'd just have to accept her odd appearance or turn his head away from the sight. In fact, she wished he *would* look elsewhere. She could almost feel his gaze on her skin. She chanced another quick glance up through her lowered eyelashes. For heaven's sake. He was still looking at her. He didn't look happy.

He and Bong and Rudolfo hadn't eaten much breakfast this morning, but they'd drunk more than a gallon of coffee. They'd also taken several swigs of water from their canteens, something they usually didn't do except along the trail. She dared another quick glance. He was still looking at her, giving her that black-browed, angry look.

She raised her chin and then nodded to let Bong help

PARADISE FOUND

her swing up into the leather saddle. Not too bad. The horse stood still as a rock under her weight. Maybe she could really do this. Bong handed the reins to her.

Left hand, she told herself. *Keep a firm grip on the reins with your left hand.* She'd read that much somewhere. Bong was now adjusting the places where she was to keep her feet. The animal felt huge and warm and really awfully comfortable. The leather saddle was firmly supporting her. It had always been fun riding the plow horses around the yard while Papa watched. Maybe this wouldn't be so bad after all.

"Mabuti." Bong spoke with his head pressed against the horse as he worked with the foot things.

Sarah looked down. "My booties?" She looked up at Markham. "All I have are these shoes and the slippers I wore to get married in. I don't have any booties . . . boots."

Markham raised his hand to cover his mouth but Sarah could see the laughter in his eyes. Well, at least he was grinning instead of looking as if he could kill someone. Oh, he thought he was so smart!

"Mabuti. That's the name of your horse. It means Good in Tagalog. Mabuti. . . . Good."

Sarah's face warmed. Never mind. Now she could start learning the language herself. She already knew one word. No. Two words. *Mabuhay* and now *Mabuti.*

"Thank you, Bong. And thank you, Markham, for explaining." She lifted her chin and smiled. "I think we can start those lessons in the Filipino language while we ride down the trail today. You can work with me for a few miles and then Bong can work with me for a few more miles. That way neither one of you will be overwhelmed." She smiled again. "I can see that neither of you feels really well this morning, so I'll try not to impose on either of you for too long."

She watched Markham's brown eyes narrow to slits.

"Going to learn the language, are you?"

"Certainly. I'd like to prepare myself for my work with the people in our village." She smiled down at Bong, who stared up at her, his mouth open. "You've learned English, Bong. I'm sure I can learn your country's language as well."

Bong nodded, but he didn't say anything for a second. Then he shook his head as if clearing it before he pointed to her foot.

"How the stirrup feel, ma'am?"

Oh, yes. *Stirrups*. That's what the foot things were called.

"The stirrups are fine, Bong. You'll have to teach me the word for stirrups in your language." The young Filipino corporal backed away, nodded and went to take up the lead for the string of pack mules and horses.

"Which native language are you planning to learn on this little trip of ours, Sarah?" Markham allowed Jonas's muzzle to move sideways to touch the mare, Mabuti, on the neck. That put Sarah and Markham almost knee to knee. "You want Bong's, or Luz's . . . or perhaps Rudolfo's?"

"This native language, of course. What they speak." Through the linen trousers she could feel the heat from Markham's leg. He was almost touching her. "And

Markham, would you have Jonas step back just a bit? I think he might be scaring Mabuti."

Markham reached out and slapped Mabuti on the rump. The horse didn't move. She didn't even turn her head to look back.

"She seems pretty steady to me. Maybe it's her rider who's skittish." He pulled Jonas a side step away. "Panpangan, Tagalog, Chabicano. Ilocano, Viscayan?" He paused and was silent for a moment as if awaiting her answer.

"Is that my first lesson?"

"Oh, no, ma'am. That's your first choice. You have to choose one."

"Choose one?"

"Yep. Choose one language. You name it and we'll see if we can't get right after it. The people of the Philippine Islands speak eighty-seven dialects . . . each so different that they are, in essence, different languages." He allowed Jonas to drift close to Mabuti again. To Sarah, the spot where the man's blue woolen leg touched her white linen one seemed ready to burst into flame.

"So, which is it you were wanting to hear, Miss Schoolmarm?" He waited another moment. "Bong speaks Chabicano. That's what they use around the Cavite area. Luz speaks Tagalog. That's common in Manila, and I think Rudolfo was born in Mindora. None of us could understand his native tongue very well."

Sarah realized her mouth was standing open. She clamped her lips together. He could have kept her from looking like a fool. He *certainly* could have told her all this much earlier.

"There is one language that the Filipinos are starting to use in every part of the country now." He drawled the words. "Sort of a common method of communication, so everyone can be understood by everyone else wherever they go."

"Well, that sounds fine to me. The most common language. Let's work on that one. Do they have a name for it? What is it called?"

"It's called English." He kicked Jonas into motion and rode toward the front of the train, his laughter trailing through the vines and trees on either side.

Although his hangover was still with him, Markham felt almost lighthearted, the grin still on his lips as he thought of the little farm girl's face. Although she was behind him on the almost invisible path, he could still see the picture of her walking so lightly toward that big fat horse. Scared, brave, looking like a clean little boy in his Sunday clothes. No. He was wrong about that. Not like a boy at all. That white shirt and those white trousers just let him see what was really female about her. And that crazy hat she loved so well. He found that so sweet and girlish of her to want to protect that stupid hat. Was it possible that she hadn't noticed that her new hat was already looking pretty dusty and more than a good bit trailworn? He smiled again, then sobered.

He took a deep breath. *Better see to it, Captain,*

PARADISE FOUND 123

that she never, ever, *learns what you talked about with Bong and Rudolfo last night,* he instructed.

"You were being a bastard, Markham," he told himself aloud. He couldn't seem to resist teasing the poor innocent who thought she was so grown up and so in control of her own destiny. The noble schoolteacher. He laughed aloud again. He promised himself he'd make their drunken behavior up to her after they'd forded the river. They'd take a good long break and he'd gentle her down again. Let Bong teach her a little Tagalog.

It was just that every time he got really close to the little widow she acted as if she were smelling something bad. Or what was worse, as if she were afraid of him.

Truth to tell, in her prickly-proud, childlike way, she was probably doing the right thing. All through the trip he'd constantly found himself wanting to talk to her, wanting to touch her . . . wanting to smooth that silky golden hair, wanting to hold her, wanting to kiss her. He felt himself hardening.

Unh unh, boy. You're trifling with trouble. He unbuttoned yet another button on his shirt, then took off his stiff-brimmed campaign hat and fanned himself with it. He put the hat back on and pulled his canteen up to his lips to drink. Maybe water would put out some of the inner fire.

After he capped the canteen, he let it fall back against Jonas's neck. He gave himself a silent order. *Do the girl a favor, Nash, and keep out of her way.* He nodded in agreement with the order. Yep. That was best. Just keep entirely out of little Sarah's way.

Ten

Snake. Oh, God, a snake! What had Markham told her about snakes? That there was one kind of Filipino snake that was sure death if you were bitten. What was it called? Never mind what it was called . . . what was she going to do now? The small snake hung right into the path that Bong had cleared with his machete. She could see no way to go around it, and the horrid black scaly thing was looped lazily around a thick vine. It seemed to be looking straight at her. Staring. Waiting.

Paralyzed, Sarah sat motionless. Ahead of her the two men and the train of pack mules and horses were still moving through the shadowy green brush. They were moving slowly, but Sarah realized they'd soon be out of voice range if they weren't already. Above the noise of their passage they'd never hear a sound. It was up to her. How could she make Mabuti back up . . . slowly? She'd forgotten the signal if she'd ever known it.

Thank God the phlegmatic animal would stand where it was forever if she would just let it. At least she'd learned that much about old Mabuti. She slipped slowly from the saddle, a fraction of an inch at a time. After what seemed like days, her toes touched the jungle floor.

Keeping the snake in view, Sarah surveyed the path they'd just traversed. Was there something, anything, she could use to kill a snake? She saw stalks of bamboo, ragged leaves, vines torn from trees. Nothing, really. Making no sound and moving as slowly as she could, she picked up a two-foot piece of bamboo as large around as her wrist. The end of the piece was newly cut and almost pointed from Bong's machete strokes. Could she use the pointed bamboo to skewer that evil thing that now owned the pathway?

She stood up once more and peered across the saddle. It was still there, still poised, still ready for prey. The snake's eyes were as green as the vine where it hung.

She simply *had* to get Mabuti to back down the path, out from under the overhanging danger. She slid around her carpetbag and toward the back of the horse and silently laid the bamboo chunk to one side. She wrapped her fingers around the coarse red-and-gray hair of Mabuti's tail and tugged gently. Gently. Nothing. Mabuti stood stolidly in the path.

The snake seemed to sway in the air above the horse's head. Sarah wiped the sweat from her eyes with the sleeve of her shirt, then wrapped still more tail hair around her hand and pulled, gently at first, then with more and more force. Mabuti lifted one foot and let it down behind where it had been standing.

Sarah closed her eyes for a second and drew a deep breath. She *had* to move the stupid horse . . . backward. She pulled with all her strength. Mabuti lifted another hoof, then another, and as Sarah pulled, the horse moved slowly backward down the trail. Within four more backward steps, Mabuti finally looked over her shoulder at Sarah as if to ask, "What's going on back there?"

Sarah dropped the clump of horsehair and smoothed and patted it back into place, catching her breath as she did so. Now the bamboo.

She pressed herself against Mabuti's body to slide forward again toward her chosen weapon. She bent under the horse's neck and reached for the pointed stick, while at the same time trying to keep the frightening reptile in sight. The snake hadn't moved . . . had it? She didn't think so. It was still looking at her with thick-lidded eyes full of green death.

She raised the bamboo missile and drew back, then launched it with all her might, point forward, at the snake. As the piece smashed into the jungle growth, birds screamed and flapped through the overhead ceiling of leaves and the vine where the snake had been now sat swaying, empty.

Was the snake on the ground? On the horse? Stalking her? Slithering under her feet? Sarah's breath rasped in her throat. She ran her gaze wildly across the path, over the ground under the vine and everywhere in the immediate area. No snake.

Maybe it was still there just hidden under some of the greenery. She searched with wide eyes as thoroughly as she could. He could still be somewhere she wasn't looking. Maybe. She shook her head. Maybe.

But Sarah wasn't searching anymore. She grabbed the leather strap at the side of Mabuti's bridle and crashed forward along the trail. She could feel hysteria rising now.

"Come on, Mabuti. Come on, girl. Let's go. Come on." The horse, shocked out of her usual lethargy, scrambled to keep up with her running, shouting mistress. "That's it, girl. Come on." When she ran out of breath, Sarah stepped into the stirrup and flung her leg over the saddle, pounding her heel into the fat horse's rump. "Fly, my beauty. Come on, 'Buti, 'Buti, 'Buti. Run. Run!"

Not until they'd almost crashed into the tail of the last pack mule did Sarah let up. When she realized that both she and her horse were unbitten, that everything was all right for now, she slumped forward onto the horse's neck, half sobbing, half crooning her relief into the stolid animal's ear.

"Good old girl. You're not stupid, Mabuti. I . . . didn't mean it . . . girl. Thank you." Her words were muffled against the horse's body and she finally allowed herself to let the tears come. She was sure the noise of their trailbreaking and the creaking, clanging outfitting on every animal covered the noise of her crying. Better that they didn't know. She really didn't want anyone to become aware that she'd just lost her dignified schoolteacher demeanor in a standoff with a tiny jungle native.

As soon as they came to a stream or a river she'd put a little water on her face and try to keep her mouth shut. The whole experience had been horrible, but she'd learned something. She'd learned she just might be able to take care of herself if she had to. She could even take care of someone else.

Markham had started back to see what was keeping Sarah when he heard her old elephant-footed mare come crashing up to the tail end of the train. He glanced back and realized the young woman was slumped over the horse's neck, either crying or talking to the horse. Tired probably. They'd stop soon so they could get ready for the river fording in the morning. Too late to try to cross now.

Actually, Sarah Collins was holding up real well. Not what he would have expected from some fancy-dressed, spoiled white girl. He almost let himself slip into a reverie about what he'd like to be doing with the blue-eyed young woman. He pulled himself up short.

He reminded himself that he had never, not in all his adult years, ever, wanted to "settle down" with just one woman. Certainly he didn't want to hitch up with some virtuous little farm girl from Iowa.

And that's what she'd expect, he knew, "settling down." Marriage, in other words. No. Oh, no. Not for him. All he had to do for Mrs. Zumwalt was to do his job and get her safely through this trip and into her classroom if they could find one and then he was free to spend his free time with some less demanding, more generous company.

The fact that she was crazy for even coming out to the Philippine Islands was none of his affair. He still said the boondocks of the Philippine Islands were no place for *any* woman, much less for educated young virgins. He shifted in his saddle and looked back at the blond hair still laid against old Mabuti's lazy red hide. Yep, she was, for sure, a virgin.

They camped early in the afternoon on the bank of the river and everyone seemed thankful for the open space where they could let the horses and mules graze on tether and the humans could still have room to cook or walk around or sleep or just sit. Supper was a fairly silent affair. Both Bong and Markham had acted as if they were listening to something outside their little circle, but both men were famished. They'd eaten every bite of the beans and rice Sarah had prepared. She hadn't felt much like eating.

She painfully bestirred herself to put more rice on for morning. If she could only make her body obey her order to bend and do it. She was in such agony she could barely move, but she wasn't about to let on. Her legs felt as if they'd been stretched on a torture rack.

She creaked into an old woman's posture above the fire and questioned herself. Could she get back on Mabuti in the morning? Maybe she'd be all right by then. She tried to keep from looking at the captain. She'd die before she'd let him know that when she walked she couldn't hold her legs together in their normal position. Would she be permanently damaged?

Perhaps permanently bowlegged? She didn't want to talk about it or even think about it.

It looked as if Markham Nash had plenty to think about. He didn't want to hear about a snake and he didn't need any dumb questions from her. He most certainly didn't need to know she was dying from riding that big fat horse. Let him just go ahead and think about whatever it was he was thinking about so hard.

As she worked, Sarah Collins Zumwalt found her own mind skittering from subject to subject as well, especially when she allowed herself to sit quietly. Thinking helped and she'd do that or any other thing she could to get her mind off the huge pain that lodged between her legs.

Bong whistled while he fed and watered and readied the horses and mules for evening, but he, too, fell silent when it came time to sit in the camp area with the captain and the little blondie lady. He watched her totter around the fire as if she were an ancient crone and he remembered his own first day on a horse. He smiled inwardly.

He looked at the captain. The black mood was on the man's face. Better just stretch out and try to sleep. The captain would call when it was his watch or when he wanted to look over the ones who followed. No hurry on that. He looked again at the captain. Killing would just suit the big American tonight.

When Bong closed his eyes, he wondered why two people who so obviously felt the drawing of a man for a woman and of a woman for a man didn't talk to one another? He loved to talk to Madalena. Maybe, now that the schoolteacher man was dead they could. . . . He didn't try to finish the thought.

Mentally he shrugged. Very strange, these two. He shrugged again. Crazy. Like all Americans.

Sarah awoke to a hand across her mouth. She struggled to get loose from the netting that bound her, but the hand held her still.

"Shut up," Markham's voice whispered in her ear. "Lie still. I hear someone out there. Don't move. Stay here. Bong and I will take care of it." The voice moved away. The camp area was solid black, no fire, no moon, few stars. Sarah pulled the netting which hung from two Y-shaped sticks more tightly around herself, then let it drop. What good was a little mosquito net going to do?

She narrowed her eyes as she thought she saw a large black shadow followed by a smaller black shadow move silently to the right of the line of horses. Markham and Bong. Oh, God, they were leaving her. And she couldn't walk. She'd never walk again. Just to try to turn over had roused such exquisite pain in her legs that she could simply do nothing but roll back over onto her back and stay that way, legs akimbo within her horribly wrinkled white linen trousers. If she didn't move, she might live.

She strained to hear. She heard nothing. Then shots. Three of them, then farther away, three more shots.

Someone crashing away through the undergrowth. One more shot, then silence. She lay petrified with pain and fear. Seconds later, the panting Markham and his dogrobber flopped down on the ground on each side of her.

"Got 'em," Markham said.

"Yes sir," Bong answered.

"Your watch, Corporal Manawe." Markham moved closer to Sarah.

"Right, Captain Nash."

She lay paralyzed with pain and fear. They'd been chasing someone. Shooting at someone.

"Who'd you chase?"

"*Ladrones,* probably."

"*Ladrones?* Robbers?"

"Don't worry. I'm going to stay right here beside you, and old Bong here is just plain hell at night. *Nothing* is going to be able to get by that old boy, eh, soldier?"

"Yes sir, Captain." Sarah thought she could see a flash of white as the Filipino smiled. *Smiled!* And he wasn't the only one. Markham was smiling, too. They were both laughing. Giggling like little boys. They were having a good time!

"Did you see that fat one running, Bong? Bet that was the fastest he's moved in years." Markham chuckled aloud.

"I see him, Captain. His running days about over, I think."

"You keep your eyes and ears open, Bong. I'm going to stay right here with my lady and get me some sleep."

"Yes, sir, Captain."

His lady? Suddenly, her legs seemed to feel much better. If he was going to stay close beside her, maybe she could rest, too, with this huge, wonderful wild man watching over her. She turned to face him and fell instantly asleep.

"Legs hurt, huh?" Markham Nash sat sipping hot coffee as he watched her crawl from under the protective netting.

Sarah glanced at the coffee cup, then up at the sky. The sun was almost up.

"Oh. I'm sorry. I must have overslept. Did you have to make the coffee?"

"Naw. Bong did it. He's fixing us a few eggs, too. We both thought you needed a little extra rest." Sarah tried to stand, but couldn't manage it.

"Here, I'll help you." He put down the cup and stood to lift her to her feet. "Takes a few days to get used to riding astride."

"I'm fine, really." She lifted her chin. "Please don't worry about me. I'll do quite well."

He smiled down at her.

"I know that. You've been a pretty good trail hand." He leaned to pick up his cup. "No complaining along the way. No screaming last night when all that brouhaha was going on. You just turned over and went right to sleep."

"Yesterday . . ."

"About yesterday . . ."

They spoke simultaneously.

"Sorry. Go ahead." He gestured politely.

"I was almost bitten yesterday by one of those snakes you told me about. It almost bit Mabuti. I threw bamboo . . ." She felt her face crumpling and hysteria rising at the remembrance. "And then last night those men came . . . *ladrones* . . . my legs wouldn't move. Oh, God, Markham." She drew a deep, gulping sob of a breath. "I was so scared yesterday and last night and you wouldn't talk to me."

"Slow down, Sarah." He put one hand on her shoulder. "What's this about a snake? Tell me about it."

After she'd told the story of the snake, he shook his head in wonder. "You and old Mabuti outsmarted a vampire snake? Hey, you're one lucky girl. Most horses would have kicked the pure-de-hell out of you just for *touching* their tail. And you drove a vampire snake away and saved that silly old nag's life! You're some pair." He threw back his head and laughed.

Sarah laughed as well before she spoke, tears still running down her face.

"Well, now it does seem funny, but I can tell you I was scared. Last night, too." She reached as if to touch him on the chest but let her hand drop. "What about *your* adventures last night, Markham? Your *ladrones*. What did you do about them?"

"Killed one, winged one, and chased the other one away with a little help from Bong's machete."

"Killed one?" Her voice rose with horror. "Winged

one? It's as if you were out bird hunting. How can you be so casual about killing and injuring human beings?"

"It was us or them, Sarah. What do you think they were gonna do to us if we hadn't gotten to them first?"

"I don't know that they were going to hurt us and neither do you!"

"I do know. They were all carrying guns. And knives, too, not to mention their machetes."

"But to *kill* them?"

"Why do you think they were snooping around the edge of our camp? I knew they were out there long before you went to sleep." He touched her tousled hair for just a second. " 'Maybe our *ladrones* had some plan for little blondie lady,' Bong said, and I agreed. We should have gotten all three of the bastards."

Sarah swallowed the words that wanted to explode out of her. She tightened her lips. *Hush, Sarah,* she told herself. After all, this wasn't Iowa. She didn't know this country, and he did. Right now she'd do well to listen more than she talked. Her turn to do something about the sacredness of human life would be through her teaching with the students in the village.

"You first, Sarah. Once you and Mabuti are across on the other side, the rest of the train can come right on." Markham gestured her toward the water's edge. "See, the Army has made us a bit of a walkway. Kinda narrow, but a horse or mule can walk it easy." He pointed to a place on the shore where it was obvious that animals had crossed before.

Within the water itself, Sarah could see nothing. Just water . . . rushing water. Where was this walkway he was talking about? Beneath her she could feel Mabuti tense. Sarah patted the horse's neck. Mabuti didn't want to go into that old river, either.

"I'll go first and lead you all across." Markham again gestured toward the water. "We're at the end of the dry season, which is mighty lucky. This won't be much deeper than up to the horses' bellies." He looked closely at her. "You afraid? No need to be. I'll take old Mabuti's reins and lead. What do you say?" He took the reins from her hand.

What *could* she say? She swallowed her fear and nodded. She couldn't make words come out of her dry mouth.

"Take off your shoes and let them hang around your neck." He slipped one of her shoes from her foot as she untied the other. Markham tied the laces together and held up her hat as he looped the shoes to dangle against her chest. "Now your hat and your shoes'll be dry. You want to hold your carpetbags up with your hands?"

"No," she croaked. The idea of holding anything in her hands while she was in that tumbling water caused her heart to pound even harder. She had to have her hands free. "All my stuff will dry when I can spread it out." They were both shouting to make themselves heard over the roaring of the water.

"Okay. Let's go." He waved his campaign hat in the air. "Bong, I'll come back and help you with the mules." As soon as Markham shouted those words,

PARADISE FOUND 137

Jonas stepped into the water. Sarah closed her eyes and held tight to the saddle when she felt Mabuti lurch forward.

You're being silly, Sarah, she told herself. *She hasn't even stepped into the water yet.* She clenched her eyelids together even more strongly at the second movement of the big horse under her. *Open your eyes, Sarah,* she ordered herself. *You're a grown woman. A grown woman isn't afraid of a little water.*

She opened one eye. Mabuti was still a foot from the water and resisting Markham's coaxing every inch of the way. Sarah leaned forward and patted the horse's neck.

"Come on girl. You and I can do it. Together we can do anything. Come on 'Buti." She could feel a ripple of muscle under Mabuti's smoothly gleaming coat. "I know you're scared. So am I. But we have to trust him, girl. You trust Jonas, don't you? He and Jonas will lead us right across." She continued the patting and the singsong reassurances until they were into the swirling water. The horse moved more quickly, as if she had taken heart from Sarah's words.

When Sarah felt the cold liquid rushing up her own leg she fell silent, but she continued to pat the horse on the neck.

Slowly, they inched their way across the unseen path that Markham had said was there. He looked back at them every few seconds. He even smiled at Sarah, but she felt as though it would crack her face to smile back. She was frozen into a machine which patted a horse's neck but was unable to talk. Feet. *Wet.* Knees.

Wet. Thighs. *Wet.* But with each step the water receded, and there it was! She could see the bank maybe ten steps ahead. They'd made it and they hadn't drowned.

She slipped from Mabuti's back and took the reins Markham offered her.

"That wasn't so bad, was it?" he asked. He sat atop Jonas and looked down at her for a silent moment. "You all right?"

"We're both fine. Aren't we, Mabuti?" She held her horse's muzzle across her shoulder and rubbed the animal's velvety nose with her hand. "She was a little frightened, but I think she trusts Jonas."

Markham nodded. "I noticed that. Old Mabuti may be smarter than I thought." He laughed and started his horse back across the river.

Sarah kept the reins in her hand as she sank down to sit and watch from a comfortable seat within a mass of jungle fern. Her legs still hurt, but the pain was somehow more distant than it had been. Mabuti munched on a plant nearby. Sarah took a deep breath.

"We made it," she said aloud, then looked down at her wet trousers. The soaked white linen had become revealingly transparent and she could see that the lower part of her body looked almost as if she were naked from the waist down. *Markham had seen her like that.*

She felt her face reddening but then she raised her chin and forced the embarrassment back. "Forget it," she told herself. "You're alive." She nestled into the thick ferns and turned her face to watch Markham emerge from the other side of the river where the pack-train waited.

Almost immediately, he took the heavy lead from Bong and stepped Jonas back into the river. Bong waited on the bank until the last of the pack mules had started across.

Sarah watched in horror as the third mule from the last seemed to lose his footing and then tried to scramble back onto the walkway. He struggled and his erratic movements tugged at the others in the train.

"Get him back up or swim him over!" Markham shouted.

Bong dove from his horse and swam toward the struggling animal, avoiding his thrashing hooves. Bong dived and surfaced.

"Legs broke." Bong coughed and tread water.

"Cut him loose," was Markham's answering shout.

"Oh, no!" Sarah's wail was wasted on the two men.

Bong swam around the mule, pulled himself up to the back of one of the other, now barely moving, pack-train horses.

His machete flashed and most of the train were freed to follow Markham's lead. Another chop with the machete and the injured mule was alone in the tumbling river, being moved downriver no matter how he scrambled to rejoin his mates.

"He's going to drown." Sarah's words were a scream. Markham looked at her and his expression silenced her.

Bong rode the animal he'd clambered onto earlier and trotted up onto the bank, the last few pack animals and his own horse dutifully following. Bong went to his mount and checked the animal's legs, then touched his campaign hat hanging from the saddle. Last, he saluted Markham. Markham returned the salute.

"Good work, soldier."

"Good work? What about that poor animal? We can't even see him anymore. He was moving too fast in the water." Sarah stood staring at the bend of the river where the animal had thrashed a moment longer, then disappeared.

Markham looked at her but turned back to Bong.

"What was he carrying?"

"Grain and rice, sir."

"We'll manage. You may be reduced to eating potatoes or bread, Corporal." Markham grinned down at the smaller man.

"I like potatoes plenty good, Captain, especially sweet potatoes." Bong grinned back at his captain.

Sarah felt tears start. She was the only one who mourned the lost mule. For a second she tried to imagine what she would do if something happened to Mabuti and she had to let her die. She shivered and shook her head. She couldn't imagine, didn't want to imagine such a thing. She lifted her shirtsleeve to wipe tears away.

Markham moved to stand in front of her. For a moment he just looked without saying a word. Sarah couldn't make herself look up at his face.

"Nothing we could do, Sarah," he explained. "If Bong could have he would have. Those mules are like his children." He paused as if waiting for her to say something. When she didn't, he went on. "We couldn't let the injured animal take the whole train with him and he couldn't use his legs. He was dead when he slipped off the walkway." He waited another moment. "Do you understand?"

Sarah nodded and accepted the inevitable. She didn't want him to see the last of her tears, so, with eyes downcast, she walked to the line of horses to stroke her fat and stolid mount on the muzzle. She glanced at Bong, and it was easy to read the sadness on his face. The accident couldn't have been helped. Even so, she felt she needed to reassure her horse.

"Mabuti, I will always save you if you'll save me," she whispered to the animal. She thought she could feel Mabuti nod in agreement.

Eleven

Markham stood staring down the trail that would eventually lead them toward San Miguel. The hand in his pocket jingled the three lonely Mexican silver dollars that he'd been able to salvage from his trip to Manila. *Gotta stay out of the city if you want to keep your pay*, he reminded himself. *Either that or get married.* The last thought came from the far reaches of his mind and he started. Why had it invaded his reverie? He frowned at the idea. Being single and broke wasn't so bad. It had never bothered him before. At least while he *had* money, he could spend it any way he wanted.

They'd spent the whole day after the crossing just tending to the animals, eating, napping and generally lounging about. They were more than halfway there and he knew the animals needed a little break. With a few more days of hard riding they'd be back at the army camp and safe, Markham figured. Maybe rainy season would be late this year. He hoped so.

But he and Sarah were getting close enough that he had to come to some sort of decision. He'd already spent a lot of time trying to think about what to say or whether to say *anything* about Robert Zumwalt to the little widow, or whether he'd do better just to keep shut.

Bong, of course, thought the "little blondie schoolteacher" should be told about the situation and about Madalena, but Markham wasn't so sure.

He'd had to smile when Sarah had come back to the clearing wearing a clean white shirt and Robert's heavy pinstriped woolen trousers after a morning bath down at the river. Probably doing penance for showing her body during the crossing. Or making sure he and Bong didn't see any more than they'd already seen. He grinned. He held the picture of her smooth, shapely legs barely veiled by the dripping white linen. What would she have done if she knew he'd already seen the totality of her? Yep. She'd sure kept their trip from being boring.

Just let it happen, he told himself. *Keep mum. Let the fates unroll as they will for the little darling. Maybe you can be there for her when she needs you for a friend.*

He looked at her bustling about the campfire she'd built just as if she were mistress in her own kitchen in Iowa. Her clean hair glowed a blond nimbus around her head, the gold outlined by the long rays of the late setting sun.

She was small, neat, hardworking. All good traits. It was the other attributes—beautiful, virtuous, and educated—which caused him to turn away from her . . . wasn't it? He squinted into the light as if to fill his eyes with another long look at the slim girl . . . the sweet woman . . . the respectable widow, Sarah Collins Zumwalt.

Why was he staring at her? He was grinning, too. But maybe he wasn't smiling at her. It was as if he had some kind of secret. As if he knew something she didn't. He'd been looking at her all day since she'd come back from her bath. She looked down at the woolen trousers. Was it the trousers? They were much hotter than the linen ones, which had felt better against her bare skin, too, but these were cleaner and Markham *had* said they'd have to ford two more rivers.

"Both just little bitty ones. Just creeks," he'd said.

She ran her hand down the side of the heavy pants. She'd stick with the black wool. At least these trousers wouldn't just disappear if she happened to get wet during the coming crossings.

Markham had been right. The next river crossing was fairly easy, just a stream, really. The journey once again settled down into the usual daily sweat, dust, pressing jungle growth, and riding, riding, riding. Sarah felt growing pride in her new ability to bound onto Mabuti's back without Bong's help, all her previous pain forgotten.

Bong had said something very nice to her—at least she thought it was nice. He had said she was different from the few American wives he'd seen at the camp since he'd been stationed there. None of them could ride like she could, he said. He'd acted as if he were going to tell her something else, but he had just nodded and closed his mouth. But he'd smiled.

Late in the afternoon, in the deepest shade as she was brushed by hanging vines or drooping leaves, she felt a bit threatened, as if the jungle were alive, as if it were an entity which watched her, touched her. The sudden stillness seemed to pulse with hidden life, waiting, watching for something, if not for her than for something or someone else. She shivered in the heat.

She looked back at the captain who'd started pushing the packtrain to the animals' limit. He rode toward her.

"Can't you get a little more speed out of that nag?"

"Mabuti's not a nag." She leaned forward and patted the horse's sweaty neck and spoke directly to the animal. "Her's a good widdle horsey." She sat back in the saddle and stroked the animal's mane. "Anyway, what's the sudden big hurry? I thought we were almost . . ."

"Time for the rains." His terse words cut into her speech. He pulled his hat down over his eyes and jerked Jonas's head around to speed toward the front of the line once more.

"I would just love to see some rain." Sarah shouted the words even though she knew he probably couldn't hear her. "Maybe Mabuti and I could get cooled off. And rain would settle the dust."

Only moments after he'd gone, Sarah felt a fat drop of water on her forehead. She felt one more on her hand, another on her cheek, then the shower seemed to dry up. She smiled. Rain, even if only a few drops, felt good to her.

Markham made them ride on and on, plodding into the late darkness of the hardwood forest. Even then he seemed unsatisfied with their progress.

"For goodness' sake, what is wrong with him, Bong?" Before she fixed supper, she helped the corporal carry water to the exhausted horses and mules. The two of them could see the captain checking each animal's hooves and legs. "Why is he acting so strange, so anxious?"

"Our sleepytime ride time over now. Rain coming, maybe tomorrow morning, *mom.*"

"I never saw a man so scared of a little rain, did you?"

Bong grinned.

"Captain not scared a little rain, missy. He maybe worry about blondie schoolteacher and a lotta rain."

"Well, he can just stop worrying about me. I'd welcome some rain." Bong grinned again and looked skyward.

"You gonna get it, sure, Missy Sarah, *mom.* Maybe come morning."

Twelve

A sprinkling of warm droplets easily penetrated Sarah's mosquito netting to awaken her. The lovely fragrance of the coming rain was more powerfully compelling than any perfume she'd ever smelled, and the softly falling water felt wonderful against her skin, cooling and soothing. This gentle shower was nothing like the wild storms she'd been used to back in Iowa.

She struggled out of her limp netting to stand and stretch so the last few fat drops of water could wet as much of her as possible. She closed her eyes and turned her face up to the welcome moisture. The air smelled just the way she imagined good wine would taste.

"You like a little shower, do you?" The words from the captain's mouth were almost a snarl.

"Oh, yes, this is wonderful." She twirled in place. "It's the first time I've been cool since I arrived in the Philippines."

"Well, get ready to be overwhelmed with joy." He pulled the campaign hat forward to shelter his face before he stomped toward the line of mules and horses to help Bong ready the animals for their day's march.

Before Sarah could even wonder at his grumpiness, he was back.

"We'll eat cold food today, little lady. Dish something out that we can hold in one hand this morning. No sitting around and gabbing." He flung the words back over his shoulder as he moved away again.

Sarah quickly tore three pieces of banana leaf. Each piece was wrapped around a ball of sticky rice and a couple of the tiny crispy fish. As she worked, the rain seemed to gather new life. The small shower became almost a full-fledged rainfall. She found it a bit inconvenient to have to work in the lightly falling rain while trying to keep their food supply dry, but she hummed as she worked. She was cool and there was no dust in the air. Now, those were two blessings she'd counted right away.

Her mother had always insisted that she start her days by counting her blessings. She knew the rain was really good for the trees and plants. That was surely a third blessing.

She took the folded banana leaf packets to each of the men and kept one for herself. She decided to save hers to eat while she was riding since Markham seemed so anxious and in such an all-fired hurry to get started.

She repacked the oilskin packets of food and the few utensils she'd been using for the previous night's meal while the rain seemed to increase in intensity. Her wet hair kept falling forward from where she'd knotted it to fall right into her eyes then cling to her cheeks.

PARADISE FOUND 149

Maybe she'd take a page out of Captain Markham Nash's book and let her wedding hat be a small protection against the streams of wet blond hair that had begun to invade her eyes and her mouth. She pulled the damp straw hat from her now-damp sleeping roll and clapped it on her head, then pinned it securely. There. That was better. At least she could see.

She bundled the sleeping roll and the net into a soggy sausage and tossed it across Mabuti's rump where she secured it and covered it with the leather pack flap.

Through the pelting downpour she could see that the corporal and the captain had both slipped rubberized canvas squares over their heads to hang from their shoulders, but neither had offered her such a convenience.

She led Mabuti to where they stood talking and pointing into the trees.

"Excuse me, Markham. What do you call the rain things you and Bong are wearing?"

"Ponchos." Markham shifted in his saddle to look at her but said nothing more.

"Well, I was wondering if you might have a poncho that I could wear?"

"Had enough of this refreshing rain, huh?"

"I'm sure it will quit soon, but, yes, for now I've had quite enough rain."

Markham looked at a grinning Bong. At a nod from Markham, the corporal moved to rummage carefully through a pack on the back of a particularly surly-looking mule. He pulled out yet another rubberized square with a hole cut in the center of the square.

"Take off hat, teacher, *mom*."

He held the yellow square up and dropped it over her head when she had the wedding hat in hand. Sarah raised the hat to her head once again, dug the gold pins in, tightened the blue velvet ribbons under her chin and pronounced herself ready to ride.

As the horses progressed down the trail, Sarah noticed that the hat and poncho served as protection from the streams of water which poured from the heavens as if from a million pump faucets. Sort of. The hat brim dripped water and began to lose some of the pert stiffness she'd been so proud of. She tried not to think about what all this water was doing to her new hat. She could, perhaps, let it dry under weights at the village. Once dry, it should stiffen right up again.

The poncho was fine against the dashing, pelting raindrops but inside the square, her wet body was being boiled, or perhaps steamed. She couldn't decide which. Certainly she wasn't baking. That was a dryer form of cookery.

When the wind flapped the edges of the poncho up to allow entry to the entreating rain, she didn't know whether to try to hold it down or help to flip it up. Up was wet, wet, wet. Soggy, soaking, sloshing wet. Down was hot, hot, hot. Heated, tropical, steaming hot. She tried for comfort's sake to settle for an even-handed arrangement.

"A few minutes of boiling followed by a few seconds of cooling baptism," she explained to Mabuti who didn't seem to be listening. The horse plodded stolidly along, head down against the now-blinding rain. Sarah decided against trying to eat her cold-rice-and-fish-ball breakfast. Maybe she'd have it for lunch.

Markham wanted to kick himself . . . or somebody, for the day they'd spent lolling beside the river. *You knew you were cutting it close, boy. If you'd made everybody ride hard and long we'd almost be there and you wouldn't be in this fix.* He frowned forward into the curtain of gray water, then glanced back at his charges. Everything was all right. At least Bong and the animals were fine.

He had to laugh, anyway. About the little thing asking for that poncho after dancing around and swearing she could never get enough of this goddamned rain. Now look at her. A miserable, sodden mess. But she was taking the whole thing in stride . . . so far. At least the goddamned rain was doing him one good favor. It was destroying that precious wedding hat. He could do without any reminders of her wedding, and the closer they got to the village, the less he wanted to be reminded of that farce with old Zumwalt. Goddamn. Should he say something to her or not? He just couldn't decide and the time was getting shorter.

Crossing this morning should be easy enough. Not enough rain had fallen to make the next little creek dangerous yet. He turned back to try to pierce the water veil in front of him. Nothing. He'd better hurry, though. The animals' hooves were beginning to bog down just a tad.

***

In years afterward Sarah was to remember the first part of their trip, the dry part, as heaven. She remembered the last part of the trip as hell. Wet hell.

To try to keep herself from the misery of not being able to escape the never-ending pelting rain for even a moment, Sarah tried to let her own mind entertain her. Her mother had always said, "A lady can endure what she must endure."

Of course, Mama had never ridden a horse through the jungle during the rainy season in the tropics, Sarah reminded herself.

Hell, as described in the sermons in the little Methodist Church back home, had always been filled with fire. Everlasting fire. Maybe the preachers were wrong? Maybe the bad place wasn't fire at all, but was really being soaked to the skin without recourse, for hour after hour after hour, day after day. No place to run, no place to dry off, no place to hide.

Lunch was another ball of rice, and she divided one broiled fish between the men, one tiny half of a leftover fish each.

At the midday stop she dished out the rice in a moment while standing on the ground, then they'd eaten the rice balls while back in their saddles. She had to start thinking about what she was going to feed the men when they camped. *When they camped?* She groaned aloud. *How could they camp in this?* She'd rather ride all night.

She patted Mabuti. "Except for the fact that you

need to rest, I mean." The red-and-gray hair on the horse's neck felt hot, coarse, and slimy under her fingers. "Oh, ugh, Mabuti. You're being boiled, too."

The river crossing was scary, but they made it. No one even suggested stopping on the other side. A couple of times Sarah slid off Mabuti and crouched by the path to attend to her needs, but the packtrain never stopped or slowed or waited for her. They continued plodding through the Hades of constantly falling rain right on into the dark gray evening. When Markham stopped to announce and indicate their campsite, Sarah felt weighted with despair. When she slid off the horse and took a long look up, the still-falling rain made her go really desperate inside.

How could she cook? How could she sleep with her body lying in ever-deepening mud and her face constantly filled with water? For sure, *this* was her punishment for every wrong thing she'd ever done.

"Get that gear off old Mabuti and we'll tether the animals to the line over there." Markham's order seemed to be given in a better-humored voice than he had used all day. Maybe he liked sleeping in the mud?

Bong seemed pretty happy, too. He was scurrying around the horses and under the huge overhanging tree. Tearing down vines? Building something? Sarah gave a shiver of anticipation as she worked. Maybe, just maybe, Bong, and now Markham helping him, maybe they were going to work one of the little camp miracles that seemed to come so easily to them.

Now she could see that they were building a tiny lean-to shelter with bamboo, vines, and *more ponchos!*

The shelter turned its back to the slanting rain so the water wouldn't reach in under the roof and wet its occupants. Extra ponchos tied across the bamboo-vine roof made the inside of the hut the one dry area within miles. She watched them spread two long pieces of rubberized canvas on banana leaves they'd spread on the ground under the roof, and there it was! Decorative-looking palm fronds hung from beneath the canvas on the roof to wick the water away from the lean-to. A house! A place where you could sit and not be pounded by rain. Sarah couldn't toss Mabuti's gear off fast enough before she ran to tether the horse.

"I'm sorry," she whispered. "You're an awfully good little horsey, but I guess you have to stay in the rain." She patted Mabuti's wet muzzle and dashed for the finished dry spot.

Bong and Markham had pulled off the saddles and packs and piled them at one end of the lean-to. They'd beat her to the space even though she'd hurried. Markham scooted over to let her sit in the middle between the two of them. He flipped the corners of one of the ground cloths up to reveal a space of muddy ground and banana leaves just in front of her.

"Your evening kitchen, madam." He smiled into her eyes and gestured toward the wet ground and the moist banana leaves flooring the dry shelter. He and Bong had shucked their ponchos and placed them at the very back of the lean-to where the roof touched the ground. Sarah pulled her poncho off, shook it toward the front of the area, then placed it in a roll atop theirs. Her carpetbags and her bedroll followed next, topped by

PARADISE FOUND 155

her thoroughly wet hat. She hugged herself in ecstasy. No rain was in her face. She was wet but she wasn't getting wetter. She might even get dry.

"I brought the cooking bag and my blanket roll and my carpetbags, but . . ." she smiled first at Bong, then at Markham, "I apologize for this because you two have done such wonders, but I don't know what to do other than give you the last of the bananas. We've already eaten all of the cooked rice, and just about everything else requires cooking."

Suddenly the thought of her own neglected breakfast occurred to her. "Oh, I'll give each of you a fish and a half ball of rice. I just thought of it." She pulled the smashed banana leaf container from her wet woolen pants pocket as if it were a jewel of great value. She divided the crumbling mass of tiny fish and flattened rice into two dabs and handed each man one.

Both reached for the fragments of food and both swallowed the crushed rice and fish in one bite.

"Um um." Markham leaned forward to look at Bong. "Good, but not enough for a hungry man. How about you, Corporal?"

Bong shook his head

"Not enough, Captain."

Sarah swallowed the slight indignation she felt at their lack of gratitude for what had been, after all, *her* breakfast. She pulled out three bananas and doled them out. Seconds later, the two she'd given the men were just a memory. She cut her own banana and handed them each half. Markham shoved the fruit into his mouth with one hand, chewed and immediately swallowed it. Bong ate his share in two daintier bites.

"Nice appetizer, Sarah, but we're hungry men. Been on the trail almost all day without food. I guess you're just going to have to cook us something." He gestured toward the muddy triangle at the front of the lean-to. "At least hot coffee, eh, Bong?"

Bong nodded solemn agreement.

Sarah looked from one man's face to the other. They looked expectantly back at her.

"Coffee? How am I going to boil coffee? Markham, you're teasing me."

Markham turned his face to look up at the makeshift ceiling. "Um. Now let's see. I want coffee and rice and a baked potato and an onion and a nice fried fish and how about some beans cooked up with a little piece of fatback? It doesn't all have to be served at once. You can serve it in courses." He looked into her eyes. "I'm not fooling you, Sarah girl. I'm hungry. Old Bong's hungry, too. He's just more of a gentleman than I am, so that's why he isn't whining at you for more supper."

Sarah stared back at the smiling brown eyes so close to her now. Two inches closer and her lips would be touching his, she thought, and she sat up straighter. Why would such a thought even cross her mind? The moment passed when she heard her own stomach gurgle. Because of Markham's teasing grin, she pretended she hadn't heard the loud rumble. Why was she always doing something childish or silly when this man was around? She was hungry, too! She'd concentrate on

PARADISE FOUND

food. And how to cook it. There were two things she'd certainly learned on this trip. Markham Nash loved to rile her up but then he would help her if she asked.

"I can cook it if you can make a fire on that banana leaf." She dared him.

"You hear that, Bong? She's ready to cook if I'll make the fire."

"Yes, sir, Captain."

"You're on then, Corporal. Last man out of the lean-to is a mangy hound." Markham flung himself backward to yank his poncho on and clap his campaign hat securely on his head, but he was behind the little corporal who was already covered and running with the two water buckets before Markham hit the outside of the hut. Sarah watched their antics with fascination. They were acting like boys let out of school. What possible miracle could they work now?

Markham returned with two buckets of stones. He poured them out and placed them in a careful stone-floored circle atop the banana leaf foundation. He covered the rock circle with wet leaves he'd stripped from bushes nearby. He also brought an armload of cut bamboo. As he worked he smiled ever so often at Sarah. His eyes held the glint of constant laughter.

"Pretty soon you'll know all our trail secrets, sweet Sarah."

"My hat's off to you, Markham, if you really can get a fire started."

"I think your hat's off because it's too wet to wear."

Sarah nodded and looked regretfully at the sick-looking straw hat hanging limply over her poncho and bedroll. The blue velvet ribbons were wet, graying strings.

"Got your matches, girl?"

She pulled the metal box of matches from her equipment sack.

"Right here. But there's nothing to set afire."

"Yet." He reached to pull out one of the packstays from the nearest pack. She saw that the two-foot-long stay was a piece of wood about an inch in diameter. Dry wood. Protected by the leather pack. She watched Markham use his bolo knife to chip long slivers of the wood onto the leaf-stone bed.

"All we need is a little paper and we can have this fire going in seconds." He looked quizzically at Sarah. "You have any paper?"

Sarah shook her head.

"How about old Robert's books that you insisted on bringing along?"

Oh, yes. The books. A loud rumble from her own stomach caused her to color. He couldn't expect her to tear up Robert's books, could he?

"I don't know which pack you put them in, Markham."

"Bong'll know. He's got the whole train mapped in his head."

"Where is he?"

"Catching us a nice mess of fish right now, I'd say. When I left him at the river he was making himself a spear."

"He's going to *spear* fish?"

"Yep. Look yonder. Our supper's still flapping on it."

Bong raced toward the lean-to, arms held high, five fish strung on a vine in one hand, one still moving on the spear in his other hand. His wide white grin caused Sarah to laugh aloud. These two men could survive anywhere.

Markham asked Bong to find the books, then he put the buckets out to catch water before he dashed from the shelter to pick up a large log that lay on the ground nearby.

In seconds Bong had placed the leather-bound books in Sarah's lap. He also brought out a handful of small, dry kindling sticks from another pack. Markham dragged one end of the six-foot log into their space and tore the bark from the wood. Bong immediately began chopping the log into smaller lengths. Inside the bark, Sarah could see that the log was almost completely dry.

Markham held out his hand for the paper. Sarah looked at the books she held. She couldn't bear to tear pages from a book. She looked again at Markham. He didn't speak but his strong hand was still out indicating that he was waiting for the essential element. Dry paper. She had to force herself to deface one of the volumes. Of course she had to, but which one?

Dostoyevski's *The Idiot? Lorna Doone?* The Bible? No. She put the Bible aside. She'd tear one of the others first. She'd really need the Bible in the school. How about Lewis Carroll's *Through the Looking Glass?* The

Adventures of Tom Sawyer? She put Alice and Tom aside because they would be fine reading for the children, too. The last two were Ibsen's *A Doll's House* and Dostoyevski's *The Brothers Karamazov*. She couldn't imagine why Robert had carried a romance such as *Lorna Doone*. Should she sacrifice it? Or *The Idiot?* She hadn't cared greatly for that one. She wanted to read Ibsen and hadn't been able to do so back home. Papa didn't approve of Ibsen. She hadn't read *Lorna Doone*. The decision was made.

She turned the Dostoyevski novel gently in her hand. Maybe she could tear out only end papers and title pages . . . keep the book readable for use in the school. As carefully as possible, she began her task. Each tear was like a blow to her heart. Before she'd handed Markham the last of the end sheets, he had a fire going and Bong had erected a tripod of some of the wet bamboo.

After coffee and fish and potatoes fried with a little salt pork, all three leaned back in satisfaction to watch the beans simmering above the leaping flames.

"Those beans can be dessert tonight, breakfast tomorrow." Markham murmured, and touched Sarah's hand. "You're a good little cook, girl. Nice to have along on the trail." His hand traced a lazy circle on the back of her hand.

Sarah, paralyzed by his touch, could not pull her hand away, and could not say a word. She could only stare into the campfire and feel the flame of his touch upon her hand.

Bong whispered a courteous sound and pulled out

his bedroll to spread himself on top of it, his hat over his eyes.

Markham pulled his and Sarah's bedrolls out and spread them one on top of the other as if for one bed. Still, Sarah could say nothing. She sat pretending to be mesmerized by the flickering fire. When he lay down, she glanced at him. He gestured for her to come lie beside him. She hesitated only a moment before she moved to fit her damp back against his chest as if she'd been doing that all her life. The thick bedrolls resting on leaves made an unbelievably soft luxury beneath her. The big man radiated rays of heat against her back, the fire sent heat to the front of her. She felt warm and dry and protected.

"I'll take the first watch, Bong." She could feel the words rumble against her body. He placed an arm across her and even though she felt her heart racing she relaxed enough to say a few words.

"Maybe it'll quit raining by morning." She felt him grunt disbelief. "We could just stay here until the rain dries up, couldn't we?"

His warm breath flitted across her hair as he rumbled out the bad news. "We probably won't see the sun for another thirty to forty days, Sarah. This is the Filipino rainy season. Once the water starts falling it doesn't stop."

Somehow she couldn't bring herself to worry. Right now there was more than enough sunshine right here in the captain's warm embrace. She slept.

* * *

It was clear that she trusted him all right. She'd come to lie against him without a word of complaint. Markham stared over her head and into the fire. He could see the aura of light on the still-falling raindrops just to the front of the fire, but beyond that, the wet darkness swallowed all the rest of the world.

For his own benefit, he inched back from the woman who fit so perfectly against him. In seconds she'd moved in her sleep to press against him once more so they were once again like the spoons in the cupboard drawer of a good Iowa housewife. He felt warm . . . yes, warm, uncomfortable, wide awake. Good thing old Bong was snoring just inches away from them. No telling what he might end up doing if he were out here in the woods all cozied up with this little beauty and it was just the two of them. With the arm he'd slung over her, he pulled her a fraction closer against himself and then he smiled. He didn't sleep.

Thirteen

"It looks like we're always leaving good places behind." Sarah dished out beans and rice to the men. "This has been such a pleasant place to stay. Do we really have to go out in the rain again today?" She absently tucked a strand of blond hair behind one ear. "I'm just beginning to feel really dry." She smiled at Markham. "Lying . . . uh . . . sleeping with . . . uh . . . being next to you kept me warm all night and my clothes are almost completely dry."

"Would you want to stay out here for the next month?" Markham smiled across his jungle-furnished plate. "I thought you wanted adventure? Riding through a wet jungle is an adventure, little lady. If we wait much longer, being bogged down in a wet jungle's going to be an even bigger adventure." He looked out into the sheeting rain. "I'd heard folks in the U.S. talk about 'gumbo' mud . . . but unless they've been to the Philippines in the rainy season they don't really know their gumbo." He finished the last of his beans and threw his banana leaf outside to wash itself. "By afternoon we'll probably have trouble keeping the animals moving.

Their feet will be inches thick with mud and clay. It's awful hard to walk through Filipino gumbo."

"How much farther is the village?"

Markham looked at Bong, who was finishing his breakfast. "What do you say, Corporal Manawe? Could we be near our village by nightfall?"

Bong nodded. "On a sunny day, Captain. But rainy day like this? We got one more night jungle side maybe. Maybe two. For us old man Manglapus for sure, unless rain stop."

Sarah gathered up Bong's banana leaf and her own and tossed them outside. Few dishes to keep clean was one of the good things about the trip as far as she was concerned.

"I went to sleep so quickly last night after we ate that I didn't have time to compliment you two gentlemen." She looked down at her hands so she wouldn't have to look into Markham's eyes. "This little hut and the campfire and everything made the end of a horrible day so very pleasant." She looked at Bong. "How did you happen to bring so many ponchos, Bong? You saved our lives."

Bong laughed and pointed to Markham Nash.

"You tell how come, Captain."

"We're carrying mail and a load of ponchos for all the soldiers in the San Miguel area. That's one of the reasons we went to Manila . . . to pick up the rain gear." He slipped his poncho over his head. "We expected to be back in camp before the rains started."

"Oh." She kept her lids lowered. It was her fault they were caught in this deluge. "I'm sorry."

He put a finger under her chin and gently lifted it. "Chin up, girl. What happened, happened. You're plumb loco to be going to this place, but you sure haven't been a burden on the two of us." He turned his eyes to the corporal. "Has she, Bong? I even think she's made our trip a little better, don't you?"

"Lots better, Captain. Good cook."

"See?" He smiled down at her.

Sarah smiled back. Sometimes he was such a big silent frowning oaf and other times he was so nice she felt she could just . . . felt she could nearly . . . felt she'd like to. . . . She squelched the thoughts before they formed into words.

"Thanks," she murmured, and reached back for her poncho, her hat, and the food bag. "If you both want to pack up, I'll get my stuff together so we can leave." She looked longingly at the dying fire. "What are you going to do to replace the packstays we used?"

"Bamboo, my dear. The general mercantile store of the P.I. jungle. You can use it for almost anything. Lucky for us, packs don't care if their stays are wet or dry."

On her second day in the rain, Sarah sat in a sweaty lump on Mabuti's back and didn't even try to "look on the bright side," as her mother and Miss Arnold had always insisted she must do. Rain was pouring on her head through the leaks in her hat. The hat was ruined. Unutterably ruined. Her horse had slowed to a plodding shamble through ankle-deep mud. Where *was* the bright side?

Nothing but vines and bushes and sticky brambles pressing in on her from every side. Trees arched and leaned and dripped overhead. This was adventure?

Involuntarily she remembered the warmth of the captain's arms. She sat up straighter. It would get cooler again tonight. At the end of the day they'd build another lean-to and she'd cook another good dinner and then she'd lie all night in Captain Markham Nash's arms.

Something fluttered inside her. Prickles of anticipation radiated into every part of herself. His body pressed against hers. His breath wafting through her hair. His words in her ear. She felt her face warming. She'd been too tired to stay awake last night, but all through the night she'd been aware that she was being embraced within the arms of a man she could trust with her life. Sometimes she'd heard him whisper something to her, but she could never come awake enough to really understand what he was saying. Tonight she'd listen. She sat up straight and smiled down at Mabuti's head as she made a decision.

She'd enjoy their closeness just this one more time, she promised herself, then when they arrived in the village she'd begin her life alone. A grown-up, widowed schoolteacher who had no need for what clearly was not meant to be, anyway. Romance was not what she'd come to the Philippines for, and romance was not what Captain Nash had in mind, either. She was sure of that. To him she was just another load to deliver to San Miguel . . . like mail or ponchos.

She dreamed and planned their best supper ever as she swayed along on Mabuti's back. Tonight she'd cook the last of the turnip greens and the turnips to go along with the beans. That would make a nice change.

The rest of the slogging ride was just water, opaque skies, dripping greenery sloshing against her face, and bits of food doled out to eat while still on horseback. She solaced herself with the reminder that each reluctant step Mabuti made was one step closer to a warm, dry haven and another night of dreaming against Markham's masculine strength. Tonight she'd listen.

She could hardly believe her eyes when three shaggy bamboo nipa huts perched upon stilts seemed to emerge from the silvery spouts of rain. The sight of the houses was a shock to Sarah. Could they have already arrived at San Miguel?

Markham rode back to her side.

"It's still early, but we'll stop here. We'll all sleep inside tonight . . . even the animals. Old Man Manglapus has a shed out back that's big enough to hold all of the horses and mules and the gear also." He looked carefully at Sarah's hat. "Just take your own personal items. They'll feed us."

"Are we in San Miguel?" Her voice exposed her inner dismay.

"Oh, no. This is a way station many of us use in rainy season or for a place to visit to get away from camp once in awhile. Old Man Gordo Manglapus and his . . . uh . . . his family make a living cheating travelers out of whatever they can. They'll get a kick out of seeing an American woman."

Sarah's heart plummeted. No hut in the jungle, no wonderful beans and turnips meal, no sleeping in the captain's arms? Disappointment made her slow to unload, even slower to crawl up the ladder to the strange-looking one-room hut that Bong indicated.

What had been a dingy-looking hut from the outside offered a pleasant surprise inside. The bright yellow bamboo walls, floor, and ceiling made the room seem sunny, even though she could see the rain sheeting past the two window openings. Through the spaces between the bamboo canes of the floor she could see the pigs and chickens who huddled in the semidry area under the house.

Two older women with babes in arms and a number of girls of various ages stared at her from their squatting or sitting positions against the four walls. A poor copy of a photograph of Aguinaldo, the Filipino leader who'd fought so bravely against the Americans, hung high on the north wall, close to the bamboo rafters. The room contained no other furniture so far as she could tell.

Sarah dipped her head in a greeting as she'd seen Luz do in Manila each time she entered a room. The women and girls stared silently.

"Mabuhay." The word felt strange in Sarah's mouth. The oldest woman laughed and bounced the baby she held. Her laughter broke the spell. All of the females, young and old, began to talk at once. To Sarah it was

like being in an airy birdcage with a flock of exotic birds who chirped and sang all around her.

One tiny wide-eyed girl crawled closer to Sarah.

"Goo morning." The child's accented greeting made Sarah smile. Her brown hand lightly fluttered across Sarah's wet woolen knee. "Goo morning," she repeated and turned her huge dark eyes up to look into Sarah's as if asking, "Why are you wearing men's clothing?"

"Good morning and good evening," Sarah answered and nodded again. The laughter and the birdlike twittering around her rose in volume. She was pleased to see Bong's head appear in the ladder opening.

"You all right, Captain want to know?"

"Yes, I'm fine, Bong. Are you and he going to be coming up in a minute?"

Bong shook his head.

"Women's house. Not for us. We stay with old man Manglapus. These women feed you pretty soon . . . after we finish our chow. You sleep here. Captain Nash say take off hat and poncho, give to me."

When Sarah removed the drenched hat and put the gold hatpins in her pocket, she could hear the gasp that rose from every throat.

"What is it, Bong? What's wrong?"

"Nothing wrong, *mom.*" The skin at the corner of his eyes crinkled and his eyes smiled into hers. "Blondie hair. Blue eyes. White skin. They like. Think you look like statue in the church." His white teeth gleamed as he chuckled. "Maybe you Jesus' mother, they say."

Sarah handed him the poncho. She wanted to say something about the two men eating without her and something about being relegated to the second sitting for supper or something about being shunted off to one side or about being deserted. She opened her mouth to air her anger, then realized she would be talking to a person who wouldn't understand her feelings in a million years.

"Can't you stay with me for a while, Bong?"

A worried look crossed his face. "No, *mom*. Not right for man to come up in ladies' house. Not at Manglapus. Other house is for men. Fine place. You'll see."

"Well, what will you do over there?"

He grinned and tipped an imaginary bottle, then turned as if to begin his climb back down the ladder.

The captain was the one who needed to be listening. And he wasn't here. Sent his errand boy. Probably getting drunk over there with a bunch of other men. Maybe some women were with them over there, as well. He'd said Manglapus ran a way station that catered to soldiers. What better way to cater?

"Bong, are all the women over here?" Sarah asked.

Bong grinned hugely.

"No, *mom*. Some women over there cook supper. Captain okay." He ducked and disappeared from sight. Sarah traced his movements through the cracks in the floor for as long as she could. He flapped her poncho and hung it on a peg that protruded from one post. It hung dripping above the small group of hogs. They didn't seem to mind the added water. He took the hat with him.

Captain okay. Uh huh. I'll just bet. Sarah felt rising rage at Markham's inconsiderate behavior. *What did he want with her hat? Over there lolling about with strange women and eating and probably drinking while she was here starving. And he knew she couldn't speak the language.* That thought caught her up short. What business was it of hers if the captain was doing everything she'd imagined? Disappointment wouldn't kill her, her mother had always said. She needed to put him out of her mind and she needed to go about her own life here in this new country. Again she surveyed the slowly darkening room. Every eye was still trained on her movements.

Maybe it was time she learned some of their language. What would be even better, maybe she could teach these women and girls some English. It would be good practice for her work at the school and it would pass the hour or so until bedtime.

She turned back to the quieted, attentive group. She pointed to her own chest and spoke the words very distinctly.

"My name is Sarah."

Bong dipped his head as he entered the larger nipa hut where Old Man Manglapus and his two women sat eating. Across the room the captain squatted on the floor with his back against the wall. Bong tossed the tattered, dripping straw hat toward the captain. The hat hit a woven palm mat curtain that hung down the middle of the room to divide the space into two parts.

"Blondie lady, okay, Captain. She ask about you."

"She get anything to eat, yet?"

"The two little boys took food over for all them women." Bong nodded and grinned. "I think teacher pretty mad about something, Captain." He pointed to his cheek. "Face got real red both sides when I said you stay this hut tonight."

Markham nodded but didn't answer. He watched the older of Manglapus's two women light the wick that floated in a gourd of oil. She was by far the better-looking of the two, but when she spoke or smiled, the three missing front teeth spoiled the effect of the smooth *café con leche* skin. The younger, smaller woman was just an ordinary-looking Filipina . . . which meant she was quite attractive to most American eyes. She was short, slim, round-faced and smooth-skinned. Her long skirt was old but fairly clean. All in all, Manglapus offered attractive merchandise . . . for most travelers.

Markham ate his chicken and rice with his hands as he toted up the sum in favor of either young woman and shook his head in a silent negative. At some other time or some other place he might have engaged one or the other or both in a bit of badinage or perhaps more serious play, but now, all he wanted to do was think about the "blondie lady" with the anger-flushed cheeks.

That little gal was mighty used to getting her own way. Probably just wanted to rag on him for putting up here. She might not be happy, but he knew she was much better off here with all these people around. Last night had just been too hard on him, too tempting.

Another night in the woods like that and he might. . . . He couldn't finish the thought.

He wiped his hands on his trousers when he'd finished the last bite of rice, then picked up the hat Bong had tossed to him. He turned the bedraggled piece of wet straw in his hands and laughed.

"Bong, do you think one of these beauties has a native hat I could buy for our passenger?" He held up the limp shreds of straw and ribbon. "This poor thing wouldn't keep rain off a drowning rat."

Bong engaged the younger girl in conversation and nodded.

"She say 'yes,' Captain."

"How much?"

Bong held up five fingers. The captain shook his head. Bong spoke fiercely with the woman, then held up four fingers. Again Markham shook his head and he held up two fingers. The girl nodded and slipped behind the curtain to return with a round hat hand made from palm leaves, such as the Filipino country people wore in the wet season.

Markham counted out two Filipino pesos into the girl's palm, and when she made an inviting gesture toward the curtained area, Markham again shook his head. She looked at Bong.

"Go ahead, Corporal, if you want to. Either lady is yours with my compliments. I think I'll decline." He lifted his hand to his forehead, "I'm feeling a bit peculiar. Might be the fever slipping up on me again. You go ahead."

Bong shook his head.

"It will be my treat, boy, if you're interested. I have a few pesos left plus a couple of dollars. Both nice-looking women."

"No, Captain. *Salamat Po,* but tonight while you be think of little blondie American. I think of Magdalena." He waved the waiting woman away and moved closer to the captain. "I was wondering, Captain. You gonna be the one tell Magdalena about El Tor in Manila or am I maybe do it?"

Markham frowned and stretched himself full-length on his side against the bamboo wall.

"I don't know, Bong. Go ahead and tell her yourself, if you want to. And what am I gonna tell Sarah . . . or am I going to tell her anything? That bastard, Robert Zumwalt. I just don't know. One of us should have killed him long before he died." He searched Bong's face. "Are we destined to end up with two hysterical women on our hands?" He was silent for a moment. "We'll probably be there tomorrow evening."

A picture of a screaming, crying Sarah raced through his mind and he thrust the picture from him.

"I'll think about it. You plan to give Magdalena the news, if you want to." He yawned hugely. "Or maybe we just won't tell anybody anything." He yawned again. "Maybe we'll just let all the information go through official channels. That's the U.S. Army way of doing things, isn't it?"

Fourteen

Sarah mourned the loss of her beautiful wedding hat with the blue ribbons, but she had to admit that the "Filipino farmer hat" Bong had offered her was a great practical improvement over her other chapeau.

The drowning rain was still falling as they rode, but her head felt reasonably dry, much different than it had been on the trail the two days before. She was glad to get away from that awful garlic-smelling Manglapus place, too. She'd made friends there and she thought she'd taught some of the young girls several helpful phrases in English, but there was something about the place that displeased her mightily. She didn't even want to try to think about why she'd been so unhappy there.

She craned her neck to see a clear space through the trees canopied overhead. No sun, only dark skies. It looked as if there would be only one more long, uncomfortable gray day in the saddle. The sound of the men's bolo knives chopping, monkeys screaming, and constant water splashing would be the only music she could look forward to. She sighed. This trip was turning out to be quite different than she had expected. Today would probably be horrible.

She'd readied Mabuti for the day's ride by herself. Both Bong and Markham were being somewhat standoffish, so she had to be satisfied with her own thoughts and her own company.

"And with yours, Mabuti," she added aloud to the slow-moving horse. "If I didn't have you to talk to, I don't know what I'd do."

Markham couldn't see much of her face because of the huge hat which covered most of it, but he could tell she was either talking or singing. Her lips were certainly moving. Probably talking to that old slug Mabuti, telling her what a great horse she was. Markham felt the usual tiny prick of envy that Sarah's sweet words were mostly for that fat old horse.

He let Jonas drift to the side of the trail so Bong and the pack animals could pass on and he could be next to the schoolteacher for a moment or two.

"I see you got yourself some protective headgear, Miss Sarah. How's it working out?"

She lifted her chin and looked up into his face. Her blue, blue eyes seemed to be calling him to account in some way, he thought.

"Good morning, Captain. Yes, much better, thank you." She paused as if waiting for his comment. When he gave none, she went on. "Bong was very kind to think of getting a hat from the Manglapus family for me."

Damn. Bong and that old nag Mabuti always got all the appreciation. *He* always received reproach.

"Yeah, well, just one of the services the Army provides for its guests." He held her gaze a moment more. As he looked, he watched the color rise in her cheeks. "It won't be long now until we'll be in San Miguel, Sarah. If everything goes well you'll get to spend the night in your own house. How about that?"

She dropped her gaze and didn't answer.

"Isn't that what you wanted? To hurry up and get there so you could settle into your own place and start building yourself a school?"

The startled blue gaze lifted again to his own.

"Build a school? Hadn't Robert already started a school?"

"No school, Sarah." He made his voice gentle, "Not yet. Robert was probably just settling in, too, in the months before you came." Now what? Should he warn her that the only school was a school for scandal? "Listen Sarah . . . uh . . ."

"Yes, Markham?"

"Listen, girl, I told you things weren't going to be what you expected." He watched her chin rise again, her back straighten. She was twisting herself into a swivet. "Now, don't go getting yourself all in an uproar." He reached to put his hand on hers.

"I'm not upset." She didn't pull her hand away.

"I'll tell you what. . . . After we all check in with the major and you have a day or two to get acclimated, old Bong and I will come along and help you get the school building set into motion." He smiled, hoping for one in return. "You saw how quick Bong got you a shelter pitched in the woods. He and some of those other troopers can do wonders with bamboo and a few palm fronds."

The small hand moved to turn and clasp his own. The gesture and her smile made him want to shout a happy expletive, but he kept his voice quiet.

"I assure you, ma'am, the Army, at least the part that I represent, will do everything in its power to see that you're comfortable and happy in your new place."

"Oh, Markham, you and Bong and Rudolfo and Luz have all done so much for me." The tremulous smile widened. "I've learned to love this country and its people. I know I was an unexpected burden to you."

He smiled in return and clasped the small hand in his a bit more tightly as she spoke again.

"Do you suppose we will ever see Luz or Rudolfo again?" She leaned toward him to whisper the next words in confidence. "I really think they were courting, don't you?"

He nodded. Courting. That meant she thought the young couple were probably going to get married. And maybe there was some truth in that.

"I expect you're right. Next trip the Army sends to Manila, we'll have someone ask around about them." He looked more deeply into her blue eyes.

Her eyes grew dreamy and unfocused. "Just think, they might even have a baby by the next time we see them."

He nodded, mesmerized into sharing her dream for the Filipino couple. "Yeah. That'd be great all right."

PARADISE FOUND

He didn't know whether to laugh or curse at her next question.

"Does Bong have a sweetheart?"

"Old Bong? Well. Yeah. I guess. He likes one of the village girls real well, but . . . uh . . . she . . . that is, things kind of got mixed up for them, I guess."

"What's her name?"

"Magdalena."

"Oh, that's a beautiful name. Maybe we'll get to attend their wedding, Markham." The blue light in her eyes softened even more. "Wouldn't that be exciting? Maybe she could wear the dress that Mama made for *my* wedding. Someone should get some use out of it."

Oh oh. What kind of a mess was he letting himself be led into here? *Better back away. Your name is probably coming up next in this girlish litany of romance among the natives.*

"Sarah. Listen everything is going to be really different than you expect here. The Philippines are very different than Iowa. People don't always marry for love here . . . lots of times they don't even marry. Just be the kind of a woman you've already proved yourself to be . . . one who can tackle anything." He loosened his hand from hers and slapped Mabuti on the rump. "I gotta go back up to the head of the train. See if you can get this rotten old bag of bones to catch up with us."

As he rode away he could hear her apologizing to the stupid horse about his choice of words.

* * *

"He didn't mean anything by it, Mabuti." As she talked, Sarah peered up once again through the umbrella of leaves. The sky didn't seem quite so dark. It was still sheeting rain, but the day had somehow brightened considerably.

". . . and you just have to remember that he's an army man, my dear. They're encouraged to be rough in their speech, but you've seen that he has a very good heart." She smiled down at the back of the horse's head. "Oh, fiddlesticks, Mabuti. I forgot to ask him about that wonderful smell that was in the air all up and down the Manila streets." She patted the horse's neck. "You just remind me about that and the next time the captain and I talk, I'll ask."

The squishing plop of Mabuti's hooves pulling out of and dropping back into the thick black mud accompanied the rhythm of Sarah's thoughts for the rest of the day. She puzzled over the revelation that Robert hadn't even started a school. She remembered distinctly the lines in his letters telling about "The school I am starting" and about "My pupils who are learning English." Had he been lying, or perhaps he had been having classes outside somewhere. It was certainly warm enough if it wasn't raining. Class under a palm tree might be fun.

She pushed aside the unanswerable questions and took up the pleasurable duty of planning a school which was to be all her own . . . and of the help which had been offered her. She'd probably be seeing the captain every day while they were building. She needed to make concrete plans.

"Small. One room to start with," she told Mabuti, "But we'll probably need to add on really soon. A nipa hut could be a schoolroom of sorts if we could somehow get a blackboard hung on one wall." She mused for a moment about where she could find desks for the children.

"They're used to sitting on the floors at home," she said aloud, and she smiled at the mental image of herself crawling across the bamboo canes of the floor, moving from pupil to pupil to see the work they'd accomplished on the "floor" slates. Real schoolroom furniture could come later. Everything would be all right. She just knew it.

The wet gray day passed, just as the others had, and when Bong whistled and motioned downward, Sarah knew she was about to see her new home. She couldn't make Mabuti speed up her "swish plop" walk through the mud, so Sarah controlled her impatience until she finally came abreast of the two men and the packtrain. They were all waiting on a small rise.

Below she could see a dozen or more nipa huts with pathways between them. Just as the pathway down the hillside entered the town, a wooden two-story house with the same type of open windows she'd seen in every Filipino house in Manila was set to the left of the trail. Next to that was a small building that had a sign on the front over the door.

"A store?" She spoke with a question in her voice, but neither man answered. She persisted. "What kind of a store is it?"

"China store," Bong answered.

"What's a China store?"

"A store run by a Chinaman. There's one like it in nearly every Filipino barrio," Markham answered with exaggerated patience as if speaking to a child. "He sells just about everything a person in a village could want. Gives credit, too, you'll be happy to learn."

"Oh, I would never do that." Sarah raised her chin. "Daddy always warned me that if I couldn't afford to pay for it I shouldn't buy it."

"You may find things are a bit different here, little lady. You'll be a long way from home out here in the boondocks. Pay doesn't always come on time when you're this far away from civilization."

"Which place is mine?" No answer. She searched the two men's faces. There was something strange going on. The horses and mules stirred restlessly as if they knew they were at the end of their journey. Bong held them back as if he understood that they weren't welcome just yet.

"Headquarters," Markham finally muttered. "We better go there first. Let the major meet you." He pointed to the far end of the settlement which offered a wooden barrackslike building. Beside that was another wooden building that looked something like a small country church. Back of the two wooden buildings was a corral and several smaller wooden buildings, one obviously a barn or stable. The open shedlike structure looked amazingly like the stable in back of the church in Manila.

It hadn't occurred to Sarah at the time that such a large animal shed was somewhat out of place at the church, but now she wondered about it. Two priests wouldn't have need for thirty or forty horses. Strange.

Smoke from several of the houses drifted into the wet air and lay like a translucent gray fog across the length of the barrio.

"Suppertime." The captain's voice was almost a whisper. "You hungry, Sarah?" He seemed reluctant to ride on down, and Sarah felt content to gaze for another moment at the place. It seemed quiet, peaceful, even beautiful. Every building was surrounded by flowering shrubs, and flame trees blazed scarlet fire all up and down the area. "We can eat in the mess tonight, if you want."

She nodded without speaking.

Markham looked back at Bong and shrugged agreement. But he continued to sit unmoving as he turned back to stare down at the tiny settlement. When he seemed to feel both Sarah and Bong looking at him in puzzlement, he shrugged again and murmured something that sounded like, "All hell's going to break loose" to Sarah's ears.

She wasn't about to question him about what he meant because he spurred Jonas and, immediately, Bong led the creaking, jangling packtrain over the rise and down the slippery path. Sarah, on Mabuti, plodded down last in line, as usual.

At the bottom of the hill, Markham waited for her while Bong continued driving the animals toward the army corral at the far end of the street.

"Markham, I want to ask you something?"

"Right now?" His voice sounded harried. "Can't it wait until we've talked with the major?"

"Well, I just wanted to ask . . . did you and Bong build the stable in back of the church in Manila?"

"The stable? In back of the church?" Now he sounded dazed. "Sarah, you amaze me. I never know what you're going to ask. Why are you asking about barns?"

"From the hill this shed here looks exactly like the one in Manila, and since the one in Manila looked fairly new, I just thought . . ."

"You're some smart little lady." He grinned. "And you're right. Bong and some of the troopers built this shed and that other one in Manila, too. I just sort of stood around and cheered the boys on." He lowered his voice to a confidential tone. "Major Firestone thought if the soldiers had a *church* as their central reporting point, it might calm them down a little whenever they got into town. The padres went along with the idea, so there you are!"

Sarah nodded and let Mabuti continue on her plodding way. Jonas pranced beside her. Now they were really in the barrio she'd be calling home. Sarah tried hard to see everything at once. The shaggy nipa huts, the few wooden houses, the store with the strangely lettered sign.

To her left the two-story wooden house with the rows of capiz-shell window shutters looked rather grand compared to most of the other structures.

"Headman lives there." Markham's voice was terse.

He pointed across the open space in front of them. "Your house." A slightly fancier nipa hut but very

PARADISE FOUND

nicely built, she thought. She couldn't wait to explore it inside. As she was surveying the cabin, a young woman appeared at a window opening and looked directly at Sarah.

"There's someone in my house."

"Yeah. Let's get on to Major Firestone's office and he can explain everything to you."

Mabuti carried her right on, but Sarah turned to look back. The Filipina was still looking at her.

"Who is she?"

"Uh, that's Magdalena. Come on. Let's get on down the street." Markham used his quirt to land several whacks on Mabuti's rump. "Get along, nag."

"Don't you dare hit Mabuti!" Sarah spoke the words through clenched teeth. Jonas sidestepped around the mare. Mabuti never looked back or broke her stride. "You're the one who should be horsewhipped, Captain Nash. What's wrong with you?"

Markham kept his face turned away from her, his hat pulled low over his eyes. Rain streamed into Sarah's face, mixing there with her tears. He was behaving just as he'd done several times in the days since they'd met. He seemed to be trying to torment her for absolutely no reason. The man was driving her crazy. She looked back at the hut he'd said was hers. Before long she'd be rid of his military ways and his strange moods and she'd be her own boss in her own house. She could hardly wait.

Captain Markham Nash preceded her when they walked through the headquarters office and into the major's cubicle. He held the half-door back for her and introduced her to the commanding officer at the same time.

"Mrs. Sarah Collins Zumwalt, Major Thomas Firestone, our camp commander."

The big redheaded man behind the desk gestured to a chair and looked questioningly at the door as if expecting someone else, and then he looked at Markham.

"Robert Zumwalt is dead, sir. Died of El Tor the day he married Miss Sarah Collins from Iowa." Markham didn't sit down, but he relaxed his shoulders just a bit. "Mrs. Zumwalt insisted upon carrying on Mr. Zumwalt's work, sir. We couldn't make her stay in Manila."

"Zumwalt's work?" The major sounded truly puzzled. "What work?"

"His school, sir." Markham grinned broadly, then looked at Sarah and sobered instantly. "Mrs. Sarah here is young, but she's a worker, sir. Great on the trail." He turned his face and winked at Sarah so the major couldn't see the gesture. "I think she'll be just what the children here've been needing."

"Hmmm." The older officer surveyed Sarah very carefully. She was extremely conscious of her bedraggled appearance, her wet trousers, her Filipino hat. She snatched off the hat, hoping to look more feminine without it. The major's eyes widened at the first glimpse of her blond hair, but he didn't comment. He looked back at the captain still standing by the open door. "Did you explain the situation here, Nash?"

"Uh, no, sir, I didn't. I thought I'd leave all that up to you, Major, sir." He saluted. "If it's all right, sir, I'd like to get on out to the stable and help Corporal Manawe get the packtrain unloaded."

When the major nodded, Markham couldn't seem to leave the room quickly enough. Sarah opened her mouth to thank him for his care on the trip, but he was gone, the lower half of the Dutch door swinging behind him. He didn't even say goodbye.

The major cleared his throat and sat in silence for a moment. He shuffled the papers on his desk before he cleared his throat again and looked across at Sarah.

"Captain Nash and Corporal Manawe treat you right on the trip down from Manila, ma'am?"

"Oh, yes, Major Firestone. I consider them to be miracle workers of a sort. They were able to . . ."

The major interrupted the start of her recital with a sigh and a question.

"Did you know Robert Zumwalt very well?"

"He was ahead of me in school, but we were schoolmates for several years, Major. My parents approved of him and thought he was a gentleman. That's why they let me come to the Philippines to marry him."

He sighed hugely this time.

"Your parents were dead wrong, Mrs. Zumwalt. Your husband was pretty much of a layabout here in San Miguel. He got in thick with the village headman and, well, I guess that there's no way to say it but to say it. The headman's daughter, Magdalena, has been living in Robert's quarters almost since he arrived." He looked directly into Sarah's eyes. She felt as if each word were a blow to her chest. "Word around the camp, now, is that the young woman, Magdalena Suarez, is . . . um . . .

with child." He looked down at his desk again. "I've just been preparing a report for the Manila office of the school board about the man."

He stood and walked around the desk to where Sarah sat stunned in her chair. "I'm awfully sorry to have to say these things to a respectable young woman like you, but you'd find out anyway. Miss Suarez is, I believe, still living in Robert's place."

"Yes." Sarah's voice was a whisper. "I saw her at the window as we rode in." All the muttered words, the strange looks, the unanswered questions, everything that had been buried was rising to the surface. Now many puzzling incidents seemed clear. She tried to think back to the very day she'd first seen Robert at the church. Had he said anything? What exactly had he expected from this kind of arrangement plus a marriage to a girl from back home? Had he thought she wouldn't accept his proposal?

The major intruded into her thoughts with what he thought to be consoling words.

"Why don't we let you have a few days' rest and then we'll see about getting you back to Manila and from there back to Iowa?" He moved to the space directly in front of her. "A nice girl like you doesn't need to be out here in the jungle in a country like this."

Sarah straightened. Go back? No. She'd made her decision. Here was where she'd stay. Now she'd be faced with an even harder decision, she knew.

"Thank you, Major, but I believe I'll stay. I came

to teach and that's what I am going to do. I'll just move into Mr. Zumwalt's house."

"You're sure?"

"Very sure."

"Well, in that case, ma'am, I'll have a trooper go on over and remove Magdalena and her belongings from the premises. No need for you to even speak to her."

A picture of the beautiful, sad-looking young woman who'd stared at her from the window rose in Sarah's mind.

"Where would you send her, Major?"

"Well, I don't think her father will have her back." He shuffled his feet uneasily. "I believe Robert, uh, your husband, paid the headman, uh, her father, a certain amount of money for her." He turned to return to his seat behind the desk. "We may be able to find her a place at Old Man Manglapus's way station."

"You mean he bought her?" The major didn't seem to hear her whispered question.

He looked over the half door and into the outer office. "Sergeant. Come in here. I have a job for you."

"No!" The word was a shout. The thought of the Manglapus way station sent a chill up her spine. Robert's child brought into the world at *that* place?

"No!" she shouted again, then lowered her voice slightly. "Don't send your men, Major . . . not just yet. I'd like to meet Magdalena, talk to her, before I decide what to do."

"Miss . . . uh, Mrs. Zumwalt, I just don't think that's a good idea at all."

"It's what I want to do, Major. Please understand."

"As you wish." The major shrugged. "We'll await your word on this. I'll have someone standing by to help you remove her when you're ready." His raised eyebrows told her he was more than slightly shocked by her request to meet Robert's mistress. "Are you really sure about meeting a woman like that?"

"I am. I would like to have my personal belongings brought over to my little house. Do you suppose your sergeant or maybe Bong or the captain or somebody could see to that?"

"Yes, ma'am." He held out his hand. "And, ma'am, welcome to the Philippines and to San Miguel. Kind of a pretty little barrio. Natives a bit strange. Independent. But we keep them in order. It's not such a bad place as Army postings go."

"Thank you, Major." She shook the offered hand. "I hope to make it an even better place if I can." She clapped her damp leafen hat back on her head and turned to leave. "I'll go find Corporal Manawe."

"I believe you'll find him waiting for you on the steps outside, ma'am. Again, good luck." He immersed himself in his papers once more.

Bong ducked his head to her as she emerged from the headquarters building. Mabuti stood patiently behind him, her back piled high with a trunk and boxes and bags.

"Poor old Mabuti girl, Bong. She isn't getting to rest and eat like the others."

"Captain say she your horse while you need. Keep

PARADISE FOUND 191

her in Army corral." He flashed her the white grin. "I give her extra oats tonight. Mabuti like oats."

"Bong, where is Captain Nas—Uh, never mind." *His job is over, Sarah,* she told herself. *He got you here, now you're on your own. Get on with your life.* "The army stable is such a well-built structure. I understand you did that?"

"Yes. Thank you, teacher." Bong's dark skin reddened slightly.

"Maybe you can help me build a school?"

"Oh, yes, *mom*."

"Well, let's go meet . . ." She stopped in her tracks. "Oh, my word, Bong. Now I understand. This Magdalena is the one you. . . . Oh, dear. I'm so sorry."

"Not your fault, not Magdalena's fault, *mom*. We okay. Maybe better now . . . now Mr. Zumwalt not come back." He flushed again. "I already tell her about him die of dreaded El Tor after you marry in church. She know she have to leave your house."

"Maybe not, Bong. Let's just get right on over there and see if we can work something out." She stepped down into the puddled, sandy street and took Mabuti's reins from the soldier.

It's been her house, too, you know. She gave the idea some thought. *Magdalena's more than a little like you, Sarah Collins. In a way, she's Robert's widow, also.* Suddenly, at that thought, the slicing tropical rain turned icy cold against her skin. She clenched her teeth to keep them from chattering. *And, just like you, she has no other place to go.*

She yanked on Mabuti's reins and the fat horse and

the Filipino corporal followed her as she strode, chin up, into the fury of the wind-driven rain, toward her hut.

When they reached the palm-thatched house, Captain Nash stepped out of the darkness and nodded to Sarah.

"I just thought I'd help you and Bong unload the boxes and bags."

"I'm not going to make her leave, Markham, at least not right now, so don't ask me." She tried to see his expression but his face was shadowed.

"I didn't ask that. I just came to help you."

"Well," she wiped rain-diluted tears away with the back of her hand. "Well. All right. I'm glad you came." She tugged Mabuti into the space under the house.

"You go on up, Bong." The captain took over the unloading from his corporal. "Tell Magdalena that Mrs. Zumwalt will be sharing the space with her for a while."

Bong nodded and mumbled, "Thanks, Captain."

"Are you sure you want to do this, Sarah?" He put his hand on her arm. "The whole army cadre has heard about you, and I'm pretty sure that by now they all know you've decided to forgive and forget. Hard to keep things quiet here. I told you there were no secrets in the P.I." He indicated the hut floor above them with his chin. "I know they all, especially the major, think you're making a big mistake."

"Maybe so, but I'm not throwing anyone out into this kind of weather. All I have to do is put myself in her place and it's easy. I know what to do." She looked at the hand on her arm and remembered how strong and warm and wonderful it had felt when flung across her waist the night she'd slept next to him. "I have to do the right thing."

She felt bereft when Markham yanked his hand away to begin untying her parcels.

"Up you go then." He pointed to the ladder. "Tell Bong I'll unload this old plug and hand the stuff up to him." He grinned and patted her on the shoulder. "I'm pretty sure he has already told her about the good little blondie American schoolteacher, but I'll translate for you if you want. Magdalena speaks a little English, but she speaks Tagalog better. I'll stick around and that'll let you get everything settled between you."

Sarah gave Mabuti a pat before she stepped under the house, untied her rain-soaked, muddy shoes and shook them from her feet, then raised her chin, took a deep breath and started her barefooted climb up to face what was going to be a very strange adventure, living with her husband's mistress.

Halfway up she felt a touch of panic rise. She looked back at Markham, but he was busily untying and unstrapping her last reminders of home so she turned back to the bamboo stairway, her stairway to a new life.

Fifteen

The first thing Sarah noticed about her new house was the glowing gold and yellow and pale green of the bamboo floors and walls. The house was divided by a pale woven straw partition. But there was something else. Something like home. She took a deep breath and smiled. The room smelled like an Iowa farm, the scent a faint reminder of new-mown hay.

The sleek, glassy rounds of bamboo felt wonderful to the soles of her feet. She smoothed first one bare foot, then the other across the floor, thinking of them to be like sleek, deliciously solid glass cylinders underfoot.

The room she'd climbed into held two polished dark wooden chairs and a gleaming, high-backed wooden bench. The chairs and the bench were carved and held shimmering white inlays of mother of pearl. A high shelf ran around three sides of the room. Her instant impression was of a quite beautiful room, elegant in an unusual way.

And so was the young native woman who sat in one of the chairs. The exotic beauty of the woman's creamy skin, large brown eyes, and shiny black hair made Sarah feel almost completely colorless. Corporal Manawe squatted on the floor to one side of the chair where the young woman sat. Both the Filipina and the soldier gave a start and leaped to their feet when she appeared. Bong smiled, but the young woman's face wore an anxious, strained expression.

"Mom." The corporal ducked his head. "This is Magdalena. She pretty good worker if you let her stay in your house."

"Just a minute, Bong. Let me take off these wet socks." Perched in the door opening, Sarah yanked off her long black cotton lisle hose and tossed them over the top rung of the ladder. She stood and reached to touch the young woman's hand. "Tell her, Bong, that I'd like her to stay but not to have her work especially. I'd just like to have her company."

"Thank you, *mom.*" The woman's breathy voice rose just above a whisper. She put her hands together at chest level and dipped her glossy dark hair toward Sarah in the Filipino version of a bow.

"Please call me Sarah and I'll call you Magdalena, if I may."

The Filipina woman's hands steepled together at chest level and her dark head nodded again.

"Bong." Sarah turned and looked down into the laddered opening. Markham was still working with the leather straps and the other ties. "Captain Nash said he was going to hand my things up to you."

Bong smiled a tentative smile at Magdalena and moved to the entryway.

"May I see the rest of the place, Magdalena?" Sarah indicated the partition. "Is that another room?"

"Yes, *mom*. Sleeping chamber."

That must be where she slept with Robert.

The thought flashed into Sarah's mind, but she was surprised that it caused her no pain. She realized she would not have liked sharing a bed with Robert, even though she had willingly married him with the understanding that she would have to sleep with him. Relief. That was what she was feeling. Just plain relief. She had to be honest with herself. She was glad she would never have to sleep with Robert in this bed or in any other.

She looked at the wide bamboo platform which held a thin mattress covered with a silken embroidered crazy quilt which she remembered had been made by Robert's mother. Several chests and a trunk lined the walls, and pegs high on the wall held a few pieces of clothing. The window openings overlooked a huge flame tree and some other flowering trees which she couldn't identify. The whole place was wonderful. Beautiful. And clean.

She knew who had been keeping the house. Robert would never have done any of the chores he considered to be "woman's work."

"How shall we arrange our sleeping?" Sarah asked as they moved back into the other room. Captain Nash and Bong stood there, surrounded by her bags and boxes. Beside Bong's wide bare brown foot, the captain's long foot covered in knitted khaki woolen socks seemed particularly American. Sarah realized that the barefooted corporal seemed at home but that the captain looked boyish and vulnerable and a bit out of place without his boots.

Markham asked the girl the question in Tagalog and Bong added a word or two. Magdalena lowered her lashes over her huge brown eyes, then nodded before she pointed to a corner of the room.

"She says she's been putting her mat here in the main room every night. She'll just continue to do that if that suits you. She says she knows Americans don't much like sleeping on the floor." Markham grinned at Sarah. "I think you just got yourself a dogrobber, girl. She sure has expressed gratitude."

"Dogrobber?"

"You know, like Bong is for me? A personal helper. Dogrobber. That's what we call them in the Army. I guess Magdalena is going to be your corporal."

"Tell her I want us to be friends."

Markham spoke and Magdalena answered, then hung her head. One tear escaped her eye and trailed down a cheek that was like pinkish tan satin.

"Oh, my God. She says she's in a family way, Sarah."

"I know that."

"You know it?"

"Didn't you tell me there were no secrets in the Philippine Islands?" She grinned at him. "Anyway, your Major Firestone had already informed me as to the status of my household."

"Oh. Yeah. I'd forgotten for a moment. There really *are* no secrets around here." Markham sighed. "The only reason we didn't know was because we were in

Manila." He glanced at Bong and lowered his voice. "Reckon that news was pretty much of a shock to the corporal."

Sarah stepped closer to the weeping woman. She placed her hand on the Filipina's shoulder. Magdalena mumbled something, then cried even harder. Sarah nodded, gazing into Magdalena's eyes as she spoke.

"Everything will be all right, Magdalena." She turned. "Tell her what I said, Bong."

Bong translated quickly and then the two young women were embracing and sobbing together.

"What are they crying about? Bong, do you know?"

"Cry because they feel happy, Captain."

"Oh. Oh, then that's all right. A little happy bawling should make all of us feel just a whole lot better."

Sarah wiped her eyes and tried to smile at Markham.

"Why didn't you tell me anything about Robert? About Magdalena? You both knew he was living with her, didn't you?"

"Well, I tried to tell you. Remember?" Markham unbuttoned the collar of his shirt. "I know I told you he was a bastard." He ran his fingers around inside the shirt's neckline. "I told you that even before you married him."

"You could have told me everything."

"Yeah." Markham grinned at her. "You were so all-fired determined to get married to the guy that I thought maybe you loved him. I didn't want to be the one who broke your heart by tattling on him."

"How many other things did you keep back . . . such as the fact that no school has ever been started in San Miguel?" She held up her hand as if to stop him from answering. "Yes, I know. You did tell me Robert hadn't built a school, but, my word! I just assumed he was teaching in his house or in the church, or some other place such as the mess tent."

"Who let *that* particular cat out of the bag?"

"Your major. He was quite informative."

"I'll bet. The whole Army cadre thought old Robert was about as useless as tits on a boar hog." When Sarah stared at him, he had the grace to color slightly. "Well, Sarah, hell. He acted like he thought the Philippines were his personal playground and the people, his possessions. And he never turned his hand to do a lick of anything resembling work. How could I tell all that to his new bride?"

"I'll just bet you're full of all kinds of secrets, Captain Nash."

"I do have one really good one." His dark eyes glinted with mischief.

"Can you share it with us?"

"Later maybe. Right now we . . ."

A Filipino voice called from below to break into their conversation.

"Goo' morning. I come up?"

Magdalena moaned and shrank back against the wall. Bong straightened and moved to stand in front of her as if trying to protect her.

"Who is that?"

"Magdalena's father, the village headman. Señor Suarez was Robert Zumwalt's favorite crony."

"The major told me that money crossed hands, that Robert *bought* her from her father."

"That's correct. He lives in the big wooden place across and down from you." All four stood in paralyzed silence for a second.

"I come up?" The voice from below again.

"What should I do?" Her tone was a fierce whisper.

"Let him come up. After all, you're going to have to be on good terms with everybody in the village. Bong and I will getting the rest of the stuff in, so we'll be right here. No need to be afraid."

"I'm certainly not afraid . . . but someone is." Sarah indicated the trembling daughter of the caller.

"Yeah. Magdalena has plenty of reason to fear him. Let him come on up and let's see what he wants. Just remember he's a snake, an oily snake." Sarah stole a glance at the hard brown gaze of the army man. His mouth turned down into a straight line of disapproval. His brows were drawn together in a frown. He really must dislike this Suarez, she thought.

"Maybe Magdalena would rather wait in the bedroom?" She whispered the words to him.

Markham murmured the translation of Sarah's question, but Magdalena shook her head, then pressed herself even deeper into the corner.

Sarah moved to the ladder opening. "Good evening, sir. Please come up."

In seconds a thin, dark-skinned man dressed in a white shirt and trousers put a bare brown foot onto the bamboo floor. He nodded at Markham and bowed to Sarah. He ignored his daughter and the corporal.

"Welcome, schoolteacher." He took Sarah's hand into both of his. "So sorry my friend Mr. Robert Zumwalt die in Manila." He lifted her hand as if to kiss it. Sarah had to yank hard to pull her fingers from his grasp.

"Thank you for your welcome." Sarah looked over his shoulder to see Magdalena continuing to crouch in the corner of the room. "I have met your daughter Magdalena already." Sarah knew her words were daring, maybe even incendiary, but she wanted to dent the man's impervious facade.

The village headman shrugged.

"She no good no more."

"Magdalena? Is that who you're talking about?" Sarah felt the blood rising in her face. Rage spun a whirlwind in her mind. "You're talking about your daughter?"

"No good."

Sarah put one bare foot a step closer to the man, but before she could say a word, Markham stepped between them carrying a large woven basket. He looked down at Sarah in passing and shook his head slightly.

Well.

Oh, all right.

She was, after all, a guest in the man's town. She stepped back and kept silent as Markham moved on into the second room to set the bag on the bed. Sarah could feel her nerves trembling with anger. When Markham and Bong had once again disappeared down the ladder, she allowed herself to speak calmly to the man.

"Excuse me, Mr. Suarez. What exactly can I do for you? Did you wish to speak privately with Magdalena?"

Suarez glanced at his frightened daughter for only an instant before speaking.

"No, Teacher."

"Then, what can I do for you?"

"You have no companion?"

"I think Magdalena will be a good companion."

He shook his head with an impatient look.

"I mean man."

"No. No man. You know my husband died in Manila."

He looked at her blond hair for a moment, then his sly glance flitted across her breasts and down the area of her groin to finally stare at her dirty bare feet. His hand instantly followed suit. His touch flashed against the length of Sarah's body.

What? Even though she knew he had just made the bold sweeping move, she was unable to make herself believe that this stranger had really touched her . . . from her head to her feet.

She gasped.

He straightened and leered.

"I be your companion," he whispered. He leaned so close she could feel his fetid breath in her hair and then she was engulfed in a cloud of garlic and stale beer. "I will 'specially like to have the blondie American teacher."

Sixteen

"Bong, I think you and your men might have saved my life. Building a shed for me like the ones you built for the horses is a wonderful idea for our new school." Sarah touched the bark-covered heavy tree trunk that stood in the center of the stable as a main roof support. "The idea of having a bunch of children in a nipa hut really scared me. A bamboo structure seems so . . . so breakable, so fragile."

"Nipa hut like the Filipino. Look weak and little, but strong as iron." Bong stood looking up at the stable's slanted roof. Sarah could see he was glowing with pride in his work.

"Magdalena told me bamboo was strong, but she agreed that the children and I might be happier in a nice wooden shed." She glanced at Bong's face to see his reaction to the Filipina woman's name. He gave away nothing. It was as if a shutter had come down to close his face. "At least that's what I think she meant."

"She thankful for you, *mom*. She learn English pretty easy, I think. Quick, too. I work with her."

"Good. English lessons would be great. But truth to tell, we already understand each other pretty well." She glanced at his face again from the corner of her eyes. "I'd like Magdalena to get out more. I don't want her cooped up in that house all the time." She took another peek. "Could you do something about that, Bong?"

"Oh, yes, *mom*." The bright smile returned. "I get her out more if you want."

"Better get over to talk to her today, Bong. Of course, right now, mornings aren't too good. She's feeling sick in the mornings, but in the afternoons and evenings she feels fine."

"Yes, *mom*. Thank you, *mom*."

"Now," she gestured at the open front, "at the front we can put . . . what?"

"Bamboo or mats or palm leaves, *mom*. We'll fix it up real nice for the little ones and their new teacher lady."

"Whatever we can use to close the school in without cutting off all the air, Bong. We don't want to boil my eager students." She paced off the distance of the back wall, looking at the earthen floor as she walked. "At least I won't have the constant worry about one of the students—or maybe the teacher—falling through the schoolroom floor." She laughed. "Magdalena thinks I'm silly because sometimes I'm afraid when I peer down through the cracks in the floor and I feel as though I'm falling."

Bong joined in her laughter. "I already know you brave lady, Teacher *mom*."

Sarah turned and picked her way across the stable to the open side, where she peered up at the sky.

"Can you work on our school building even if it is raining? And what do you want me to do to help you get the place ready for the students? I'm pretty good with a hammer."

"Not the American *teacher!* Not work on building school!" Bong displayed shock at the idea, then laughed. "A little rain not keep us soldiers from work. You just wait. We finish, *mom.*"

"Did Captain Nash tell you what to do, or did he say he would help with the school?" Sarah wanted to bite her tongue. She couldn't seem to keep herself from thinking or talking about Markham.

She and Magdalena had had long conversations using English and sign language to talk about the two men, Markham Nash and Bong Bong Manawe. It was as if they were driven to talk about them and used each other as sounding boards.

Sarah wondered what Markham would have done if he had seen Magdalena's father touch her the night she'd moved in. No one knew about the man's shocking behavior except her. Magdalena probably hadn't even seen the man's flashingly vulgar move. Since that lecherous introduction to the headman, she'd stayed well away from Señor Suarez, but she'd continued to be civil to him in public when she couldn't avoid a meeting. Magdalena was really terrified of her father. She knew that.

"Yes, *mom.* Captain Nash, he tell us to make the school and he help plan building for you."

What did that answer mean? That Markham would be around when they were building the school? That he would merely be supervising from headquarters? She'd not seen the man since the first night when she had joined him at the officers' mess for supper. Magdalena had prepared all her meals since then. Maybe she could invite him and Bong to eat at her house.

Surely that would be the decent, courteous thing to do, wouldn't it? Sort of a "thanks be" for all their trouble? Of course, there was really no way she could pay them back for everything they'd done for her, but she *could* be hospitable. Her mother and father would say that was the right thing to do in any case.

"Bong, would you and Captain Nash like to have supper at my house this evening?" She turned her back to the shed opening to issue the invitation.

"I hope you're accepting for me, Corporal Manawe. I do love Magdalena's *sinigang*." The American man's voice came from just behind her. Sarah whirled, and the hem of her gray cotton gown almost touched Markham Nash. She felt her pulse speed.

"I, too, hope we're having *sinigang* if it's a favorite of yours. What is that *sinigang*, by the way?" She smiled up into the captain's face.

"It's a kind of a clear vegetable soup with fish or shrimp in it. Got little yellow flowers in it, too. You'll like it." He groaned at the picture in his mind. "A bowl of *sinigang* could even make me give up one of my mama's good dishes." He touched Sarah lightly on the shoulder. Her world stood absolutely still. The masculine heat of him penetrated her skin. "We accept, Madam Teacher. Okay, Bong?"

"Okay, Captain."

"I'd better hurry on home and alert Magdalena to your choice of food, Captain." She turned her face toward the corporal. "We'll have plenty of rice, too, Bong." She'd said she was going home, but she knew that so long as that strong, sunburned soldierly hand was touching her she was helpless to move. "I'm sure Magdalena knows how to cook rice the way you like it."

Bong's white smile split the smooth butterscotch skin of his face. She knew that the smile was his acceptance before he again bent to his work. Sarah paused and looked at his back as he gathered tools into a box. She worried about him and Magdalena. What were they going to do? She knew they loved each other. She and Markham would have to talk about the problem. Maybe tonight.

Markham looked down at his hand resting on her shoulder. *Why am I touching her?* He didn't move his hand. *You know the answer to that question, boy. Better get your mind on other things!* But he let his hand continue to rest lightly on her shoulder.

He'd been rushing frantically through the paperwork that had been allowed to pile up while he was gone, but this morning when he'd spied her chatting with Bong, he had just decided to hell with it, shoved the remaining papers into a drawer, tossed duty out a window and rushed out of the office and into the horse shed. She was wearing the gray cotton dress. Her tiny figure simply shouted womanliness to him. She'd worn that same dress every day since they'd arrived. No evidence of a corset. Yet. He grinned.

He'd watched her making the rounds of the major's office, the chapel, the Chinaman's store, even the site they'd arranged for the school, her golden hair shining through the foggy haze from under that black lace mantilla she'd commandeered from somewhere. She'd also been to nearly every hut in the village.

Bong had reported that she was trying to drum up student's for the school. Once he'd watched her hurry into her house with that old bastard Suarez right on her heels. Whatever she'd said to the man, he'd switched directions in a hurry. Standing on the first rung of the ladder into her hut she'd parried her closed umbrella against the man, as if it were a weapon. He'd have to ask her about that particular run-in. Suarez was probably bothering her about Magdalena.

To Markham, the little red plaid umbrella she carried everywhere was far from a weapon. It was the lighted beacon that his eyes had searched for each day as he labored to fill in the miles of required forms. He gave an inner smile when he glanced at the little red bumbershoot, closed up and leaning against the wall in the far corner of the stable.

Bong picked up the wooden toolbox and shifted it to his shoulder. He dipped his head to Sarah, then shifted his gaze to Markham as if asking permission to leave.

PARADISE FOUND

Markham nodded back. The corporal was on his way to the building site to get the other men into gear, Markham surmised. Even though he'd had to do some arguing with the major, Markham was going to see to it that she was sure enough going to get herself a school, one way or another. The Army could do without Bong and the other men for the few days it would take to build the shed so she could set up the stupid school. That was the only thing she seemed to want.

"Got the other troopers ready to work, Corporal?"

Bong nodded and stepped out into the rain.

Bong. And that damned Magdalena. What were they going to do about those two? They'd need to discuss that problem soon. Maybe tonight.

Bong took off his hat, dipped his head, then spoke to her as she worked over the tin basin of wash water.

"Mabuhay, Magdalena."

She hardly glanced up from where she squatted next to the laundry rock, but he knew she could see him from the corner of her eyes. Her hands slowed but continued to scrub the piece of cloth she was holding. A slight smile etched itself at each corner of her mouth.

"Mabuhay, Bong Bong."

Her voice was so beautiful. Almost a whisper. So womanly. So civilized. The Tagalog language always sounded like a song when she spoke it. He didn't want to disturb her, but he'd promised himself that he'd talk to her plainly now that there was no one else around to hear.

"I hope you are well, Magdalena."

"Very well, thank you."

"The child? Does it seem well, too?"

She nodded, head down, her cheeks reddening.

"We must talk about our future, Magdalena. I have told you I am willing to take the child as my own." He moved a fraction of an inch closer to her. "It is as I said before. What cannot be helped must simply be put aside. Let us allow our lives to go on." He closed his eyes and took a deep breath as he threw away his pride. "I need you with my body and with my soul."

"What can we do, Bong? I live with the lady schoolteacher. She needs me. She is my mistress now since her husband has paid my father for me. She has not given me permission to be with you." She raised her eyes to his. "I cannot have such bad manners as to ignore her. Perhaps she will give her blessing if we ask . . ." She again blushed and looked down at the washing. "And we must think of the Army, of the captain. What of him?"

"You are right, my heart. We must go about this gently." He shifted in place and looked to see if any villagers observed them before he quickly touched her shoulder, then as quickly withdrew his touch. "It is true that they are Americans, so we can not know what they will decide." He smiled at her quick intake of breath. He was glad to see that his touch still meant much to her. "Such an erratic people. But I am no longer afraid of the captain as I once was. And I have observed that the blondie teacher woman is much like the women of our barrio in some ways." He fanned insects away with the brim of his hat. "I believe she has innocence in her heart." He fanned the brim of his hat again.

Magdalena stole another quick glance at him. Her brown eyes told him many things without speech.

"Of course, like all Americans, they are somewhat crazy, but their craziness is not always the bad kind. Both can be very kind if they wish to be." He nodded and paused a moment for thought. "Sometimes I don't understand them. Americans seem to be bold when it is wrong to be bold and timid when it is wrong to be timid."

Magdalena nodded agreement. "I have noticed that they don't mind touching each other when they are in public. Men touching women, I mean. The Captain Nash touches my teacher lady and she looks pleased." Magdalena looked around as if she were a bit frightened at her own boldness in speaking of the Americans who were their employers. "And in private they are very formal," she whispered. "Almost as if they do not know each other."

"Well, what is worse?" Bong nodded and continued her train of thought. "When they could do as they wish . . . that is, when no one is around or when they think they are quite alone, they then act as if they must keep well away from each other." Bong let his hand pass quickly across Magdalena's shoulder once more. "In public, they are without shame, in private they act stiff, awkward, as if they do not know what to do . . . as if they are afraid of each other."

"Aye, *Dios*. What you say is true." She tossed the

rinsed garment into the waiting pottery bowl with the other things she had washed. She had to laugh just a little. "Ah . . . anyway, what can you say, Bong Bong? They are, after all, Americans."

"Yes. *Our* Americans." He was silent for a second. "We must show them some respect and be patient about our own needs."

"Perhaps we can ask and they will give us their blessing?" Magdalena dared to look directly at him. Her hands trembled with the excitement of the intimacy of their meeting. Bong realized that sharing this moment with him was enough to last her for many days.

Bong loved it when he had the opportunity to look deeply into his beloved Magdalena's dark eyes. Her glance was like a deliciously sweet cup of cold water taken in the middle of the hot day. He had thought it over. He nodded at her suggestion.

"The captain will come to eat with the teacher lady tonight. I will come also. She has asked me to spend more time with you. Does that frighten you?"

She shook her head and smiled at the dress in her hands.

"The captain has talked much of *sinigang*."

She nodded again.

"Then I will eat *sinigang* and rice with you this night." He let his voice lower to a murmur. "I have brought you a golden trifle from Manila. I will give it to you tonight when the captain comes."

"You and the captain will come to our hut tonight? Together? Truly?" She stood, suds dripping from the cloth in her hand. "Perhaps we can make our desires known to them while we are all together? Perhaps tonight?"

Bong nodded and stood also. "Yes. Perhaps tonight."

The candlelit room seemed so cozy to Sarah. The three of them sat at the banana leaf supper spread that Magdalena had prepared. Magdalena stayed near the stair, ready to climb down to get whatever else was needed. When Bong had carried up the heavy tureen of *sinigang,* Sarah had been very pleased to hear the captain's hungry murmur. The soup did smell good. Hot and spicy. Magdalena had explained that the yellow flowers Markham had talked about were squash blossoms.

"Your squash blossom special, Captain," she murmured when Bong carried the soup up. After Bong seated himself, she felt even more pleased. To have the two men sitting there ready to dip out balls of rice from the pile on the center leaf put Sarah right back out onto the trail with the two of them. She reached for a helping for herself, and the back of her hand brushed the back of Markham's reaching hand. Her hand tingled and she drew back quickly.

"Excuse me, Sarah. Go ahead."

"No, no, Markham. You're our guest. Please."

Bong glanced quickly at Magdalena as if to say, "See how they are. They are frightened to be near each other." She veiled her smile of understanding with her hand and lowered her eyelids from the heat of his loving gaze.

"This is tasty-looking *sinigang,* Magdalena." Markham called to the young woman crouched in the corner nearest the ladder.

"We have everything we need now, Magdalena. Water to drink, soup, rice, bread, fruit. Come sit down here with us." Sarah gestured to the place beside herself.

Magdalena answered with a quick negative shake of her head.

"Why not? Let's all eat together."

Again the negative gesture accompanied by a shy smile.

"Mom. Is our custom. Woman wait. Not eat until all finished." Bong grinned sheepishly at his explanation.

"Well, we do that, too, back in Iowa, on Christmas, or Easter, or some big day like that, but there are only four of us here." Sarah motioned again to Magdalena. "Besides, I'm a woman and I'm sure not going to wait while you and Captain Nash here hog up all Magdalena's good cooking."

"Different, *mom.* You would not wait. You American schoolteacher lady."

Sarah looked at Markham in bafflement.

"Markham, would you give these two an order in Tagalog so we can all relax and enjoy our meal and our time together?"

After a few words from the captain, Magadalena scooted herself a few feet closer to the dining circle.

"There. Now, this is what I call a good meal." Sarah filled earthenware bowls from the tureen and handed them around to the others. "I just knew I'd find some use for Grandma's spoons if I brought them with me." She handed each person a silver spoon. "These are real silver and this is my first party meal in my new house, Markham. I'm so pleased."

"Just hope your evening party doesn't ruin your standing in the community, Sarah girl." Markham dipped his spoon into the hot soup and licked his lips in anticipation. "You do want those folks to send their girls to you to be taught, don't you?"

"How could all of us eating supper together ruin my reputation?" Sarah's spoon froze on its way to her mouth.

"Well, little innocent, what you've got here is a woman of dubious reputation, an officer fraternizing with an enlisted man—even worse, a *native* enlisted man—and a good-looking young American widow. All four of these folks sitting around together in the dark in a very private place, more or less." He rolled his eyes in delight and dipped again.

Sarah gasped with indignation. "That's not the way it is at all."

"How do the people of San Miguel know what we're doing up here? They can imagine anything they want. Good stuff, Magdalena." He waved the spoon in the air as if including the whole community. "All those people in that particular setting could have the makings of a spicy bit of gossip, Mrs. Zumwalt, Blondie American Teacher."

Good-looking young widow. Sarah smiled down at the sticky rice ball in her left hand. He thought she was good-looking!

"The people with whom I have supper really has no bearing on whether I'm a good teacher or not." Sarah made the declaration, then lifted her chin and fluttered her eyelashes to look into the captain's eyes where the gleam from the candle was reflected twice. "This is Magdalena's home and she's allowed to see her friends here. As for you, Captain, I'm in your debt so deeply that a year of *sinigang* suppers could never repay you."

The evening passed with plenty of good talk between Sarah and the captain, with deep silences between the two young Filipinos. While they ate, Markham brought out a flask which he shared with Bong. Both Magdalena and Sarah declined when he gestured the drink toward them.

"American bourbon," he explained. "Not the native rice wine, nor even *tuba.*" He lifted the flask again as if to be sure they really did not want to accept his offer.

Again both women declined.

"What's *tuba?*"

"Wine made from fermentation started in the heart of the palm tree. Palm wine."

"Even the whiskey hasn't made Bong very talkative, Markham. Are they having a good time?"

"Don't worry about them not saying anything, Sarah. Filipinos usually don't talk while they're eating," Markham explained. "In fact, I think he has just given her a present which I helped him pick out in Manila. It has his initials on the back."

"Oh, how touching." Sarah smiled at the corporal and glanced at the shining face of Magdalena who was looking down at a tiny gold cross on a thin gold chain which now hung around her neck. Inspecting further, Sarah imagined she could begin to see the rounded bulge of Robert's baby below the waistline of Magdalena's Sunday-best native dress with the butterfly sleeves.

Sometime within the next five months, arrangements would have to be made about the child. Sarah peeked at the expression on Bong's face. He didn't seem anxious or worried.

She forced the troublesome thoughts from her mind. This was her first party in her own new house. She was determined to enjoy it. She took another spoonful of the delicately rich-tasting *sinigang*. The shrimp were just right in the clear onion-vegetable broth. She swallowed with pleasure. Markham was right about *sinigang*. She prayed he wasn't right about what the townspeople were saying. She'd just let the future take care of itself.

"Tell me, Markham, when you and Rudolfo and Bong were drinking that night on the trail, what were you three talking about that included my name?" Sarah waved her hand as if he had interrupted. "Now don't tell me you weren't discussing me. I heard my name."

"You really want to know?"

"Yes. I do. You hurt my feelings dreadfully that night."

"I know, Sarah. I apologize. We paid for it next morning though. Remember? It was all that *tuba* that Bong passed around."

"Oh, yes, I really enjoyed watching your suffering." She smiled sweetly. "Now. Back to your comments at the campfire, Captain, if you please."

"Well," Markham leaned back on one elbow. "When Bong talked about Magdalena and Rudolfo talked about Luz, I felt as if I had to talk about someone, so I talked about the blondie schoolteacher."

"I already know that much." Sarah leaned forward impatiently. "I want to know what you said."

"You're sure you want to hear this?" Markham took a drink from the flask.

"Indeed I do."

"Well, I told them about . . . you're really sure you want to hear this?"

Bong and Magdalena had shifted away from the banana leaf supper table and were conversing in low tones in their own language. The Filipina's new gold necklace twinkled with points of candlelight from the darkness of their chosen corner. Bong was smiling at the beautiful Magdalena and she was smiling back at him. Sarah thought they seemed to be enjoying their whispered conversation greatly. She'd never seen the two of them conversing so freely together. She turned her attention back to the captain.

"I want to hear everything, Captain Nash. Speak up."

"All right. If you're sure?" He looked his question once again. Sarah nodded testily as if to say, "Get on with it."

"I told them quite a tale about seeing this little pink corset with lace ruffles round the edges come flying through the air toward me right through the jungle." He took a bit of rice and looked innocently across at Sarah. "Of course, I had to explain to them what a corset was."

Seventeen

Oh, my God! The piece of shrimp in Sarah's mouth instantly turned to cardboard. He'd caught the corset? Had he seen her cavorting through the jungle in her hat, shoes, and stockings? And with those monkeys? Sarah felt her face flame. She looked at the bamboo rounds of the floor and wished the cracks between the rounds would widen to let her or the captain fall right through. She didn't care which one fell. She just wanted to be out of his sight.

She couldn't look up at him. She couldn't eat. She couldn't even chew the bite still in her mouth. She couldn't move. She'd never speak to the man ever again.

From the corner of her downcast gaze she could see the captain calmly dip her grandmother's silver spoon into his soup bowl. Even when he spoke again she couldn't lift her eyes to his.

" 'Course, I told them that with a figure like yours, a corset was just gilding the lily anyway, so to speak."

She'd kill him and then never speak to him again.

"I want you to know I didn't tell them about seeing you dancing for the monkeys in your altogethers.

While wearing hat, shoes, garters, and stockings, of course." He gave a hoot of laughter. "The monkeys seemed to enjoy the performance almost as much as I did."

His words burned like acid. *He'd been laughing at her all these weeks.* And with good reason. She lifted her chin. Nothing to do now but pretend he'd never opened his mouth. Once he was out of her house she would just never look at him or speak to him or think about him ever again. If she could just get through the rest of the evening with him in her house she promised herself to avoid him at all costs in the future.

"More soup, Captain Nash?" Sarah admired the cool firmness of her tone.

"Oh, back to Captain Nash, are we?" He chuckled just a little. "Honest, Teach, I wouldn't share our secret with anyone else. I thought it was charming, you chousting about stark naked, uh, *almost* stark naked, in the middle of the jungle."

"*Our* secret!" Sarah couldn't help the words that blurted themselves across the banana leaf table.

"Well, *you* did it and *I* saw you. Doesn't that make the whole thing *our* secret?" He laughed again. "I bet my mama would have said you were cute as a bug in a rug." The reflections in his brown eyes were really of the white candle, she knew, but through the haze of her embarrassment, the shimmering images seemed to turn into two naked white-skinned girls frolicking about. They seemed to be wearing broad-brimmed hats.

She clenched her fists in her lap. *Change the sub-*

ject. Act as though you haven't heard a word he said. The directions seemed to come inwardly in her mother's voice. Triggered by mention of *his* beastly mother, probably.

"Captain, I've been really concerned about Bong and Magdalena. Can we get them married? Or do they *want* to be married? Or do you know?" She looked at the grinning soldier across from her. She could throw her glass of water in his face or empty the tureen over his head. No. Better not. Chin up. Plow right ahead. "Her father is certainly going to be of no help."

Mention of the village headman sobered Markham instantly. His smile disappeared.

"That old bastard. He'd sell her again if he could, but since she's not salable, I'm pretty sure he doesn't care what happens to her."

"She can, of course, stay right here, but I think the two of them are in love." Sarah's fingers felt awkward as she smoothed the starched collar of her white shirtwaist. Mama's advice was working. They were at least off the subject of the stupid pink corset with the stupid pink lace. "They may want to get married. What do you think?"

"I'll talk with Bong, Sarah. I guess there's no big hurry."

"I'll be working at the school site tomorrow." She was silent for a moment. "Bong says he doesn't want me to do anything, but I can't just sit around and wait for other people to build my school. Maybe I could talk to him then?"

"Or maybe we both could."

Sarah heaved a sigh of relief. It seemed she'd succeeded in changing the subject. Perhaps, just perhaps, she could put her trailside indiscretion behind her.

"I think they are discussing our future," Bong whispered into Magdalena's ear. "Perhaps things will work out much more quickly than we expected."

"They are both good people," Magdalena murmured. "Still, do not forget that they are Americans. Sometimes Americans do not understand until they are approached directly." She touched the gold cross with pride. "Subtlety seems lost on them."

"I'll agree that they are very forward in their speech and behavior."

"Yes. Correct behavior and good manners seem to escape them at times." Magdalena put her hand over her mouth as if to keep from further comment on the two Americans.

Bong nodded, and where no one could see, his right hand smoothed and caressed Magdalena's back. She seemed pleased with his touch and leaned back slightly to accept his unspoken lovemaking.

The morning after the party, at the building site, Sarah realized that Markham had ordered Bong to let her take a direct part in the building, but she didn't care that the order had had to come from him. Just so long as the school got built.

She handed a board to the captain so he could wield

the saw. For a second she looked at his huge hands that worked with such delicacy. Somehow the work had become fun. The smell of the newly sawed wood, the shouts in their language from Bong and his three helpers. Being near Markham. She bit her lip at that thought, but she couldn't help admiring the tall, smiling man. He was odious, of course, no question. But his smile . . . well, his smile . . . it was almost like the sun coming up. Warm, beautiful, covering everything!

She sneaked another look at him. Honestly. He worked so well with the soldiers under him. And he really hadn't referred once to *their* secret. Maybe she could just forget her indiscreet moments, if he had.

They worked without talking once they hit the rhythm that suited them best. Sarah carried and held and weighted down boards. Markham measured and sawed and hammered. She could see about a dozen brown-skinned children peering and poking about, getting closer to the actual construction at every moment. The smell of the cut bamboo and of the damp earthen floor seemed like barnyard fragrances from her Iowa farm days.

Sweet perfumes of unknown exotic jungle flowers wafted through the air to mix with the leftover reek of cooked garlic and dead fish. That particular smell was purely Filipino and she'd learned to love it. She knew that for the rest of her life she would be carried back to this wonderful place anytime she smelled flowers or fish or garlic.

On the trail Markham had explained that the Filipinos thought all Americans smelled bad. She'd certainly

PARADISE FOUND

noticed that the water buffalo snorted with distaste and backed away from her anytime she came near. The visiting children seemed to carry all the local odors with them. They all wore flowers and even the babies ate garlic, or so it seemed.

Sarah's welcoming smile and friendly *mabuhay*, caused them to giggle and duck back and hide behind the flowering trees and thick palmetto greenery nearby, but she could hear their high-pitched chatter.

Markham suddenly threw back his head and roared out a song in Tagalog. She could hear the children's answering laughter, then several of the bolder youngsters ambled closer to the half-built shed as if being called by the man's song.

"What are you singing?"

"It's a children's song. I've heard mothers singing it to their babies. I don't know what it's called." He grinned. "Probably sounds pretty silly coming out of the mouth of an American soldier."

"Tell them to come back this afternoon and I'll have something for them." She was pleased that the dark-tempered captain could be so tender and funny with the children. "I'll try to get cookies made or something."

Markham's shouted message caused the brave ones to scamper back to the safety of the brush, but the children didn't really go away. They stayed close by and watched their very first school being put together board by board.

* * *

Lucky boys and girls. They'll get to be with her every single day. Markham looked up from his sawing chores to admire the way the gray light of the rainy day became sunshine when it was filtered through the gold of Sarah's hair. The black mantilla hung from a peg on the side wall. The ugly thing reminded him of a spider's web. The happy-looking little red plaid umbrella hung from the same peg.

Sudden insight poured into his consciousness. *Mourning.* That's why she was wearing gray all the time. Probably hadn't brought a black dress or she'd be trailing around in that. Of course, while they'd been building her little academy she'd covered the gray cotton with an old-fashioned white cotton apron. Dollars to doughnuts it had belonged to her mother. But it was the constant wearing of the gray dress that gave away her thinking.

Now he understood why she was wearing that black thing on her head everywhere she went. Only the oldest women in the village wore black mantillas, and they always had someone they were mourning. That bastard, Robert . . . he was still reaching out from the grave to influence her.

"We'll finish with the outside walls tomorrow, Sarah. We must start thinking about what you'll need inside."

What did he care that she was playing the widow? He was only helping so the children could have a school and so he wouldn't feel responsible for the teacher . . . who was really not much more than a child herself. Got this thing over with, he could return to his real job. Yeah. That was it. He was hurrying this project so he could get back to his real job and quit feeling responsible for this Iowa innocent.

"Another week or two and you and your school should be up and running, little schoolmarm." He raised the saw in a half-salute and she returned the gesture with a proud smile.

"We'll start with just the benches first since they're easier to handle, Markham." Sarah stood back to admire the seven smooth, handcrafted wooden benches which the soldiers had just carried into the snug classroom. "Soon we can have a meeting and ask the fathers and mothers to build some sort of desks or tables for the children."

She looked up at the high ceiling. She hoped the open space above the palm thatch on the front wall would allow air to enter but no rain. Someday maybe they could plan for real floors, but there was nothing wrong with solidly packed earth for now.

Magdalena had insisted on coming to help push the roller that Bong had made to smooth the ground in the classroom. Sarah watched her as she passed across the floor in front of the tall windows. The windows on the three sides away from the thatched front had hardwood and capiz shell shutters that could be opened or closed as the weather dictated.

"It looks like a real school," she said in delight, whirling in place like a little girl playing a game. She made herself walk sedately to the front of the classroom. She was afraid Markham would remember her capering that very same way he had in the jungle. She'd have to remember that she was a widowed schoolteacher now, and she must act accordingly.

"Well, isn't it a real school?" He grinned.

She knew he loved to tease her, but he had worked harder than anyone to get the place ready. She was impressed and delighted that the structure was framed up with solid Philippine mahogany. They'd be completely finished soon. Markham had said next week. Oh, she could hardly wait. She smiled back at him and gestured to the smoothly rolled earthen floor at his feet.

"With floors of the finest dark marble!" She trilled the words as if in song. She pulled a bench close to the back wall. "If you'll help me get my penmanship cards up on the walls, I'll feel we've gone a long way toward teaching these little sweeties some English." She gestured toward the brown faces that filled every window opening. The tinier children sat on the shoulders of their older brothers and sisters. They were all there now, every day, watching and commenting. They all giggled when she pointed to them. Not one child had yet set foot into the classroom itself. She frowned. She had talked it over with the captain, but she still couldn't understand why they hadn't yet come inside.

"I told you not to worry, Sarah. Most of the parents don't think girls should go to school. They'll come around when the Army commandant orders them to get their sons *and* daughters into the school."

"Will he do that?"

"Oh, absolutely."

"How can you be so sure?"

"I know the new commandant very well."

"The new commandant? Major Firestone?"

"Nope. The new one. Major Markham Allenby Nash, acting commandant, as of the first of next month." He kept his head down and busied himself with taking over the roller from Magdalena. "Got my new orders this morning. And I know exactly what the new man's going to do." He pulled the homemade sheepsfoot roller to smooth the ground at the place where she wanted to stand. "Let me get this space pounded down some before you start your tacking." She was already standing on one of the benches in order to reach high up on the walls for the display of the cards she'd so carefully brought from Iowa.

"Oh, Markham. A promotion. I'm so thrilled for you."

He turned and spoke to Magdalena in Tagalog.

The young Filipina left the room without a word.

"What did you say to her, Markham?"

"I told her this roller was too heavy for a little mother like her and that she'd be helping a whole lot more if she would bring us all something to eat, the U.S. Army footing the bill, of course."

"Oh, good. I am a little hungry. And I've been worried about her pushing that heavy thing. The baby will probably be here in a month or so, I think." She peered out over the heads of the children to see Magdalena hurrying up the puddled street. "I've just been so excited I'd forgotten about eating." Sarah stood tall on the low bench and looked down at the campaign hat that now stood just below her eye level. It was nice to look down on *him* for a change. "Aren't you excited?"

The brown eyes glanced up, laugh lines already telling her he was teasing again.

"About what, Madam Schoolmarm?"

"About your promotion, of course. That's wonderful news."

"Are these the cards you want?" He lifted the pile of dark green letter cards toward her. Sarah pulled out the A and the B, then put the rest of the cards on the bench at her feet. She could just envision all the children reading and writing the ABC's on their slates, if they *had* slates, or chalk. If they didn't, she'd get some somehow. She held out a letter and admired the smoothly printed card's Spencerian perfection for a moment, then looked down into Markham's smiling face.

"We've spent entirely enough time on my school. Tell me more about your promotion."

He pushed his hat back and his smile died.

"It might mean they're getting ready to transfer me to some other godforsaken hole in the P.I., or maybe somewhere else." His brown gaze caught hers and held it. "I kinda hate to leave until I see the little 'blondie schoolteacher' settled and happy in her job."

In disbelief, Sarah saw the packed earth waver as he said the last word. The walls swayed and the benches shifted. Alphabet cards spilled across the floor.

"Markham!" She heard her own scream as if it belonged to someone else. "What is it?" She felt herself launch out into empty space.

Two muscular arms caught her, enfolded her, pulled her close, held her.

"It's an earthquake, darling. Just an ordinary earthquake. You're all right." The floor was solid once more, the walls stilled, several of the benches lay on their sides, the scattered cards stared up from the floor. She watched Bong bend to right one of the benches. "I'm not going to let anything happen to you, little Sarah. Don't you know it's my job to take care of you? By order of the U.S. Army." She felt his breath on her hair.

She didn't move, couldn't move. The captain's . . . no, no, the *major's,* arms were the only really safe haven in this strange, unsteady new world she'd chosen to venture into. And now her only security might be leaving! She leaned even closer to him and let the tears come.

Eighteen

Just as Markham had prophesied, even though Major Firestone remained in command for the time being, once Markham sent word out to the families in San Miguel, all the children came. Some came with their *yayas,* which Sarah learned was one of their words for child nurse or nanny, or with their men servants, or with a relative, but they all came, even Magdalena's younger brother. Every day they came . . . at the times each of them preferred, rather than at the time set by Sarah, the *maestra.*

"Why won't they come to school on time, Markham?" she wailed. "Some days there are only two or three children there when I ring the bell. A few come only after the midday siesta." She leaned on his desk to be sure he understood her appeal. "And, Markham, why, oh why do they bring their nurses or their other servants or their adult relatives?"

"You must learn to be patient, Sarah. We'll get them all to come on time eventually. To Filipinos time doesn't have the value it does to us." He grinned at the gold watch pinned to her chest. "We could get each one of them a watch." Sarah felt that he kept his glance on the piece of jewelry a moment longer than necessary and she had a quick vision of a pink corset flying through the air. His smile widened and his gaze lifted to her face. "You know, Schoolteacher Lady, they don't have clocks at home, most of them."

Oh. Of course. She hadn't thought of that. She remembered the bare cleanliness of the houses she'd visited. Usually not much more than a tintype or two of parents or grandparents in their best clothing posed for a visiting photographer. Almost no furniture. Perhaps one wooden chair or bench. No clocks.

"You're right. Well, I know how to settle the time problem. We'll get a loud bell and ring it fifteen minutes before schooltime, then again when classes start."

"That's a good idea, but I thought you had a bell."

"Just the little dinner bell that Mama gave me. That's to use inside the classroom. We need a big, loud, outside bell." Involuntarily, as she spoke, her eyes traced and retraced the sculptured outline of his firm mouth. His lips looked just the way a man's lips should look. "Could the Army find us a bell, do you think, Markham?"

"Maybe. I'll see what we can do. I'll put Bong and Sergeant Gilbert onto that chore."

Even though the weather was clearing, she had the little red umbrella clenched in her hand and resting on his desk. *Why is she staring at me? At my lips?* Her look made him want to . . . to touch her. He turned slightly and rose to stand at the open window of his office so he wouldn't be directly under her gaze. He was mighty glad that his skin was so sun-darkened that she couldn't see the heat he could feel rising in his face. He started to walk to the door to call the sergeant, but he turned back. He'd better tell her now so she wouldn't feel abandoned.

"Sarah, I'm going to have to take the troops into the field on maneuvers, then we have to swing by Manila on official business. Since the rains have pretty well let up, it won't take us long."

Was that dismay on her face? She couldn't be upset just because he was leaving. It was probably just that she'd gotten to depend on him for the school. "Don't worry. Bong asked if he could stay here close to Magdalena, and I thought . . . well, under the circumstances, he might need to be here with her."

Sarah nodded, but she looked distracted.

"I doubt we'll have another earthquake for several months. And Firestone and Bong will stand ready to help you if you need any assistance." He held out his hand as if for a formal handshake. "It'll just be me and Jonas, and all those other old boys who are crazy to get into town. We'll be traveling pretty fast. I shouldn't be gone more than a week."

She looked even more dismayed. "Is someone else going to be riding Mabuti?"

Damned horse. She thought more of that nag than she . . . "That old bag of bones? No trooper would be caught dead on your old mare. No." He touched her chin with the side of his hand. "We'll leave the lovely Mabuti right here for you."

For a second he thought of their days together on the trail. In a way, it had been splendid. In another way, it had been misery. In any case, he knew he wouldn't be joining the troopers in the fleshpots of the big town. In their time together this little woman had put some kind of hex on him. He'd just hang around the Army headquarters until he got everything fixed up, then he'd round up the celebrating soldiers from their camping area in the churchyard and head on back home as fast as he could get the men through the jungle. Hell. He'd make it a point to pick up all those slates she was always pining for. How much room could slates take up, anyway?

"When are you leaving?" She left the umbrella on the desk and walked to join him at the window. She placed her hand into his.

"Right away. We need to go while Major Firestone's still around to hold this place down." He grinned. Her little hand felt right in his big paw. It was so small he was almost afraid to really shake it, might hurt her. Damn. She smelled kinda nice. A little sweaty like everyone smelled except in the rainy season, but the scent from her body was different, sweeter. There was something else, something kind of flowery and a deeper note . . . like something good to eat, maybe. She smelled deliciously blonde. He took a deep breath of the tantalizing fragrance of her.

He forced his mind back to what they were saying. Never mind sniffing around the little widow, he warned himself. He took another deep breath. It was just that he hated to go off and leave her here, practically alone in the barrio, before she'd really gotten started and established in her schoolwork. Yep, that was it. Anyway, the major would be here and Bong would be here for her if she needed him.

She could see the trace of pride in his face even as he said, "Danged nuisance. But it's an order. Gotta see these people in Manila. Get this new appointment made official." He dug the toe of his boot into the floor of the office and looked down. "We'll probably leave tomorrow, first light. You won't know me when I get back, girl. I'll be wearing gold leaves on my tunic."

She wanted to laugh. He was so puffed up, so transparent in his pride. She, too, was thrilled at his new appointment, but, even more, she felt wildly disappointed that he was leaving. The warmth of his handclasp sent tiny thrills up her arm. She held on to his strong hand as if it were a lifeline thrown her in the midst of a strange sea. She clutched his hand more tightly. How could he just up and leave her?

Don't be so silly, she warned herself inwardly. *This officer is not here for your personal comfort, anyway. You wanted to be on your own, didn't you?* She held the big hand and looked down to see her white thumb lying bright against the darkness of his sunburned fist. "Well, now you really have what you wanted." She put her left hand around their handshake.

"We'll all miss you, Markham." She closed her eyes against the tears and held on to his hand for dear life.

* * *

PARADISE FOUND

She was holding his hand with both of hers! Oh, hell. Was she crying?

He'd run those horny old Army boys' legs off getting them to Manila and back. Were the tears for him or was she just feeling weak at the thought of going it alone . . . of being without her usual army protection?

Anyway, when he got back maybe they could talk. Get things straightened out between old Bong and Magdalena. Hell, he and Sarah would get things straightened out between themselves. He'd just have to explain what the oak leaves meant to him, how army life *really was* for a career officer who loved the service. How a wife could just be an anchor dragging down a man's climb up the ladder. Not that she wanted to be a wife again anytime soon, probably.

He leaned forward to let his lips encounter unruly blond wisps of hair that rose in the breeze from the window. He let his eyes close for a moment at the touch of the golden silk.

"Don't cry, little Sarah. When I come back we'll have us another scandalous *sinigang* party and we'll talk about . . . everything." He wrapped his other hand around hers and around both their clasped hands. "Hey, how about if I find out what's going on with Luz and Rudolfo while I'm in town. Would you like that?"

He watched the blond head nod though tears continued coursing silently down her cheeks.

"Aw, don't cry, Sarah honey. If you'll smile I promise I'll bring you something nice from the big city."

* * *

"Ps-s-st." Magdalena turned her smiling face at his call. "My captain goes to Manila tomorrow."

She stood, her smile wiped away by the fear on her face.

"You will go with him?"

"No." Bong stepped into the shadows under the nipa hut where she had been preparing the evening meal. "I asked to stay and he agreed that that would be best, but he leaves at first light taking most of the soldiers with him."

She looked stricken.

"He says he will bring your cousin Rudolfo back to the village with him if he can. Luz also. Would that please you?"

Magdalena smiled widely and nodded.

"I promised the teacher I would stop by and see you every day. Did you know that, my little bird?" He smiled to try to soothe her. She had opened the collar of her dress for coolness and it pleased him that the golden cross he had given her dangled about her neck even as she worked. "There is no need for your worry. I will be right here. We will have time to be alone, perhaps."

She caressed the mound of her belly where the baby lay.

"I know we can only comfort each other. Surely there can be no lovemaking because of the baby, but just to lie quietly beside you would make me very happy."

She nodded. "Very happy. It would make me very happy, also."

"Do not be afraid. I think when my captain returns they intend to ask us to be married. Will that please you?" He touched the spot where the cross touched her chest.

"Oh, Bong Bong," she gasped with pleasure. "Yes."

"I will see you tomorrow." Bong ducked back out into the light of the deserted street and raced toward the enlisted barrack.

Bong returned much sooner than Magdalena had expected. When she saw him running back from the barracks she tried to pretend that she was busy, that she wasn't thrilled he was returning so soon. It was difficult to hide her smile, but she gave him the dignified welcome that an honored guest deserved even if he had just gone and come back.

He was out of breath, but he steepled his hands at his chest and greeted her in the correct manner. She could see that he, too, was having to suppress smiles and words that wished to bubble out of him in the helter-skelter way he'd learned from the Americans, but he controlled himself.

When the formal greetings were out of the way he grabbed her hand. She pulled away and glanced in every direction. What if someone should see them?

"Never mind that now, my Magdalena. I have news. Portentious news. The American chaplain and my captain are even now awaiting us in the chapel. We are going to be married before the captain leaves."

Magdalena looked down at her everyday clothing. "I am not prepared, Bong Bong. Do you mean this very minute?"

"This very minute." His grin showed his teeth. She loved the glint of happiness in his eyes. He did truly love her and he truly didn't care that she was not dressed in her best. She scraped the fire out and without another word they walked hand in hand toward the American priest and the American church and a new life. She would tell the blondie teacher at another time. Teacher would be happy for her, she knew.

"We will sleep separately for now, Bong Bong?"

"Yes, if that is what you want."

"That is what I want. We will tell after the men return from Manila. Now it will be our secret."

He nodded agreement and squeezed her hand. "You will belong to me," he whispered.

In the chaplain's office Markham explained what had happened to Magdalena at the hands of the deceased Robert and told him of what Bong had agreed to do concerning the coming baby.

"He says he will treat the child as his own if he can just marry his Magdalena at last." Markham held his hand up, palm out, as if swearing to what he was saying. "And I can tell you that Corporal Bong Bong Manawe is a man of his word. He's my personal dogrobber and I've trusted him with my life more than once." He let his hand drop. "He loves Magdalena and he knows she can't help what her father did to her."

"Whatever you say, Captain. This is all a bit irregular, but I'm glad to be of help to your friends." The padre picked up his equipment and they walked together toward the mess hall which doubled as the chapel. "This may be most unChristian of me, Captain Nash, but I can't help thinking that Robert Zumwalt did the right thing, by letting the cholera take him off so quickly, I mean."

Markham nodded grimly.

Bong and Magdalena arrived at the building at almost the same time as the two American officers. Markham introduced everyone.

"Do we need another witness, padre?" Markham looked at several of the uniformed troopers sitting at tables in the hall. He beckoned to one of the men. "Sergeant Bustos, would you come over here a moment?"

Bong kept his eyes on Magdalena; Magdalena kept her eyes down. The Filipino sergeant saluted. "Yes, sir."

Markham returned the gesture. "Sergeant Bustos, you know Corporal Manawe, don't you?" The sergeant looked at Bong, then nodded. "Do you know his fiancée, Magdalena Suarez?" The man looked at Magdalena and nodded again. "The chaplain you know, and you certainly know me." The uniformed man shuffled in place and looked somewhat puzzled.

"We're holding a wedding here, Bustos. We want you to be one of the witnesses. Can you do that?"

Bustos smiled widely and nodded again.

The wedding party moved to the front of the room where the chaplain had had an altar set up. In a matter of minutes Magdalena Suarez, wearing her faded cotton work dress, was made Mrs. Bong Bong Manawe and the corporal became her husband.

While he stood behind the wedding couple to witness their ceremony, Markham couldn't help smiling dreamily at the picture of a little blond schoolteacher that rose behind his eyes. With a start he dismissed the notion immediately. God, no. Marriage was not for him, not even with the little blond darling.

In the single room that usually housed Captain Markham Nash, Bong and Magdalena sat on the edge of the captain's cot. They spoke in Tagalog as polite people should when at home.

"I'm afraid, Bong Bong."

"What are you afraid of?"

"I'm afraid to be here. We should not be in this room. What if he comes and finds us here?"

"Magdalena, my dear, I spend much of my time, every day, in this room. I am the one who keeps order here." He smiled down at his new wife, then put his arm about her shoulders. "The captain has given us permission to have what the Americans call a honeymoon. That means we have private time together. We have the rest of the afternoon to be together, so there is no reason for you to be afraid."

"He lives differently than most Americans, I think."

She gestured at the austere room. "A cot with an army blanket, a small metal chest, a pair of boots and a hat, a chamber pot, a little wooden table and chair and nothing else. He lives very plainly."

"I've worked around or for a good many American officers, dearest one." He rose to glance out the wood-shuttered window above the table before he again seated himself beside her on the cot and took her hand. "It has been my impression that in the rooms where pictures and gimcrackery abound, you'll probably find a less capable man."

"You've studied these American Army men very carefully."

"Oh, yes. That is because as a part of the U.S. Army my life may often depend upon the character of the man I serve." He shuddered with distaste. "One new young officer even had a red coverlet and pictures of unclothed women in his room." His eyes swept the shining waxed floors, the clean surfaces in the room. "Nash is a true army man. His mind is upon his duty, just as it should be. He has character and I trust him. In a fight he is the man I would choose to stand at my back."

"I know my schoolteacher likes him, though she doesn't speak of him. Does Missie know we were married today?"

"She was at the school as usual, so I don't think so, but I am certain she will approve when she learns of it."

"Maybe not. How can we know?"

"Put all this worry away from you, Mrs. Manawe.

Let us talk of our future. I know you want us to live separately as we have been doing and I have agreed." He pressed a chaste kiss upon her forehead. "Now let us decide how soon we can live together as a married couple?"

"Let me talk with my American teacher, then we can discuss this. Are we to have our own room for living together, my Bong Bong?"

"Yes, Captain Nash has assured me that he would help me with the cost of such a place. He has also promised that I will build it for us with the help of several troopers." He was pleased to see the smile that touched her eyes. "We will be allowed to build our own room on the far side of the parade ground. That way you will be distant from your father and protected by the U.S. Army." He touched the black silk of her hair. She was relaxing somewhat, but he realized she had more to discuss before they could simply be themselves.

"Have you something else that concerns you, my dove?"

She smiled gratefully at him.

"It is my little brother. I am concerned about Sonny Boy. He is growing up without the correct guidance. Already he is nine years old and has only his *yaya* to answer to, since my father is so often gone and I do not dare go to my father's house."

Bong tried to control his face and contain his anger at the mention of the behavior of his beloved one's father. Even here, on his honeymoon, that odious person intruded. It was selfish of him, he knew, but he wanted Magdalena to think of him alone this afternoon.

He took her hand.

"Let me give your concern some thought. Perhaps we can find answers by consulting our Americans." He patted the cot with his free hand. "In the meantime, are you tired, my Magdalena? Let us take our ease upon the bed. We can talk as well while lying down." He pressed her gently against the pillow and stretched himself beside her.

Ah, the beauty of her smile. She understood what he wanted and her smile told him she agreed to lay aside care. Perhaps they could not be truly man and wife this afternoon, but they might explore their love just a little. Whatever happened here in the captain's room would be only as *she* wanted it to be. He would never force himself upon her. He would be as gentle with her as was the morning breeze with the opening flower.

On the second morning after the Army cadre left, Sarah stood in the doorway of the new school, hopelessly ringing the little handbell. Only two little girls so far and none on the way she could see. How in the world would she get the children of San Miguel to school on time?

She tried to remember what life had been for her during her grade-school years. Miss Arnold. Fun. Boring. Giggling. Hard work. Friends. Awful. Wonderful. Now it seemed all of a piece . . . just the right kind of a life for a little girl. She'd loved Miss Arnold. She'd loved school. She'd even gone to her classes a few times when her mother had told her she wasn't well enough and should stay home. She'd never missed a day. What had made her so determined to be sitting at her desk whenever the school was open?

Not the boring. Not the awful. But she'd loved the hard work, the fun, the giggling, the friends, everything wonderful. Perhaps that was the answer.

Make the hard work fun, allow for some giggling and see that something wonderful happened among friends every single day . . . especially at the beginning of the day. *No one would want to miss a day like that!*

She'd put her plan into motion this very minute. Those who came to school late would miss a barrel of fun! She turned back to the two girls and a tiny boy who had slipped in unnoticed.

"Okay, children. I'm going to teach you a song. It's called 'Pretty Red Wing.' It's by a man named Thurland Chataway. Maybe we'll even dance a little." She dipped and whirled across the front of the room under their wide brown stares.

She stopped and turned to face them. She began to sing aloud. " 'Now, the moon shines tonight on pretty Red Wing . . .' " Her clear contralto voice filled the classroom and floated out through the openings in the classroom walls. " 'The breeze is sighing, the nightbird crying.' " As she sang it through the second time, it occurred to her that pretty Red Wing was an Indian maiden . . . maybe from Indian Territory? She wondered if Markham knew the song.

In minutes, her singing and her gestures had enticed

the three tiny, punctual scholars to join her. " 'For afar, 'neath his star, her brave is sleeping . . .' "

When they seemed to have learned the melody, if not the pronunciation of the words, Sarah bowed to the small boy and led him to the front of the room to dance to the strains of their new song. Meanwhile, several other out-of-breath children had raced into the melodic temptations of the classroom. More followed. Standing against the back wall, a forty-year-old *yaya* smiled and opened her toothless mouth to join in with, " 'While Red Wing's weeping, her heart away . . .' "

Three more children danced with a chosen partner, a few others danced alone.

"One more turn and we'll get down to the fun of working on the alphabet," Sarah told them, and she started the song again, then smiled widely at her big-eyed partner who had staunchly refused to give her up to an older girl or to another boy who had tried to cut in to share a dance with the maestra. "We'll sing and dance the ABC's, maybe."

She wished Markham Nash could have been there to see the children speeding through the classroom door to join their friends' musical moment. His deep voice would have made "Pretty Red Wing" just that much more fun for everyone.

Plans for "morning fun" time whirled through Sarah's head as she tripped through the dance with her solemn partner. Finally, when they all flopped laughing onto the benches, Sarah took a deep breath and explained, "That was the chorus, children. Can you say 'chorus?' " She laughed at their enthusiastic mangling of the word chorus. "Tomorrow, *mañana,* we'll learn the verse. Can you say 'verse?' "

Ah. That was an easy one. Children, *yaya,* and man servant bellowed the word.

"BERSE."

Their answer made her smile so much that most of the class shouted the word one more time for her pleasure. "BERSE."

A few then shouted, "Red Ring." All giggled.

The few latecomers stepping through the door looked disappointed, yet hopeful. Maybe they'd get in on some of the fun?

Sarah felt like clapping her hands with pleasure, so she did, and many of the children joined her. *Caught you, my little ones.* Sarah inwardly rejoiced in her plan's success. She had a feeling that *everyone* would be on time the next morning for the first verse of "Pretty Wing." And she knew that the rest of this day would be wonderful. Perfect.

She stood and pointed to the cards with a thin stick she'd asked Bong to sand for her. As she pointed to each letter she sang its name: "A, B, C, D, E, F, G . . ." Today they'd all learn to sing the alphabet in English. She couldn't help herself, she giggled with pleasure and her pupils followed her lead. A real school, at last.

If only Markham Nash could have been there.

At home that night Sarah sang the verses of "Pretty Red Wing" for Magdalena. Soon the hugely pregnant Filipina was singing some of the song also, assisted by the eavesdropping children who danced around the ladder below Sarah's hut.

There once lived an Indian maid,
A shy little prairie maid,
Who sang a lay,
A love song gay,
As on the plain she'd while away the day.

She loved a warrior bold,
This shy little maid of old,
But brave and gay,
He rode one day,
To battle far away.

Now the moon shines tonight on pretty Red Wing,
The breeze is sighing,
The night bird crying,
For afar, 'neath his star,
Her brave is sleeping,
While Red Wing's weeping,
Her heart away.

Next morning Sarah had to laugh. The children and many of their attendants came tumbling in, on time or well before time. Only a sad few were late. It was clear that none of them wanted to miss any of the morning fun. Mentally, she thanked all those teachers back in Iowa who had tried to make school and learning interesting and even thrilling for that little Sarah and her classmates.

"Pretty Red Wing," and the dancing that went with it, was repeated and extended to learn the second verse. Sarah marveled at how easily both children and adults learned English words if they were set to a melody. Probably they didn't know *what* they were singing about, but they did have a grasp of the words of that particular song, whether they seemed to them to be nonsense syllables or not. She promised herself that she'd have Markham come and explain the meaning of the song in Tagalog just as soon as he returned.

In the evening when she returned home, escorted by several of her students, she saw Bong sitting in the shade below her house, talking to Magdalena. As if a candle had been lit and thrust before her eyes, she realized that Bong and Magdalena, too, could come to the school, if they would, and explain the song. They needn't wait for Markham. He might be gone for weeks. She hadn't forgotten how long their trip through the jungle had lasted.

"Good morning, Bong. Hello, Magdalena. How is everything with you two."

"Very well, *mom.*"

"All fine, *mom.*"

"Bong, could I ask you to do me a favor?"

"Surely, *mom.* What favor you want?"

"I was hoping you, and maybe Magdalena also, would come to school with me tomorrow. I need you both to explain a song that my students have learned in English. A Tagalog translation would be very helpful. I think the children would be pleased to know what the song says." She smiled at Magdalena. "Magdalena already knows part of the song."

"Pretty Red Wing." Magdalena said the words and Bong looked blank.

"You sing about birds?"

"Red Wing is the name of a young girl, an American Indian girl, and the song is about her." She gestured to the children who stood just inside the shade cast by her hut. "Sing with me, children."

The children sang, joining Sarah and Magdalena, and Bong listened. He grunted when they were finished.

"What is this weeping that little Red Wing do?"

"That means she was crying, Bong, because her soldier, her warrior, had gone far away from her."

"Nice song, *T'cher*. We'll come to school in the morning." Bong gave her an abbreviated salute.

"Oh, thanks, both of you. It'll be fun having you there to explain the song to them. If we had some slates we could do some writing, too. I guess we can write with sticks in the sand outside the classroom."

"You like little Red Wing, huh, *mom?*"

"I like little Red Wing? Oh, yes. It's a popular song in America."

"No, I mean maybe you do this 'weeping' for your soldier, the captain, because he gone. We all miss him, too. He'll come back soon. He said we'd have a party when he got back." Bong smiled at Magdalena. "You not need to weeping, *mom.*"

Sarah laughed and made her climb to her house. Magdalena followed and Bong waited below.

"Bong wish speak with you, *mom*."

"Of course, Magdalena. Ask him to come on up. I didn't realize he was waiting for me." While Magdalena called the corporal, Sarah unbuttoned her high collar and removed her shoes. She sat on the floor with her back against the end of the wooden bench and, with a gesture of her hand, invited Bong to take a seat on the floor in front of her.

"You wanted to say something to me, Bong?"

"We both want to say something to you, *mom*." He put his hand on Magdalena's shoulder. "Magdalena, she afraid to say it to you."

"You're afraid to talk to me?" Sarah was shocked. "I thought we were friends."

"I did something without asking, *mom*." Magdalena lowered her gaze. "Maybe you might be angry, *mom*." She flicked her glance toward Bong as if asking him for help.

"The captain arranged it, *mom*. The day before he and the troopers rode off to Manila." Bong took Magdalena's hand in his own. "We married, *mom*. Captain had Chaplain marry us in the mess hall. Sergeant Bustos was the witness."

Sarah gasped.

"You got married and didn't invite me?"

"No time, *mom*. You were in the schoolhouse with the pupils and Captain getting ready to leave. He arranged with the padre." Bong pulled Magdalena toward him with an arm around her shoulder. "So we say yes and here we are." Bong looked proudly at

Sarah. Magdalena continued to look down. "Mr. and Mrs. Bong Bong Manawe."

"Oh, Bong, Magdalena. I'm so happy for you. I only wish I could have been there." She looked directly at Magdalena. "Do you want to move out of our house, Magdalena?"

"No, *mom*. I stay here."

"Don't worry, *mom*. I'm not moving in on you two. Captain say he help me build a room for us on back side of the parade ground. Then we move in together."

"Oh, Magdalena. Congratulations, to you both. Count on me to help with the building of your new house."

"Now, children, since you know the song and what it means, we are going to do a little writing and spelling." Sarah turned and smiled at Bong and Magdalena. "It was really nice of Sonny Boy's big sister and her husband to help us with understanding our song." She applauded her two helpers and encouraged the children to do the same.

Bong turned as if to leave.

"One more thing, Bong. Could you please tell all the children to find a stick and meet me out in the shady road in front of the school? We're going to learn to write and spell *Red*. Ask them to sit in the shade." She giggled and hugged Magdalena.

The students made a semicircle around the teacher as Bong arranged them. Each made a smooth flat surface in the sand in front of himself or herself as Magdalena instructed.

"Ready?" Sarah asked and lifted her stick to write RED in letters three feet tall in the dirt of the road. She turned back, and using her stick as a pointer, she spelled the word aloud. R-E-D. She pointed at them, then again wrote the word "RED." Most of the children followed her lead and printed the word on their own sand slates. Again Sarah wrote the word, except this time she wrote it in the air as she said, "R-E-D, red." She pointed her stick at the children and all followed her direction by writing the word and spelling it in the air in front of them.

She traced the word on the ground and shouted the word, RED. The children did the same.

Sarah danced a step and sang, " 'The moon shines tonight on pretty,' " she paused and they filled in, " 'Red Wing.' "

She nodded and smiled. "Good. *Mabuti, mabuti,* children." Thank Heavens for my good old horse, she thought, I'll never forget their word for *good.*

The children cheered her use of their own language.

She sang again and the students watched her closely. When she got to *Red* she stopped and they sang the word as she traced it in the sand.

Bong and Magdalena moved away up the sunny street, chatting and laughing together. They didn't touch each other. After all, they were in public.

The students learned to write and recognize the two words, Red Wing, that day. After school they rushed home to teach the English words to grandmothers and baby sisters. *Red Wing* was written on the wind . . . and in the sand and with grains of rice that night.

Sarah went home tired but happy. By the end of the week she just knew that all of the children would be able to read and write the first sentence of their song. *The moon shines tonight on pretty Red Wing.*

Nineteen

By the fifth day after Markham had gone, Sarah was pretty sure the problem of the morning laggards had been solved. Everyone in the barrio knew "Pretty Red Wing." Sonny Boy Suarez, Magdalena's little nine-year-old brother, had brought several friends to serenade her with the song just the night before.

She walked home today as she had done each afternoon, with her usual "honor guard" of about ten children, each trying to be the one walking closest and holding on to the *maestra Americana*.

Some shouted "American Lady Teacher" as they paraded along the village pathway, others called out to "Blondie Lady Teacher," or combinations of these and other English words they'd learned. The smaller or slower scholars contented themselves with an occasional "hello" or "good morning" or "good evening."

Mothers and other relatives of the children leaned from windows along the way and fathers stopped work to smile proudly at the evidence that their particular darling was a favorite of *the maestra* (Was not their little Juanita at this very moment walking hand-in-

PARADISE FOUND

hand with the blondie teacher?), and it was also plain for all to see that now their Juan, or Gilberto, or Maria Luisa was becoming quite accomplished in this new language, this English.

Sarah was thrilled when a wrinkled *abeula* (grandmother) or a smiling parent hazarded a loud "Good Morning, T'cher" during the late-afternoon parade home.

On the fifth day since the Army cadre had been gone, Sarah made the climb up into her house with a sigh of relief. She had had no idea that teaching would prove so difficult and exhausting. And she'd never realized that the lack of privacy of a teacher in a small village would be so frustrating. She was always pleased when Magdalena slipped out to meet with Bong and she could have the house to herself for a short while. But even then, there were always some children playing in the area at the bottom of the stair under her house.

She supposed it would seem a desirable profession to the outside world—monthly salary, work that was not physically taxing, especially if she could get help from the children in keeping the room clean, carrying water, and helping with other chores. People saw with envy what they thought were free weekends and long weeks off in the summers.

She smiled as she remembered her father's enumeration of all the good points about teaching. She would dare him now to take such a job himself, to spend just one week in a classroom. She'd wager he'd be screaming to get back to his farm long before the week was over.

She unbuttoned the first three buttons of her gray shirtwaist, laid the collar tabs back, then fanned the deep "V" of white skin she'd bared. She used the Filipino farm hat that Bong had handed her on the trail because it stirred the breeze so well. The movement of the air on her chest was almost as refreshing as a cool drink. She sat idly fanning herself for a moment, then pulled several tortoiseshell hairpins from the sweat-dampened chignon at the nape of her neck and let the blond strands fall before she ran her fingers through the heavy mass to lift it high on her head and repin it into an uncombed topknot. The small breeze generated by the palm leaf hat-fan felt heavenly on the back of her neck also.

One of the most shocking things she'd observed in the Philippines was the daily bath that was taken both morning and evening. Everyone, rich and poor, seemed to bathe that frequently. She and her family were considered finicky clean with their Saturday bath. Here, the poorest citizen bathed at the public well or pump by pouring the water over hair, face, skimpy clothing, and body.

Now she, too, looked forward to her evening bath. She couldn't bring herself to bathe below the house as Magdalena and others did, but she at least carried her own bucket of water so Magdalena didn't have to wrench the heavy vessel up the ladder. Just the thought of the bath to come soothed her. She'd noticed that each day now seemed hotter than the one before.

She and Magdalena sat smiling and fanning, quiet for a few minutes, each at ease with the other. She

PARADISE FOUND

watched Magdalena absently fingering the gold chain that held the cross Bong had given her. She usually kept the trinket hidden under her clothing.

A shout from outside drew Magdalena to the window. Sarah looked up at her and stopped the palm leaf hat in midfan.

"What is it?" Sarah could now hear the pounding of horses' hooves. She pulled herself up. Excitement flooded her. Maybe Markham was back! She threw the hat aside and dashed to the window just as Magdalena began drawing the wooden shutters closed.

"Who is it? Why are you closing all the shutters?"

"Ladrones." Magdalena's whisper sounded as loud as a shout in Sarah's ears. "Robbers. We must hide, *mom.*"

"Robbers? Oh, my word. The school. I have to go protect my school." Sarah started down the ladder stairway.

"No, *mom.*" Magdalena protested. "No go. You stay."

At the foot of the stairs Señor Suarez stood waiting. He grasped her arm in his hand. She hardly noticed what he was saying. She stood transfixed by the loud cries from up and down the street and by the billowing dust and smoke and the pounding sounds of the swirling herd of horses ridden by the invading bandits.

Already she could see flames coming from the China store, catty-cornered from her across the dirt street. She looked quickly in the other direction, toward the Army headquarters. As she watched, seven of the Filipino soldiers poured out onto the parade ground not far from the school. Most had only bolos or small knives in their hands; one who obviously had been sleeping was dressed in his underwear and carried no weapon. She searched for Bong but couldn't see him in the group.

"Come. I will protect you, Blondie Lady." Suarez's garlic breath engulfed her.

"Let go of me, sir. I have to get to the school." She shouted the words into his face. "You take care of Magdalena. She's upstairs."

She shook her arm from his grasp and raced from the shadow of her house to slip into the palmetto growth behind the long row of nipa huts. She pushed back the nausea that her fear had brought on.

She'd try to keep herself hidden while she made her secret way back down toward the school building. She had to make it. She felt the tide of bile again rise in her throat and she forced it back. She couldn't let these ruffians do any harm to her precious new school. Not now. Not when she was just beginning to be successful.

Crooks and malfactors! Someone had to stand up to people like that. She'd make her father proud. She'd just stand right there in that doorway she'd helped build and she'd tell those invading outlaws that she was an American citizen and that the school building was American property. They wouldn't dare shoot an American woman . . . would they?

"Somehow they must have realized we were unprotected," she murmured. She pulled her skirts and petticoats up from the left side in back and from the right side in front. She then anchored the billowing yards of cloth by tying the lengths tightly across one shoulder to meet in a knot beneath her breast.

She bent low and forced her way through the vibrant greenery that tried to hold her back. She quietly shoved herself through the shadowed tunnel she was making in order to reach the far end of the street. She hardly noticed the slashes the razor-edged palmettoes landed on her smooth white thighs above her gartered black cotton stockings.

Her blood seemed to surge through her, each frightened pulse like the crash of a wave pounding against a beach. In her ears the sound of her own heart beating was as loud as the shouts that echoed up and down the village street.

"Who could have told them?" She frowned in puzzlement. Maybe they'd seen Markham and the others leaving. It was almost as if they *knew* that the American soldiers were gone and that the Army men had taken most of the garrison's guns for maneuvers.

Twenty

Sarah stopped behind the last two huts in the row of houses so she could look out between them. She could see her new schoolhouse clearly from where she stood. She could also see a corner of the Army parade grounds. Where had the Filipino troopers gone? Nobody was stirring at either place. To catch her breath she leaned against one of the hardwood tree trunks that helped hold this particular family's nipa hut up out of the mud during the rainy season.

Now, the rainy season long finished, the earth beneath the house was shaded, but it was dry and dusty, without even a slough for the mother pig who stood squealing on the hard dirt floor. The animal screamed her displeasure so loudly it was as if she knew the bandits had come for her and her piglets. She strained at her braided vine halter and jerked away from her babes' searching mouths. Something was wrong and the mother pig knew it.

Sarah slipped into the shadowed area under the house and looked up to see if the hut's inhabitants were anywhere about. Their usually open door was closed tightly, their ladder drawn up against the troubles of the street. She leaned out to glance up at the always open windows of this house and those of the other huts. Closed. All closed. Right up and down the street, each house displayed wooden storm shutters, closed and locked from the inside. Even as she watched, someone at the Suarez house continued closing the rest of the shutters on the upper floor of the two-story building. Probably nine-year-old Sonny.

She saw one of the blue-uniformed Filipino soldiers dart across the street. It looked as if he were racing toward her house. She thought the man might be Bong, but she couldn't tell for sure because he disappeared from sight before she could actually see his face. The intruders acted as if they hadn't even noticed the lone soldier.

The shouting and a few gunshots now seemed to be concentrated toward that end of the street where her nipa hut sat. The China store blazed. She could smell the flames. She was sure that the kerosene barrel and other oils the Chinaman sold would create more havoc. Sure enough, as she watched, several small explosions called an end to the barrio's most indispensable merchant. The bandits hadn't yet touched the large Suarez house so far as she could see.

Sarah untied her skirts and let them fall to her shoetops again as she stood trying to calm her breathing. Everything and everyone on the village street was quiet except for the tormented squeals of the pig under the house where she stood. The only noise came from the circling horses, the shots, the shouting of the *ladrones,* and the crackling and small popping noises from the fire at the store.

She took one last deep breath and poised herself to make the dash across the open area of the street to the schoolhouse when a hand closed around her arm and a knotted loop of rope slipped over her head and tightened about her neck. She did not need to twist around to look at her captor. She had already reluctantly inhaled her captor's foul-smelling breath as it eddied against the side of her face.

Suarez!

"Take your hands off me, sir." Sarah used her one free hand to try to fend the man off. He only stepped closer.

"I take care of you, Blondie School Teacher." His words were a husky whisper in her ear. "Not safe out on street." He gestured from behind her at the riders who now circled in the road in front of the burning store.

"Let me go at once, señor." She continued to tug against his grip on her arm. The hemp of the roughly woven rope felt as if it were afire against the sweaty bare skin of her neck.

"Come. We hide in the bush, *maestra*. I keep you from trouble."

"I'll scream."

"Go ahead. You scream, *mom*. We see who help you."

She knew he was right. The people in the small houses were all much too busy trying to save their own heads to worry about the American schoolteacher.

She straightened her back and lifted her chin. She could certainly outtalk this sleazy excuse for a man.

"What do you want with me, Señor Suarez? I shall certainly report your shocking behavior to the commandant if you don't let go of me this instant."

When the man stepped from behind her, she could finally see his face. His grin reminded her of the grimace of an animal . . . a small, sneaky animal, like the weasel that her father had set traps for in the barn. Her father. Iowa. Their barn. Oh, how she longed to be standing beside her father inside that Iowa barn at this very minute.

"Señor Suarez, you're going to be in a world of trouble for this."

The village headman stepped even closer to her to rub his body against her thighs, his hand upon her buttocks.

"I don't think so, T'cher. Maybe you like love with me, Blondie Lady. Maybe after we try, you want more." The sun glinted on his two gold teeth. "Maybe. We see what you say when we through."

"Not in a million years, you awful little man."

"You like sleep with my Magdalena. You only like women? Try me, why not? You might like better with me. Your husband, he like me . . . like my little girl, too. Maybe you like me, too." He released a cloud of fetid garlic breath into her face. "You only know if you test." His gold-trimmed grin was twisted, somehow demonic.

Horror rose in Sarah's mind. He thought she was. . . . He thought she and Magdalena were. . . . He was saying that Robert had. . . . She was unable to even finish the thoughts that his words stirred.

"You unnatural excuse for a parent!" She turned and swung her free hand to smash against his grinning, evil face. She swung again and slashed her fingernails down his cheek as hard as she could.

He dropped his hold on her arm and stepped back. She could see the three reddening lines stand out in welts against his dark skin. She yanked backward, but he didn't let go of the rope. She scrabbled with both hands to try to loosen the tightening loop.

He was still smiling when he slammed his clenched fist into the side of her face. She felt blackness rising and tried to fight against it. Suarez pulled her hands behind her and tied them together with the free end of the thin rope with which he'd almost throttled her.

He loosened the loop around her neck just enough so she could breathe, then pushed his face into hers.

"No more American trick. What you do, I do worse. Understan'? I am *el jefe*. I am your village headman. I am the boss here. You hit me, you get hit harder, you pull rope, you cut off own air. Understan'?"

Sarah nodded and tried to force herself to stay upright. She was beginning to understand all too well.

"We go now." He giggled at his next thought. "What Robert would say about his blondie wife now, you think, Señora Zumwalt? Maybe he like to play our little game, too. What you think?" He laughed again. "Me and him and Magdalena, we play plenty games."

He looped the rope casually through the crook of his elbow, as if it were the arm of a well-dressed lady he had agreed to escort into the dining room. He then turned and sauntered toward the heavy jungle. Sarah knew if she resisted she'd be choking again within seconds. The rope's harsh manila fiber had already burned a sweaty necklace of stinging pain around the skin of her neck. She stumbled forward to follow the village headman into the jungle. There was nothing else she could do.

Suarez stayed about four feet ahead of her. He didn't look back and he made no effort to clear a way for her. Limbs whipped back into her face and branches shoved the rope into her face. Her dress and petticoat caught on everything as she moved. With her hands tied behind her, she was defenseless against the plants. All she could do was follow and duck, or move to the side if she saw something coming her way. She tried once to see if anyone from the barrio was observing, but she had no time to tell. She had to match the headman's pace or suffer the same miserable choking she'd already experienced. Once she thought she heard Magdalena's name shouted but she couldn't be sure.

Within seconds her face and arms, her bared chest and her ankles were scratched and bleeding from the whipping plants. One of her best black cotton lisle stockings had caught and ripped on a stiff nettlelike plant. The garter on that leg was now at her ankle and tattered remnants of the woven stocking dragged behind her shoe. More than once, the dragging sock caused her almost to fall. Suarez trudged on and never looked back.

Was this really the person Robert had been most

friendly with in the whole village? What had they done together? What sort of person did that make *Robert?* Had she ever really known him at all?

She felt a touch of relief when they moved in under the tall canopy of trees. She was still oozing sweat from every pore, but at least they were out of the direct sunlight here. Now she would just need to watch for tree branches or vines that might come swinging back against her. He had led her to a wide and obviously well-traveled path. Suarez looked back at her and smiled.

"I will be your companion, Blondie T'cher," he trilled. "You will surely be glad you come with me. We have good time."

"Where are we going?"

"Party. You will see."

He had a place in mind. Maybe when they were again face-to-face she could talk to him, make him see the folly of his behavior.

And what about Robert? Her schoolmate Robert. Her dead husband Robert. Had Robert really been a cad and a villain all along? Even in Iowa? Or had the tropics caused him to change? She could almost hear her mother saying, "Birds of a feather flock together, Daughter."

Now she understood the anger that had been in his voice every time Markham Nash had mentioned Robert. Markham had seen a side of her dead husband that she had never known. She gasped for breath, tripped and fell to her knees. Scrambling to her feet, she ran a few steps while still bent over at the waist. Suarez would not wait for her to recover her balance. She felt as if she were splintering into a thousand pieces. Fright made her tremble as if she were cold. She shivered once more. She might never see Markham again. She was going to die in a strange country, never to see her mother or her father or her friends in Iowa again.

Panic rose in her chest and she felt an involuntary sob begin, but she savagely pushed it back.

No little-girl bawling, she told herself. *You've got to think, to plan, to talk this creature out of whatever he has in mind for you.* She knew no one was coming to rescue her; she had only herself to depend upon. *You can outsmart this greasy lout,* she tried to convince herself.

It might be days before Markham and the soldiers came back. Bong was taking care of Magdalena, but they wouldn't know where to look for her. The other village people probably wouldn't search for her. Of course, Magdalena would worry and so would Bong. She didn't know what might have happened to them. She hoped Bong had made it to the hut and to Magdalena. It was too close to the end of Magdalena's time for them to do much of anything but wait each day for the baby to come. No searching through the jungle was possible for her. She needed to be close at home now.

Sarah marched stolidly through the maze of forest growth, her neck wearing a blazing ring of fire.

She'd bide her time and do whatever she had to do to stay alive. She had to see Markham one more time . . . to tell him . . . to tell him . . . she didn't know what.

Maybe to tell him that she didn't want him to go away and leave her alone in the village again. And something else. . . . If only he had been in his quarters today, none of this would have happened.

Close your mind to the bad things that are happening to you, she told herself. *There's good here as well.* She could almost hear the words in her mother's voice.

She looked up at the dark-green canopy of treetops looped with pale-green vines. It all looked like it had the first few days with Rudolfo and Bong and Markham. She'd been almost too nervous then to really see it. So beautiful. Birds everywhere. Orchids. Chirping and whistling sounds that stopped as they neared and began once more as they passed. Maybe there were monkeys watching here as well.

She took a deep breath of the richness of this verdant world. While she was walking she could push down her fright and panic by trying to think what to do. The jungle was alive . . . and so was she. She planned to stay that way.

Her dragging stocking tangled in a mass of sticky vines and she crashed awkwardly to the jungle floor but Suarez simply continued walking. She struggled to her knees and then to her feet and tried to keep up with him.

"I tripped on some vines," she called loudly. "I couldn't help it, señor. Could you loosen the rope just a little?" As she shambled toward him, she pretended to be gagging. "Please?"

The Filipino man stopped and waited for her, then, without speaking, he used both hands to spread the

PARADISE FOUND

rope enough to let the loop lie loosely against her shoulders. Then he leaned to kiss the wide rope burn that circled her throat.

Sarah couldn't control her shudder.

"Ah, don't feel bad." He kissed the burn again. "Maybe you learn to like me, perhaps yet."

She shook her head but didn't answer and he continued his leisurely stroll, now holding her upper arm in a firm grip. He spoke as if they were strolling through a park and continuing a talk they'd started long ago.

"Robert tell me American women different. That true?" He grinned at her. "He say American women better lovers. That true?" He shook her arm to goad her to enter the one-sided conversation. "He say Magdalena like piece of wood in bed. That true?"

The shock of hearing a father talking intimately about his daughter's sexual activities with another man, with Robert, was almost more than Sarah could bear. Robert, her husband, and this village politician had been cronies . . . and far more than that, apparently.

Sarah grit her teeth. Those two . . . weasels had discussed bedroom secrets with each other, had even taken part in some unusual sexual frolics. They'd not only talked about Magdalena in the most intimate way, but they'd conjectured about *her*, Robert's future wife, as a bed partner, as well!

"Robert say you was going to be better than Magdalena. That true? Is true you better lover?"

Sarah made a silent vow. *If I ever get away from this carrion, I will do everything in my power to see that he never sees or speaks to me or to Magdalena or the baby. Ever.*

An explosion of long-repressed rage roared in her head. She'd never really understood murder before, but now she knew in her own heart and blood and sinew why some women had found themselves able to kill. She could murder this man if she had the opportunity, she was sure.

A rising hill of huge rocks and boulders lay in their path. Suarez tightened the rope about her neck and dropped his grasp on her arm to begin the climb.

There was a path, yes, but Sarah didn't know if she could climb the steep trail or not. Not with her hands tied behind her. She needed to buy time. The craggy climb upward seemed a trap . . . even to the small man who led her like an animal. She could see his visible doubt about whether or not to go to the right or to the left or to try to go straight ahead.

"Help me, señor, please."

"You young and strong. Help yourself." He was breathing heavily and his eyes held a baffled, beaten look. He stood panting on a rock shelf just above her. Maybe she could talk him into untying her wrists, at least.

"I could help myself," she explained after she had made her plea, "but I could also help you make the climb."

"I know. You want run away from me."

"I give you my word." She nodded and smiled reassurance up toward him. "You untie my hands and I'll help you get up and over this rock cliff." *And* then

I'll run away as soon as I can, she added silently and crossed her fingers in the age-old childhood sign that said she was holding something back.

Suarez led her to the edge of the rock where he stood.

"Turn around. I fix." She turned her back so he could reach down to her hands. She could feel him fiddling with the rope. There. One hand free. But what was he doing with the other one? She was able to turn and was horrified to see that he was tying her right wrist to his left.

"You no get away from me, T'cher. I see to that."

He was right. She would not get away. At least not right now. Later, who was to say? She had to think of something. The ride with Markham and Bong through the rain-soaked jungle had been a Sunday school outing compared to what was happening to her this day. The last few hours had been the worst ones of her life. She shook the circulation back into her left hand, then pulled herself up to stand next to the little man who awaited her on the ridge.

The rest of the two hours of climbing were fairly easy. Sometimes she almost lifted the village headman onto the next foothold. Sometimes he held on to her for balance. Sarah finally realized that he was so unsteady because he had been drinking. He must have sneaked some liquor while they were struggling up the pile of boulders. That was probably the reason for his halting behavior. Fierce joy filled her at the realization. A drunken jailer would be easier to fool than a sober and watchful keeper.

By the time the sun sat low in the sky, they stood at the top of the last heap of gray rock and looked down at the trail sloping before them. At the base of the sloping path was a camp of some kind laid out against a sheer rock cliff. Heavy jungle ringed in the open space to the left of the hidden lair.

Only one bare-chested man lay stretched out as if he were sleeping. He rested on a pile of cut bamboo fronds, but there was plenty of evidence that others had been there. Horses hobbled to a manila rope line, a campfire, saddles, and harnesses told the story. Meat cooked on a spit and pottery jugs were piled against the stone face of the cliff. The far side of the camp looked as if it might be a sheer drop into nothingness.

"Friends," Suarez grunted and pointed. "We go down now, meet friends. I bring you long way to meet friends." He turned his head slowly and smiled at Sarah. "They want meet my blondie schoolteacher." She felt as if the sweat on her body had suddenly turned to ice. Who were these people this man called his "friends"?

"There's only one person down there. Where are your other friends?"

"They come soon." He laughed.

Sure enough, as they walked down the last fifty yards of the sloping path, men began riding and strolling into the camp area. Filipino men. All ruffians, by the look of them, Sarah thought. They dropped heavy-looking bundles against the cliff wall and took the pottery jugs toward the fire. Several headed to a nearby stream to bring buckets of water. Sarah thought longingly of dipping the water to pour it over her herself.

Only cool water could soothe away some of her discomfort.

The largest man had a scar that cut from his eyebrow across his cheek, then under his chin. He looked to Sarah just like what the Methodist minister back home had often described as "Evil incarnate."

Suarez walked toward the cruel-looking man and spoke words Sarah couldn't understand, then the headman grinned back at her before he placed the rope into the hands of the glowering man with the scar.

Suarez spoke English to her.

"I tell him I bring him a present. You."

Twenty-one

Suarez gestured toward the wicked-looking gang leader.

"I give you to my friend."

Sarah's heart sank. Hope died within her. She was a gift meant for this creature. "God," she prayed inwardly. "Let me die first."

The scarred man barked an order at her. She lifted her chin and stood as straight as she could. If she were going to die, she'd do it with dignity. She would not be a coward, no matter what happened. She was an American schoolteacher. President McKinley's emissary to the Filipino people. She stared the scarred man in the eye.

He turned to Suarez and spoke.

"He want you to sit down and be at home." Suarez laughed. She knew he understood her fear. Her anguish seemed to please him.

"Sit down?"

"Yes. Over on the tree trunk by the fire. He going to give you some coffee." Suarez giggled joyfully. "He want you, American Blondie School Teacher, to feel welcome in his . . ." Suarez searched for a word. "In his home, even."

The taller man was already leading Suarez and Sarah to what appeared to be the seat of honor in the camp. The scarred man barked orders to his subordinates and they rushed to do his bidding. One man put an American Army blanket on the tree trunk. Another poured hot coffee into a tin cup which he handed her as she seated herself. Suarez seated himself next to her.

"I speak the English for him," he explained to her. "I tell you what he want me to tell you."

The village headman seemed proud that he had been selected to interpret for the commanding taller man.

"He say, 'Would you like water?'" Before Sarah could answer, Suarez spoke again. "He say, 'You maybe want something to eat?'" Suarez now became almost courtly as he spoke the words she had heard at least a hundred times before from the Filipino families whom she had visited in the barrio.

"He like to know what you think of our country." Suarez nodded at the man as he spoke again, then turned once more to Sarah to interpret. "He also want to know, where your companion is."

Sarah understood full well that the man was asking who her lover was, but she would just stick with her usual way of answering when she was asked that very question by the village people! "The children are my companions during the day and my friend Magdalena Suarez keeps me company in my house at night."

Ah oh. She froze in silence for a moment. Perhaps

the last part of that answer had had something to do with what Suarez had said earlier. Did all the people in the barrio believe she and Magdalena were. . . . She shook her head. She'd think about that later. Now, her plan was to try to make friends with this attentive ruffian if she could.

"Yes, please. I'd very much like a glass of water."

She remembered one of Markham's first dictates, "Never say no to a Filipino's offer of food. That is the height of bad manners and, what's worse, it's rude to your host or hostess." He'd grinned and said, "Eat and drink whatever they give you and say nothing."

She looked at the meat turning on the spit.

"I would love to eat . . . that is, after all the men have finished their food, of course. Tell him, Mr. Suarez, that the roast his helper is cooking smells wonderful."

Suarez nodded enthusiastically. "A delicacy in our country. Dog meat real spicy. Your husband Robert like it. It go good with the drink."

Sarah's stomach turned over. Maybe the hungry men would eat it all before she was offered any. Whatever happened, she'd do what she had to do.

The men began to pass the rust-colored pottery jugs, jugs like the ones Markham and Bong and Rudolfo had used on the trail. Suarez took a jug from the scarred leader and drank deeply. He passed the container to Sarah. She lifted the jug and took a minuscule amount of the liquid into her mouth but kept the jug to her lips and pretended to swallow several more times. When she lowered the jug and passed it back to Suarez, she heard an admiring murmur go up around the campfire. She'd apparently passed one test.

She tried to keep from rubbing her lips or spitting. The liquid had tasted quite awful. Nasty. Bitter. Gritty. No telling *what* was in that jug. The stuff burned her throat raw. Her eyes watered, but she maintained her composure. Drinking something else might help.

"Mr. Suarez, may I have another dipper of that good water, please?"

A man came running with more water for her. She thanked him and drained the gourd dipper. There. That was better. The men surrounding them watched her every move. They seemed to be continually making a tighter, more attentive circle around her. She felt despair take over. If they kept their eyes on her every single moment, there was no way she could get away from them.

The scarred man stepped close enough to touch her. She saw his hand move toward her. She wanted to shrink back, to scream. She stiffened her backbone, instead. His hand lifted a strand of her hair. He held the strand out for all to see, and he seemed to be explaining her hair's texture, color, and weight as if he were lecturing on the subject. All the men in the circle nodded and murmured understanding of the statistics.

"First time they see blondie hair," Suarez explained. "All Americans is blondie."

"You know better than that, señor. You've seen the Americans in the Army. They have hair color of every shade." She surveyed Suarez's oiled hair. "Captain Nash has hair that is blacker than yours."

Suarez interrupted her. "Put out your arm."
"What?"
"Hurry up. Put out your arm, man say."

Sarah dubiously extended her arm. They hadn't hurt her yet. What now? She couldn't help it. She closed her eyes.

She felt fingers lightly smoothing her arm, breath from several mouths touching her skin. She opened her eyes. The scarred leader and several of his henchmen were leaning over her forearm, examining it thoroughly. They murmured and exclaimed among themselves as they looked. One prodded gently and smiled at his friends. He nodded and others came to take their turn to look.

"What are they doing?"

"All Americans hairy. Men like to see blondie hair on arms. See white skin."

"Oh." These men weren't hurting her. They were acting a whole lot like the children had acted when they were just getting acquainted with her. She had finally realized she had been a being from another world for the little ones. Maybe she was just as strange for these men.

"Some say you ugly." Suarez laughed. "Other say you like a flower. Most flower had little bit of hair on them, anyway, like on you." He took a drink from the jug, but he didn't pass the vessel on to her. "I say hair on arm okay. You pretty woman."

The behavior of the men puzzled Sarah. They were acting as if she were their honored guest in their well-appointed drawing room, a stranger whom they were trying to make feel at home. They were studying her, but they weren't hurting her.

As they examined her, they passed the jugs among themselves. One handed her another cup of coffee. A second one placed a native cigar on the log within reach of her hand. He said nothing, but it was clear he was giving her a chance to smoke if she cared to do so. She was apparently not required to drink any more of the liquor. Several who had just finished bathing and had not had a turn at her hair gathered to examine the strand displayed by their leader earlier. Each touched her hair, combed it through their fingers and commented on it. Sarah sat as still as a stone. Maybe they would let her go?

One look at the welts down the side of Suarez's face told her that any thought of going back to San Miguel unscathed was only wishful thinking. *He* had plans for her if none of the others did. He was cutting the rope that held them together. She could hardly believe he was actually cutting the rope. Usually Filipinos were so frugal they would work an hour on a knot rather than cut a string or a rope. What now? Sarah shook her newly unbound hand and flexed it. She wanted to be ready for anything.

"You be first. You stand up and sing."

"Sing?"

"All party have entertainment. It time for entertainment now. You sing."

Sarah rose and looked around at the circle of men. The scarred man had taken a seat at the other end of the tree trunk. Each man in the group looked at her expectantly. They really did want her to sing! She took a deep breath. Papa's favorite. She'd sing "After the Ball." She closed her eyes, and just for a second she was standing with each bare foot planted on Papa's big shoes and he was holding out each of her hands as he sang and danced around the kitchen with her. Her mother sang and watched the two of them. She opened her eyes. All the waiting *ladrones* still sat staring at her.

" 'After the ball was over,
After the stars had gone,
After the dancers were leaving,
Just at the break of dawn . . .' "

The audience of cruel-eyed men swayed in time to her singing, enraptured by a song they couldn't understand, a song sung by a woman who probably looked like a picture in a book to them.

"Again yet!"

She sang the song again. They nodded and swayed some more. When she'd finished, they applauded. Two men rose to take their turn at the entertainment. One placed a bandana on his head. He knotted the cloth in each of the four corners, and Sarah understood from their gestures that he was acting the part of the woman for the pair. They danced to the music and the beat the other men furnished. Sarah applauded wildly. Suarez stood and sang a song in a minor key. Several of the men wiped their eyes as he sang.

"I sing love song in Spanish."

Sarah nodded understanding when Suarez again seated himself. She had a wild thought. If she could teach children to sing "Red Wing" she could probably teach these rough men as well. The jugs hurtled around the group again and yet again. Sarah stood. She turned to Suarez.

"Tell them I will teach them an American love song." His announcement was greeted with nods and words that she thought were assent. She began the song, and they listened attentively. She chose one of the smaller men from the front row to sing each line of the chorus after her. Soon all the men were roaring the song, line by line. They were getting noisier. After awhile Sarah nodded and bowed and asked for another drink of water and returned to her seat on the log. She could hear the song being practiced by several of the onlookers.

Two men stood and sang the chorus of "Pretty Red Wing" by themselves. Their friends shouted approval. Sarah applauded. The two sang two more Filipino songs. The small man she'd chosen earlier did a jiglike dance as the other men clapped.

The scarred one rose and pulled his bolo from its scabbard. Sarah crossed her arms against her chest. What now?

He stepped up onto the tree trunk and began his declamation. Loudly, then very softly, his voice wove a spell on his audience. He added broad gestures. He was telling a story or reciting a poem, Sarah surmised. At several points in the rendition, the audience shouted the words with him. He frowned when they did that and they grew silent and let him have his solo turn.

He turned to Sarah, raised his machete as if it were a sword and brought it swiftly down to chop into the trunk. He smiled. At least she thought it was a smile. He bowed. Sarah bowed back and clapped as loudly as any of the men in his gang.

What kind of primitive, civilized, curious, childlike, artistic, cruel, courteous people were they, these Filipinos? She hated most of what had happened today and yet she knew that she would not have wanted to miss what had transpired in the robbers' camp. Maybe something was wrong with her?

"Now, I see what your body like, Blondie T'cher. Maybe too much blondie hair." He took another long, long drink. "You b'long me, again." As he drank and talked, the men sang as a group.

During the singing one of the men nearest the firelight rhythmically tossed a golden trinket from hand to hand. Sarah stared. Her heart almost stopped. A cross. On a chain. She knew she'd see the letters "B.M." on the back of the cross if she could look at it. She desperately wanted to examine the golden cross but knew she mustn't try. The sight of the tiny cross pulled her up short.

What had she been thinking of? These weren't just a bunch of nice but rough and ready men. These were the *ladrones* who had invaded the village. *Her* village! These were thieves, rapists, and murderers. What had they done with Magdalena?

Suarez tugged at her arm. Since she'd been rejected by the leader, he had his mind set on taking her into the darkness for his own purposes. What was she going to do with this horrible little beast?

"Come, Señor Suarez. Let us have a drink first.

Please pass the jug." She motioned to the fired clay vessel at his feet.

He looked delighted, then puzzled.

"You like our *tuba?*"

"Oh, yes. We have nothing like this back in Iowa."

"Where Iowa? In New York? In California?"

"Closer to New York, I believe." She gestured. "Please. You have your drink first, sir."

Her father had once told her that a happy drunk man was much less dangerous than an angry sober man. Perhaps this was where she would test his theory.

She raised the jug and then returned it to Suarez. "Thanks. Do have another drink, señor."

He tipped the jug to his mouth once more, then stood. He gestured toward the jungle. He yanked the army blanket from the tree trunk and threw it over one shoulder.

"You, me, us, we go now, yet." He staggered, straightened, and made a wobbly trail toward the palmetto bushes. He turned and bowed to the men at the fire and all called encouraging comments toward them. "They say you goo' woman, still yet."

Sarah hefted the jug.

"I'll just take us something to drink, señor."

"Goo'. They true. You real goo' woman."

His speech was beginning to be barely coherent.

Should she dare hope? What could she do? Her mind searched frantically for a plan, a way to escape whatever it was this man wanted. She would just have to be ready for any opportunity. For a second Markham's smiling face rose in her mind, but longing for him was useless. She must do something on her own. And quickly.

Nausea rose in Sarah along with overwhelming fear. She could smell the Filipino village headman's breath and his sweaty body. He was moving closer to her and touching her, one hand smoothing her buttocks.

"I put blanket there. You lay self down on it now." She stopped and looked at the man. There was little moon and the night was almost black. The flickering light from the robbers' campfire gave just enough illumination so she could see the man's eyes and his two gold teeth and the gleam of the flames on his sweat-bathed skin.

He dropped the blanket, smiled broadly and reached for the jug she held. Then he made a courtly bow and a sweeping gesture of command toward the dark square of the U.S. Army blanket. Sarah felt her blood congeal in her veins. There was nothing else she *could* do. She sat down.

Twenty-two

Sarah sat still, her chin raised, her back stiff. The army blanket beneath her felt somewhat comfortable, even springy because it covered low jungle growth. She stared sightlessly down at the gang of men near the fire and she could feel the darkly ominous figure of the man swaying and muttering above her. She told herself that if she didn't look at Suarez, he might forget what he had planned to do. Certainly screaming wouldn't help. The men in the robber band below seemed to think it was perfectly fine for this odious creature to have led her through the jungle like an animal on the end of a rope. They'd even congratulated him when he'd removed her from the firelit camp area.

She had to think of something, but she was so frightened she couldn't think logically. She stared hard at the still-celebrating robbers, as if examining them carefully could give her an answer or possibly the remnants of some sort of plan.

There was one thing to be grateful for. She didn't have to have even a single mouthful of old Rover. She could see that some of the men were already eating the roasted dog, others were sleeping or had, perhaps, passed out from the drink. The scarred man sat on the log she'd just left. He strummed a guitar and sang softly to himself. All of the men were so far away from where she was sitting that she could hear only a word or two or a single note from the guitar now and then.

Beside her, Suarez stood unsteady on his feet, still drinking from the jug and muttering in both English and in his own language.

"You drink." He handed her the jug.

She pretended to take a long, long drink, then handed the pottery vessel back up to him. The smell of the stuff in the jug was so bad she had to force herself not to gag on the odor alone. Instead, she smiled and fluttered her eyelashes. "Now you must drink, señor."

"I drink." He lifted the jug to his lips. As he drank, he stumbled forward and fell and the jug rolled toward the camp. No one seemed to notice the clatter it made as it banged against rocks. Suarez didn't seem to miss his bottle. He sat in a crumpled heap for a moment, then threw his body against hers, knocking her flat against the rough blanket.

Sarah wanted to scream or cry and fight. She knew she could do none of those things. The other men were too close for her to make a lot of noise. They would probably come at once to investigate, perhaps even to hold her while the drunken headman had his way with her.

Maybe they were all going to do what Suarez had said *he* was going to do. Maybe they were planning to take turns and Suarez had taken first turn. If only Markham had been there when the *ladrones* came in. But, of course, she was silly to even think such a thing. His absence was the cause of their arrival, surely. She'd certainly figured that one out. They had come *because* the army men weren't there. Unquestionably the attack on San Miguel was Señor Suarez's doing. He must have gotten word to his outlaw friends that the coast would be clear during the next few days.

Even though she was scared out of her mind, she wasn't going to allow herself to cry. He was on top of her and she could just let him do what he said he was going to do . . . or she could show some spunk. Her mother hadn't taught her about gumption for nothing. She'd show him what Iowa girls were made of. She'd fight. That's what she'd do. She shoved silently against the weight of the man, kicking at his legs, tearing at his face.

He lay against her, not fighting back, not holding her. He was a leaden lump pinning her body to the blanket. She shoved again. He mumbled some words she couldn't understand. She strove desperately to move from under his bulk. Although he was a small man, he was almost covering her, seemingly as heavy and hard to maneuver as a corn sack full of grain.

Perhaps he felt so heavy because he was completely sodden with drink. Papa had been right, she thought. This man probably wasn't going to be any more trouble. Not to her. Not tonight. If she could get untangled from his corpselike embrace maybe she could slither quietly off into the jungle and be back in the village—or somewhere—before the others ever realized she was gone.

She shoved his arm from her shoulders.

"Lay still, Blondie Americana." His voice was so slurred she had trouble understanding the words. She lay stiff and silent for a moment. What could she do? Panic paralyzed her for a moment.

His breath stank like rotten meat. She tried to turn her face away from the odor. He didn't move. After another silent second she took a deep breath and kicked at the leg that pinned hers to the ground. With both hands she shoved at him until he turned onto his back. A loud snore rose from his throat. She pulled more oxygen into her lungs. That made her realize that she'd been holding her breath.

When I talk to Papa again, I'll tell him he was right about drunks, she promised herself.

She rose to one elbow and surveyed the camp area. Several of the robbers were sleeping. She'd have to be brave and chance it while most of them were really drunk or still celebrating. She might never get another opportunity. Tomorrow morning would most certainly be too late. Using her elbows, she inched herself backward on the blanket, then off the blanket and onto the littered humus of the jungle floor.

Sweat rolled into her eyes and blurred her vision. It didn't matter anyway. The night was so black that, in the direction away from the fire, she could barely see her hand in front of her face. She remembered Markham's comment about the jungle sheltering them as well as if they were in a dark cave.

Fear pounded through her when a rough-fibered vine caught against one shoulder, scratched the length of her wrist, and wrapped itself about her arm and the top of her body, seemingly determined to keep her pinned to the moldy, leaf-covered earth just at the edge of the gray blanket.

She stopped her movement for a moment and lifted her skirt to wipe her eyes. She was almost off the scratchy blanket, except for her legs. Suarez muttered once and was quiet again. The men in the camp who remained awake seemed calmly undisturbed. No one looked in their direction. She remembered that she had been able to see nothing but blackness at the edge of the jungle from where she had been sitting at the fire. Maybe they couldn't even see her or Suarez? She straightened, sat up and yanked the offending vine from her arm. She hardly noticed the new scratches the vine tore across the top of her wrist.

"Better not stand up even if they can't see." She murmured the words.

She lowered herself to the ground, turned and began to crawl on her hands and knees. Rocks and hard chunks of wood and other greenery, and once a needle-sharp thistle of some kind, bit into her palms but she made steady progress.

Finally, she stopped and wiped her face again. The sweat made the scratches on her cheeks burn like fire. The rope burn on her neck had gone beyond pain into torture. She tried not to think of a bath with the cool water sluicing down over her head and neck and shoulders. She forced herself to look back at where she'd been. Suarez and the blanket were several feet behind her.

Low bushes kept her from seeing exactly what was happening in the camp, but it seemed quiet. Before she turned back to resume her crawl, Suarez flung himself over and spoke his words clearly: "Blondie Lady."

She turned into stone. Could he see her? Was he going to come after her? She froze for another second. No. The rasp of his snore let her heart beat again. She crawled a few more yards across the litter of jungle cover. Fear crawled with her. Plants above her reached for her hair and her clothing as if to slow her movement.

The steamy air and her exertion caused a river of sweat to mold her soggy dress and petticoat to her body. She took a deep breath. She had to stand up. She wasn't going to get anywhere at all on her hands and knees.

She heard her skirt rip when she stood, the cloth caught by a dry palmetto leaf as she rose. The noise she made rasped against the quiet of the jungle. She felt herself paralyzed in place. Had he heard? Had he awakened? Her blood pounded and she recognized the copper taste of fear on her tongue. Did she dare walk? Run? And which way should she go?

She forced herself to take one small step, then another. Now she could see the drunken man as only a black lump against the glow of the flickering firelight. The humusy, soft earth seemed to swallow her feet. For a long second she felt as if she couldn't move. Vines twined at her legs, branches tore at her face. She forced herself forward. Every breath was full of a sweet flower fragrance, like jasmine, perhaps. She took more tiny steps. She was determined to get through this tropical hell somehow.

Which way to go? She had no idea, but she knew she wanted to move as far away from the village headman and his outlaw friends as she could, as quickly as she could.

"Never mind direction. Just keep moving away from the fire," she whispered to herself. "Don't stop for anything." In the morning she would be able to find the village. Right now she had to save herself any way possible.

Her on-the-trail conversations with Markham rose up to haunt her. She could almost hear her own silly words. "I came here because I didn't want to stay and live a boring life in Iowa. I want adventure, excitement!" She'd wondered at the time what had passed between the two men when she'd said that. They'd looked at each other and both had smiled. Now, after a day like today, she realized that there was such a thing as too much excitement! Adventure in itself wasn't what she really wanted. What she really wanted, still wanted, was to teach and to be with people who knew her, respected her and loved her.

Faced with the kind of excitement she'd had to endure during this twenty-four-hour period, she'd realized that in her drive to escape a monotonous existence, she had laid her life open to happenings she'd never dreamed of, never wished for. Her apprehension increased as she pondered what the future might have in store for her if she should ever make it out of this dark and silent strangeness.

Should her future lie in Iowa? Or had she only exchanged boredom for constant fright and anger in this foreign place? Maybe. Maybe she had made a huge mistake. Maybe her safe homeland was where she really belonged. That's where Markham and everyone else around the Army cadre seemed to think she should be. *Oh, Markham, where are you?*

The suddenly frightening sound of something moving across the dry clutter in front of her stopped her again. She held her breath for a moment. Just an insect or a little animal, she reassured herself and continued walking, testing each foot of jungle ground before she put her weight down on it. The violent urge to run, *run,* surged through her, but she held herself in check. She had to keep feeling her way. If she panicked like a runaway horse, there was a good chance she could step into a hole or fall off a cliff or smash into a wall of rock. She remembered Miss Arnold's favorite saying: "Slow but steady wins the race."

Her foot touched a log, a fallen tree. A place to rest and decide what to do next. She turned and sat down on the log to catch her breath, letting her mind drift to Captain Markham Nash. *Major* Markham Nash.

For the first time she was able to admit to herself that she felt something for him . . . that she loved him . . . even though she knew quite well that he just thought of her as another burden the Army had handed him. The remorse that filled her at that moment was more painful and more real to her than the physical wounds the vines and branches had exacted from her as they tore at her hair and her skin.

The slashes on her skin would heal; perhaps her heart would not.

The shrill cry of a night bird pulled her up from the log. She stood and stepped over her resting place. She had to go on. She had to stay alive to see Markham, to talk to him one more time. How much time had passed she had no idea, but the jungle around her was pitch black and the blackness was thick with silence. This blackness was different than the darkest night in Iowa. Back there, even when there was no moon, a person could see a few feet ahead as she walked.

Had she been walking for minutes? Hours? She couldn't tell. She'd keep walking until she could walk no longer. What if she fell into a hole? Walked off a cliff? Never mind. Better that than what the men behind her had had planned for her.

As she trudged through the undergrowth, arms outstretched in an almost useless attempt to defend herself against the tearing vines and branches, she made a vow. She would make one attempt to talk to Markham. Maybe he deserved honesty from her. If it seemed that they couldn't both feel love, then she'd have to go back to Iowa just as soon as passage could be arranged. Decision made, she lifted her skirt to again wipe her face before she took another step.

Of course, there was the school. She took another step. A jade vine slapped her across the face. She tore at it with her hands and kept moving. She couldn't go back home until she'd made sure that the little school she'd worked so hard to establish was running smoothly, that the children had a teacher and that the teacher who replaced her understood how best to teach barrio children. Then, perhaps, she'd be ready to go home.

That's what she'd do. She kicked at a grasping nettlelike plant. The sting of the nettle was no worse than many of the other wounds she'd received today. She stiffened her backbone and clenched her teeth to seal the promise to herself. She'd get herself straightened out with Markham, see to Bong and Magdalena's wedding, attend to the baby's welfare, and after she'd gotten the school firmly up and running, *then* there would be nothing to keep her from returning to America and civilization.

She reassured herself that there was one really good thing she'd done in the Philippines. Her school and her students were wonderful. For a second she let herself relive the joy she'd felt in the classroom when she'd tricked the children into running to school earlier than they'd planned. "Pretty Red Wing." The singing. The dancing. Had it only been this morning? Or lifetimes ago? So much had happened since then.

After what seemed hours of walking, Sarah stumbled and fell against the trunk of a huge tree. She felt around in the dark and realized that another tree grew only about an arm's length from the first. *Maybe I can rest here for a while,* she thought. She wedged herself into the space between the two trees and curled herself into a ball. She tried to make herself as small as possible. She just couldn't walk any farther, not through all that thick growth. Maybe the heavy underbrush would screen her from any searching *ladrones*.

She couldn't hold back her sobs. She let the tears flow, but she stifled any sound. She was hot, scratched, and cut, the tiredest she had ever been in her whole life. Her neck was on fire. She was hungry and she was scared and she was alone. She had been so stupid that she hadn't even known, really known, the man she had actually married in the church in Manila. In Iowa he'd seemed just a pleasant schoolmate. Had the Philippines turned him into a monster or had he always been a hidden bad apple? For a second her mind returned to the cross the robber had tossed so casually from hand to hand.

What had happened to Magdalena? The young Filipina was almost ready to have her baby. Had the man who had the cross harmed little Magdalena in some way? And what about Bong?

She wrestled herself into another position and tried to see the sky, but she couldn't. Of course. Only darkness. That was nothing different, she told herself. Apparently she'd been doing everything in the dark for months now. She seemed to have botched everything she had come to the Philippines to do. She had almost been killed and maybe her friends were dead and now she had realized that she was in love with a man who didn't need or even want a wife.

She shifted to rest her back against the largest tree trunk. She knew she couldn't sleep here in this wild place. She'd always thought a jungle would be full of sounds. Animal cries. Bird songs. Insect clickings.

This heavy silence still surprised her. No. No sleep. She needed to be watchful. She wouldn't sleep. Not in a million years, but she was so tired and so scared, she didn't think she could walk any more until she could see where she was going. She supposed this would be as good a place as any to hide and wait for the morning.

She sniffed and scrubbed her fists into her swollen eyes. She forced back any more tears that might want to flow. She was through with crying. Crying wouldn't help. She was fighting for her life now. She had to live so she could make her way back to Iowa and the people who really loved her.

She'd stay here in the little nest she'd made between the trees, just until the first show of light, then she'd be off and running like a shot. She scuffled to button the top three buttons at her neckline, then reached down to straighten her shredded gray cotton skirt as best she could. She raised her arms to try to neaten her hair but she realized there was no use trying that. Her hairpins were long lost somewhere in the bush.

She let her hands drop and she laid her head of tangled hair down upon a protruding root of the sheltering tree. She closed her eyes and allowed a memory picture of Markham's brown eyes and his teasing smile as she'd last seen him to lull her into quiet. Her breathing slowed and her limbs relaxed.

Sleep overtook her in less than a second.

* * *

... Was that Robert over there? What was Robert doing, wandering around in a robbers' camp in the Philippine jungle? He was wearing the tweed jacket that he'd worn to school for several years.

Sarah felt pleased to see that he was here. He had come to take her somewhere, she knew. She watched him a moment, then, at his gesture, followed him across the camp area around the fire, back of the log where she'd been sitting and into a rocky cave. The floor of the cave was a series of descending flat stones. She realized she had never been in such a place. It seemed cool and damp.

The strange greenish light that filled the rocky place added to Sarah's trepidation. Robert's shadow moved down into the bowels of the earth ahead of her, and he did not look back, nor offer to help her down the rocky stair. He was, in fact, ignoring her.

"Robert!" Her voice echoed slightly against the stone walls of the place, but after her call, Robert continued his journey with only a slight hesitation. "Robert, wait for me. Where are we going?" When he didn't answer, she went on, but she began to want to turn back, to be out of the strange greenish light, to be away from Robert. It was clear he didn't need her, but something forced her downward, dogging his footsteps.

"Why am I doing this?" she asked herself aloud. It had become abundantly clear by the way he looked and acted that Robert really didn't want her with him, didn't want her following him, actually felt burdened by her presence.

After a few more steps, she entered a rounded stone

room, a cavern that was also illuminated with the hazy green light. Robert was waiting for her there. He inched around her and stood on the step just above her to lean against the wall and look down at her.

"Can't you take a hint?" he said. "I don't need you. I don't want you." He took a step upward. "You just stay here, Sarah. I'm going back up." He smoothed his tie and put his hands in the pockets of the tweed jacket. "Don't follow me." He leaped lightly up the stone steps and was gone from her sight, returning to the surface.

Sarah's heart lurched. She took a deep breath. He'd led her to a strange place like this, then deserted her . . . insisting he wasn't responsible for her welfare. What was she going to do now? Tears were running down her cheeks she knew. She could feel them, but strangely enough, she was unable to wipe them away because she was not able to raise her hands to her face . . .

Twenty-three

What was that?

Sarah was suddenly awake. She stared straight up. A pinpoint of light pierced her eyes and she raised her head. Where was she? The sun was well up. She felt the leaf-covered ground beneath her hand. Ugh. Suarez. She let her aching body flop back down onto the floor of the jungle. Memories of her kidnapping and of the evening in the robber camp came flooding back into her mind. Anguish brought her upright. *Oh.* Pain forced a groan from between her lips. She was sore all over. *Keep quiet!* she warned herself inwardly. She sat listening. She knew she'd heard something. Some *sound* had awakened her.

The *ladrones*. Suarez. What if they showed up? What should she do? She stood, then leaned over to pick up a piece of a fallen branch. The roughness of the bark against the palm of her hand made her feel safer. She gripped the makeshift club tightly with both hands. Maybe they wouldn't find her, but if they did, she was going to go down fighting.

She stood poised, ready to strike, her heart hammering in her chest. In the silence of the moment, her empty stomach gurgled loudly. The growling, rippling sound was like an explosion in her ears. She pressed the butt of the branch against her complaining stomach.

Dumb, dumb, dumb. Anyone for miles around could have heard that stupid gurgling.

As if in answer to her thought, the tiny noise that had been nagging at the edge of her consciousness became a bit louder. Footsteps. A person. No. A horse. Two horses. Both walking very slowly, very carefully. As if the riders were searching for someone. She raised the stick again. They were getting closer by the second. She resolved to die before she'd go with Suarez or any of the other men again.

She peered through one half-opened eye. She couldn't see clearly, but she made out the form of a horse and rider through the heavy brush. A second horse walked a few feet behind the first. It looked as though the man on the horse was guiding the animals directly to her hiding place. Of course. She was such a dolt she'd left a trail that even a *drunk* could follow!

She gripped the club more tightly and clenched her eyes tightly shut at the same time. *I'd rather roast in hellfire than ever again go anywhere with that poor excuse for a man,* she resolved.

"I don't think you'll be able to hurt me with your eyes closed like that."

Joy coursed through her. Her eyes snapped open.

"Markham! How did you find me? How did you know where to look? When did you come back from Manila? What happened to Magdalena?" The words tumbled out quickly as she pulled herself from her hiding place. She dropped the stick and tried to smooth her hair into some semblance of order. "Where's Bong? Is the school still standing?"

Markham was already off Jonas, and in one long stride he'd reached her and closed his arms about her. She put both arms around his waist and leaned into his chest, eyes closed, a smile on her face. His embrace was everything she had needed. Safety, security, friendship . . . and maybe something more.

For a long second they stood, silently melded together. Markham spoke first.

"Are you all right, Sarah?" He leaned back just a fraction and tipped her chin up with one hand. "Did they hurt you?"

"I'm scratched and I'm dirty and I'm a bit frazzled and ropeburned, but no, I guess I'm really not hurt." *Oh, he smelled so good.* She tried to lean into that comforting masculine chest once again, but Markham wasn't having that. He held her chin and lowered his lips. She stared at the sculptured lips. He was going to kiss her. She hoped he was going to kiss her. Gently, then more strongly, he let his mouth cover hers. *He is kissing me,* she thought dreamily. The incandescent heat from his lips radiated from her head down to her toes.

He lifted his face and smiled down at her.

"Hey, Miss Schoolmarm, that was mighty nice, but let's try it again. This time you just open your mouth a tiny bit."

Oh. Was that how it was done? She stretched to put one hand at the back of his neck, and when his lips touched hers, she was ready. She felt his breath against her mouth, then his lips slanted across her own, then his tongue pressed its way into her mouth. Her whole body felt as if it were filled with little stars. Her whole body yearned to get closer to him. He was the one who could cause the rapture she was feeling. She molded herself to him and she felt as if she were a creature with liquid for bones. When he took his mouth away she wanted to cry out with disappointment and longing. *"Again"* she wanted to say, but she didn't.

"We'd better get on out of here." He looked over her head, then back at the trail he'd taken. "I expect the troopers can take care of the *ladrones,* but I need to take you home." He brought his gaze back to her and seemed to be studying the lines of her face. She felt the sudden quiver of her lower lip as she drew in her breath. She wished he wouldn't look at her. Not just now, anyway.

"I know I look a sight." Again she smoothed her tangled mop of blond hair.

"You look exactly right to me."

He searched her face as if it held a secret he needed to know. His breath was warm against her cheek, then on her mouth once more. He kissed her, slowly, with relentless, building intensity.

God. He'd thought he'd find her dead or raped or hurt badly in some other way but no, there she was, gallant little thing with a stick in her hand and her eyes clenched tight shut. He wanted to laugh with relief, but even more he wanted to kiss her.

Her lips, even as parched-looking as they were, were all soft, sweet innocence. He wanted the velvet that he knew was inside, the honey of her being. He wanted her . . . all of her.

"That's right, darlin', open just a little and let me taste paradise."

Markham led Jonas and the other horse toward a fallen log and beckoned Sarah.

"Mabuti!" Sarah patted and smoothed the fat mare's jaw. "You brought my old 'buti for me." The horse nodded her head as if answering Sarah's greeting.

"Well, I didn't know who I'd find with you or what shape anyone would be in or . . . I was afraid . . ." He slapped Mabuti lightly on the neck. "I know you're glad to see her, but let's let old Jonas carry us both home."

He boosted Sarah to stand on the log. "Wait. I'll pick you up after I'm on." He mounted the horse and bent to lift her to a seat across his lap. She sighed, put her arms around him and leaned into his strength. He clicked at Jonas and the big horse stepped away with Mabuti following on her long lead. He offered his canteen and she moved out from his chest long enough to drink, then snuggled against him once more.

"I thought you were never coming back from Manila." Through the woolen army tunic she could feel his heartbeat against her cheek. He smelled sweaty, manly, wonderful. She took a deep breath of the remembered scent. "You took so long."

"I felt the same way. It was mighty hard to finally get all those wild old boys rounded up to make the trip back through the woods." The rumble of his voice held the deep timbre of a bass drum. She pressed closer to be nearer the reverberation of his words. A sudden thought chilled her. She stiffened within his embrace.

"Is everyone all right? Did they burn the village? Is my house still standing?"

She could feel the touch of his lips on her hair. "Oh, God, Sarah. I'm so glad you're all right. Some of the barrio people were hurt, but no one was killed. They only burned the Chinaman's store. They didn't kill him." She could feel his thighs tense. "Magdalena's in your nipa hut. It's okay."

He wasn't telling her everything. She could tell by the deepening of his voice.

"Was Bong hurt? Is Magdalena sick? Is she having the baby?"

He shifted slightly in the saddle and put his free arm across her lap. He cleared his throat. She knew that was exactly the way he always acted when he wasn't telling her everything.

"Markham, I want you to quit thinking of me as a little girl. You don't have to protect me." She shivered within the sanctuary of his arms. Maybe she really didn't want to know. Maybe he was right. Maybe she *was* still a child who needed, even wanted, to be kept in the dark about the sorrows and griefs of life. No.

Whatever had happened, she had to face it. "Tell me the whole story."

"Well, we're almost there. You'll find out everything when we get there, anyway." He lifted his free hand to embrace her. "Poor little Magdalena was hurt bad when I took off from there to search for you. They'd mistreated her . . . they. . . . Well, they raped her, Sarah. Several of the bastards took turns." He tightened his hold on her. "Bong's with her." He cleared his throat again.

"Oh, poor Bong," Sarah murmured her sympathetic concern.

"Yeah. He's sworn vengeance on all of the robbers." Markham's voice lowered to a whisper. "Poor Bong Bong. He howled like a mad dog when he learned what had happened to his wife. I wouldn't want to be in those old boy's shoes."

They made the last kilometer of the trip in silence, each wrapped in thought. The village main street was completely empty. She could see the school building standing unharmed at the other end of the line of houses. The school and all the rest of San Miguel lay shrouded in a pool of silence.

At the foot of the ladder that led up to her living quarters, Markham used one hand to help her slide down to stand beside Jonas. She lifted her chin and looked up at the soldier. He wasn't getting off.

"Aren't you coming in?"

"I'm just going to report that we found you and put these two horses into the stable, then I'll be right back." He stretched a hand toward her hair. "I missed you, little towhead, every moment I was gone. And Major Firestone has been out of his mind with worry about you since the *ladrones* rode off. I've got to let him know you're all right." He touched her hair, then tapped Jonas's hindquarters to move him and the phlegmatic Mabuti on toward the army parade grounds. "We need to talk, Sarah Collins. About us. You and I have things to say to each other," he whispered over his shoulder.

His whisper wafted down the silent street and she nodded agreement. True. They must talk. She had to find out how he felt, although she thought she knew. He was a career Army officer who had no need for a wife. She thought she knew that, but she had to find out for sure. They had to get things settled before she could ever make that long ocean voyage back to the United States and her parents' Iowa farm.

She glanced at the still-shuttered Suarez house, then just quickly across at the blackened shell of the Chinese merchant's burnt-out store, before she began the slow ascent into her own house. She would never understand how such a corrupt creature as Headman Suarez could ever have sired such a lovely young woman as Magdalena and such a pleasant lad as nine-year-old Sonny Suarez. Sonny was a joy in the classroom. Quick, well behaved. Totally different, both of them. Maybe Magdalena had learned from her mother, but Major Firestone had told her that Magdalena's mother had died when Sonny was born. Perhaps Magdalena had been more a mother than a sister to him. She shook her head in puzzlement. Another thing she'd have to ask Markham about.

Before she had gone up two more steps she heard Bong's long, piercing, grief-stricken cry. The cry sounded like the shriek of an animal in pain.

Dear Lord help them all.

That was surely the sound of a bereaved one's lamentation of mourning, even if she couldn't understand the language. She stopped, then continued her climb, the bamboo ladder a golden blur through her tears.

Magdalena was dead. Sarah just knew it. And what about the child?

Twenty-four

Blinking away sun blindness, Sarah stepped up on the ladder so her head and shoulders were in the room. Both hands on the top rung of the ladder, she surveyed the shadowed place she thought of as her parlor. Bong knelt at the foot of Magdalena's sleeping mat, his back to Sarah. A plump Filipino woman bent above Magdalena's still form, then lifted something and turned toward Sarah.

Luz! Although the woman seemed much rounder, fatter, than she had at the parish house, Sarah recognized the tiny maid from Manila. Luz held the small bundle toward her and smiled.

Sarah moved on up the ladder and Luz again offered the bundle.

"Baby gir', *mom*," the plump little maid explained.

"Oh, Luz. I'm so glad to see you." Sarah reached to embrace the young woman with one arm as she took the child with the other. She tried to clear tears from her eyes so she could see the baby without impediment. She unwrapped the swaddling wrap to search the babe's every perfection. Creamy skin, red and a bit puffy now, but the child would be beautiful, Sarah could tell. Huge deep blue eyes, a tiny, perfectly formed little body, hardly larger than her favorite cat back in Iowa when it had been just a kitten. Sarah counted the toes, then the fingers. Five of each. She pressed the day-old child against her breast. The child felt warm and wonderful. The wobbly head held in the palm of one of her hands seemed to hold the essence of life, helpless human life. Tenderness for the child almost swamped her.

"Bong?" The uniformed man rose and half bowed, then turned and disappeared down the ladder without a word. Of course, the baby wasn't his so it was understandable that he didn't feel about it as she did. The brown satin skin of his face had been set in hard lines that she hadn't seen there before.

"Magdalena?" Sarah moved to the mat and stared down at the body of the young woman. A pang of despairing guilt clenched in her chest. If only she had stayed with Magdalena instead of running to protect the schoolhouse, maybe she could have saved the young woman somehow.

"She die. Hurt too much." Luz crossed herself and muttered something Sarah didn't understand. "Bong go kill men now." Luz crossed herself again. "Rudolfo go, too."

"Bong and Rudolfo went to kill the *ladrones?*"

Luz nodded. Sarah nodded. She understood because she'd felt the same primitive anger she'd seen on Bong's face surge through herself when she was captive in the jungle. She surprised herself by thinking she would like to help him find the ones who had injured the lovely Magdalena and then help him kill them . . . starting with Magdalena's father.

She felt a twinge of fear. There had been a great many outlaws. Maybe as many as fifty or sixty. Or maybe not so many as that. Perhaps her fear had multiplied the numbers? She'd better tell Markham, anyway. One person, or even two people, wouldn't have a chance with that crowd of wicked men.

She held the baby closer and stared down at her dead friend. What had sweet Magdalena ever done to deserve the kind of life she'd been handed? Sarah tried to quell her own inner rage by pressing the baby even more firmly against herself. Suddenly, she loosened her grip and looked down at the little face. Anger wouldn't be good for the baby. She would have to be aware of things like that from now on. She'd always have to be aware of how her feelings might affect the baby. She smiled at the tiny girl, then at the little woman.

"But Luz, how did you get here?"

"Captain, he bring. I cook for soldier. Rudolfo help with soldiers' horse." Luz smiled broadly. "We married." She crossed herself. "In the church. Me and Rudolfo have to marry when Father find us together on my mat." She grinned, unashamed. "I plenty glad Father catch us. He make us marry on the very next day, he so upset."

"Oh. Congratulations." She let her gaze drop to Luz's rounded belly. Another baby? "Oh, Luz, I'm so glad." Sarah wanted to laugh with joy and cry with sorrow. A Filipino friend regained . . . a Filipino friend lost. She

PARADISE FOUND

handed the baby to Luz, then knelt at the side of Magdalena's mat. "How long has she been dead?" She looked up at Luz and reached again for the baby.

"Just now die." She kept the baby in her arms. "You want me take baby?"

"Oh, no." Sarah reached again for the child and Luz relinquished her. Sarah clutched the baby girl as closely as possible. "I want to hold her." She looked at the baby's face and then at the child's mother. She could see Magdalena's features and Robert's coloring. The child's thick brush of hair was a clear, golden brown. "She's such a beautiful girl baby."

"Maganda." Luz agreed.

"I will keep her myself." Sarah moved the child to the crook of her arm and rocked her. "She will be my baby now." She tipped the child as if to let her see the face of the dead Magdalena. "See, baby? Your mother. But I will be your mama now, little girl."

She let the waiting tears spill over. Magdalena had been more than a helper, more than a friend. And now she was gone. Sarah made a silent promise. *Magdalena, I won't let your baby forget you. I'll tell her all the wonderful things that I know about you. I will care for her as if she were my own.*

"I'll take her for my very own." She spoke aloud. She swiped one hand across her cheeks, then glanced up at Luz.

"You keep Filipino baby, *mom?*" Luz let the shock spread across her face. "You? Blondie Americana with brown baby?"

"She's not plain old *brown,* Luz. She's kind of a

beautiful *café con leche* color, don't you think?" She rocked the child again. "Anyway, even if she were purple I'd want to keep her." To herself she added, "As for Suarez, he may be her grandfather, but I'll never let that criminal anywhere near this child." She spoke aloud to the corpse of the young woman. "And that's a promise, Magdalena."

Sarah allowed Luz to hold the baby long enough for Sarah to get herself bathed and groomed and changed into a clean dress, then held out her arms to take the child again.

Almost before she'd finished buttoning the white buttons down the front of her dark-blue cotton dress, the American Army padre and the Filipino ladies of the town began to arrive to prepare the body and the lights and the food and the hundred other rituals of a village funeral. They all looked at Sarah from the corners of their eyes but no one tried to take the baby from her. They spoke with Luz and with each other and some practiced their words of English on Sarah.

"T'cher."

"Goo' morning."

"Blondie baby, blondie t'cher."

Sarah tried to be a good hostess, but she felt as if a crushing weight had lifted from her shoulders when she finally heard Markham's voice. He was speaking with the men who had gathered below before he climbed up into the house. She realized she could understand a word or two of the Tagalog he spoke. Wistfully, she recalled her resolve to learn the language of the people. Now it was too late. She would certainly have no use for Tagalog back in Iowa.

The baby in her arms cried out and stretched fitfully. The sound frightened Sarah. It forced her to think about the unthinkable. Could she take the baby back to Iowa? But more important at this moment was how she was going to feed the tiny orphan. She jiggled the infant and patted her back to try to soothe her. The air in the room thickened with the smoke from the incense and the myriad of candles. The smell of roasting meat drifted up from below.

One of the young village women who had been nursing her own baby gently placed her child on her lap, then lifted Magdalena's baby from Sarah's arms and put her bare breast to the hungry child's mouth. She smiled at Sarah as if to reassure her that she wasn't trying to steal the child. Sarah nodded understanding, steepled her hands and murmured thanks in Tagalog. *"Salamat Po."*

Sarah watched Markham pay his respects to the body laid out on the mat in the middle of the room, several candles standing lit at Magdalena's head and feet. He held his campaign hat across his heart, his head bowed. *He's thinking some of the things I've been thinking,* Sarah told herself. *He's blaming himself a little, probably. Both of us wanted Bong and Magdalena to be happy, but they never had a chance.*

He turned and searched the room with his eyes before he smiled at her. He slid through the praying, chatting crowd, nodding and speaking in Tagalog to the female mourners before he reached the corner where she sat on the dark wooden chair.

"Awful close in here with all these people and those candles, little lady." He fanned himself with his campaign hat. "It's not the custom for the men to stay inside with the body. Want to go outside where we can get a breath of air?" As Markham stood looking down at her, she could see the sadness written in his eyes.

"I'm afraid to leave the baby." She gestured to the young woman who sat nursing the child, her back against the side of Sarah's chair.

Markham spoke to the nursing woman. She smiled, nodded and spoke a few words.

"She'll put the baby in on your bed and have one of the older girls sit with her while it sleeps. You'll see. Everything will work out all right. Come on. We need to talk."

Sarah stood and felt pain radiate through every part of her body. She held on to the arm of the chair to help herself rise.

"Have you given the baby a name?" he asked, helping her toward the ladder. "You need to stretch to get all those kinks out."

"No name, no father, no mother. Poor little girl." She went down first and waited for him at the bottom. "I'm going to keep her." She spoke the words without looking at him, then let her gaze drift up to see if she could read his thoughts.

Markham grinned down at her. "I sorta figured that

out, Miss Schoolmarm. I reckon you realize that taking on a child is going to be a whole lot of trouble?"

"It's my duty," she said and set her lips. He would never want a woman with a baby, a baby that wasn't even her own. But someone had to raise Magdalena's child.

The little girl was now her responsibility, just as Magdalena had been her responsibility . . . responsibility she had not lived up to. She wouldn't make the same mistake twice. Caring for the child would be the one thing she could do to make up to Magdalena leaving her alone to be ravished by her countrymen.

"Well, why not keep the baby for your own?" Markham questioned as they walked through the crowd of *tuba*-drinking men. "It could be done." Markham nodded to the men, but he kept them both moving through the crowd. He took Sarah's hand when they had walked far enough away from the cluster of male mourners and slowed their pace down the sunlit street. "You can do it if that's really what you want to do."

"I do want her."

"It would be a lot easier for you to take care of the baby here in the Philippines than if we were all back in America." He tipped his campaign hat further over his eyes and looked down at Sarah. Sunshine glinted on her clean hair. The scratches and bruises that had been so dark against her skin this morning were hardly noticeable now.

"Do you think so?"

He nodded. "Taking in someone else's child is a pretty common custom in Filipino families." He squeezed her hand gently. "Kinda like us Indians. Those families who have no children can ask for, and get, a child from an aunt, or a sister or a friend." He laughed. "Sometimes a person can get children even if he or she didn't ask for one . . . especially if there is a little bit of money or a big house, or a good job or something." *I don't want to scare her,* he told himself, *but she's going to have to face what's going to be required of her as the baby's mother. I feel the same kind of responsibility she must be feeling. I owe Bong so much . . . my life, several times over. But he wouldn't want this baby, would he? Not Robert Zumwalt's baby. No.*

He stopped and turned her to face him.

"Are you sure you want to take on the task of mamahood?" Her clear blue eyes looked earnestly into his own. She nodded "Yes." God. He couldn't think straight. This little farm girl had him in the palm of her hand. She was so good, so. . . . He looked down at the rounded tops of her breasts covered by the virginal blue cotton gown and again forgot what he had been thinking. *The old tropical fever must be rising through my brain,* he told himself.

"I wouldn't want anyone else to take over raising her. After all, Robert was her father. Doesn't that make me the logical person to care for her?" Her clean hair somehow held the scent of sandlewood. "Besides . . ." Her cheeks reddened a little. "I want her. She is such a darling. She looks like Magdalena."

She'd never shirk from what she thought of as her responsibility, but how am I going to feel about taking on two little women instead of just this one? His hand seemed to move of its own volition, to smooth her sun-gilded hair. *And how's the Army going to feel about me taking on a Filipino orphan as a daughter? I'd better give this whole situation some thought before I blurt out anything about love or marriage. That doesn't mean I can't kiss her once more, though. Does it?* He bent to brush his lips against hers in the lightest of caresses. When he straightened, her hand raised, and her fingers touched her own lips as if in a question. Her eyes seemed troubled.

"I have been wanting to talk to you, Markham." Her hand dropped. "Out in the jungle while I had more than enough time to consider . . ."

He hardly heard her words he was so intent on tasting her mouth again. He bent and captured her lips, drawing her sweetness to himself. He wanted to groan with longing. He could feel himself harden, and he drew her strongly against him so that she could feel his hunger. She didn't pull away. His heart thudded in his chest. She had raised to her tiptoes as she wrapped her arms around him so she could hold herself against his manhood as closely as possible.

What was he doing?

He loved her.

But did he want to marry her? Father someone else's child?

He'd have to think about that.

Shouts and hoofbeats from the other end of the street broke into their private moment. Creaking leather and jangling metal fittings added to the din. Down-at-the-mouth *ladrones,* mounted on horses, a number of riderless horses and mules, and the cordon of U.S. soldiers moved slowly down the hillside trail. The village headman rode with the Army cadre, as if he had been part of the round-up mission to bring in the outlaws.

All up and down the street, village residents hung out their windows or scampered down their stairways to see what was happening.

As the crowd of men neared them, Markham raised his hand to stop their forward movement. He returned the salute of the sergeant in charge.

"Is this all of them, Sarge?"

"Yes, sir, Major. All except the seven still at the campsite."

Markham took two deliberate steps to glare up at the village headman. "Off that horse, Suarez." The man visibly paled and fell, more than slid, off the back of the unsaddled animal onto the dusty street. He held onto the reins and the other trappings of the horse as if he needed help standing. Markham gestured toward him.

"Sarah, you want this guy put in the stockade with the rest of these snakes? Next week someone can

PARADISE FOUND

take him on up to Manila to appear before the adjutant general."

Sarah stared silently at the frightened little man. Why had she been so afraid of a weasel like him?

"Sarah?"

She shook her head.

"No, I don't want him in jail, but I don't want him anywhere near me or the baby. I don't think he should be anywhere near Sonny, either."

"Baby my grandchild. Mine," Suarez muttered. "Sonny Boy my child."

Sarah touched the sleeve of Markham's tunic. She whispered her question. "Can we do this without going before a judge or anything official?"

"We sure can." He nodded. "We're occupying this country and the Army is the law. Judge and jury, too, if necessary."

"Then I don't want him anywhere around me or the children."

"Hit the trail, Suarez. You're no longer welcome here in San Miguel."

"But, sir. I am village headman."

"Not anymore, you're not. You're just a bum."

Markham turned his back to the man and started toward Sarah.

Sarah saw the quick movement of the Filipino man's hand and she screamed a warning.

"Markham. He's got a knife!"

Markham whirled, and before the knife could leave the man's hand, Markham's fist landed squarely on his chin, lifting the former headman's feet from the street and laying him out in the sand.

Markham looked down and addressed himself to the cringing man. "Don't even go near the place that used to be your house, Suarez. The Army has just confiscated your property and given it to the Chinaman so he can open a new store." He glanced across at Sarah. "Your personal belongings will be given to your son and granddaughter. We'll find a home for Sonny Boy. And you . . . you're lucky you still have your life." He jerked the man to his feet with one hand. "Search him, Sergeant Bustos, and keep any weapons you find, then send him on his way."

As the sergeant did his duty, Markham continued. "Don't show your face in this barrio again or you're a prisoner. You understand, Suarez?"

A Filipino soldier shouted the translation of Markham's sentencing for the benefit of the villagers. Applause and cheers rose on both sides. The defeated man walked slowly away from the road and disappeared into the jungle. Markham made an almost imperceptible slashing motion across his neck to the sergeant of the Filipino squad. Immediately, Bustos left his horse and raced to follow the deposed headman.

"Not very popular, was he?" Markham took her hand and looked down into her face.

"What will he do?"

"I don't give a damn . . . and neither should you. Sergeant Bustos will take care of everything, Filipino to Filipino." Markham smiled down at Sarah. "The sergeant will see to it that he doesn't hang around any-

PARADISE FOUND

where near the village. He probably has money stashed away somewhere, or cronies in Manila. He'll be all right. He'll be crawling on his belly for a while, which is the way it should be."

Sarah sighed. Everything was so rough, so violent, out here. Better some unpleasantness for Suarez, though, than letting that little weasel have her baby. She'd do anything to keep the baby safe.

"You gotta toughen up that soft heart of yours, Teacher," His eyes were soft with amber lights. "Or else you might really get hurt." His deep voice was almost a caress.

Only by you, she answered inwardly.

He strode to the American sergeant to give further orders. As the two army men talked, Sarah slipped toward the line of Filipino soldiers where Rudolfo sat grinning a greeting.

"Oh, Rudolfo. I'm so glad you and Luz decided to come with Major Nash. I wanted so much to see you two again."

"We wish to see you, too, *mom.* Luz and me marry." His cheeks reddened. "Soon we get baby."

She congratulated Rudolfo enthusiastically, then looked at the group of Filipino soldiers who sat their horses near him. "I thought you went with Bong. Where is he?"

"He fight. They *pito* men left for him to fix up."

Pito? That word meant 'seven,' didn't it?

"You mean he's in the jungle fighting with seven men?"

"Yes, *mom*. One at the time. What the *caballeros* from Spain call *duelo. Con bolo.*"

"*Duelo?* He's fighting a duel with each of the seven robbers left behind? He's fighting them with machetes?"

"Yes, *mom*."

"Markham." She felt as if her voice were lost under the noise of the restless animals. "Markham!" This time he turned his head to look at her.

"Bong may be in trouble. Rudolfo says he is dueling with seven of the outlaws."

Markham nodded and gave a grim chuckle.

"Sarge told me. It isn't Bong that's in trouble. It's those bastards that attacked Magdalena who are going to be sorry they ever came into this town." He saluted the sergeant once more and gestured to the men to carry on. The cortege moved on toward the army stockade. "Sarah child, by the time old Bong Bong Manawe is through with those misbegotten misfits, they'll be little more than bloody ribbons."

"But, Markham, one against *seven?* I'm so scared for him."

"Oh, they left a couple of troopers behind to corral the bystanders as he works each one over. He had my permission to take them on."

"But aren't you even concerned?"

"Yeah." Markham shrugged. "I don't want him to *kill* all of them, but since I'm not up there to quell him, who's to say what will happen to those seven reptiles?"

"I mean concern for Bong." Sarah shook loose from

his touch. She couldn't believe he was laughing. It was just like the night he and Bong had chased the men from the campsite.

"Hey, when a machete-wielding native gets the blood lust and decimates the population with his bolo knife, they call it 'running amuck.' I think the term was coined right here in the P.I." He placed his arm around her shoulders and coaxed her into the shadow at the side of the street.

"And girl, if I ever saw blood lust it was surely riding old Bong when he asked permission to take those culprits on, personally." He squeezed her shoulders in reassurance. "If you're gonna worry about anyone, worry about the bad guys. They're probably really hurting right about now. I'm pretty sure old Bong is running amuck at this very minute."

Sarah couldn't control her shudder. Some of the things that happened here made safe Iowa look so secure, so civilized, so . . . she almost didn't let herself finish the thought . . . so dull.

Twenty-five

Should she tell Markham she thought she was in love with him? Or should she do the ladylike thing and keep silent? She knew her mother and Miss Arnold would most certainly opt for the silence. She could almost hear them speaking in unison. "It's a man's place to do the asking, Sarah dear."

He drew her arm through his and she thought the two of them were just wandering aimlessly through the cleared area under the huge trees in back of the army encampment. At least to her it seemed they were walking merely for the sake of a need for privacy. "There are no secrets in the Philippines," Markham had told her.

Anywhere in the village that they might show themselves they could be sure that people would be trying to talk to them and crowds of children would follow them as well. She was surprised that in moments she could see that their walk seemed to have a definite goal.

Markham wanted to know everything that had happened on her frightening night as Suarez's prisoner and she wanted to know about Manila and the priests and about Luz and Rudolfo. They also needed to make plans for the baby and for Sonny Boy Suarez, who was being cared for by the woman who had worked for the Suarez family for years. They talked of everything . . . everything except the one thing that was most important to each of them.

Markham hesitated a bit when he gave her Rudolfo's version of the forced marriage to Luz because the priest had walked in on them while the two of them were making love on her mat. She could tell he hadn't wanted to tell her straight out what the two were doing, but Sarah laughed and told him that Luz had already given her every detail.

"Rudolfo said that he was going to marry her anyway." Markham chuckled. "Luz was already pregnant, but Rudolfo just didn't like the idea of some Spanish aristocrat telling him what to do and when to do it." Sarah loved the humor of the pictures Markham's words painted and she told him so, but her next question stopped his laughter.

"While you were in Manila did you go to the graveyard?"

He gave her a look of disgust.

"Are you still harping on old Robert Zumwalt? Why the hell would I want to go to that bastard's grave?"

She shook her hand from his arm. Stiff-lipped, she refrained from looking at him when she spoke.

"I did, after all, marry the man, Major Nash."

"Major Nash now, is it?" He smiled at her resolute stance. "Come on, Mrs. Sarah Collins Zumwalt. I want to show you something." He again took her hand and he led her through the heavily forested flatland. With the other hand he held a bolo to slash at the intruding vines and plants. Then he coaxed her up a small hill to an open space where he gestured toward a low cliff.

Sarah stared. She drew in her breath, stunned.

"Oh, Markham. It's beautiful. I didn't know there was a waterfall back here. I can't believe it. There are orchids everywhere." Her eyes sought his. His brown eyes glowed at her wonder. "This is really paradise." She smiled at him. "Sometimes you're so angry about Robert that I think you've forgotten he was a human being, too." Her look almost forgave him his impolite attack on the dead man.

"I hate to admit it, but I guess part of my anger is just old-fashioned jealousy." Markham knelt on a wide, flat rock upholstered with soft moss. He patted the space beside him.

"Sit here with me. I've never seen anyone else back here, so I always think of it as my private place. It's almost as pretty as the territory was when I was a kid living outdoors."

"Certainly more beautiful than Iowa." She smiled and completely forgave him his indiscreet joke about Robert. "Although Iowa has its own type of beauty, understand . . . just not so lush as all this." She gestured with both hands at the flowering jungle scene.

For a few moments they sat silently, drinking in the clear elegance of the falling waters, the circle of blue sky above. Pale pink, deep fuschia, every shade of purple, and millions of trumpet-shaped white flowers streaked with gold hung against the different shades of green that grew on every side of the tiny pool below the fall. Up above the falls on the highest side of the cliff a huge flame tree blossomed crimson fire against the pale sky. Sarah could hear birds sing and sometimes she could hear small animals darting through the underbrush at each side of the crystalline curtain of water.

Markham leaned back on one elbow.

"You like it?"

"It's overwhelming, but I love it. Thank you for bringing me here. It's so comfortable. So cool. It even smells cool. It's so quiet. It's almost like a church but better than a church." She let her glance fall to her lap. "It is a thousand times better than anything I've ever seen." She put her hand on his. "Markham, I needed something like this after all the horrid things I've seen recently."

He removed his hat and placed it to the side, then he took off his uniform tunic and rolled it into a bundle.

"Lie back on this. Since we're in an open space here, we can see the Filipino sky."

Sarah did as she was asked. An unusual tropical languor stole across her limbs. She realized she was drawing in a variety of subtle fragrances with every breath: sometimes sweet, sometimes spicy. For the first time in two days she relaxed. The frightening hours among the *ladrones,* the even worse time alone with Suarez, Magdalena's death. . . . All those things that were mad or frightening were truly over. She was with Markham. She was safe.

"Markham . . . may I ask you something?"

"What do you want to know?"

She had to smile inwardly when his expression became wary. What was he expecting her to say? She murmured her question.

"What was that wonderful yeasty, fresh-bread smell in the streets in Manila?"

"You're asking me that *now?*" His face became a map of surprise.

"Yes. The Philippine Islands are such a study in contrasts, including all the odors. Everything here smells really wonderful or really awful."

"I guess it was the *copra.*"

She rolled over to face him and smiled.

"I know you think I ask too many questions, but what is *copra?*"

"Dried coconut meat . . . and I don't think you ask too many questions. I just wonder at the subjects of the questions sometimes." He turned to face her. "I wonder what's going on under that little blond thatch, because usually the question you've just asked has nothing at all to do with the place we're in, or what we were talking about or anything that has happened to you at all." He touched her nose with his finger. "It's your mental processes that puzzle me."

She couldn't keep looking into those masculine brown eyes that sparkled so close to hers. They made her feel strange. Fidgety. As if they could see straight inside her head. But she couldn't let him see into her heart. She turned onto her back again. When she turned away, he stood up.

"Want to go in?"

She saw that he was slipping off his boots and stockings. When he reached forward to unbutton his khaki woolen trousers, Sarah sat up.

"What are you doing?"

"I like to swim here when the heat gets to me. Want to go in?"

"Certainly not."

"Suit yourself." He raked off his underwear and stood at the edge of the rock for a moment, his back toward her. Sarah gasped and stared.

He raised his arms. She could see his powerful back muscles ripple beneath his darkly creamy satin skin. Hours in the sun had covered his face and his neck and his lower arms with an even darker silk. She wanted to look away, but she couldn't. Tall, strong bones, every inch of him perfect. He was gorgeous! When he bent and suddenly surged forward like a knife cutting the water, she gasped aloud. She had seen every part of him. *Every part!*

She leaned back, closed her eyes and smiled to herself. It was only a glimpse, but that was fair, wasn't it? Of course, that was only fair. He had seen every part of her when they were on the trail, hadn't he?

Perhaps she dozed or maybe she kept her eyes closed for only a moment. Time lost its meaning in this wildly beautiful place.

The stream of water splashed across her face brought her fully awake. She turned her head to look into the army man's smiling brown eyes. He held the edge of the rock ledge with one hand and dashed more water across her face with the other.

"Hey, Teacher. Come on in. The water's fine."

"No thank you. I've just had my bath, sir, but I'm glad to see that you're enjoying yours. What I want to do is just lie here with my eyes closed and be lazy."

He sprinkled a few more drops of water on her.

"Better stop that." She spoke without opening her eyes.

"I will . . . if you'll move just five inches to your right."

"I'll fall in."

"No, you won't. You'll be right at the edge. Close enough for me to kiss."

Oh. Yes. Good. She wanted another kiss. Or something. Maybe she could get up enough nerve to tell him she was going back to Iowa . . . unless he could persuade her to do otherwise?

She edged closer to him, but she couldn't look directly at him. He laid his hand across her waist and bent his head to touch his wet cheek to hers.

"See how cool you'd be if you were in the water?"

"Yes. It's tempting, Markham, but I think one of us has to observe the proprieties, don't you?" She felt her face flush even warmer from the touch of his chill skin against her own. Now. Better tell him now.

"I've been thinking about . . ." Her declaration was cut off when his moist lips covered hers. His mouth

PARADISE FOUND

felt cool and hot at the same time, the lips satin cool, his tongue heated. His tongue traced her lips and then darted inside her mouth to challenge her tongue. She opened just a bit. If only she could get a little closer to him. When she turned toward him, he groaned with desire.

His hand moved from her waistline, slowly, excruciatingly slowly, to run his palm under one breast. Both breasts hardened to a point. She could feel it. Both were hungry for his touch. His fingers and his thumb twined around one uncorseted nipple, then moved across to the other. Sarah held her breath. She'd needed that so badly. But it still wasn't enough.

Their kiss went on for long, searching moments. His mouth tasted sweet, spicy, masculine. He tasted like Markham. He tasted like love.

This. This was what she wanted. This and more. This joining was what she could never hope for in a life spent in Iowa. This longing, this answering to longing, filled her whole being. But it wasn't enough. Why not go ahead? Let whatever was to happen, happen.

Don't hold back, something inside her whispered. *Love the man. Let him love you. He desires you now, even if he can't commit to you forever. At least you'll have this one time to remember.*

"Come up here, Markham. Come lie beside me." Her voice was so low, it carried only to the ear of the man whom she wanted. The man who wanted her.

Markham shivered in the water. She was calling him to lie beside her on the stone ledge.

"Are you sure, Sarah darling? Really sure? If I come

up there now I may reach the point of no return." He fluttered a kiss across her throat, down her chest, to her cloth-covered breast. She drew a deep, shuddering breath. He could hear her heart with his lips.

"Markham. Please." The whispered plea propelled him to the two stones he'd always used as his ladder from the pool. His body was growing. He lifted himself to stand above her.

"Look at me, now, Sarah."

Water beaded his taut skin and sparkled against the sun. She caught her breath. He was huge. His skin was wet tan satin, diamond drops decorated the black hair that wreathed the tan, then lavender, then deeper red of his engorgement. His manhood stood out proudly from his body. Like . . . something like the stallion Jonas and yet different from him and from all the mating farm animals she'd ever seen.

She touched the mossy space beside her.

"I'm sure."

He knelt and lifted her to sit facing him.

"If I hold you in my arms there will be no turning back."

She nodded understanding. Acceptance. Anticipation. She raised her face for his kiss and twined her arms about his neck.

"I love you, Markham."

That was more than he could stand. He pulled her into his arms and lowered her to the stone bed. He groaned against her neck then kissed her again. With one hand he lifted the damp skirt of her dress and her petticoat. She wore nothing under the heavy ruffled petticoat. He glimpsed a golden tangle of curly hair.

His hands fumbled with the tiny pearl buttons that went from the collar to below the waist of the blue cotton dress.

"Let's get you out of this thing. I want to see you, all of you." He tore the buttons loose and lifted the crumpled mass of cotton cloth over her head as if she were a present he couldn't wait to unwrap.

She was all white and rose and golden curves. She clung to him. Her mouth moved against his. She was saying something, but he couldn't hear because his pulse pounded so loudly in his own ears. He had to force himself to hold back to keep from plunging his hardness into her.

Slow down, boy, he told himself. *Slow way, way down.*

She felt no shame, no worry that she was yielding her virginity to this man. This was what she wanted. Her hands pulled him onto her even as he moved atop her. Only Markham Nash could make her complete. She knew that. She'd never love anyone but him. This was what she was meant to do. Long years from now, back in Iowa, she'd have at least this one time to remember.

She let her hand smooth the line of his back. He raised his head as if he were listening to something far away, his eyes unfocused, his eyelids heavy.

"Sweet Sarah," he breathed as he again lowered his

head for another long kiss. Her hands moved in circles on the muscles in his broad shoulders. He murmured something else, but she couldn't quite hear. Had he said, "I love you?"

She stiffened at first as if to reject him, then felt fright tremble through him. She forced herself to relax. This *was* what she wanted, wasn't it? She was feeling things she'd never felt before, imagining things she'd never imagined before, learning what she'd never have again. The heat between them increased with each heartbeat. She felt something deep within her fold and tremble and search for the man.

She tugged him delicately to rest between her legs. She'd instinctively parted them for him. It was almost as if she could not bear another moment without him inside her. She was not afraid, she reminded herself. She'd banished her uncertainty. She had to feel this man inside her before she could be whole. She had to love him with her whole body.

He paused and gave her a tender look.

"It might hurt just a little, darling girl. Are you still sure?"

"Yes." She didn't have to think about her answer. This was Markham Nash, the man she loved. This was perhaps the only, only chance she'd have in her whole life to feel what love was really like. "I want you inside me."

His groan was one of male surrender. He rose and eased himself slowly, slowly, into the honey of her being. The small barrier was swept aside in a few seconds of pain that she forgot in the midst of the shimmering love that he brought with it. They were a perfect fit, tightly entwined in the way that real lovers were meant to be. The way she'd known *they* would be.

Markham moved easily, slowly, letting her desire build around him. He had to keep a tight rein on himself the way he kept a rein on Jonas when the stallion wanted to run.

Torture. Delicious torture. He moved in slow rhythm within her and echoed the same movements in the kiss he gave her.

Her hands kneaded his back and made hot, sweet brands upon his skin. He looked at her closed eyes and her rapt expression. She, too, was rushing toward the goal that love held before them. He could see it in her face.

So be it.

He began deepening his thrusts. Her eyes opened wide with the first shock of pleasure and he could hold back no more. He had to quicken his movement to meet her at the top of her long, shattering climax. He, too, lost himself in her velvety depths, let her inner contractions caress him to draw every drop of love from him.

For long moments they lay still, sharing the last tiny inner flarings of their lovemaking. He was still atop her when she gave a small scream and pushed him off. She sat up, frowned, then desperately scrambled to grasp for her dress and petticoat.

"What's wrong, Sarah?"

She didn't answer, just shook her head and slipped the garments over her body and fumbled with the endless buttoning and tying. Tears formed in the corners of her eyes.

"Did I hurt you, darling?"

She shook her head and pointed upward toward the rock cliff above them without turning her face in that direction. He glanced up.

Three young Filipino faces smiled down at them.

One of the three little girls called, "Goo' morning, T'cher."

Twenty-six

"Oh, Markham, I wanted to talk to you about staying on here in San Miguel or about leaving . . . about going home. Now there's no question. I'll have to leave." Sarah spoke with her head bent, her gaze toward the ground. "So I suppose there is nothing more to discuss."

Her mind was in a perfect torment. If he didn't marry her now, the gossip would rage all around her in the barrio. That was sure, and some of the talk might, probably would, make it back to the Central Educational Office of the school board in Manila. *Or even to her parents in Iowa!* But she couldn't mention any of her fears to him. She couldn't blackmail him into loving her. He had to want her freely or she had to leave. There was no other way. And she had no time now. She must leave or allow herself to be disgraced by the talk.

"Come on, Sarah. We don't have to run just because a couple of your students spied on us." He stopped and faced her in the road. "I've told you before, girl, there aren't any secrets in the Philippines." He tapped her chin lightly with his knuckles. "These children who live in one-room huts with several generations of family often see and hear much, much more than American children ever do." She continued to walk. "Those little ones weren't shocked or surprised. They've seen it or heard it all before." When she wouldn't stop, he tugged at her arm. "Slow down. Let's talk."

"I have to get home." Still, she couldn't bring herself to look at him. She kept up her hurried pace. "I shouldn't have stayed away from the baby so long, anyway."

"Come on, Sarah. I can't talk to you when you're loping along with your head hanging down like a broken-spirited mare. Look at me. What's all this about going home? I assume you mean home to Iowa?"

"Listen, Markham, I can't talk with you now." She sent a meaningful glance at the interested crowd of Filipino men and boys who filled the space below her house and the street outside. "We'll talk later when we can have some privacy." She put her hand on the stair that led up to her house. The fermented smell of *tuba* was strong on the air. "I have to think. I've got to make plans for me and for the baby. I expect I'd better start making plans for Sonny Boy, as well." She looked into his eyes. A quiver of desire ran through her. He'd been so wonderful at the pool. Oh, Lord, she wanted him again. Had she turned into a completely wanton woman?

She turned her head away from the compelling brown eyes. If she looked at him too deeply or too long he would be able to read her heart. The offer had to come from him. It had to come freely without coercion. She lowered her gaze to the bamboo ladder where her hand rested. "I'll see you at Magdalena's funeral in the morning." Before he could say anything further, she had started her climb.

"I'll see you in the morning." Markham muttered. Hell, he'd forgotten to tell her about the slates and slate pencils he'd brought from town. He'd tell her in the morning.

He nodded again at the gathered men. When they offered him *tuba* he refused as politely as he could. The smell of the homebrewed drink made his stomach roil just a bit. He turned away from her nipa hut and trudged toward the army post compound, head down, like a pony whose spirit has been whipped out of him. He walked the same way he had accused her of walking.

She's right, he told himself. *She should go back home to Iowa.* That was the best place for a respectable young woman like her. He'd taken her virginity, the one physical quality prized above all others by both women and men. She'd done it for *him.* He lifted his head then lowered it again. By God, she was sweetness itself. She was like a fine wine that had invaded his blood and his mind and caused him to do and say some very strange things. Pray God he hadn't given her a baby.

Quick thoughts about the way she'd looked at the pool, of the way she'd felt in his arms, of the way he'd loved her etched themselves in his brain. He felt desire rising and he tried to squelch the feeling.

Put that hot blood on ice, he advised himself. *The girl is doing the right thing. She knows what she wants. Even if I do love her I just have to put my own feelings aside for a moment and think about what's best for her. So . . . Iowa it is.* He lifted his head and straightened his shoulders. *To really love a woman is to want what's best for her.*

He pulled out one of the new khaki-colored handkerchiefs from his back pocket and swiped it across his forehead. Sweating and chills. Bones aching a trifle. Just like last night. Probably a touch of the old fever coming on.

Sarah spoke and nodded at the chatting and praying women who still filled her living room. With a nod of gratitude she lifted the baby from the young Filipina mother's arms and carried the child to the curtained-off bedroom. She'd have to have Markham try to make arrangements with this young woman. Maybe she could be a wet nurse for the child until Sarah could figure out something else.

What did women do back in America when a baby's mother had no milk? Cow's milk? No. Goat's milk. She'd heard about that somehow. How soon before babies began to eat real food? Luz would know.

The little girl slept soundly beside her, obviously well satisfied with the substitute mother's milk. Sarah let her hand feather across one of the tiny palms and it closed about her finger. The motion made her feel as if the child had closed a hand around her heart. She wanted desperately to lift the baby and clutch it to her, but she let the child sleep on, undisturbed.

She needed to start making all the necessary arrangements for leaving. Markham would help. Her breath caught at the thought of his name. If he didn't want to marry her, and it was clear that he didn't, then there was nothing else she could do. She had to go home. The disgrace and all the laughing gossip would be more than she could live with, and she didn't want the baby to have to live with shame, either. She need only pray that she herself was not now with child. Even if she were, she could handle that. She could take care of everything if only she were back safe in Iowa.

She looked down at the sleeping face. What would her parents think of this half-Filipino baby? The farm people who were their neighbors? Miss Arnold? She lifted her chin and straightened her spine as if she were standing in the aisle of the Methodist church back home. Of course, they'd all love the pretty little thing. She could make them love her. She was sure of that. Robert's parents might be really happy to welcome a granddaughter to take the place of their lost son. She looked at the baby more carefully. No. They probably wouldn't want to hear about Magdalena and Robert, so they probably wouldn't love the baby, her pretty little Dionisia.

She smiled at the remembrance of the solemn meeting with all the little girls at her school. It had been a wonderful spelling lesson for them, choosing a name for a baby girl. The boys were to choose a boy's name this very week. Oh, the boys would be so disappointed. They'd badly wanted to welcome another little man into their midst. Now they'd have to learn to spell a girl's name instead.

After long deliberation and much listing and crossing out in the soft earth they'd been using as a slate, and finally voting, the girls had chosen the name Dionisia, and Sarah had agreed. It was a pretty name. She'd certainly call her Dionisia. Magdalena would approve of that choice, she knew. Dionisia Magdalena Zumwalt. Yes. She could call her Joanie or maybe Maggie. The name would be both Filipino and American, just as the baby was.

"What am I going to do about you, wee little Joanie?" she whispered, then she, too, fell into an uneasy sleep with the sounds of the funeral litany and the droning mourning songs from the next room as background for her dreams.

Twenty-seven

The first two letters of "Mess" and the last two letters of "Hall," showed on each side of the painted cross which had been hung temporarily above the door on the outside of the wooden army building. This was the place she had been invited to that first night after she and Bong and Markham had ridden into the village. The dining tables had been moved back and the benches had been placed in rows at the front.

Sarah entered and walked to a bench near the front. She felt as if every single person in the room were looking at her and commenting to his or her neighbor. *"There's the woman, the teacher, who was making love with the major in the jungle yesterday."* Sarah pressed her lips together, lifted her chin and straightened her spine. She would forget all that for now. Today she would think only of Magdalena.

The service for Magdalena began almost as if they had been waiting for her. It wasn't at all like the funeral services Sarah had been to back home. She stood and knelt when the others did but she felt as if she weren't really in a church. She was somewhere in a floating world.

Magdalena's body was in the mahogany box at the front. She knew that. And the Army padre was a preacher. She knew that, too, but she felt as if she were dreaming and the dream was running much too long. She'd wake up soon and Magdalena would be humming as she boiled the rice and Sarah would call down to her as she found herself getting ready to go to school. In a few minutes Markham would ride by and shout greetings. Bong would certainly walk somewhere near where Magdalena was working to say something very quietly in Tagalog to the young woman. Sarah wanted it to be that way again. She wanted her morning to be just as it had been three days before. She wanted her life to be just as it was before the robbers came, before everything had changed.

The baby, her Dionisia, was the only good thing that had come out of all of this. Leaving her at Maria's house had bothered Sarah, but she couldn't expect the young mother to desert her own husband and family to come and feed Dionisia every few hours. She'd done what she had to do. She'd left the baby with Maria on the understanding that she would visit frequently since she wanted the baby to know her.

She felt frantic about having to do such a thing, but she didn't know what else to do. Markham could give her some advice. He always gave her good advice. He could help her decide what to do about the baby. She tried to find Markham in the crowd without making her search obvious, but she couldn't see him. He was the tallest man in the village. If he were in the room she would be able to see him for certain.

He hadn't come!

He didn't want to see her again!

Surely he'd come to the graveyard. Oh, yes. The graveyard. He had probably had to work this morning, but he'd be at the gravesite later. Sarah knelt as the rest of the mourners did, then looked at the back of the room when everyone rose. There was Bong. She just knew that Markham would come to show Corporal Bong Bong Manawe respect, if nothing else. She was sure that he'd be there when they actually buried Magdalena.

When the boys' choir stood to sing, the sadness she'd been holding inside herself seemed to burst through the inner dam she'd built. Sarah tried to stop the tears, but she couldn't. She sobbed for Magdalena, for Bong, for Dionisia, for herself, and for all the dreams and plans that had gone awry for everyone. Nothing would ever be the same again.

Luz and Rudolfo came to walk with her when the funeral was over.

"You cry too much, *mom*. We walk with you."

"Luz, what was that beautiful song the boys sang at the end?" Sarah asked.

"Called 'Panis Angelicus,' *mom*," Luz answered. "It say Magdalena go to sleep with the angels."

"So beautiful," Sarah murmured, and a few more tears fell before she could lift her chin and stand tall to ready herself to face all the rest of the mourners at the gravesite.

Bong moved in behind them. His voice was hoarse with emotion as he spoke to Sarah.

"Magdalena, she love you, *mom*. She say we need respect you. You good blondie American woman."

"Oh, Bong. I'm so sorry. If I had just stayed at home maybe I could have protected Magdalena somehow."

"No, *mom*. You stay in house they just do same thing to you." He walked in silence for a moment. "You put your heart at rest, *mom*. I already pay off the men who do this thing, *mom*."

Sarah shuddered just a little at the darkling tone of his voice before she nodded understanding. From the corner of her eye, she saw Luz cross herself repeatedly. Rudolfo gave a short grunt of laughter. Bong was telling her in his own way about his duels with the seven robbers who had been singled out for him. Sarah kept her mouth shut. She didn't dare ask him what had happened to the seven evil men. Best change the subject, she thought.

"I named the baby Dionisia Magdalena." She turned back to look at his solemn face. "Markham told me you and Magdalena had married. That means you can keep her baby if you want to, I suppose. But if you'll allow me to do so, I'd love to keep Magdalena's little girl, Bong. Is that all right with you?"

"Yes, *mom*. Magdalena would want that. I want, too. I don't have any place for a baby."

They were silent for the rest of the short walk. At the gravesite Sarah searched the crowd for the tall officer. She did not see him.

Of course. He was staying away because of her, because he didn't want to see her again. That was it, wasn't it? Or maybe it was only because he had had the duty? Colonel Firestone had attended the funeral, hadn't he? So Markham's absence from the funeral could mean that he'd had to stay behind to attend to army business, couldn't it? She knew Bong wouldn't volunteer the information. She took a deep breath. It was a blow to her pride that she was the one inquiring about him, but it couldn't be helped.

She would have to ask.

"Bong, where is the major? I can't believe he didn't come to Magdalena's funeral."

"Oh, *mom,* I was going to tell you. Major pretty sick. He right now in the infirmary. He not able to come today. Can't walk around. Got the fever plenty bad."

Twenty-eight

Sarah's heart stopped.

"Fever?" Her voice quavered the horrid word.

"Yes, *mom*. Major he sick like a dog, he say."

Sarah stared unseeingly at the Army padre who still spoke words above Magdalena's grave. She took a deep breath of the sweetly fragrant *ilang-ilang* flowers that lay on the polished wooden coffin. Robert had died. Magdalena was dead. And now Markham was going to die. She was sure of it.

She was suddenly hurled backward to the day she'd arrived in Manila, to her strange wedding to Robert. Again it was as if she could hear the Army doctor saying, "I'm sorry, Mrs. Zumwalt, but there's nothing you can do. He probably won't last the day."

"NO!" The word exploded from between Sarah's lips causing the others at the grave to turn and stare. She compressed her lips and straightened her spine. She would have Bong take her directly to the infirmary the instant the funeral was finished.

She bowed her head with the others as the priest prayed in Latin. Maybe she could have saved Robert

Maybe she just hadn't tried hard enough. Most of her guilt lay in the fact that she'd felt relieved she would never have to live with Robert Zumwalt. Should one feel relieved . . . *pleased* that one's husband was dead? Perhaps she hadn't tried hard enough to help Robert stay alive. If she hurried, maybe she could still do something to save Markham's life. She couldn't, she *wouldn't,* let him die. The feelings she had for him were very different from the ones she'd had for Robert.

Four men from Bong's squad used ropes to lower the wooden box into the grave, then the padre made the sign of the cross. He bent to take up a pinch of earth between his thumb and his finger to toss it in on top of the casket. He looked questioningly at Sarah.

"What is it, Bong? What am I supposed to do?"

"You put dirt into grave, too."

"But I thought that was for family. . . . Oh, maybe *we* are her only family since Sonny Boy isn't here. You must put earth upon her casket also, Bong." She bent and took a handful of the sandy soil and tossed it in. "Goodbye, Magdalena," she murmured.

She watched Bong squat and dribble his handful of earth slowly, slowly. He whispered something. She realized he was saying his goodbyes to his wife.

When he stood, the four young soldiers stepped forward with shovels and began to fill in the hole. Soon everyone had said a word to Sarah or to Bong, then they all drifted away to return to the village.

Sarah touched Bong's arm.

"Do you need to stay alone with Magdalena for a moment?"

"No, *mom*. She not here anymore. I know Magdalena gone."

"Well then, would you take me to the infirmary immediately, Bong? I must see the major."

"For army men only, to go inside infirmary, *mom*."

"Pooh. Do you think I care a snap about the Army's silly rules? Take me there this minute."

Bong looked at Luz. "You better take *mom* to infirmary, Luz. Major have my balls for sure, if I bring her in there."

"Sure. I not afraid. I take."

"Let's hurry."

Rays of impatience radiated from Sarah's head down her body and into her legs. She felt the strong impulse to run, just the way she had sometimes felt at home as little as a year ago. Now she had to observe the rules of grown-up respectability. A teacher did not run on a public street. But she wanted to. They could walk fast. She pulled Luz along with her.

"Not too fast, *mom*." Luz grinned up at her. "I pretty fat now, legs not work so quick." She patted her belly. "Baby maybe come soon if her mama hurry too fast." Sarah felt a twinge of guilt. She had been trying to hurry the little maid a bit more than necessary.

"Anyway," Luz continued when Sarah slowed their pace. "No hurry. Major not go nowhere, not right now."

Oh, God. He was that sick. They all knew he was going to die. They just hadn't told her. The Army wouldn't know of her interest in Markham anyway, so they would not feel they had to inform her.

The last few yards to the small wooden building seemed to take forever. Luz pointed and Sarah raced the last few yards, thrust open the door and stepped into a square room with three cots ranged along the south side wall. One person lay in the middle cot, but no one else was in the room. The room smelled of strong antiseptic.

"Where's the doctor?" Sarah spoke to Luz behind her.

"Don't know, *mom*."

"Go get him and bring him here, Luz." As she stalked toward the narrow bed she pulled off the black mantilla and began rolling up the sleeves of her dark-blue cotton dress. She leaned over the sleeping man.

"Markham. Markham Nash. Major. Can you hear me?" She shouted her words to try to bring him back to the world of the living.

His eyes fluttered open.

"Sarah. Anyone who couldn't hear that tone would have to be either deaf or dead. What're you doing here?"

"I've come to help make you well."

"I doubt you can do that. The fever just has to . . ."

"Don't be a doubting Thomas, Major. You'll have to cooperate with me." Tears welled in her eyes. "Oh, Markham, help me by helping yourself." A few droplets fell onto the shoulder of the surprised-looking officer. She let her hands flutter out palms open, and her voice rose to make a dramatic declaration. "I can't let you die. If you die I think I'd want to die also."

"Now, little schoolmarm. Calm down. This fever is just . . ."

"Don't give in, Markham. Fight it. Luz has just gone for the doctor. First thing, I'll get some water and start sponging you off." She stepped to the bucket of water that rested on a bench near the door. She dragged the bench and carried the bucket toward his cot. "That's what Mother did when we had fevers back in Iowa." She raced back to rummage through the cabinet that stood at the other side of the door. She pulled out a linen towel. "This should do."

"Sarah, you aren't supposed to be in here. This is a restricted area." He started to sit up, but she pushed him back down.

"Do you think I care about some silly little Army rule when you're sick and you need me?" She looked at him with astonishment. He was trying to pretend to be feeling better than he was. She just knew it. He didn't want to frighten her, was all.

She drew the sheet back and dipped the towel into the bucket of water. Markham smiled a weak smile and allowed her to unbutton, then draw off his long johns so she could sponge every part of him with the cool wet towel.

It did feel kind of good. He'd have to keep himself from grinning or laughing while she played angel of mercy. He'd just bet that no one had explained about the old fever he'd picked up in Cuba which occasionally came back to plague him. Then it struck him. *She thought he had cholera!*

He moaned with pleasure when she gently wiped his chest with the damp cloth.

"Oh, Markham. Am I hurting you?" He could see the tears spring to her eyes again. Poor little thing. He probably shouldn't tease her.

He closed his eyes and moaned again. Luz stepped into the door. Sarah glanced up at her.

"I'm so glad you're here, Luz. I'm sponging his body down to lower his fever."

Markham groaned lightly.

"Markham, darling. Don't die. I'm going to have Luz get the padre. We'll be married before you go. I want to be Mrs. Nash a thousand times more than I ever wanted to be Mrs. Zumwalt."

He sneaked a peek through slitted lids. She meant it. She was planning another deathbed honeymoon. He groaned a bit louder and put his hand on her.

"Oh, you're burning up with fever." She dropped the towel back into the bucket. "I think he's dying, Luz. Get the padre. And where's the doctor?"

"Doctor say he already been here. No use look in again."

"He's given up on him!"

Markham groaned.

"Quickly, Luz. Fetch the padre. Tell him Major Nash and I want to be married. Right now!" She looked down at Markham's faint smile. "There. See? That makes him happy, Luz. Get the priest."

Well, why not? he thought. This girl had certainly

proven she wasn't going to be thrown off balance by any rough station or primitive fort where he might be stationed. She'd stood up damned well in some bad circumstances. And she was a lot of fun to tease. He was crazy about the little schoolmarm. Might as well admit that. He'd had to turn on his side and put his hand and leg forward so she couldn't see what she was doing to him right now with all her gentle sponging.

"Marry?" He made his voice a weak croak.

"Yes. We'll be married, my darling. I'll try to keep you alive, but if you insist on going, I'll at least have your name."

"My name?" Another trembling croak.

"Oh, my Lord. Now he's forgotten who he is. I'll kill that doctor." Sarah lifted the towel, wrung it out and again started her cooling ministrations. "Do you know who I am, my darling?"

"Yes. You're my little wife-to-be."

She smiled tenderly down at him and leaned to kiss him lightly on the lips. "I believe you're somewhat cooler," she announced.

Not all of me, he thought, and turned onto his stomach.

"Could you wear your pretty suit?" He let his voice sink to a whimper so that she had to lean over to hear him. "And could you throw away that ugly black thing you've been wearing on your head?"

"Of course, dear." She continued swabbing his body. "As soon as someone else comes, I'll run straight home and change." She dropped the towel into the bucket at Luz's reentry. "Oh, dear, Luz, he isn't wearing any clothes . . . but I suppose in an emergency that doesn't matter. Please come and take over. Swab him gently with the damp cloth. That helps bring the fever down."

"Padre say he come pretty shortly, *mom*." The little woman panted a bit as she talked from all her rushing.

"Oh, good." Sarah turned and looked down at her patient. "He seems a bit better, but I'm still scared." She showed Luz how to hold the cloth to cool him. "He could die at any instant, so just keep swabbing. That's all we can do. I'll put on my wedding suit and be right back." She turned at the door and smiled. "He wants me to wear the suit my mother made me." She ran from the room.

Luz clicked her tongue and grinned.

"Shame on you, sir. You let little blondie woman worry about you."

"I know, Luz. I just couldn't resist." He lifted the sheet once again. "You can quit that stupid swabbing. Rinse out the bucket and go get us some clean drinking water. And call Bong and Rudolfo to witness the goings-on."

"You really marry the t'cher?"

"You bet, Luz. You think she'd make a good wife?"

"Oh, sure. She be good wife but she like little girl some ways, sir, Rudolfo say." Luz shrugged and picked up the bucket. "All Americans crazy, anyway, Rudolfo say."

"That's right, Luz." Markham sat up and wrapped the sheet around himself. "We *are* crazy. Might as well be crazy together." He stood and reached for his uniform when the Filipina had gone from the room.

Newly washed and combed and wearing the light-blue-striped lavender woolen skirt and jacket, Sarah felt quite grown up and extremely fancy, but she also felt very hot in the heavy suit. She carried Magdalena's palm-leaf fan for her "something borrowed." She wore the patent-leather slippers which were a bit shabby looking, but still passable. She was especially sorry that she had ruined her pretty straw hat on her ride through the forest. Her head was bare with her silky blond hair pulled into a high pompadour with chignon.

"Markham. You're up, and you're dressed. Do you think that wise?" She fanned her way across the floor. "We can be married with you lying comfortably in bed. Please don't tempt fate."

Markham slumped against the bed. He let his shoulders droop.

"Just wanted to be sure everything was right for you, dearest, seeing as I haven't much time." He coughed and bent nearly in half. "I want you to have good memories to live with, memories of our special moment." He coughed again and gasped a little. "I want you to have perfect memories of our wedding ceremony."

"Oh, Markham. Please, please sit down, or better yet, stretch out on your bed."

"Well, I will, if you'll sit there with me."

"Of course, my darling. I'll do anything you ask."

PARADISE FOUND

They sat together on his bed. Sarah fanned him with the palm-leaf fan. They remained silent for a moment before Sarah sighed and spoke.

"I thought about bringing the baby, but it seemed so hot for her. Since she's too young to remember anything, I thought she would be better off with Maria. As soon as you get better we need to talk about her taking your name, don't you think?"

She directed the fan on herself. "I'm so miserably hot. It must be dreadful to have a fever in this climate, Markham. Please let me sponge you with cool water until the minister comes."

He patted her shoulder weakly. "Now you know what us army boys have to go through every time we get dressed up."

"I just love my suit." She lifted the peplum on the jacket. "Really, it's quite stylish." She turned to look into his eyes. They seemed as clear as usual, with that bright little gold spark deep inside the dark-brown which she had often thought of as the signal he was teasing her. Maybe he was feeling better.

Could she have had something to do with saving him? She smiled happily at the thought. "Now I'll love it even more, but I would never wear it again in this climate for any amount of money." She pulled out a lace-edged linen square and patted her upper lip. "Probably I shouldn't be sitting down. I'm afraid I'm getting my skirt and my jacket all wet."

She cut her eyes toward him. He let his chest sink in and he closed his eyes and flopped loosely in her direction.

"I'm getting pretty hot, too, Teacher Lady."

"Oh, dear." She leaped from the bed to race to the door to look out. "There. The padre's coming. He and Luz are just loafing along." She opened the door more widely. "Father, come quickly. I think he's slipping away again."

Bong and Rudolfo walked into the room and the priest and Luz followed.

Bong looked down at the prone major. Markham opened his eyes and winked at Bong, then closed them again and groaned. Bong laughed and turned his laughter into a fit of coughing.

"Oh, Father, we want to get married. Here. Right now." She held on to the chaplain's sleeve and pulled him toward Markham's bed. "Will you do the ceremony now, sir?"

The man bent over the patient.

"Is that what you want as well, Major?"

"Oh, yes, sir. Hitch us up right and proper before it's too late." Markham smiled sweetly up at the priest. "I think I can stand up for the whole shebang, Father. If we do it right away."

The chaplain placed his book and other items on the cabinet against the wall, arranged Bong, Rudolfo, and Luz as best men and matron of honor, put his long white stole around his neck and beckoned to Sarah.

"I guess we're ready, young lady."

Sarah bent to help Markham rise.

"You really don't have to get out of bed to do this." She felt happiness warring with anxiety inside her

PARADISE FOUND 361

chest. Was all this fuss and bother going to make him worse?

He put his arm around her shoulder and leaned heavily against her, using her as if she were his crutch.

"I can do it with your help, my little cornflower."

She shot him a sharp look.

He gave a weak smile.

"Well . . . Iowa, corn, blue eyes. They all seem to flower in you, Sarah." His voice seemed stronger to her. "Come on, little schoolmarm. Let's do it."

They shuffled in tandem to stand in front of the preacher who spoke as loudly as if he were in a Paris cathedral.

"Dearly beloved, we are gathered together today in this place in the sight of God and man . . ."

Sarah shivered inside her woolen suit. Her mind was a jumble of thought and emotion. Everything from the first ceremony in Manila to Miss Arnold's eyes when she heard about the second marriage, and maybe about the second widowhood. Sarah stole a quick glance at Markham. He still had his arm around her, but he was paying close attention to what the padre was saying. Where his arm rested it was as if she were on fire. Could she be catching his fever?

Her first "I do" came out as a whisper.

The rest of the wedding went so quickly that she hardly realized that they were nearly married. Markham slipped his army ring on her finger, and when the padre announced, "I now pronounce you man and wife!" Sarah gasped. It was all over. She was married and she had missed most of it.

"You may kiss the bride." He beamed at the two of them.

Markham put his other arm around her and drew her close. When he bent, his lips felt warm, his mouth sweet and his kiss exciting. He didn't smell sick. He tasted wonderful, and for a moment he seemed his old self. When he lifted his head and smiled down at her, he said, "Congratulations, Mrs. Nash."

Sarah's heart turned over. They were well and truly married, whatever happened next.

What happened next was that the Army doctor slung the door open and stomped into the infirmary.

"What the hell are all you people doing in here? Major, you get back into that bed and the rest of you lot clear out. I should have you troopers up on charges!"

The padre maintained his dignity.

"Doctor, I've just married Major Nash to the widowed schoolteacher."

"Well, it's done, isn't it, Chaplain? Now, I want my patient back in his bed and I want all of you gone. Now!"

Markham grinned, kissed her lightly again and whispered, "Come back after dark" before he walked obediently toward his bed. "Thanks, friends, for standing up for me."

The Filipinos, the chaplain, and Sarah all allowed themselves to be shooed out the door. They stood silently on the grass outside the infirmary for a moment before anyone spoke.

"Come on, everyone," Sarah tried to maintain her

PARADISE FOUND

dignity. "Come to my house and we'll have a small reception. Do come, padre."

The gray-haired man shook his head. "This is undoubtedly one of the strangest days of my life. I think I'll decline your invitation to the reception without the groom, but still I thank you very much. I believe I need to closet myself with my prayers for a while."

"Father, we really are married, Markham and I, aren't we?" Sarah fanned the palm-leaf fan. "Everything was legal?"

"Oh, you're legally married all right, ma'am. If you and your witnesses will come by my office tomorrow I'll give you the papers for your files."

Sarah nodded and fanned a bit harder.

"Will the marriage be legal in Iowa?"

The chaplain stepped back a step as if to ward off any more strangeness.

"Yes, yes, my dear. Perfectly legal. Anywhere in the world. Now, if you'll excuse me." He turned and sprinted away behind the horse corral.

"Come. I will fix good stuff to eat," Luz announced. The four friends moved down the dirt street to Sarah's nipa hut to celebrate her marriage.

Much later, when they'd eaten the *menudo* (blood/liver soup) and all the *flan* (custard with caramel sauce) that Luz had prepared, Sarah brought out a bottle from the bedroom and held it high in her left hand. She grasped a small packet in her right hand.

"I thought we could drink the rest of Robert's whiskey. We'll all drink to the health of the major." She held up the small packet. "And I have a present for you, Luz, in honor of the new baby." She extended the bottle toward Luz.

"I no drink, *mom*. Priest say no good for baby." Luz passed the bottle on to Rudolfo, who took a healthy slug, then handed it to Bong.

"Long and happy life for Major and his wife." He tipped the bottle up.

"Oh, Bong. I do hope you're right. Maybe our marriage has given him heart. Maybe he'll fight to live."

Bong and Rudolfo looked at each other and grinned. Bong shrugged his shoulders.

"Major some fighter, all right, *mom*. If you need a fight, Major the very one to call." He took another long drink. "I drink to little blondie wife who have to live with Major now. Maybe you gonna learn a lot about fighting." He raised the bottle again.

Sarah reached for the whiskey.

"Oh, let me drink to everything you've said. I do most fervently hope that I will eventually be allowed to live and be happy with Markham." She held her breath and took a swallow of the stuff. "I love him so very much." She gasped and took another swig. "I don't know if I can wait two more hours before I get to see him."

"You see Major tonight?" Luz looked surprised.

"Oh, yes. He asked me to visit him after dark."

Rudolfo and Bong again looked at each other and chuckled.

"Almost dark now, *mom*. I think you and Major have honeymoon tonight." Bong stretched his hand for the bottle before Sarah could take a fifth drink.

"He did seem to be getting well, didn't he?" Sarah took the bottle back.

"Yes, *mom*. I think maybe he be real well tonight, *mom*. Feeling good."

"You say you got something for me, *mom*?" Luz peered at the small paper-wrapped package in Sarah's lap.

"Oh, yes." She handed the packet to Luz. "These are for you to keep or sell. Whatever you want to do. They belonged to my grandmother. They're real gold."

Luz looked a bit puzzled.

"They're hatpins, Luz. Keep your hat on your head. Or do whatever you want to do with them. I know that this is a bit strange for a baby present, but I just don't have anything else of value to give you. They should be worth quite a few pesos."

Luz nodded and smiled. "Thank you, *mom*."

Rudolfo nodded thanks, too, before he took another swig.

"Markham says we will have to live on officers' row now." Sarah looked around the gold and green of her living room. "I have an idea, Luz. If we really do move into army housing, why don't you and Rudolfo move in here?" She patted Luz's stomach. "The new baby will be coming soon." She stared at the young Filipina's belly. "Why, Luz, maybe you could help feed Dionisia? After your baby comes?" She passed the well-diminished bottle on to Bong.

"Maybe so, *mom*. Me and Rudolfo like house." She shoved a bare foot along the bamboo floor to prod her husband. "Don't we, Rudolfo?"

Rudolfo almost dropped the bottle.

"Oh. Yes, *mom*."

"Luz, aren't you and Rudolfo cousins of some sort to Magdalena?"

"Oh, yes, *mom*. Our grandmothers sisters."

"So that makes Sonny Boy Suarez your cousin also."

"Sonny Boy?"

"Magdalena's young brother. He seems such a fine boy, well mannered and smart at school. Even though I don't care for his father, I can't help liking Sonny." She looked into the opening of the almost empty bottle. "Sonny is staying with the Suarez maid, but she has at least six children of her own and only a very tiny hut. I was thinking . . ." Sarah touched the little woman's forearm. "If you could bring Sonny Boy into the house here with you, it would solve another big problem." She turned her gaze toward Rudolfo to be sure he understood what she was saying before she turned back to Luz. "I could give you a little money each month for Sonny's keep and for wet nursing my baby. That way you could afford to stay home and take care of the family. Let some other village lady take your job with the Army."

Luz was already nodding enthusiastically when Sarah asked Bong to explain everything she had said to Rudolfo.

"He say many thanks, *mom*. They take in littl

PARADISE FOUND

cousin anyway but nice to have blondie lady giving money for children. Americans pretty generous even if they do act funny."

"Thank him for me, Bong." Sarah swayed and let a tear drop from her eye.

"Bong. I know you'll never forget Magdalena, but I hope in time you'll find someone else to love. Then you can have a houseful of children, too."

"Maybe not, *mom*. I no marry. I go where Major go. Major always need a dogrobber. Now you Mrs. Major, maybe I help you too, *mom*." Bong took a drink and handed the last remaining whiskey to Sarah. "Drink to wedding night, Mrs. Major."

Sarah turned up the bottle and drank the last spoonful of whiskey. That mouthful didn't taste half so bad as the first one had, she told herself, although it still burned going down. She giggled and stood up. She felt extremely lightheaded and her black patent-leather slippers seemed to wobble in place. Everything around her appeared to move just a little. The whole experience was rather pleasant. Now she knew why men drank.

"I think I'll just go on over to the infirmary and visit my husband."

"We walk with you, *mom*. You maybe celebrate marriage too much to walk by yourself."

"I do feel much better, Bong. Much cheered. And I'm sure Markham is going to be feeling worlds better as well. I won't mind spending the night sponging him down with cool water if only he will try to get well."

"Yes. You right, *mom*. For sure he going to be feeling *much* better when you get there. 'Specially after you been there a while." He and Rudolfo laughed boisterously and each clipped the other on the shoulder with a fist. Luz only smiled.

Twenty-nine

Sarah giggled and opened the door of the hospital room, then gestured to Luz that she should go in first. Luz stepped up ahead of her into the dark infirmary building holding high a lard bucket with a candle in it. Holes pierced in the tin container sent out flickering rays of light to partially banish the darkness.

"Is that you, Sarah?" The question came from the shadows at one side of the room. Markham. Sarah loved the deep velvety quality of his so-masculine voice.

"Yes. And Luz. She came with me." She laughed again. "She wouldn't let me come to the infirmary by myself."

"Is she drunk, Luz?" The officer stepped into the stippled light. He was barefooted and wearing only his long johns and his khaki uniform work trousers.

"Maybe a little, Captain."

"Luz, don't you know? He's a major now." Sarah took the candle lantern from Luz. "The four of us celebrated our wedding, Markham." She twirled the bucket slightly and tiny dots of light danced about the walls near the door. "It looks like fireflies," Sarah murmured. "Just like fireflies."

Markham lifted the lantern from Sarah's hand and set it on the cabinet where the priest had laid his things earlier.

"We'll keep the fireflies, Luz." He grinned and pointed to the door and Luz smiled also, then nodded before she left.

When the Filipina was gone, Sarah put her hands up to his bare shoulders and looked searchingly at his face. "How do you feel? Are you all right, Markham?" The light painted tiny gold dots on his dark skin. She traced her fingers through the spots. "You're gold splattered."

"So are you, little schoolmarm."

"But are you still dying of the fever?"

"No. And I never was. I had a touch of fever from my time in Cuba, but the doctor says that I can get back to duty in a couple of days."

She moved closer to him.

"You were teasing me. That really wasn't fair of you. I was so frightened, Markham."

"I know."

"Did you want to fool me?"

"Well, you seemed to be having such a good time thinking you were marrying me on my deathbed that I decided I'd just let you go ahead with your plans." He bent and brushed her lips with his own. "You're quite an organizer when you think something needs doing, Mrs. Nash."

At his words, Sarah could feel the warm, fuzzy feelings she'd gotten from the whiskey receding more and more beyond her mind's reach with each minute. She wished the feelings would stay. Maybe she didn't need cold hard reality. Maybe she wasn't going to like what she would hear him say next.

"Oh, Markham. Did I force you into this wedding?" She lowered her eyes. She tried to let her hands slip from his shoulders, but he wouldn't allow them to go. "I was being silly, wasn't I? I suppose I should be ashamed."

"Sarah, it's pretty hard to *force* me into doing anything." He lifted her face with his hand and smiled down at her. "I guess you'll learn more about that as the years roll by. As for shame, I'm pretty sure you have no reason for feeling that."

"Why *did* you marry me?"

"I love you, silly girl. You mean you still don't know?"

Sarah's heart turned in her chest. *He loved her!*

"I love you, too, Markham, but why haven't you told me that before?"

"Oh, my sweet, I thought I shouldn't influence you. I thought that if you wanted to go back to Iowa, that that was the best place for you." He pulled her close to him and murmured into her ear as if telling her a secret, "To tell you the truth, I didn't know if I was a very good candidate for marriage and instant fatherhood."

"What changed your mind?"

"Looking up at those big blue eyes spilling tears onto my shoulder because you thought I was going to die." He smoothed her hair and began to pull the tortoiseshell hairpins from the blond topknot. The pinpoints of candlelight shifted constantly and coated their faces with moving flecks of magic. "I've known from the first day we met that life with you would never be dull."

Sarah stared into his brown eyes, mesmerized by his glance as well as by his words.

"Besides, I'd had several hours lying here alone to think over our situation." He tossed the tortoiseshell hairpins onto the cabinet and drew her loosened hair into a silken fan over her shoulders. "You've always been honest and straightforward with me about everything. I figured I'd better be the same with you."

She nodded. "I'm so glad you decided that."

"Magdalena and Bong had such a short time together. That made me think, also." He ran his knuckle through one of the silky fans of hair. "I've dreamed about touching your hair." He lifted the golden mass from her right shoulder and let the pale silk drift through his hand. "Especially when I've been trapped behind the desk. Seemed all I could do was think about you . . . about what I wanted to do with you."

His whispered words seemed to burn a passage into Sarah's soul. Markham Nash loved her! He'd dreamed about her! He'd wanted to touch her!

His hands moved to the row of buttons on her dark blue dress. "I see you've changed to something cooler than your pretty suit." He released each button from its captivity.

PARADISE FOUND

"I'm glad I got married in it, but I simply couldn't wear it any longer than was necessary."

He finished the last button. "Now I feel like a fool. Bong even told me I was a fool. Why, girl, we could have been loving each other months ago." He bent and kissed her forehead as he worked.

"Maybe we needed time to come to a decision, Markham. Both of us. I've been stupid, too. Thinking like a child, as if I were still back in Iowa."

"That's one of the things I love best about you." He drew the cotton dress off her shoulders and let it whisper down to fall in a circle about her black patent slippered feet.

"That I'm stupid?"

"That you've a goodness, an innocence. Like a child, maybe, but you always try to do what's right." He fumbled at her waist for the strings that tied her petticoat. She reached to her left side to help him. The starchy white ruffled slip crinkled down to rest atop the blue cotton circle of her dress.

She took a deep breath of relief. For the first time since she'd realized that their lovemaking had become a public piece of gossip, she began to feel sure of herself, sure of him. This was her husband and he was saying, in all the ways he knew how, that he loved her, that he wanted her, that they would be all things to each other.

"Now you," she said. She unbuttoned the fly on the front of his trousers. As she fumbled with the buttons she could see and feel that his hardened manhood was straining to be released from its woolen prison. Again she was surprised by the size of him and by his pulsing aliveness.

Before he could reach to do it, she'd pulled her own cotton shift off over her head and sent it flying in much the way she'd thrown her corset in the jungle. She took his hand and allowed him to help her step over the heaped cloth circle that surrounded her.

He stared and groaned deep in his throat.

Sarah loved hearing that sound. Maybe he hadn't meant the same things she'd meant when she'd said "I do," but one thing he *had* meant was this delight with her face, her hair, her body. The kind of love that her parents shared could come only after years of sharing and caring. She knew that.

In years to come she'd have to remind herself to let this strong, independent, man of hers have his liberty so she could keep him by her side. Let the ties be voluntary. Let him learn to anchor himself into their marriage and then she'd be there for him. Time enough for all that in the years to come. But now, tonight, their time together was beginning.

She took a step toward him.

When he smiled the desire she saw in his face flooded her with joy. This kind of love was what she, too, wanted. What she needed right now.

He took her lips hungrily. She opened her mouth as he had taught her and tasted the sweet richness of his searching kiss. She twined her arms about his neck, then let one hand sweep up through the heavy blackness of his hair.

She dragged her mouth from him.

"I love your hair, too, Markham. I've often thought of running my hands through it."

"Now we have time for everything." He took her right hand and held it in the air with his own, as if they were ready to dance. "My God. Look at you. A tiny gold-speckled goddess." She could see a brighter gold spark alight deep in the back of his brown eyes.

He led her to the shadowy corner where he'd thrown the straw tick and his muslin sheet off his cot and onto the floor.

"See? I was getting our wedding bed ready, my darling." He dropped to his knees and gazed up at her. "Let me just look at you for a moment. I've been waiting all afternoon for this."

He leaned forward and lightly kissed the neatly curling blond thatch between her legs.

"I could have killed that doctor earlier, but I'm claiming you now, my little golden wife." He kissed her again. "I'm branding you for my own."

She tugged at his hands to lift him to his feet once again, then she dropped to her knees. She leaned toward him and left an arch of tiny kisses on the black fur that framed his manhood, pushing the insistent maleness of him to the side and down in order to do so.

"And I'm claiming you, also, my dark hero, my husband. I choose to belong to you."

In her heart she knew that this murmured exchange between them was more of a marriage ceremony than had been the legal one earlier in the day. They were truly making their promises now . . . for each other and for no one else.

He knelt to face her and Sarah trembled against him. She'd already had a taste of this man and what he could do to her. Passion leaped in her. Her nipples hardened, and between her thighs she could feel a yearning, a pulsing call that made her ache, made her want to cry out to him.

His mouth covered hers, and as he kissed her he laid her compliant body down upon their wedding bed. His tongue thrust his demands into her. She could feel his arousal harden still further.

The glimmer of candlelight was behind him now and she saw his strong body silhouetted in darkness against the moving luminescence. His dark presence loomed above her, almost overwhelming her. The small amount of light seemed caught in the tawny depths of his eyes. He was playing with her. She waited breathlessly for what he would do next. He bent for another kiss.

Their bodies grew heated and wet with sweat after only a few kisses. Sarah's hair felt much as it had in the forest after the rains started.

"I'm so hot!" Involuntarily the words burst from her.

He laughed. "So am I, darling, but I think we're talking about two different things." He rolled a little away from her. "Romantic though my bed-on-the-floor idea might have been, I can see it wasn't practical. I'm pretty sure this room was built by some damn Yankees who were expecting snow within months. Let's get the hell out of this hotbox."

"But where will we go? I think Luz and Rudolfo are in my house."

He nuzzled her moist neck, then licked it. "Um um. Sweet and salty. Your sweat tastes as good as it smells." He stood up and lifted her up. "We'll go where you started all this."

Sarah felt her face flame.

"I started it?"

"Aren't you the one who patted the rock and said, 'Come on up here, soldier'?" He laughed as he strode to pick up their clothing. "Let's get outside where the breeze can touch us. A cool dip in the pool would be a good way to start married life, I think." He tossed her her dress and petticoat. She searched for the short shift.

When they were ready, he folded the sheet and took two pillows from the beds.

"Blow out the light, little darling. No use letting the world in on our honeymoon. It's mighty hard to be alone in this country, but let's try." They stepped outside the door and drifted soundlessly across the damp grass and the pounded earth floor of the compound. Markham lifted his finger to his lips in the age-old schoolteacher's sign for quiet.

Sarah giggled, then clapped her hand across her mouth. She carried the now darkened lantern.

When they'd moved up and into the forest, Markham relit the candle inside the lantern and they made the rest of the walk with the company of fireflies.

At "their" rock they spread the sheet and laid out the pillows as if on a bed at the finest hotel.

"I love this place," Sarah whispered. "It's so beautiful."

"And cooler, too. Come on, schoolmarm. Let's go into the pool and get rid of our travel sweat." When they'd undressed again he showed Sarah how to climb down the step like rocks. The water rose like cool silk around her knees, then her thighs, then her belly.

"Can you swim, my darling?" He tread water as he helped her to come down the natural stone ladder.

"Papa and Mama thought young ladies shouldn't go swimming in public, so I never learned." She had an instant of wondering what her parents would think of their new son-in-law, then the magic of the place took over.

"Hold on to me and I'll take you for a ride around the pool." He lifted her onto his back as if she were a child playing piggyback. He pushed off and his strong back muscles moved against her hard-nippled breasts. She let her whole body sink into him to ride him through the black water.

"I used to be afraid of water," she said dreamily into his ear. "I guess I won't ever be afraid of anything again if you're with me." She kissed the space below his ear.

He took a deep, heaving breath. "Time to get out now," he announced. He helped her up the steps and followed closely behind her. She could feel his hardness against her legs as they climbed. "Time to get warm again," he announced, and turned her to him when they reached the flat surface of the big rock. He

PARADISE FOUND

took her face in his hands and murmured, "I love you," before he kissed her.

On their bed of muslin across stone, he sipped for long moments at each of her breasts in turn, then ran his tongue in a moist line of fire down the center of her belly and into the valley between her legs. He touched the rippling guardian of her sex with his tongue then suckled the honey of her. She was dissolved with love, plunged into a whirling pleasure of feeling, of wanting. She thrilled at what he did, but she wanted more. She wanted him inside her.

"Markham. Please. I want . . ."

He raised his head and slid upward on her.

"I know what you want."

He raised himself on his arms and held himself aloof from her. She could feel his manhood throbbing, heavy against her flesh.

"Touch me, Sarah." He rolled to one forearm and with his free hand took her hand to press it to encircle the pulsating organ. It felt so strange, so alive to her sensitive palm and fingers, almost like a separate entity. Heated, corded with veins and hard muscle. Yes. That was what she wanted.

She moved quickly to touch her lips to his life root . . . now to be her own. He cried out at the touch of her lips and told her he could stand no more when she placed her mouth over the moist tip of him.

"Come on up here, Mrs. Nash." He pulled her roughly to lie once more on her back on the sun-warmed rock covered by unbleached muslin. "I've dreamed of this every hour since I first met you."

He groaned and thrust himself into the very center of her being. Inside her he held himself still until she began to move and enfold him with her sweetness. She molded herself to him and drew him into her with the longing made flesh again.

He set the rhythm and her hips rose and fell to meet it. Each began to move more swiftly until they could take no more. Her back arched and she called his name and then she felt the beat and pulse of his own shuddered convulsions at the same moment he spoke.

"Sarah. Sarah, darling."

They kissed a lingering sweet kiss of promise of more, and at almost the same moment they both dozed, the day's fatigue sweeping them before it. But Sarah roused herself and fought sleep. There was that one question she wanted him to answer. She forced herself awake and into speech.

"Markham."

"Hm-m-m."

"Markham. I want to ask you a question."

He opened one eye and gave a half smile. "The answer is yes. I brought you both slates and slate pencils from Manila. And yes, I also brought you a bell, a big loud brass bell. The priest at the church sent the thing to the little widow for her school with his blessings. Now can you close your eyes?"

"Oh, Markham, you darling. The children will be wild with happiness, and the bell will help them be on time every day for sure." She kissed his chin and the corner of his lips. "But no. Thrilled as I am by your news, those weren't the questions I wanted to ask."

Markham opened both eyes. "Something to do with rock formations in the Philippines? Or perhaps how to say 'good night' in Tagalog, madam?"

"No, neither. But remind me. You can answer those two questions at another time." She raised herself to her elbow and traced a design on his chest. "I just wanted you to tell me what else you said about me. You know. When you and Bong and Rudolfo were drinking and talking about me that night on the trail? You told them about my corset, I know, but what else did you say? You three talked and laughed for such a long time."

"You really want to know?"

She nodded.

"Are you sure you want me to reveal that secret conversation?"

"Markham!"

"Well. If you're sure you want to know." He looked the question with his raised eyebrows. "You're sure?"

"Yes, yes, yes." She pounded him lightly on the shoulder. "Tell me. Tell me. Tell me."

"Well, Bong and Rudolfo were bragging about Magdalena and Luz and their excellent womanly qualities. When I spoke of your qualities as a woman they reminded me that all Americans were crazy."

"What did they think you were?"

"A dark-skinned man who spoke Tagalog."

"Oh, yes." She put her head onto his shoulder as if to return to sleep. "I'm glad you defended me."

"I *didn't* defend you. Did I say I did that?" He tangled his hand in her wet hair and pulled her closer. "I agreed with them. That you *were* crazy, I mean."

"Oh." Her word was almost soundless.

"And that I liked that, I told them."

"Oh, Markham, you didn't."

"One more thing. Crazy or not, I told them I was going to marry you." He chuckled and closed his eyes and went back to sleep.

Sarah stared wide-eyed into the star-studded bowl of the sky.

He'd told the two men he was going to marry her and, sure enough, here they were, married! Who had tricked whom? Her heart thudded with joy. Maybe he'd caught *her*. She closed her eyes, ready to dream of their life together.

Both fell into exhausted slumber, their bodies still entwined.

The thundering splashing falling water made night music for them as they slept. Neither Sarah nor Markham heard the few words and the teasing sweet laughter from the throats of their friends.

As the Americans' slumber deepened, Luz and Rudolfo and Bong stole away to their own sleeping mats, secure in the knowledge that this marriage was well and truly made.

As some people say: There are no secrets in the Philippines.

HISTORICAL ROMANCES BY PHOEBE CONN

FOR THE STEAMIEST READS, NOTHING BEATS THE PROSE OF CONN . . .

ARIZONA ANGEL	(3872, $4.50/$5.50)
CAPTIVE HEART	(3871, $4.50/$5.50)
DESIRE	(4086, $5.99/$6.99)
EMERALD FIRE	(4243, $4.99/$5.99)
LOVE ME 'TIL DAWN	(3593, $5.99/$6.99)
LOVING FURY	(3870, $4.50/$5.50)
NO SWEETER ECSTASY	(3064, $4.95/$5.95)
STARLIT ECSTASY	(2134, $3.95/$4.95)
SWEPT AWAY	(4487, $4.99/$5.99)
TEMPT ME WITH KISSES	(3296, $4.95/$5.95)
TENDER SAVAGE	(3559, $4.95/$5.95)

Available wherever paperbacks are sold, or order direct from the Publisher. Send cover price plus 50¢ per copy for mailing and handling to Penguin USA, P.O. Box 999, c/o Dept. 17109, Bergenfield, NJ 07621. Residents of New York and Tennessee must include sales tax. DO NOT SEND CASH.

Taylor—made Romance From Zebra Books

WHISPERED KISSES (3830, $4.99/5.99)
Beautiful Texas heiress Laura Leigh Webster never imagined that her biggest worry on her African safari would be the handsome Jace Elliot, her tour guide. Laura's guardian, Lord Chadwick Hamilton, warns her of Jace's dangerous past; she simply cannot resist the lure of his strong arms and the passion of his *Whispered Kisses*.

KISS OF THE NIGHT WIND (3831, $4.99/$5.99)
Carrie Sue Strover thought she was leaving trouble behind her when she deserted her brother's outlaw gang to live her life as schoolmarm Carolyn Starns. On her journey, her stagecoach was attacked and she was rescued by handsome T.J. Rogue. T.J. plots to have Carrie lead him to her brother's cohorts who murdered his family. T.J., however, soon succumbs to the beautiful runaway's charms and loving caresses.

FORTUNE'S FLAMES (3825, $4.99/$5.99)
Impatient to begin her journey back home to New Orleans, beautiful Maren James was furious when Captain Hawk delayed the voyage by searching for stowaways. Impatience gave way to uncontrollable desire once the handsome captain searched *her* cabin. He was looking for illegal passengers; what he found was wild passion with a woman he knew was unlike all those he had known before!

PASSIONS WILD AND FREE (3828, $4.99/$5.99)
After seeing her family and home destroyed by the cruel and hateful Epson gang, Randee Hollis swore revenge. She knew she found the perfect man to help her—gunslinger Marsh Logan. Not only strong and brave, Marsh had the ebony hair and light blue eyes to make Randee forget her hate and seek the love and passion that only he could give her.

Available wherever paperbacks are sold, or order direct from the Publisher. Send cover price plus 50¢ per copy for mailing and handling to Penguin USA, P.O. Box 999, c/o Dept. 17109, Bergenfield, NJ 07621. Residents of New York and Tennessee must include sales tax. DO NOT SEND CASH.